EXILE IN PARADISE

Their lips met, tentatively, experimentally, and suddenly Jade surprised herself, as well as Pieter, by the intensity and depth of her own feelings. She had known that she found him attractive, but she was startled by the upwelling of her own desire.

She had been accustomed to feigning passion during her brief unsavory period as a concubine, but now a tidal wave of emotion swept over her, uprooting her. Even as Pieter's hands caressed her, exploring her body, she was doing the same to him—relishing the experience, driving herself to more incredible heights.

They forgot time, place and the blazing tropical sun. All they knew was that they wanted each other, that they had to have each other...

Books by
MICHAEL WILLIAM SCOTT

Rakehell Dynasty #1
Rakehell Dynasty #2: China Bride
Rakehell Dynasty #3: Orient Affair
Rakehell Dynasty #4: Mission to Cathay

Published by
WARNER BOOKS

The Rakehell Dynasty
Volume IV

Mission to Cathay

MICHAEL WILLIAM SCOTT

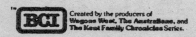

™ **BCI** Created by the producers of
Wagons West, The Australians, and
The Kent Family Chronicles Series.

Executive Producer: Lyle Kenyon Engel

WARNER BOOKS

A Warner Communications Company

WARNER BOOKS EDITION

Produced by Lyle Kenyon Engel

Cover design by Gene Light

Warner Books, Inc.,
666 Fifth Avenue,
New York, N.Y. 10103

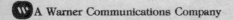A Warner Communications Company

Printed in the United States of America

First Warner Books Printing: January, 1984

10 9 8 7 6 5 4 3 2 1

For
My Grandchildren

Mission to Cathay

BOOK I

I

The mansion, like the Rakehell family that had lived in it for generations, was unique. Located near the foot of Pequot Avenue overlooking the estuary of the River Thames in New London, at the point where it flowed into the end of Long Island Sound and the open Atlantic Ocean beyond it, the large, white, two-story house was a symbol of the power and importance of the great Rakehell dynasty.

Looking toward the town of New London from the beach behind the house, even the casual observer could see the many buildings of the Rakehell and Boynton shipping complex, the huge industrial plant where clipper ships that circled the globe had been constructed. Before them there had been brigs and schooners, and more recently there were the modern steamships that were coming increasingly into vogue. The United States had been plunged into the horrors of the Civil War earlier in the year of 1861, and new buildings had been thrown up for the construction of the ironclad warships that the

Union was convinced would soon add a new dimension to naval warfare.

But the war was forgotten, at least temporarily, as Jonathan Rakehell, who had succeeded his late father, Jeremiah, as chairman of the Rakehell and Boynton board, sat at the head of the dining room table and looked at those who had assembled for supper. Gray-haired, his face deeply lined, he looked down the length of the table and grinned at his slender, still-blond wife, Elizabeth, fifteen years his junior, who sat opposite him. A glance was sufficient to tell her his thoughts. They enjoyed a sense of communion as rare and sensitive as their love for each other, and she knew, without being told, that he was proud beyond measure of his son, daughter, and their cousin, who were also gathered at the Rakehell table and were busily engaged in animated conversation.

Seated on Jonathan's right was his elder child, Julian, who looked enough like Jonathan himself in his mid-twenties that viewing him was like turning back the clock. Julian was tall and slim with an athletic build. He had the typical crisp brown Rakehell hair, hazel eyes, and the prominent long jaw and chin that marked all male members of the family. Julian was in charge of the operations of the company and held the title of president, which he had well earned. He was a worthy successor to the long, honorable line of New England shipbuilders, and his father was satisfied with his performance in every respect.

To Jonathan's left sat his daughter, Jade, and as he stole a look at her, his heart filled with joy. She was all that he had expected of her, and she far more than fulfilled her rich promise. She was even more beautiful than her lovely mother, Lai-tse lu, who had died so tragically a generation earlier. Jade was living proof of the Chinese adage that the child of an Oriental and an Occidental who loved each other was incomparably good-looking. Her hair, a rich blue-black, hung in a thick straight mass below her shoulders and served to frame her oval face that so clearly reflected the mixture of East and West. Her eyes, beneath delicately shaped brows, were dark and limpid but reflected her lively intelligence and her strength of character. Her lips, full and deep red, were reminiscent of an overripe cherry and were a strange blend of sensuality and self-control.

Although she had many Western clothes in her extensive wardrobe, she had chosen to wear to supper a Chinese Cheongsam. Its stiff high collar emphasized her long neck, and the magnificently embroidered silk of the upper portion of the garment brought out her broad, sloping shoulders, her high, full breasts, and her incredibly small waist. The slit skirt of the Cheongsam was particularly appropriate and served to emphasize her long, slender, perfectly shaped legs.

Her light laugh sounded like the pleasant tinkling of temple bells, and the illusion was further enhanced by the musical sounds of the gold, silver, and jade bracelets at her wrists as she gestured expressively with her long tapering hands.

Many women, had they been endowed with Jade's beauty, would have been content. But she, like her half-brother, Julian, possessed a boundless, restless ambition. She served as the head of the all-important Oriental operations of the Rakehell and Boynton company and was no figurehead. Hundreds of employees in Hong Kong, where she made her headquarters, and in Canton, where she lived at the lovely old estate of her grandfather, Soong Chao, a merchant whose acumen she obviously had inherited, were prepared to swear that there were no traders in the East who were her equal. The competitors of Rakehell and Boynton had passed the same judgment on her.

Beside her sat a dark young man, with subtle Oriental features, who was closer to her and to Julian than anyone else on earth. Their cousin, David Boynton, the son of Jonathan's close relative, business partner, and best friend, Charles Boynton, had been virtually raised with the two Rakehells. He and Julian had climbed the rigging of sailing ships under the supervision of stern boatswains when they were scarcely able to walk, and both had earned their masters' papers by the time they had reached their majority.

The son of a half-Chinese courtesan who had sacrificed her life for Charles Boynton, David had been educated in England and had inherited his present position as head of the English operations of the company. When his father and stepmother, Charles and Ruth Boynton, took up residence at their country estate, he remained in London and became master of their town house in Belgravia.

Intense and hypersensitive, David spoke with the clipped drawl of an Oxford University graduate and dressed in the most fashionable clothes that his London tailors could make for him.

He had often been the object of private debate between Jonathan and Elizabeth. "I don't care how British he appears to be," Elizabeth had said. "He's part Chinese, and I'm afraid that's a stigma in England."

Jonathan had shaken his head emphatically. "But he's a major stockholder and head of the British branch of a very large and successful shipbuilding and commercial trading company," he said. "There are very few men in England who are his financial peers, I can assure you."

"No matter," Elizabeth had replied stubbornly. "There are no snobs on earth worse than the upper-class English, and I'm sure that David is tolerated, rather than accepted, in the circles in which he moves."

Her husband had looked at her curiously. "Has he ever complained to you?" he had asked.

She'd shaken her head so vigorously that her wavy blond hair had danced. "Hardly," she replied. "And even more important, he's never indicated the least unhappiness in his dealings with Julian or Jade, either. I know because they've told me as much. But I wouldn't expect anyone who'd been reared by Charles and Ruth ever to complain about anything."

Now, scrutinizing David Boynton carefully, Jonathan thought that perhaps his wife was right. At the same time, however, he had to admit that nothing in the attitude of the young man revealed that he was less than contented with his life or any phase of it. He and the two young Rakehells were laughing heartily at some private joke that Jonathan and Elizabeth completely failed to grasp.

"It strikes me," Jonathan said severely, "that the younger generation is very rude."

The laughter died away. "Sorry, Papa," Julian said, "but I just dropped my fork and Jade quoted Molinda on the subject."

Still giggling, Jade repeated the comment in Mandarin, the language of the upper-class Chinese.

Elizabeth was blank, for she knew no Mandarin. She well knew, however, that Molinda was a remarkable woman who had been the chief of operations for Rakehell and Boynton in the Orient for a generation, and had been Jade's mentor and guide in the years that the young woman had been living in the Far East. The woman was Balinese and French by birth and had been sold to the Fat Dutchman, an enormously wealthy, highly successful trader in the Netherlands East Indies, who had purchased her as a slave girl when she had been very young. Through her astuteness, she had won her freedom and had become associated with Jonathan and Charles. Yet she had managed, at the same time, to remain on close terms with the Fat Dutchman. Now she worked in an advisory capacity for the Rakehell and Boynton firm, leaving much of the day-to-day operations to Jade and enjoying her newly found free time for travel and relaxation.

Jonathan chuckled, then turned to his wife and translated what Jade said. "The wise man," he said, "walks as lightly as a hummingbird skims the surface of a flower, but he trumpets like an elephant to advertise his presence."

Elizabeth smiled. Being married to Jonathan for many years, loving him and all that he stood for, she had come to greatly appreciate Oriental wit.

"I've been meaning to ask you, Jade," Jonathan said, "how is Molinda doing?"

"As nearly as I can judge," his daughter said, "she's having a wonderful time. She spends weeks traveling for pleasure all over the East, and when she comes home to Hong Kong, I honestly think she's reached the point, after leading such a hectic life, that she relishes doing absolutely nothing."

Elizabeth entered the conversation actively for the first time. "What I've never understood," she said, "is why Molinda has never remarried. She's only in her middle forties, and she's still one of the most attractive women I've ever known in my life."

"You don't understand Molinda," Jade told her. "She'll never remarry, I'm sure, because she has virtually no respect for most men. She was forced to endure relations with too many of them in the years when she was enslaved by the Fat Dutchman, and since that time—to be blunt about it—she's used her sex appeal as a weapon in business. A highly successful weapon.''

Elizabeth nodded thoughtfully.

"As a matter of fact," Jade went on, "the only men I've ever heard Molinda speak of favorably are Papa, Uncle Charles, and her husband, whose death left her genuinely grieved. I think she was also disturbed when the Fat Dutchman died, but she seemed vastly relieved to be dealing with his niece, who took over the business. I must admit," she added, "that I prefer trading with Anna van der Luon to doing business with her uncle."

"She operates much as her uncle did," Julian said. "When I last visited the estate outside Djakarta in Java, I was offered my choice of harem wenches, and from the little I saw, the stable of girls is as extensive as it was in the Fat Dutchman's day."

David smiled without mirth. "I've heard," he said, "that Anna has actually expanded her uncle's household. I'm told that she keeps a number of male servitors there for the purpose of serving important women guests."

Jade nodded and said in an offhand way, "Oh, I can vouch for that, David. She offered me my choice the last time I was there and couldn't seem to understand that I wasn't interested in any of them."

Jade was sophisticated beyond measure, Elizabeth thought—far more worldly than she herself had been in her early twenties. But that was all to the good. Thanks to her experience, she would not be subjected to possible hurt as easily as her innocent elders had been.

Julian glanced first at his father, then at his stepmother, and decided to brave their possible wrath. "There's a rumor making the rounds in the business," he said, "that Anna also has added a number of eunuchs to her staff."

"So I've heard," Jade replied calmly. "She uses them for her personal pleasures, I believe."

Jonathan saw that Elizabeth's curiosity had been aroused and that she was about to inquire how eunuchs could possibly be of service to a woman. So he decided to interrupt the conversation decisively.

"Instead of frittering away time in gossip, which leads us nowhere," he said, "I find it far more useful to be brought up-to-date on the political situation in Cathay. I've been waiting for the details ever since Jade arrived here this morning."

Recognizing the note of command in her father's voice, Jade instantly sobered and began to speak crisply. "The Taiping Rebellion goes on and on," she said. "Insurgents are up in arms over the shortages of food and the crowded conditions, as well as the presence of so many foreign devils—or Fan Kuei, as you know they are called. They are disgusted with the emperor's inability to do anything about conditions in China, and a great many cities, and even entire provinces, are still held by the insurrectionists."

Jonathan shook his head. "That's astonishing," he said. "The rebellion has gone on for at least ten years now."

David sipped his wine and remarked softly, "The emperor isn't your friend the way Tao Kuang was, Uncle Jonathan. The emperor is now Hsien Feng, Kuang's fourth son, who succeeded him and has disgraced the Chrysanthemum Throne. The fact that he's been incapable of stamping out the rebellion has proved that he's weak and ineffective."

"Far worse than that," Jade said, fingering a long earring of closely set diamonds, "were the consequences of the second great war with the foreigners just two years ago."

Elizabeth was thoroughly familiar with the state of affairs they were talking about. In the autumn of 1859, Peking, the capital of the Middle Kingdom, had been occupied by seventeen thousand British and French troops. This was the second time that Western nations had gone to war with China, and the issues were similar to those in the first war: China had reneged on trade agreements, and Britain and France were demanding what they felt were their rightful prerogatives.

"It's true, isn't it," Elizabeth asked, "that the people of China blame the emperor because the British and French looted and burned the Summer Palace?"

"The malaise runs far deeper than that, I'm afraid," Julian explained. "Under the terms of the Treaties of Tientsin, in which the

United States and Imperial Russia have taken a part, along with Britain and France, eleven more Chinese ports have been opened for trade. Foreign legations have been established in Peking for the first time, trade routes have been opened in the interior, and Christian missions are now allowed there.''

There was a hint of sorrow in Jade's smile. ''You neglect to mention, Julian, that a foreign staff has been hired for the maritime customs service, which means that Americans in Chinese employ will be dealing with Americans, British subjects will be dealing with Englishmen, and so on. The Russians have been given territory north of the Amur River, and I'm told the tsar has gone so far as to establish a new city, which they're calling Vladivostok.''

They were interrupted by the serving of roasted beef, with potatoes, onions, and carrots that had been cooked in the pan. This was a traditional Rakehell dish, and Elizabeth was the sort of housewife who carefully upheld family tradition.

Jonathan waited until the serving maid had left the dining room. ''I haven't visited Cathay in a number of years,'' he said, ''but what I fail to understand is how the Hsien Feng Emperor can keep his throne after he's been so thoroughly disgraced.''

''My biggest news,'' Jade said, ''is that the emperor has gone into isolation and is seeing literally no one.''

The others at the table stirred. David leaned forward. ''Do I assume correctly that his son, T'ung Chih, will succeed him on the Chrysanthemum Throne?''

Jade nodded. ''To be sure, although he's only a child and someone will have to rule in his place.''

''Who?'' Julian demanded, drumming on the table with his fingertips.

''I'm not familiar with the inner workings of the Imperial Palace,'' Jade replied firmly. ''No foreigner is. But to the best of my knowledge, the emperor's brother, Prince Kung, is the leading candidate to become the regent until the young emperor is of age and can take over himself.''

David spoke quietly in his upper-class English drawl, but his eyes were sharp. "May I ask the source of your information?" he inquired.

"Indeed, you may," Jade replied, "provided that you keep in mind this is privileged information and it must go no farther than the family. My informant is Prince Kung himself."

Jonathan nodded approvingly. She was indeed his daughter and Lai-tse lu's.

Julian's expression remained unchanged. "Obviously you know the prince," he said. "How well do you know him?"

Jade's features looked Western rather than Oriental as she grinned at her brother. Then, looking down at her plate demurely, she murmured, "We are acquaintances, nothing more."

Jonathan was privately relieved. He knew virtually nothing about his daughter's private life, and it was comforting to hear that she had not become the mistress of Prince Kung.

"He's sincerely devoted to the welfare and future of his country," Jade said. "He's a very earnest man, and although his education, like that of so many members of the royal family, has been rather circumscribed, he is extremely eager to learn all that he can. I've sent him scores of books in the past couple of years. What I like best about him is that he has inherited one unique trait of the Tao Kuang Emperor. He is perfectly willing to employ foreigners in order to bring the Middle Kingdom into the modern world."

"Hooray," Julian said, and David went through the motions of applauding.

"It appears to me," Jonathan said carefully, "that there will be new opportunities opening in Cathay for Rakehell and Boynton if Prince Kung becomes the regent for the boy emperor."

Julian began to eat his beef with great enjoyment. "Exactly my feeling," he said. "We'll be in a wonderful position to take advantage of the new treaty. Think of all those ports that we can now visit and of the merchandise for which we'll have markets!"

David remained unimpressed. "I prefer to wait," he said.

Julian looked at his cousin incredulously. "Wait?" he demanded. "In the name of all that's holy, why should we wait?"

David, as usual, marshaled his facts in an unemotional manner. "Let me remind you, Julian," he said, "that this country of yours is currently embroiled in a civil war that is threatening the entire economy of the Union. The navy has commandeered a number of our ships, and you well know from the building operations, the New London yard is making new ships almost exclusively for the navy these days. Frankly, without government help and cooperation, I don't see how it's possible for Rakehell and Boynton, or for any other American company, to take advantage of the new treaty conditions in the Middle Kingdom."

"You forget, my boy," Julian replied hotly, "that we are not exclusively an American company. Our British branch is almost as big and is in equally solid financial condition. I propose that we aim our biggest thunderbolts at Cathay from your side of the Atlantic, rather than from this side, where admittedly we're crippled at the moment."

As usual, talk at the Rakehell supper table had turned to business, and Elizabeth tapped her water glass with her spoon. "I don't in the least mind business discussions at noon dinner," she said, "but I've forbidden them at supper. You'll have to continue this later, gentlemen."

Julian and David subsided, and Jonathan was relieved. Neither had sought his help, so he volunteered nothing and very much preferred keeping his mouth shut. The active day-to-day and month-to-month operations of the company were in the hands of the younger members of the firm, and though he could advise them, he preferred not to settle their disputes. They would have to work out their differences themselves, just as he and Charles had worked out theirs over a period of so many years.

After dinner, Jonathan and Elizabeth retired to the parlor, she to begin reading George Eliot's latest book, *Silas Marner*, he to review the company ledgers. Though he was not involved in the day-to-day affairs of the company—preferring to enjoy his latter years with Elizabeth, spending time at home or traveling through the ever-growing United States—Jonathan refused to be a mere figurehead.

He and Elizabeth would advise the younger generation, just as his father and Missy Sarah had done before their deaths.

The young people, meanwhile, had gone out for a walk on the beach. Jade discarded her high-heeled slippers, Julian and David removed their boots, and as they strolled in the sand along the shores of the Thames Estuary, where they had learned to swim and had enjoyed so many picnics in their youth, they were flooded with memories.

Problems of the present that pertained to business matters were far more important to Rakehells and Boyntons than was any nostalgia for the past, however, and Julian inevitably reverted to their discussion at the supper table. "I still feel," he said slowly, "that we should be in a position to move and to strike rapidly in the event that Prince Kung takes charge of the Middle Kingdom as regent. We stand to gain a great deal if we move boldly and quickly."

"Sadly," David replied, "you keep forgetting that the United States is hobbled by the unfortunate war that's broken out here."

"I've already explained to you," Julian said in annoyance, "that we can utilize the facilities of the British division of the company to act rapidly."

"The point I'm trying to make," David replied with asperity, "is that we take the risk of losing what we already have. If the regency doesn't work out as we've anticipated, we can lose the very substantial profits that are being earned regularly and steadily by the British division. For all practical purposes, we've got to rely on my operations and on Jade's to see us through to the end of hostilities here in America."

"If we do as I suggest," Julian said icily, "we'll more than make up for any losses that the American division may incur in the years ahead."

David stopped short on the hard sand and shook his head slowly as he stared at his cousin. "You've always been obstinate," he said. "In fact, you're as stubborn as a bull."

Julian began to lose his temper. "I'd rather be a stubborn bull," he said, "than a stupid ass."

David's eyes flashed, and he clenched and unclenched his fists rapidly. "I see no reason," he said, "to become personally abusive."

"You started this, not I!"

"Like hell I did!"

Jade looked first at her brother, then at her cousin, and sighed. They were the best of friends, but both were accustomed to having their own way and were infuriated by opposition. What was more, they occasionally reverted to their early rivalries, and on these occasions they were inclined to behave like boys rather than men.

"It's a trifle on the cool side tonight," she said, "but I think a swim might be helpful. It's guaranteed to reduce the temperature of overheated blood."

The young men paid no attention to her and, glaring at each other, automatically adopted basic defensive postures in the martial arts.

Jade became alarmed. Both were experts in Oriental unarmed combat, having been taught the arts since earliest childhood, and she was afraid they might become so carried away that they would do each other bodily harm. Julian was tall, rugged, and—typical of a Rakehell—powerfully built. David, although somewhat shorter and lighter, was exceptionally wiry and made up for his lack of physical strength with his unparalleled grace and speed.

"Stop it this instant, both of you!" Jade commanded. "We're trying to decide a matter of business principle, not annihilate one another."

Julian gave no sign that he even heard his sister's plea. "For the sake of your continued good health, David," he said, "I strongly urge you to apologize."

"It's you who must either voluntarily or involuntarily express sorrow, old boy," David replied.

They inched closer together, each of them seeking an opening that would give him an initial advantage in combat.

Jade looked at them in despair. In moments they would be engaged in a brutal fight and would be fortunate if they didn't suffer broken limbs or even worse damage. They had forgotten her existence, so great was their growing anger, and had ignored her attempts to pacify them. She had only one alternative. She, too, had learned the martial arts and was an expert in them, and she had to utilize her knowledge quickly and authoritatively in order to prevent serious damage.

Approaching the pair, she lashed out at them simultaneously, striking their upraised arms so that they were forced to lower their hands to their sides.

Taken completely by surprise, they staggered backward and gaped at their totally unexpected assailant.

Having started the physical fight, Jade knew she had to finish it, and she did not hesitate. Taking advantage of the long slit in her cheongsam, she turned sideways to the pair and launched a devastating stiff-legged kick, first at Julian and then at David.

Both of the young men went sprawling on the ground.

Taking advantage of the initiative she had gained, Jade stood over them, ready to knock them to the ground again if they persisted in their belligerence. "I hope you've had enough," she said. "If not, get up and I'll give you a real taste of sand."

The tension in the air was so thick it almost acquired a physical presence of its own.

Suddenly David exploded in loud laughter. He was joined almost immediately by Julian, and the pair roared so hard that tears streamed down their faces and they had to hold their sides.

At last they struggled to their feet, brushed themselves off, and advancing simultaneously on Jade, hugged and kissed her.

She remained far from mollified, however, and continued to glare at both of them.

"You really are extraordinary," David told her and began to laugh again.

"I pity the poor devil you marry," Julian told his sister and threatened to collapse as a new gale of laughter swept over him.

"I'm glad I'm providing both of you with so much amusement," Jade said tartly. "But I really think it's time you behaved like responsible adults instead of little boys who are spoiling for a fight."

"I'm afraid she's right," Julian said, shaking his head.

"As usual," David added, and extended his hand.

Julian grasped and shook it. "We'll work out our differences sensibly in the morning. Does that satisfy you, Jade?"

A sniff was her only reply.

Julian and David looked at each other a trifle sheepishly and then communicated without words, a knack they had acquired through many years of close association. With one accord, each of them caught hold of one of Jade's arms, and they began to propel her down the beach.

"We were starting out on a walk . . ." Julian said.

"For old times' sake . . ." his cousin added.

"And in spite of an unpleasant interruption, walk we shall," Julian concluded.

In the parlor of the mansion, Jonathan Rakehell was looking out the window prior to going upstairs to bed, and glancing out at the beach in the moonlight, he saw his son, daughter, and their cousin strolling arm in arm. All three were laughing and appeared to be having a wonderful time. He smiled warmly and reflected that the company that he and his cousion, Charles Boynton, had inherited and had expanded so dramatically was in safe hands.

II

Anna van der Luon was in a highly agitated state, and everyone on the staff of the extensive jungle estate of her late uncle, the Fat Dutchman, outside Djakarta, the capital and principal port of the Dutch East Indies, well knew it. The woman, a faded blonde in her late thirties who still had a good figure despite the fact that obesity had been one of her late uncle's most outstanding physical characteristics, paced the length of her book-lined study restlessly, pausing occasionally to glance hastily at one of the ledgers that she opened and quickly shut again at random. Her loose-fitting gown flapped endlessly as she marched, and she ran a hand incessantly through her shoulder-length hair, tangling it further. As usual, she paid no attention to her appearance.

In his office farther down the hall, Count Pieter Sabov, the handsome young Russian nobleman whom the late Fat Dutchman had befriended and had hired as a bookkeeper, knew of Anna's nervous state, which was caused by the imminent arrival of some very important visitors. Experience with Anna in recent years had taught Pieter that he was going to suffer an unpleasant afternoon.

The concubines, as beautiful and as luscious as they had been in the Fat Dutchman's day, remained in their own quarters and were silent, neither gossiping nor joking. Clad only in the wraparound ankle-length skirts that were typical of the island of Java, they knew that when their employer was like this, it was best to stay out of her way.

Even more apprehensive were the long-haired eunuchs, clad like the concubines, with their faces daubed with cosmetics and their nipples rouged.

The girls knew it was their duty to serve business guests whom Anna invited to the estate. But the eunuchs were less fortunate, in that the mistress of the household sometimes utilized them for her own pleasure and, being more familiar with them than she was with the girls, was inclined to abuse them when she was out of sorts.

Even the small, wiry, brown-skinned men who composed the security force and kept strangers from straying onto the estate and prevented the escape of the concubines and eunuchs were ill at ease. The moods of Anna van der Luon affected them, too, and she often fired men and hired new ones whenever the whim struck her.

Pausing in her incessant pacing, Anna tugged viciously at a bell rope located on the wall behind her desk.

After a time the door opened, and a woman of about forty came into the room. Wearing cosmetics applied as carefully as those the concubines wore, and attired in a wraparound skirt, she was allowed the dignity of a breastband, as well.

Erika von Klausner had changed appreciably in the years that she had been enslaved by the Fat Dutchman. A German noblewoman who had become the enemy of the Rakehells, she had tried to do away with their trusted employee Molinda and, as a result, had incurred the enmity of the Dutchman, who had forced her to join his household. Over the years she had entertained countless business visitors and had been especially popular with the Orientals and Malays who found her pale skin a novelty. Gradually, as her looks and her waist-length red hair had faded, she had found other ways to make herself useful in the household, and now she carried the badge of authority that marked her as the mistress of the concubines, a long whip from which three strands of stout leather protruded.

But Erika von Klausner was anything but content with her lot, and she bided her time, waiting for an opportunity to dispose of Anna van der Luon and to take control of the large trading company herself. At the moment, that opportunity seemed to be right at hand. Erika had managed to win the loyalty not only of the concubines—who were deeply grateful that their mistress seldom used the whip on them—but also the loyalty of the Javanese menservants, who knew that Erika would reward them handsomely if they went along with her plan to do away with Anna van der Luon. The fact that the Fat Dutchman's niece was in such an agitated state also meant her guard would be down. Today seemed to be the day to strike.

Entering the study without knocking, Erika lowered herself to a sitting position on the floor, then touched her forehead to the tiles in a gesture of obeisance. "You called me, madam?" she inquired politely.

Anna removed the stopper from a cut-glass decanter and poured a generous quantity of *genever*, a potent liquor that she imported from Holland, into a glass. She downed the drink in a single gulp before she replied. "I did," Anna said brusquely. "A ship is putting into Djakarta this afternoon with a delegation of merchants from Canton on board—the first such group ever to leave the Middle Kingdom for the purpose of arranging foreign trade. I've been fortunate enough to secure their promise of a visit for forty-eight hours, so I want every concubine in the house to be prepared to greet them and to accede to their slightest wishes." She pondered for a moment, then added, "You'd best have the eunuchs ready to greet them as well. I know nothing about the preferences of these Chinese, and one or two of them may prefer a half-man to a real woman."

"I understand, madam, and it will be done as you wish," Erika murmured. Instead of making another obeisance and departing, however, she continued to stand facing the mistress of the estate.

"What do you want?" Anna demanded brusquely.

Erika made no reply and reached into the top of her skirt.

The pale blue eyes of the Dutchman's niece bulged in horror as she saw the other woman draw a thin, supple, double-edged knife of the type used by the security guards. Before she could call out for help or escape the fate that awaited her, the shaft of sharp steel plunged through the cotton fabric of her dress and penetrated deep into her heart.

Anna van der Luon died without making a sound, and her body slumped to the floor.

Erika looked at her without pity; if there was any expression in the glittering green eyes, it was a hint of triumph. "At last," she said under her breath, "at last." After spending more years than she cared to remember as a helpless courtesan, then as a supervisor of others in a similar predicament, she was at last free. But her work was not yet done, and her goal was yet to be accomplished.

She went to the door, opened it, and beckoned surreptitiously.

Within moments, two of the short, brown-skinned armed guards came silently into the room. They immediately noted Anna's body and nodded to each other; obviously all was going according to plan.

Erika reached down, opened the slit of her skirt, and removed a leather bag strapped to her leg. For years she had been accumulating whatever money she could—gifts from customers whom she had pleased, tokens from the Fat Dutchman, and since she had been placed in charge of the girls, her regular wages. Now she unhesitatingly handed each of the men a small pile of gold coins. For the moment, at least, she was out of funds, as poverty-stricken as she had been the day that the Dutchman had made her his captive.

The guards counted the money and dropped the coins into little leather pouches. Satisfied that she was keeping a bargain, they wiped a small puddle of blood from the tile floor, then covered the dead woman's face with a cloth. Without further ado, they carried her from the room.

There was no doubt in Erika's mind that they would keep their end of the bargain. They would dispose of the corpse, and no one would ever know what had become of Anna van der Luon.

Plucking the current ledger from the pile of books on the edge of the desk, Erika hastened to her own quarters, where she picked up a vial that contained a mixture of lemon juice and blond dye that she had prepared for this very day. Then she unhesitatingly went to the suite that tradition decreed was the private quarters of the ruler of the Fat Dutchman's shipping empire.

Closing the door behind her, Erika von Klausner allowed herself a momentary sign of weakness and leaned against the wood. Her scheming and conniving, her commission of a cold-blooded murder, at last were paying dividends. She was already a free woman for the first time in more years than she cared to count, and within a very short time, she would assume her rightful place as one of the wealthiest and most powerful women on earth.

Hurrying into a tiled chamber where she had taken the precaution of having the concubines fill a large tub with water, she applied the mixture of dye and lemon juice to her hair, letting it soak in for some minutes before she rinsed it out. Looking at her reflection in the mirror, she grimaced but was plainly satisfied. She had been transformed from a fading redhead into a blonde. Next, she went through the wardrobe closets that contained Anna's belongings and made a sour face. None of the nondescript, ill-fitting cotton dresses that the woman had worn were suitable, and she knew she would have to put some of the more accomplished concubines to work with needle and thread to make her a proper wardrobe as rapidly as possible. In the meantime, she would continue to wear her own snug-fitting skirts and breastbands. At least they showed off her still-trim figure to good advantage.

Rapidly patching her makeup, Erika immersed herself in the ledger and read it avidly for the better part of an hour; then she returned to the study and seated herself behind the desk in the huge wicker chair that the Dutchman himself had once occupied. Sighing in gentle triumph, she rang for Count Pieter Sabov.

Shortly the door opened, and he entered the room, trim in open-throated shirt and trousers of white linen, his feet clad in a pair of rope-soled shoes.

Erika eyed him narrowly, having anticipated his reaction when he saw her behind the desk. As a matter of fact, she had been observing Pieter Sabov for some time and knew him as well as he knew himself.

As she well realized, he had fled from the imperial court in Saint Petersburg, having incurred the anger of the tsar, which was a common occurrence for the unfortunate members of the court. The Fat Dutchman had hired him as a bookkeeper after he had come to Djakarta as a penniless refugee, and he had become a valuable member of the household. In addition to everything else, as Erika well realized, she wanted him. In Russia, even as a very young man, he had been a high-ranking soldier in the tsar's army, and he carried himself with impressive grace and self-confidence. What was more, he was uncommonly athletic in build, and his youthful virility had a definite erotic appeal for her.

A look of surprise registered briefly in Pieter Sabov's pale blue eyes when he saw that in place of Anna van der Luon, the slave mistress was seated behind the desk, and he knew it could not be accidental that her hair was now blond instead of a faded red.

Erika felt certain he had guessed the significance of the transition, and she merely smiled as she filled two glasses with Anna's favorite liquor, *genever*. Handing him one, she remarked casually, "Anna van der Luon has departed. I have taken her place."

He calculated rapidly, his face betraying none of his feelings. "Yes, madam," he murmured. He recalled all too vividly his days of penury as a refugee from the wrath of the tsar, and he wanted, at all costs, to avoid a return to that situation. He would go along with the new turn of events, at least for a time, until he figured out how he could use the situation to his own advantage. He had already acquired some money from his work for the Dutchman and then his niece. Now perhaps with Erika von Klausner he would be able to acquire the additional funds he wanted before he went out on his own again.

He was reacting precisely as Erika had known he would. It would be easy enough to control him. "When we're alone," she said, "please continue to call me Erika, as you've done in the past. In the presence of others, however, I prefer to be known as Anna van der

Luon. You might say that I am assuming her identity in order to expedite and simplify the transfer of a very considerable estate.''

His eyes widened, and he averted his gaze. He recognized the boldness of the maneuver in which she was engaged but decided not to comment on it. "I understand, Erika," he said softly.

"Not quite yet, you don't, but you will soon," she told him, and sipped her own *genever*, which, oddly, she was enjoying for the first time. Its taste, she decided, had to be acquired.

"I've long had the feeling," she said, "that your talents are not being utilized to the full. Now I'm in a position to rectify all of that. Effective at once, you are promoted to the post of manager of this property. In addition, you'll become my junior partner in the administration of my fleet of ships and trading company, and you'll naturally share in the profits.''

The gleam of avarice that she read in his eyes told her that she had judged him correctly. He, too, had suffered a severe loss of fortune in life and welcomed the opportunity to regain his wealth.

"Beginning the day after tomorrow," Erika told him, "we shall make a comprehensive survey of our entire financial position. I see by my calendar that we have nothing on the agenda for at least a week thereafter, so we'll have ample time to survey our overall situation together and to decide on ways to improve our position.''

"Good," he said vigorously. "I shall look forward to it.''

"Our most immediate and pressing concern," she said, "is the arrival later today of a delegation of imperial Chinese officials from Canton.''

He became alarmed. "Weren't they familiar with the—ah—previous occupant of your post?''

"They were not," she replied firmly, "and there's no need for them to ever learn that she's been replaced. If you will be good enough to make sure that the customary banquet is being prepared for them in the kitchen, I'll make sure that the concubines and the eunuchs are prepared to greet our guests royally.''

He grinned at her and rose slowly to his feet. "Your confidence strengthens mine," he told her.

She smiled at him, not realizing that her features had become so hardened that her expression was enigmatic. "You anticipate no problems, then, with household servants who may become overly curious?"

Pieter quietly patted the hilt of the short sword that he habitually wore. "There will be no problems," he assured her.

"I've tried to learn all I could about my predecessor's way of life," she said quietly, "but there are certain areas in which I've had to make surmises. For example, I've guessed that you and she were—shall we say—intimate."

He shook his head. "As she was not the most appealing of women, I'm glad to say that your guess is mistaken. For whatever her reasons, she preferred the company of eunuchs."

Any woman who preferred a half-man to Pieter Sabov was mad. Rising from her seat, she walked across the room, then turned to him and demanded, "Do you find me attractive?"

He took his time examining her, letting his eyes roam from her head to her feet and back up to her head again.

Erika gloried in his scrutiny, well knowing that her figure was as trim and supple as that of a concubine half her age. The lust in his eyes answered her question.

She responded by walking up to him, so close their bodies were touching. With a silent invitation, she allowed him to fondle and kiss her as he pleased.

Their intimacy would provide the cement that would bind their partnership close together and would enable them to overcome the unseen handicaps and risks they would face in the difficult days to come.

The pungent, sweet scent of gardenias and jasmine filled the air, the concubines lolled gracefully on the cropped grass, and not even the grotesque eunuchs, clad, as usual, like women, disturbed the serenity of the scene. Erika von Klausner, who actually was thinking of herself now as Anna van der Luon, surveyed her domain from her oversized wicker chair with its thronelike back, and sipping a frosted glass of *genever* and soda, she felt at peace within herself and with the world.

The miraculous truly had taken place. Not once had her identity been questioned, and she had managed to negotiate a contract for trade with the delegation from Canton that was the largest ever achieved by the Dutchman's company. When it came to dealing with the local officials who had done business with the real Anna van der Luon and would surely recognize an imposter, Erika had Pieter conduct the meetings, explaining that his employer was temporarily incapacitated.

"I'm very proud of all of you," she announced to the subordinates who had accepted her rise to the position of their mistress without a question or a murmur. "We did wonderfully well with the Chinese delegation, and I know that you are responsible for putting the merchants in a receptive mood. Even those of you who didn't directly service them were thoughtful and considerate. Therefore, all of you are being rewarded with new skirts. The bolts of material will arrive from the Djakarta waterfront this very afternoon, and you each may select two lengths of any bolts of cloth you wish for yourselves."

The concubines were pleased and spoke happily among themselves, none of them realizing that Erika was cleverly buying their continued loyalty.

"There are two of your company whom I particularly wish to commend," Erika said. "Agloia, will you step forward, please?"

A sultry black-haired girl rose from the position in which she was reclining and sauntered forward slowly, her hips swaying.

"Your conduct obviously left nothing to be desired, Agloia," Erika said approvingly. "The head of the delegation actually wanted to buy you from me and was sorely disappointed when I told him you were not for sale. Here is your reward for serving him so well." She removed a diamond and pearl ring from her own hand and slipped it onto the girl's slender finger.

Agloia couldn't resist preening.

Erika swiftly but lightly drew a hand across the girl's bare breasts as a message to the whole company that she could do whatever she wished with them, then sent her back to her place. "Tongla!" she called.

One of the eunuchs, a caricature of a woman, rose and came forward.

"Tongla is living proof that honesty pays big dividends," Erika said. "She so pleased the tea merchant from Canton who chose her that he presented her with a handsome necklace of coral. You'll note that she still wears it because she rightly offered it to me, and I granted her permanent possession of it."

Reaching into a purse at her waist, Erika withdrew a coral ring that matched the necklace and handed it to the eunuch.

The overwhelmed Tongla cooed with pleasure.

Acting on sudden impulse, Erika reached out and pinched the eunuch on the buttocks through the thin fabric of his skirt.

Tongla's loud squeal of pain and humiliation caused the entire company of women and eunuchs to giggle at length.

"There, there," Erika said in vast amusement. "Your next lover may think your black-and-blue mark is irresistibly attractive." She drained her drink, rose, and went into the house.

Pieter Sabov, working in his shirtsleeves, was laboriously adding a long column of figures. "I get exactly the same results every time I add these figures," he said excitedly, "but I still find it difficult to believe. Our profits from our deal with the Cantonese are going to be enormous."

Erika hugged him, then sank complacently into her wicker chair behind the desk. "This is the first deal I've ever managed myself," she said. "I think we'll always achieve results like this."

Pieter shook his head in wonder. "If you're right," he said, "we'll soon be as large and wealthy an enterprise as that of the Rakehells."

At the mere mention of the Rakehells, a startling transformation took place in Erika. Color rose to her face, her eyes glittered, and her fists became clenched so tightly that her shoulders and arms became rigid. "There was a time," she said venomously, "when the Dutchman's company was infinitely larger and stronger than Rakehell and Boynton, and so was a shipping company in Hamburg for which I once worked."

Pieter was astonished by the viciousness of her undertone.

Although Erika did not realize it herself, the mere mention of the word "Rakehell" had sparked a violent series of reactions within her. Many years earlier she had toyed with the idea of marrying Jonathan Rakehell and had become infuriated when he had rejected her. He had become her most implacable and hated enemy, as had Molinda, who was employed by him, and her feelings toward both had multiplied after her attempts to do in Molinda had failed, and the Fat Dutchman had punished her by forcing her into enslavement. Her warped thinking had solidified through the long humiliating years of her enforced captivity, and she was convinced that Jonathan Rakehell was personally responsible for the suffering she had endured.

"Pieter," she said, "you see the beginning of the woman I have become, just as you're aware of the woman I was. As much as I've craved my freedom, as much as I have longed for the riches and the power that finally have become mine, there is one thing that I have wanted even more. Something that has given me the strength to go on when my situation seemed hopeless and my future appeared bleak. My hatred for the house of Rakehell, my absolute determination to even the score against them, has kept me alive and kept me sane."

Pieter, who was coming to know her, thanks to the intimate relationship she had thrust upon him, was surprised by the depth and intensity of feeling that she displayed.

"Jonathan Rakehell may be beyond my reach now," she said. "He's given up traveling to this part of the world and he's not that active in the business since he's become the chairman of Rakehell and Boynton. But he has children who are active in the business, a son and a daughter. I intend to make them suffer the way their father forced me to suffer! I intend to see that Jonathan Rakehell's children—as well as his company—come to ruin."

"May I ask how you will accomplish that end?" Pieter asked as respectfully as he could.

But Erika was so inflamed she took no note of Pieter's servility. "We are going to America," she announced, her voice breathless. "There, in their own territory, we will wage a war against the Rakehells from which they will never recover!"

III

Surrounded by the mounted armed guards, who had been her constant companions since the Rakehell and Boynton clipper had landed her at the Chinese port city of Tientsin, Jade decorously rode her horse sidesaddle through the broad, dusty streets of Peking, the imperial capital of the Middle Kingdom. This was her first visit to the city since the war with England and France that had shaken Cathay to its roots, and she marveled at the changes that she saw. In some ways, Peking was the same as it had ever been, and in others, it was vastly different.

The small, simple clay huts that were the dwellings of the poor still seemed to stretch endlessly to the horizon and gave the optical illusion of going all the way to the Great Wall that had been erected to keep the Manchurian invaders out of the city. That effort had failed, and the Manchu dynasty now ruled the land, as it had for centuries.

The air was filled with fine particles of dust, a phenomenon peculiar to Peking, and Jade's eyes smarted and she swallowed with some difficulty. These reactions alone told her that she had returned to Peking.

The young woman and her party rode through a gate set in a towering stone wall and accepted the salutes of soldiers, in rumpled uniforms of imperial chrysanthemum yellow, who were armed with ludicrously old-fashioned flintlock muskets. As Jade well knew, she was about to pass through the section of Peking known as the Imperial City.

Here were located the massive stone buildings that housed the various government departments, and clerks worked by the tens of thousands in earnest anonymity, guiding and directing and supervising every aspect in the lives of the people who constituted the most populous nation on earth. There were no major industries in Peking; strictly a government center, its business was exclusively that of administration.

But something new had been added to Peking since Jade's last visit, and she gazed with interest at the huge compounds, each surrounded by a high wall of its own and each of which occupied the equivalent of several square blocks. These were the foreign legations that had been established since the war, and she was fascinated to see the flags of the United States, Great Britain, and France, of Germany, Imperial Russia, and Portugal flying over the various compounds.

As one who was herself half Chinese, Jade could sympathize with the citizens of Peking, who, she felt sure, were humiliated by the presence of the foreigners in their midst. Not only were outsiders actually living in the imperial capital for the first time in recorded history, but each of the legation compounds was considered to be foreign soil, a literal extension of American or British—or whatever the nation might be—territory where the laws of that nation, rather than those of China, prevailed. The governments of the Western nations were being shortsighted as usual, she reflected. In their greed to acquire Chinese territory, they were riding roughshod over the sensibilities of the people of Cathay and were building trouble for themselves in the future. But they could not look that far ahead, and only those who had the welfare of the Middle Kingdom at heart could feel apprehensive about the shape of things to come.

The government was dominated by the Corps of Eunuchs, a remarkable organization that comprised the best brains available in the nation. Promising youths were taken into the corps, subjected to cruel surgery, and then rigorously trained for the posts of high administration, which were occupied exclusively by members of this elite band who devoted their entire lives to furthering the cause of the emperor and his subjects.

Ultimately the party came to another high, thick wall, beyond which could be seen the pagodalike upturned edges of the tile roofs that loomed behind it. Here lay the Forbidden City, the very heart of the empire. Here were the palaces of the emperor, his wives and concubines, the princes and princesses of royal blood, their innumerable retainers, and the government officials who administered their affairs. It was said that many individuals in the armies of servants who waited on members of the royal family spent their entire lives behind the walls of the Forbidden City.

Both the Tao Kuang emperor and his sister, An Mien—whom Jade had met when she was a little girl—had died years ago. Wu Ling and her American husband, Dr. Matthew Melton—whom Jonathan had introduced to the imperial court—were not in residence in the Forbidden City at the moment, for they were visiting some of the remote provinces of China, helping the people living in rural areas.

Imperial guards armed with curved, double-edged swords halted the new arrivals, and the leader-of-one-thousand—the officer in charge—questioned Jade regarding her identity and the contents of the packages carried by the packhorse directly behind her mount.

The mere mention of her name was sufficient to identify her. As the officers in charge of the troops of the imperial guard well known, Jonathan Rakehell had been made a gift of a permanent dwelling of his own in the Forbidden City, and the right to use it had been passed to his children. As to the packages carried by the packhorse, she explained them readily.

"They're gifts for Prince Kung," she said. "I'm bringing him some books, as well as some other gifts."

There was no need for her to explain further. The sixth son of the Tao Kuang Emperor surely was the only member of the royal family who could read in English, French, and German, and he was recognized as a scholar equal to a mandarin of the first rank. As for the other gifts, these were newly manufactured Western guns that Prince Kung had requested from her.

The staff had kept the little house, adjacent to the royal palace, immaculately clean, and the servants filled a porcelain tub with hot water and a variety of scents so that Jade could luxuriate in a bath and rid herself of the grime of the road that she had accumulated on the journey from Tientsin.

When she emerged from her bath and a servant helped her dress and arrange her hair, she sent a messenger to the palace to notify Prince Kung that she had arrived and sought an audience with him. She was still seated at her dressing table mirror when the prince sent word back to her that he was eager to see her at once.

She had deliberately chosen Western clothes for the interview and had selected a pleated skirt of white silk, a blouse of the same material, and high-heeled shoes. With the exception of an enormous ring of carved jade that had been a gift of the Tao Kuang Emperor to her late mother, she wore no jewelry.

She made her way to the far end of the garden and opened the door that separated her father's property from the palace. Then, slipping into the mammoth structure through a side door, she quickly made her way down a familiar corridor to a suite on the second floor, which she entered without knocking.

Seated on a huge cushion of silk was the burly Prince Kung, who was surrounded by the books that Jade had brought him over the years. He was eagerly scanning the books that had just been delivered and, in his haste, was reaching for them one after another, following a quick perusal. He was so preoccupied that he didn't hear her enter.

His visitor cleared her throat delicately.

He looked up, recognized her with a quick smile, and did her the honor of rising to his feet, which was an unnecessary gesture for royalty.

The reason Jade had elected to wear Western attire became readily apparent when she dipped in a polite curtsy to the prince. Had she been wearing Oriental attire, she would have been required to obey the inviolable Chinese custom of prostrating herself on the floor before him.

He extended his hand in a friendly greeting. "I am more grateful to you than I can tell you for the gift of these books," he said, addressing her in English and pausing occasionally as he searched for an appropriate word. "Plainly they were purchased with great thought in mind, because, without exception, they deal with the subjects that interest me most: political and military affairs."

"I hope you enjoy them, Your Highness," she replied demurely. "The Middle Kingdom was ever-present in my thoughts during my sojourn in America."

He sat, then waved her to a place opposite him on a cushion similar to his own. "Is it true that America is suffering from a civil war?"

"I'm afraid it's all too true," Jade replied. "The issue responsible for the break is the insistence of the Confederacy—the group of southern states that have formed their own nation—on keeping the institution of slavery, although the causes are far more complex than that."

"Who will win?" Kung demanded.

Jade was lost in thought and replied carefully. "I believe the Union will win," she said, "because of a far greater industrial potential and output. She has the factories—including the munitions plants—to achieve victory. The Confederacy is much like the Middle Kingdom and is basically agricultural."

He nodded somberly. "That is why we require many industries of our own and must start building more plants and factories as soon as possible."

A manservant in imperial yellow pajamas slipped into the room and served the couple with tea.

Jade could not help noticing that the cups were exquisite and were made of porcelain so thin and delicate that they were semitransparent.

"What news is there of the Taiping Rebellion, Your Highness?" she asked.

The prince sighed ponderously. "Ten years ago," Kung said, "a mystic, H'ung Hsiu-ch'üan, founded an organization which he called the Heavenly Kingdom of Great Peace. He began his operations in Kwangsi Province and the spirit that he inculcated in the people spread like a swift-moving fire."

He was outlining the origins of the Taiping Rebellion, with which Jade was already thoroughly familiar, but she kept in mind that it would not be politic to interrupt a prince of the royal blood.

"H'ung's rebellion could have been crushed with great ease," Kung said, "if it were not for the presence at his side of Yang Hsiu-ch'ing, who is an able military planner and a genius in the fighting of battles."

Again Jade nodded. She needed no one, not even a prince of the realm, to tell her that thanks to the superior generalship of Yang, the Taiping rebels held vast portions of the Middle Kingdom, including such important cities as Anking, Soochow, and most important, the former imperial capital, Nanking, which H'ung and Yang now used as their own capital.

Kung saw her expression. "I am determined," he said, his voice hardening, "to drive the rebels from the land of my ancestors, no matter what the cost."

She knew he was sincere and was very much relieved.

"The cost, I fear, will be high," he continued.

Jade looked at him blankly.

"I suppose you have heard," he said, "that during your absence from the Middle Kingdom the Hsien Feng Emperor departed the land of the living and has joined our illustrious ancestors."

"I learned the news when I landed at Tientsin," she replied.

He nodded solemnly. "Under the terms of the late emperor's will, a board consisting of eight regents was named to rule the country. I was one, and the Empress Yehonala, who was the concubine of the emperor until he married her, is another. Six high-ranking officials, all of them rich in wisdom and in governing experience, also were named. All six have now died. They were either poisoned or strangled in their beds.''

Jade involuntarily gasped.

''It is small wonder that you are shocked,'' he said grimly. ''The Dowager Empress Yehonala is as ruthless as she is ambitious, and she allows nothing to stand in her path. She is determined to rule the Middle Kingdom alone until her son comes of age many years from now.''

''But she hasn't dared to have you assassinated, I take it,'' Jade said.

He shook his head and smiled sourly. ''The generals of the army and the admirals of the navy are my friends and my supporters,'' he said. ''If anything should happen to me, I believe they would join forces with the rebels, and Yehonala would lose her throne, as well as her influence. Her son, if he survived, would be reduced to the role of a beggar. I believe I'm safe, at least for the moment, although there's little doubt in my mind that the woman will nevertheless plot against me.''

Jade's huge eyes narrowed. ''What makes you so certain?'' she wanted to know.

''She loathes all Westerners, whom she regards as barbarians,'' he replied, ''while I consider them to be civilized men from whom the Middle Kingdom must learn much if we are to take our place as a great power in modern society.''

''You're very wise,'' she told him and was about to say something more but hesitated.

''Speak up!'' he demanded. ''Never fail to be candid and honest in all of your dealings with me.''

''Very well,'' Jade replied, and sipped her strong, aromatic tea, which was so lacking in color that it looked like a cup of pure water. This was the special tea brewed for the exclusive use of the royal family, and it was available to no one else in the Middle Kingdom or in the world beyond it.

''Your Highness undoubtedly knows that many stories are told about the Dowager Empress Yehonala,'' Jade said. ''It is rumored that in the days of her concubinage she slept with many high-ranking army officers in order to curry favor with them, and according to a rumor that has reached the ears of members of at least one of the patriotic secret societies, she is again up to her old tricks. In fact, it is said that she is even having an affair with the chief eunuch of her household, who is no eunuch at all but merely poses as one.''

Her revelations did not surprise Kung, who merely nodded, wisely refraining from asking how she happened to be privy to what was being said in secret society circles. He knew that her father had taken up arms with the powerful Society of Oxen in the Opium War against the British two decades earlier, and that she had been reared by a prominent member of the Society of Oxen, as well. But if she had any connections with the organization now, she was certain to deny her membership if he inquired. So he remained bland, nothing in his manner indicating that he suspected there was more in the background and personality of this lovely young woman than met the eye.

''Have you heard any rumors,'' he asked lightly, ''to the effect that the Dowager Empress Yehonala and I may join forces in the near future?''

Jade was stunned. ''I have heard no such story, and if such a tale were to come to my attention, I would laugh at it,'' she replied flatly.

''I would urge you not to laugh,'' he told her quietly.

She stared at him in openmouthed disbelief. ''Surely you're joking, Your Highness!'' she protested.

Kung shook his head and adjusted his heavy Western-style spectacles on the bridge of his nose. ''As long as Yehonala and I are at odds and stand opposed to each other,'' Kung said, ''the rebels will flourish and will strengthen their hold on the cities and provinces they have captured. Only when we two coregents unite and work together will it be possible to defeat the rebel hordes.''

She took her time digesting his words. ''What you say is undoubtedly true, Your Highness,'' she replied slowly. ''But I scarcely need to warn you to beware of the woman. Make whatever terms you must with her in order to achieve the common goal of smashing the rebels. But beware of poison in your cup and the knife that strikes while you are asleep.''

"I assure you, I shall be cautious," he said, and suddenly he grinned at her. "You are going to see Tseng Kuo-fan while you're in Peking?"

"How did you know?" She could not conceal her surprise.

"It has come to my attention that you and the young general are old friends," he said. "So I assumed that you would pay him a visit."

He was being diplomatic, although Jade didn't know it. Actually, he had been informed by his omnipresent secret police that Jade Rakehell had been the mistress of General Tseng Kuo-fan during the period when the officer had commanded the Canton garrison. In view of her possible connection with the patriotic secret society, her ties with the young general assumed considerable importance. He was experienced in warfare, having fought the British and French ably and skillfully, and he was a firm believer in the need to modernize the arms and armaments used by the Chinese if they hoped to hold their own against late-nineteenth-century foes.

"I was acquainted with him when he was stationed in the south," Jade said, "so I thought I'd pay my respects to him while I'm in Peking."

The prince nodded casually, nothing in his manner revealing that he considered such a meeting significant.

"Is it permitted for me to inquire, Your Highness," she asked, "when you and the Dowager Empress intend to reach an accommodation?"

The prince became cautious. "Let me say only that I anticipate a meeting with her in the very near future," he replied.

"I shall be in the city for another day or two," she said, rising and curtsying preparatory to taking her leave. "I hope I shall hear good news from Your Highness before I sail to Canton to resume my business there."

When she had gone, Prince Kung sat still, absently leafing

through one of the books that she had given him. Jade Rakehell, he decided, was well worth cultivating in the present situation. She was of far greater importance than he had ever imagined.

General Tseng Kuo-fan was one of a new breed of Chinese leaders. Taught the languages of the West in his youth by Jesuit missionaries who had not neglected his military education, he had joined the Imperial Army as a junior officer while still in his teens. His advancement had been rapid, based on sheer merit, and he was one of the few Chinese who had enjoyed a career of distinction in the recent debacle against the British and French.

The appearance of his headquarters indicated his personality. The brass buttons on the uniforms of the sentries outside the small palace at one end of the Forbidden City were shined, their boots were polished to a high gloss, and most important, they were armed with modern rifles and bayonets. The difference between them and the troops of the standard Imperial Army was marked.

Jade Rakehell announced herself to an aide and was instructed to wait in an audience chamber where a dozen or more people already were waiting in the hope of gaining an audience with the general. Her wait was short, however. She had no sooner sat and made herself comfortable, ignoring the surreptitious stares of the others, when a door at the far end of the high-ceilinged chamber burst open.

General Tseng, a brace of pistols in his belt and a sword at one side, wore a handsomely tailored uniform of imperial yellow with scarlet piping, the distinctive mark of his corps, and a delighted grin appeared on his face when he saw Jade.

At thirty-five, the youngest and most athletic of the high-ranking officers of the Imperial Army, he looked years younger.

"Jade!" he shouted in English as he strode across the room. "I thought you were still in America."

Before she could rise, he swooped down on her, lifted her to her feet, and ignoring the presence of other visitors and at least a dozen of his own subordinates, he kissed her breathlessly. "Come along and bring me up-to-date on your news," he said, linking an arm through hers, and only when they reached the door did he halt.

Turning regretfully to those who'd waited so patiently for him, he said, "I'm sorry, but perhaps one of my assistants can take care of you. I'm afraid I'm going to be occupied for some time to come." He conducted Jade down a corridor to a private suite, and seating her before a low table whose legs were handsomely carved lions of stone, he insisted on first ordering a meal for her.

His memory was remarkable. He remembered that she was very fond of a dish that consisted of sliced chicken with sliced hard-boiled eggs, smoked ham, Chinese lettuce, mushrooms, and onions, as well as water chestnuts and bamboo shoots. He recalled, too, that she was highly partial to a dish of shelled oysters, shredded pork, and minced scallions, which were lightly stir-fried. Orders having been given for the meal, he sat opposite her at the table and again addressed her in English.

"Now," he said, "let me look at you." He inspected her with such care that she grew embarrassed.

"I haven't changed that much in less than a year," she protested.

General Tseng laughed. "You've become even more gloriously beautiful since I last saw you," he roared.

"Must you shout, Kuo-fan?" she asked. "Do you want your entire army to know that we were once lovers?"

His laughter rattled the delicate figurines that stood on a low, graceful table beside him. "I'd like the whole world to know it," he declared.

"Well, I wouldn't!" she retorted. "I have a reputation as a lady to protect, and I would just as soon not be reminded that I was indiscreet and inclined to be rash in my youth."

The general subsided, and although he continued to regard her fondly, he lowered his voice. "What brings you to Peking?" he wanted to know.

"You—among other things," she replied. "I've been anxious to speak with you, and while I'm about it, I wanted to assess the political situation myself. There are rumors in the south that Prince Kung and the Dowager Yehonala are at dagger points, but I've just come from a visit with His Highness, and I'm inclined to believe now that he and the empress will bury their differences."

The general nodded confidently. "So they will. At least for the time being. Kung has the unqualified support of the better part of the army, including my corps, but several of my colleagues are reluctant to take up arms against the mother of the boy emperor, even though there's little doubt in their minds that she's responsible for the murder of her fellow regents. The situation isn't very healthy, but it promises to improve."

"It must improve," Jade replied with heat. "Not only do the foreigners who've moved in since the war drain away the better part of the profits from the tea and cotton trades, our major exports, but the continuing presence of the rebels in so much of the country further enfeebles us."

He stared at her; she was the only woman he had ever known who was thoroughly conversant with the complex political and military situation in the Middle Kingdom. "You'll be relieved to hear," he said, "that the days of the rebels are numbered."

"Oh?" She was polite but alert.

"Assuming that the regents are able to strike a bargain," he said, "several of my colleagues and I are in the process of forming a new striking force, to which we've given the optimistic name of the Ever-Victorious Army. We're going to go after the Taiping rebels with every resource available to us, and if we have the support of the people, I'm sure we'll win and recover the lands that the emperor has so shamefully lost."

Jade rose to her feet, went to the door and closed it, and then returned to the table. "The time has come for me to take you into my confidence," she said. "I'm going to pass along to you a secret that is known only to my brother and to our cousin: You shall have the unqualified support of the patriotic secret societies, especially that of the Society of Oxen. As you can imagine, they have many members currently living in rebel-occupied territory, so their support should be particularly valuable to your corps."

General Tseng firmly banished from his mind the undeniable fact that Jade was both beautiful and desirable. There were far more important matters at stake. "Do I gather correctly," he asked softly, "that you're acting as an authorized spokeswoman for the Society of Oxen?"

Jade nodded complacently, and there was a hint of amusement in her voice as she replied, "Since the days of Lo Fang and of Kai, my mentors, I have been a member of the high command of the Oxen."

He was thoroughly bewildered. "How is it possible," he said, "for one who is a mere woman and is prominent in a foreign firm of shipbuilders and traders to achieve a high place in the Oxen?"

"Let me answer you as best I am able," she replied flatly. "As to my being a mere woman, I can ride a horse as well as your best cavalrymen, and I will match any marksman in your corps in a contest with either rifles or pistols. I can navigate and sail a clipper ship safely across vast stretches of ocean, and I am adept in the use of the martial arts. As to your other charge, it is true that I am a Fan Kuei—a foreign devil. It is also true that my grandfather, Soong Chao, gave his life for his country in the Opium War. My father, Jonathan Rakehell, fought side by side with the men of the Middle Kingdom in that war, and my mother, Soong Lai-tse lu, contributed a fortune to help bolster the imperial treasury. I have no need to prove my patriotic attachment to this country."

He rose abruptly, and he brought his heels together and bowed. "I owe you an apology, and I offer it to you freely and sincerely," he said, speaking in Mandarin. "I spoke in haste, but you're right. No one can quarrel with your credentials."

Their food arrived, saving her the need to reply, and she ate gracefully with the ivory chopsticks she was provided.

General Tseng, watching her, shook his head in wonder. Jade was totally Chinese one moment, just as she was completely Western the next. She was the only Eurasian he had ever known who had absorbed all that was important and vital in the cultures of both East and West.

"I've been authorized to inform you," Jade said, "that at an appropriate time after you begin military operations to reconquer territory from the rebels, operatives of the Oxen who are currently living in rebel-held territory will get in touch with you and will keep you informed regarding the military strengths and dispositions of the forces of General Yang.''

"That will be very useful," Tseng conceded, and then asked curiously, "Why have I been chosen as the recipient of such valuable information?''

Jade smiled fleetingly. "You were selected," she said, "on my recommendation. The Oxen are unique among the patriotic societies because we believe in action at all costs. When there is something to be done, we cannot tolerate procrastination. You have by far the best record of any high-ranking officer in the army. You believe in results, too, and I assured my colleagues that you would not fail us.''

"I thank you and the Oxen for your faith in me," he said, and bowed to her.

"All of us," she said, "must live up to our responsibilities. China has suffered much and has gone through great travail in years past, but now she faces the real test that is going to determine the place she will take in the society of nations. We who are equipped to carry the burden for her must do so, and must insure that she does not falter on the path.''

It was not accidental that Prince Kung wore the red-piped chrysanthemum-yellow uniform of general in chief of General Tseng's corps for his momentous confrontation with the dowager empress. He elected to go unaccompanied to the interview, rather than to be escorted by a retinue of subordinates.

It was enough, he told himself as he strolled down the long, silent corridors of the imperial palace, his footsteps echoing through the vast spaces, that he wore the purple sash of a regent. That made him the highest ranking man in the whole of the Middle Kingdom, and he needed no subordinates to prove his authority.

The corridors remained deserted, and no sounds were heard from behind the closed doors of apartments and suites. Even that section of the palace that housed the prince's concubines was unusually quiet, the girls remaining subdued because they, like everyone else, feared the outcome of the prince's interview.

It was remarkable, he thought, that the commission of a few simple murders by Yehonala could have created such fear, such a lack of ease. Everyone in the Forbidden City was afraid of her, and if the truth were to be known, he was a trifle apprehensive himself. He had first known Yehonala when she had been a concubine in the service of his brother and had let him know, with subtlety, that she was available to him, too, if he wanted her. He was glad now that he had resisted temptation and had turned her down, or like so many of the unfortunate devils who had made themselves subject to her wiles, he would have had his throat slit from one ear to the other.

The quarters occupied by the dowager empress were somewhat more extensive than his own, but Prince Kung didn't in the least mind. Since the boy emperor lived with his mother, it was only natural that she should have more space. What mattered was the power and influence that she exerted as coregent, not the number of rooms that she and her retinue occupied in the imperial palace.

Coming at last to the audience chamber of the dowager empress, Kung pushed open the heavy jade-inlaid door without bothering to knock.

Awaiting him inside was a lovely young concubine on the staff of the dowager empress, a girl clad in several layers of tissue-thin, semitransparent silk.

His upper lip curled in disgust. Surely Yehonala didn't think that he could be influenced by a seductress in matters as important as those that they currently faced.

The girl promptly threw herself to the floor and prostrated herself before him. "Will my lord and master be good enough to come with me?" She asked.

He indicated that her lord and master was not unwilling to follow her, but taking no chances, he gripped the butt of the American-made Colt repeater pistol that Jade Rakehell had brought him as a special gift.

The concubine led him through chamber after chamber, all of them empty, and the prince could not help wondering what was in store for him. Surely the dowager empress was not stupid enough to have laid such an obvious ambush for him; if something happened to him here, in her quarters, the generals in command of the principal army corps would surely revolt, and not only would she lose her regency, but her son would be deprived of his throne.

At last they came to a chamber, heavy with the odors of incense burning in several pots, and lighted by softly glowing oil lamps. A rich, thick rug, on which an imperial dragon was embroidered, covered the better part of the floor, and one side of the room was piled high with cushions and bolsters of silk in every color of the rainbow.

The prince expected the concubine to remove her layers of silk and offer herself to him. Instead, the girl again prostrated herself on the floor and then hastily backed out of the room, leaving Kung alone. So much, he thought with amusement, for the seduction scene that he had imagined.

He sensed rather than heard a movement behind a complex of lacquered screens, and again grasped his pistol.

Slowly, the Dowager Empress Yehonala moved into the open and stood between two oil lamps. Her incomparable, perfectly proportioned body gleamed in the light, and for a moment, Kung thought that she was wearing only gold body paint to cover her nudity. He was relieved beyond measure when he realized that she was wearing a gown of very thin silk cloth of gold that fitted her like a second skin. Diamonds, emeralds, and rubies blazed on her fingers and at her ears, and she resembled a statue rather than a living woman, so heavy were the cosmetics that plastered her face. The effect of a mask was further enhanced by the lacquer that she wore on her hair, and her face was devoid of all human expression.

"We meet at last, Your Highness," she said in the accented Mandarin that revealed her lower-class origins.

The prince was the one of the few people in all of the Middle Kingdom who were not required to prostrate themselves in her presence, and he remained erect and unmoving as he nodded pleasantly to her. "Your Imperial Majesty appears to be in the best of good health," he replied dryly.

She knew that he was mocking her, and her eyes flashed dangerously, thus destroying the illusion that her face was a mask.

Kung chuckled. "I received your invitation and hastened to accept it at once," he said. "It isn't every day that I'm invited to visit the Dowager Empress Yehonala."

Her eyes narrowed, but she refused to become further provoked. "Please sit down, Your Highness," she said, gesturing toward a deep mound of cushions. "What kind of tea do you prefer?"

He cleared his throat delicately. "With all due respect, Your Majesty," he said, "I will have nothing to drink and nothing to eat. I remember all too well the fate that our fellow regents have met in the recent past."

She raised a pencil-slim eyebrow. "Surely you don't imply—"

"I imply nothing," he replied briskly, "and I make no accusations." The prince seated himself on a mound of cushions in such a way that he could see both of the doors that opened into the room. He shifted the weight of his pistol and opened the flap so that he could withdraw the weapon rapidly if it should prove necessary. Smiling blandly, he remarked, "You and I are coregents now, and that fact speaks for itself. I wish both of us long and fruitful lives. If anything untoward should happen to me, no matter what the cause, I'm afraid that the generals of the army, who are my good-friends, would be inclined to vent their frustration on Your Majesty, and that would mean that there would be no regents to look out for the country and the welfare of the boy emperor. You can imagine the chaos that would inevitably result."

"I have an especially active imagination," she replied sweetly as she gracefully lowered herself and kneeled on a cushion beside him. "It's possible for me to envision the scene that you've outlined, and I will readily grant you that such chaos is unthinkable for the future of my son."

"As well as the future of the Middle Kingdom," he added forcibly.

"To be sure," she agreed. "It's plain that nothing must happen to either of us in the foreseeable future. You and I depend upon each other; it behooves both of us to do all in our power to protect each other from possible enemies."

Her message was clear, and the prince smiled as he nodded.

"Your Majesty echoes my own thinking," he said. "Together we are invincible, and we can crush any foe in the Middle Kingdom who stands in our path. I include the Taiping rebels. Only if we are divided will we falter and lose our way."

Yehonala extended a slender hand on which the nails, easily an inch and a half long, were covered with a glistening black lacquer. "I'm glad that we have reached a meeting of the minds," she said.

He took her hand and held it. "So am I," he said. "It makes the task much easier for both of us."

She made no attempt to withdraw her hand.

Her new meaning was all too plain. As part of her bargain with Kung, she was offering herself. He debated the question briefly and decided that there was little to be gained and much to be lost by engaging in an affair with her. Though their intimacy would enable him to keep a closer watch on her, it would also give her increased opportunities to do him harm. He well remembered what happened to her other lovers.

The dowager empress inched closer to him on the cushions, and her hand remained limp and submissive in his.

"We shall have ample time to become—ah—better acquainted," he said, releasing her hand and moving away from her. "Our first task is to organize our joint forces for an assault in strength on the Taiping rebels. They have bled the Middle Kingdom long enough."

She reluctantly concentrated on the business at hand. "It's true," she said, "that if the rebels had been subdued when the English and French foreign devils attacked us, we would have defeated the English and French."

That was untrue, as he knew all too well. The defeat of the Chinese forces had been caused by the superior arms and training of the British and French. But he was in no mood to argue the point with the woman. Let her think what she pleased and do what she would, provided that she cooperated with him. "Together," he said, "we will triumph. You may be sure of it!"

IV

The lobby of the New Castle Hotel in San Francisco was typical of that city's great and gaudy hostelries. The chandelier of cut-glass crystal, in which it was said that one thousand tapers burned simultaneously, glittered and set the tone for the entire inn. Red velvet draperies hung over the high windows, servants in uniforms that were supposed replicas of those worn at the Palace of Versailles during the reign of Louis XV were everywhere, and the atmosphere reeked of money. That was only to be expected in a community where the gold rush of the previous decade had produced countless new millionaires.

The patrons and staff of the New Castle Hotel ordinarily were blasé, unimpressed by demonstrations of wealth. But the arrival of the faded blonde, accompanied by the handsome young man about fifteen years her junior, created a stir. The woman wore a cape of ermine and was followed by a retinue of servants, carrying, by conservative estimate, at least fifty pieces of luggage. She stood, ignoring the stares of the curious, while her escort registered for them at the desk.

"You have our reservations, I believe," Count Pieter Sabov said in accented but clearly understandable English. "Madam Anna van der Luon and party."

"To be sure, sir." The manager bowed and rubbed his hands together. "For the report that I must make to the United States immigration authorities, may I know the name of the vessel that transported madam and her party to San Francisco?"

"She traveled on board the *Java,* a clipper ship of her own fleet," Pieter replied frostily. "Madam van der Luon has come to your country on strictly private business, so we shall be eating all of our meals in the suite. Similarly, she refuses all interviews with the press and does not wish to be bothered by reporters. A magnum of champagne on ice is to be kept in her bedchamber at all times, and another is to be available in her sitting room. Tomorrow madam will receive the three leading dressmakers of your city in succession. Any three whom you choose, and please instruct them to bring samples of their wares. We will go upstairs now, sir, if you'll be good enough to have someone show us to our suite."

The manager personally led the party up the New Castle's grand staircase, and Erika, one hand on Pieter Sabov's arm, was conscious of the crowd that was gaping at her from the lobby below.

While Pieter directed the corps of porters who were struggling with the luggage to place the right suitcases and boxes in the appropriate rooms, Erika allowed the manager to show her through the many rooms of the suite. At last she and Pieter were alone, and the servants she had brought with her were led off to their own far more modest chambers.

Sighing, Erika threw her fur-trimmed coat onto a chair and sank gratefully onto a divan.

Pieter opened a bottle of champagne resting in an ice container and filled two glasses, handing one to her.

"I never knew," she said as she sipped her wine, "that great wealth could be so exhausting. I'm learning, however, and it grows easier all the time."

"We needn't have taken such a grand suite, you know," he replied.

She disliked his reproving tone and frowned. "You know full well why I took this suite," she said. "I consider it imperative that we duly impress the young lady who is going to call on us. How soon is she due?"

Pieter tugged at the chain of the gold watch that had been one of her recent gifts to him and looked at it. "She won't be here for another two hours," he said.

"Good." Erika extended her glass to him, and while he refilled it, she lightly ran her free hand up and down the inside of his thigh. "That will give us ample time to make love right here," she murmured. "Be good enough to remove your clothes."

Still unaccustomed to her abrupt sexual demands, he flushed, gulped the rest of his champagne, and hastily refilled his own glass.

Erika regarded him in amusement. "Please me," she said, "and you can wallow in as much champagne as you can drink. Now, hurry and take off your clothes!"

The red-faced Pieter had no choice and hastened to undress. He knew she relished exerting her power over him, particularly after being forced to spend so many years as a courtesan on the Fat Dutchman's Djakarta estate. He loathed himself for giving in to her whims and for accepting treatment that reduced him to the level of a male concubine; however, he received ample financial rewards, and it would not be long before he would be wealthy enough to part from Erika for all time, a free man who never had to do anyone's bidding again.

Erika leaned back on the divan and watched him lazily. When he stood in the nude before her, she crooked a finger and beckoned him to come closer.

Pieter was all too familiar with the routine that would follow. She would continue to amuse herself at his expense and would deliberately arouse him; this in turn would arouse her and then he would be commanded to make violent love to her. He had to close his mind to all thought and let her do what she pleased. It was the only way he could get through the difficult scenes that followed.

*   *   *

Alexis Johnson moved through the lobby of the New Castle Hotel and up the grand staircase with the grace and ease of a young woman who was very certain of her beauty. Her flame-colored hair was piled high on top of her head, and her long gold earrings accented the perfect oval of her face and the clarity of her chiseled features. She had made a fine art of her use of cosmetics, and only an expert would have known that she had used rouge to bring out the ripe fullness of her mouth, and kohl and shadow to emphasize the intensity of her emerald-green eyes. She had a knack for wearing clothes, too. Although her dress appeared modest, it did full justice to her ripe, full figure. She was exceptionally tall, but it was typical of her to wear shoes with towering heels to further accentuate her height.

A few moments later, she and the woman posing as Anna van der Luon took each other's measure. Erika could not help being reminded of the girl she herself had once been. Her hair had been Alexis Johnson's color, and she had carried herself with the same arrogance based on complete self-knowledge.

"Will you do the honors, Pieter?" she asked blandly.

"Of course," Pieter Sabov replied, and poured a glass of champagne for the visitor.

Alexis was conscious of the exceptionally handsome young man, but her sixth sense told her that he enjoyed a special relationship of some kind with her hostess. Thus she took no chances, and the fleeting smile she bestowed on him by way of thanks was as impersonal as it was rapid.

"Perhaps," Erika said lightly, "you'll also attend to the initial payment, Pieter?"

He nodded, reached into a wallet that he carried in an inner coat pocket, and removed from it a crisp one-thousand-dollar bill, which he handed to the young woman.

Alexis scrutinized the money at length to make certain that it was not counterfeit, and satisfied that it was legitimate, she folded it and put it into a tiny silk reticule that dangled from one wrist. "You have an advantage over me, Madam van der Luon," she said. "You know why you've summoned me here, but I'm still completely in the dark. All I know is that the detective agency that got in touch with me said they were in your employ and that it would be well worth my while if I called on you.''

''I assure you that you won't regret this afternoon, nor will you regard this visit as a waste of your time,'' Erika said. ''Before we proceed, I wonder if you'd be good enough to fill us in a bit on your background. The detective agency sent us a brief biography, but I find it's always preferable to hear what an individual has to say.''

Alexis folded her hands in her lap and pondered the question. She looked and behaved like a perfect lady. ''I attended a good school in the East,'' she said, ''one of the best in the Philadelphia area. I came west to join my father, at his request, when he was searching for a strike in the gold fields. Unfortunately, he died a pauper and left me penniless, so I had to fend for myself.''

Erika exchanged a shrewd look with Pieter. ''You appear to have not only survived but to have prospered,'' she said.

Alexis's smile was hard, and her voice became brittle. ''I always survive,'' she said. ''I despise weakness, and I do whatever is necessary to do in order to stay alive.''

Erika nodded slowly. Here, indeed, was a kindred spirit. ''I know exactly what you mean,'' she said.

''My first employment—the only work that was open to me,'' Alexis said, ''was as a dance-hall hostess in a saloon in the gold fields.''

''That must have been thoroughly unpleasant work,'' Erika commented.

The younger woman smiled faintly. ''I've known better,'' she replied lightly, ''far better. I don't recommend the work to anyone who dislikes being mauled by woman-hungry miners.'' She brightened. ''It wasn't too long, however, before I was promoted to the post of poker dealer, and my fortunes have improved steadily ever since that time. I've worked my way back up in polite society, and I'm accepted in certain circles now where my past is unknown. What else would you like to know about me?''

"I think we've heard quite enough, don't you agree, Pieter?" Erika asked.

Pieter Sabov, who found the interview and the reason behind it unsavory, nodded glumly.

"To what extent," Erika demanded, "are you ruled or influenced by conscience?"

Alexis met her gaze stonily. "I refuse to commit murder, mayhem, or any other act of violence," she replied, "and I will do nothing contrary to the law. Under no circumstances do I care to run the risk of being sent to prison."

"I don't blame you, and I certainly wouldn't ask you to run any such risk," Erika said sympathetically.

Alexis appeared satisfied but waited warily.

"The assignment I have in mind for you is simple but will not be easy to execute. As you're about to hear, it is not illegal in any sense of the word. I'll want you to travel to New London, Connecticut, which is the home of a man named Julian Rakehell."

The young woman pondered. "He's a high-ranking official, I believe, in the shipping and trading firm of Rakehell and Boynton."

Erika was delighted: Alexis was even brighter and more clever than the agency had indicated. "Correct," she said. "He's the president of the firm. I want you to become acquainted with him—I don't care how you go about doing it—and get him to fall in love with you and marry you."

Alexis whistled softly under her breath.

"Wait," Erika commanded. "That's only the beginning. After you're married to him, you'll reveal your rather lurid past to him and subject him to complete social disgrace. The Rakehells have as high a standing as any family in New England. I'll want you to make sure that by the time you're done with Julian Rakehell, that fine reputation is destroyed."

"Assuming I'm able to accomplish all that, which is a tall order," Alexis said, "I'd be also bringing social disgrace and ruin on myself, wouldn't I?"

"There are compensations," Erika told her firmly. "For one thing, naturally, I'll attend to all of your expenses, including those of a suitable wardrobe, appropriate travel, and so on. When you've accomplished your mission successfully, you shall receive the sum of one hundred thousand dollars. The money will be deposited here in a San Francisco bank, and it will be made available to you the minute you've followed the plan that I've outlined.''

Alexis stared at her to ascertain whether she was joking.

''Madam van der Luon,'' Pieter said, ''is one of the wealthiest women in the East. We don't ask you to take our word regarding her standing. I suggest you check at your own bank or, better yet, with the Dutch consulate here. As for the one hundred thousand dollars, I urge you to come with me when I make the deposit of that sum in a local bank so that you may assure yourself that what we promise is authentic and not some sort of dream.''

''If you don't mind,'' Alexis replied slowly, ''I shall certainly do all of those things.'' She was silent for a time, pondering the strange offer. ''May I ask why you have this peculiar vengeance in mind for Mr. Rakehell?''

''Let me just say,'' Erika told her, ''that his father was directly responsible for many years of intense suffering and degradation that I was forced to endure. As a consequence, I hate the very name of Rakehell and will do anything I can in this world to bring unhappiness to anyone who bears that name.''

Again Alexis was silent. ''You've been very shrewd in your choice of me as an instrument of your revenge,'' she said. ''Obviously you know that my own background has been sufficiently difficult that I've lost all true social standing and can never recover it.''

''Precisely right,'' Erika told her, ''and the only respectable men who would marry you would have to be from the Atlantic coast and would have to know nothing of your past. But the fee of one hundred thousand dollars that you'll be paid will give you independence and will provide you with balm for the indignity that you'll be forced to endure when you become young Rakehell's wife.''

''I know the man only by name,'' Alexis said. ''The task of persuading him to marry me may be beyond my abilities. What do I receive if the scheme fails and he doesn't marry me?''

''You'll have your wardrobe, of course,'' Erika told her, ''and you'll have enjoyed a sojourn in New England. But you won't receive one penny of the one-hundred-thousand-dollar reward. I'm taking a considerable risk in this enterprise, and either you have sufficient confidence in your own abilities to carry off the plan or else you're the wrong woman for the job."

"I see," Alexis said, and was silent. Suddenly she grinned, and her face became radiant. "What the hell!" she exclaimed. "I'll do it. I've taken bigger risks than this in my life, and the rewards are far greater than any risks involved."

Erika rose from her seat on the divan and solemnly shook hands with the young woman, while Pieter poured fresh champagne for all of them.

"I'll provide you with the information we've accumulated on the Rakehells in New London from the detective agency," he said, "and I'll provide you with transportation to the Atlantic as soon as you're able to leave."

"One hundred thousand dollars," Alexis mused, "is more money than I've ever known in all my life. More money than I've ever dreamed I'd possess." She rose and picked up her glass. Standing with her feet apart, her breasts outthrust, and her jaw jutting forward, she raised her glass and then drained the contents. "Never fear, Madam van der Luon!" she said. "I'll carry out this scheme of yours to the letter. You can depend on it."

V

The Honorable Drusilla Smythe, the ash-blond twenty-three-year-old daughter of the Earl and Countess of Dudley, was entertaining members of her own generation at her parents' fashionable country home outside London, and a large group of England's most socially elite were gathered for the event. The Dudleys were noted for their hospitality, and tables on the lawn beneath Japanese lanterns were laden with hot and cold foods of every description, while liveried footmen circulated through the crowds serving champagne, sack, and a variety of wines.

The staff functioned smoothly, seemingly as effortlessly as the well-oiled engine of a Rakehell and Boynton ship. The housekeeper and the butler, both of them vastly experienced, kept watch on the proceedings and anticipated requests before the guests themselves became aware of them. Foods such as the cold rare roasts of beef that proved popular were replaced from the kitchens, while the dishes that were shunned were quietly removed.

It was fortunate that the help knew its business so thoroughly, because the young hostess was neglecting her duties. Looking ethereal in a gown of pale blue gauzelike silk, Drusilla—as any number of her guests realized, and as her parents certainly knew—was totally absorbed in one of her guests, David Boynton, who had recently returned to England after his sojourn in America.

They ate supper together, then strolled at length in the extensive gardens for which the Dudleys were renowned, and ultimately they sat on a stone bench, with the moonlight playing on Drusilla's attractive features.

"The significance of steamships is very simple and easy to understand," David said earnestly, delighted to have found such an eager, receptive audience. "Ever since man has begun going to sea, he's been subject to the winds and the tides, and the weather. No matter what the ship, and there have been all kinds, including our own marvelous Rakehell and Boynton clippers, they have been subjected to the elements. No one has ever known precisely how long any given voyage would last. Now all that is a thing of the past. The steamship, driven by engines, doesn't depend on the winds and the tides. When we schedule a voyage to begin on Monday and end a week from Thursday, it begins and ends on schedule. It may be several hours early or late, of course, but almost invariably it reaches its destination when it's supposed to get there."

"I had no idea," Drusilla said, and looked at him with shining eyes.

"I daresay," he replied, "most people don't." Suddenly he caught himself and shook his head. "Do forgive me, Drusilla, for going on like this. I know it isn't considered polite to talk about one's work and to enthuse over one's vocation, but I'm so caught up in the shipping industry that I find that I live, breathe, eat, and sleep ships. It's a family curse."

She laughed, clasping her small hands together. "It seems to me to be a very nice curse," she told him.

He grinned at her. "You're kind to say so."

"I know you hold master's papers for clipper ships," she said. "Do you also have the right to act as captain of a steamship?"

David smiled again. "Do you ride to hounds?" he demanded. She was bewildered. "Of course."

"Exactly the point I'm trying to make," he explained. "You have certain family traditions and learning to ride is one of them. Well, we have traditions in my family, as well, and we not only build ships, but everyone in the family is qualified to command every last vessel that comes out of our yards. So to answer your question briefly—indeed, I hold papers to command a steamship, as well as a sailing ship."

Her curiosity was aroused. "Tell me," she said, "that gorgeous cousin of yours, Jade Rakehell, who last visited here a couple of years ago, does she hold papers to command all of these different kinds of ships, too?"

David grinned and shook his head. "No, she doesn't," he said, "but only because the world isn't yet ready to award such authority to women. But I can assure you, Jade is capable of sailing any vessel that comes out of our yards, from a clipper ship or a schooner to a passenger steamship or even an ironclad man-of-war."

"Growing up must have been very difficult for her," Drusilla said.

"On the contrary," David replied warmly. "She had a wonderful childhood. We all did."

She looked at him thoughtfully. "You know, David," she said, "I envy you. I really do. Your upbringing was so very different from that which most of us have had. You lived in America and in the Orient from the time you were a very small child, and you're as familiar with them as you are with England, and you know so much about so many things that are different and exciting."

Her enthusiasm left him flustered and he was tongue-tied.

Drusilla put a hand on his arm. "Oh, dear," she said. "I didn't mean to embarrass you."

Conscious of her touch, he became scarlet. "That is—that is quite all right," he muttered.

She breathed tremulously, then said, "We really should be getting back to the others. I'm neglecting them shamefully."

"I'm to blame," David insisted.

"Never mind," she said. "I'm having the best time ever." She took his arm and they laughed softly as they walked down the path toward the manor house and the other guests assembled on the lawn.

In their early fifties, Sir Charles and Lady Boynton were thoroughly enjoying themselves. After his father and mother had died a few years earlier, Charles retired from the Rakehell and Boynton firm and fulfilled a lifelong ambition to enter politics by becoming a member of Parliament. He and Ruth maintained an active social life in London, where they kept the house in the fashionable Belgravia section of town, and they enjoyed summers in their country house in Sussex, where they were currently residing during a recess of Parliament.

Ruth discovered that the climate and soil of Sussex were just right for her flower garden, and she grew several varieties of roses that were the envy of all of her neighbors. Charles, not to be outdone, had his own vegetable garden, and he not only grew enough to fill their own table, including that of their extensive staff, but he also had enough produce to give away to friends and neighbors.

Long accustomed to getting an early start on the activities of the day, they took full advantage of their summer holiday by going into their respective gardens for an hour or two of work each day before breakfast. Pruning and weeding, Ruth was particularly delighted at the enthusiasm that her husband showed for his activity. He worked as hard on his brussels sprouts, radishes, and cauliflower as he had labored for years in making Rakehell and Boynton one of the leading forces in British shipping and commerce, and as he now worked as a member of Parliament.

Ruth glanced at the gray-haired, wrinkled Charles, who was a year or two younger than his cousin, Jonathan Rakehell. The difficult years, when the mercurial Charles, dashing about the face of the earth making spectacular deals and attracting the attention of women because of his magnetic personality, were behind her now, and she and her husband had at last achieved the solid base for their marriage for which she had longed. Their contentment had been earned, well earned, she reflected, as she trimmed bits of dead wood from a rosebush.

Suddenly Ruth heard the drumbeat of a horse's hoofs approaching at a gallop and she was surprised. There were few visitors to the estate at this early hour of the day, and whoever was approaching seemed to be in a hurry.

Charles was the first to recognize the rider and rose hastily to his feet. David was hatless, his cape streaming behind him in the wind, and it was apparent, at a glance, that he was still attired in evening clothes. He waved to his parents, grinning broadly, and rode his horse to the stables at the rear of the main house.

His stepmother—the only mother he had ever known—was deeply concerned, and leaving her garden tools behind, she hastened to follow him. "What on earth do you suppose has happened?" she asked.

Charles, walking rapidly beside her, chuckled aloud. "From the looks of him," he said, "the boy has had quite an evening at the Dudley girl's party. I suspect from his white tie and tailcoat that he hasn't yet been to bed."

"Oh, dear," Ruth murmured, and her concern mounted.

David was emerging from the stable as his parents approached the building, and he enveloped his stepmother in a bear hug, then vigorously embraced his father and shook his hand. "I'm famished!" he told them. "I hope I'm in time for breakfast."

Discovering that they had not yet eaten, he linked his arms through theirs and started to lead them toward the dining room.

"Wait!" Ruth commanded. "I'm too grubby to sit at the table, and I need to wash first."

A laughing David released her and continued toward the dining room with his father.

Sir Charles glanced at him obliquely. "You seem very pleased with yourself this morning," he observed.

"I am, sir; most assuredly I am," his son replied. "I'll wait until Mama joins us before I discuss my news."

"Very well." Charles and David washed their hands at a small cistern on the terrace outside the dining room, then they entered through the French doors. Charles took his place at the head of the massive oak table in the dining room and noted, with satisfaction, that there was no need to tell the butler that David had come home and would join them for breakfast; a place was already set for him.

"We didn't expect to see you today, David," Sir Charles said. "We thought you were heading straight back to London after the Dudley party."

"So I was, sir, but I decided to make the detour and drop in on you and Mama first."

Ruth joined them, and the ritual of breakfast began. They were served with eggs, bacon, and sausages, with kippered herring and fried Channel sole, with lamb's kidneys sauteed with peppers and onions, and a large variety of hot and cold cereals. There were hot scones dripping with butter, and the cook did not forget that David had a weakness for toasted black bread with plenty of butter.

The young man ate ravenously, and Ruth, confining herself to a soft-boiled egg and two slices of dry toast, marveled at his appetite. Whatever had impelled him to drop in on his parents had in no way impaired his desire to eat.

Satiated at last, David settled back in his chair with a large mug of coffee, made from the beans that were imported for the family from the Dutch East Indies, and smiled expansively at his parents. "Don't be too surprised," he told them, "if one of your fondest wishes comes true in the fairly near future. Mama, you've told me for several years now that the time was right for me to marry and settle down, and you, Papa, have hinted rather broadly that you thought it would be good for me and for business if I'd find a wife. Well, I think I've found one."

Charles drew in his breath and held it.

"Do we know her?" Ruth wanted to know.

David's smile became self-conscious. "Drusilla Smythe," he said.

His parents exchanged startled glances. "You proposed to her and have been accepted?" Charles demanded, his tone sharper than he knew.

David, unaware that his father was perturbed, shook his head. "No, sir, that would be somewhat premature. I haven't asked the Earl of Dudley for her hand, and I don't intend to speak to him until Drusilla and I have reached our own understanding. Which, in my opinion, is imminent."

Again, Charles and Ruth looked at each other.

"There's a magical quality to a garden in moonlight," David said, "and I know that Drusilla felt exactly as I did last night. I've never before been in love, really, so I'm not sure that I know the symptoms, but whatever they are, I think I've caught them."

Again the older couple exchanged looks, and Ruth frowned.

This was going to be both difficult and delicate, and Charles cleared his throat. "Ever since you were very small, David," he said, "we've followed the principle of giving you your head and letting you make your own decisions—and your own mistakes. We've felt that you'd learn best by trial and error, and would stay away from a hot stove after burning your fingers a few times."

David looked at him in bewilderment, his smile slowly fading. "I'm afraid I don't understand," he said.

Ruth took a deep breath. "How well do you know Lord and Lady Dudley?" she wanted to know.

David shrugged. "I have chatted with them from time to time, mostly about inconsequential matters," he said. "They're enormously wealthy, and they have no interest in shipping or in trade or in the political affairs of the countries of the East—all of which fascinates me. So I daresay that I haven't had too much, really, in common with them."

"Oh, dear," Ruth breathed.

David turned to his father for an explanation.

"Have you ever noticed anything odd or forced in their attitude toward you?" Charles asked.

David shook his head. "No, sir."

Ruth realized that the issue had to be met squarely and without subterfuge. "I'm not sufficiently well acquainted with Drusilla to know whether she shares her parents' attitudes," she said, "but what we're trying to tell you flatly is that the Dudleys are bigots."

David stared at her in stunned disbelief.

"Mama is right," Charles said. "Their attitude is typical of a certain breed of English aristocrat, whom you've encountered countless times in your sojourns in the Orient. They regard themselves as vastly superior to people of any other race, and they're inclined to look down their patrician noses at anyone who has any hint of Chinese in his ancestry."

"They've always been very cordial to me," David protested, "and I swear that Drusilla doesn't mind in the least that I'm part Chinese. She not only treats me as she treats any of her other friends, but she was warm and vibrant and alive in the garden last night. I'm not imagining the relationship, I swear to you!"

Ruth wanted to warn him not to let his enthusiasm interfere with his judgment, but she decided to say nothing. David appeared certain in his own mind that Drusilla Smythe bore him no prejudice because of his part-Chinese background, and it was impossible to argue with a view that he expressed with such definitive certainty. She hoped, desperately, that he wouldn't be hurt, but he was a man, not a boy, and it wasn't her place to interfere.

"When are you leaving for London, David?" she asked.

"I thought I'd go soon after breakfast," he said, "unless you have something else in mind."

"If you could spare the time to wait for an hour or two," Ruth said, "we could ride together in my carriage. I've got to go to the city myself to do some errands that will keep me there for a day or two."

"By all means, Mama, we'll go together," he replied.

She nodded and let the subject of the prejudice of the Dudleys drop. Perhaps there would be an opportunity on the way to the city, or in London, to renew the conversation and to persuade him to protect himself from possible harm.

Lord Dudley, heavyset and slow-moving, was well aware of his daughter's hour-by-hour schedule throughout the day. So, shortly before she was expected back from her regular morning canter on her mare, he deliberately opened the door of his study. She would pass the room on her way to her own quarters upstairs, and it would be easy enough to fall into conversation with her.

Lighting a *segaro* of dark West Indian tobacco with a sulfur match, the Earl of Dudley picked up a pen and opened the ledger on his desk. He appeared to be hard at work.

Within a short time, he heard his daughter's footsteps as she approached down the corridor, and dipping the quill pen hastily into a jar of ink, he began to write in the ledger.

"Good morning, Papa!" Drusilla called cheerfully through the open door.

He feigned slight surprise, but his pleasure was genuine. "Well, my dear, how are you? I see you've survived your party festivities."

"Yes, and I want to thank both you and Mama for being so wonderful. It was a perfectly marvelous party."

"Come in, Drusilla, come in." He jabbed the pen into a jar of sand and beckoned.

She came into the study, tapping her riding crop against the side of a leather boot. "I hope my friends and I didn't keep you up too long past your bedtime," she said.

He smiled at her benignly. "It doesn't hurt in the least for me to go to sleep late," he said. "I'm not so old and decrepit yet that I can't tolerate a late night now and again."

"I'm glad to hear it, Papa." Drusilla had never been particularly close to the earl, and being somewhat in awe of him, she was faintly ill at ease in his presence. She had been reared on the theory that an appropriate distance was maintained between generations, and any attempts to bridge those gaps made her somewhat apprehensive.

"All of your friends appeared to enjoy themselves," the Earl of Dudley said, and blew a thin cloud of *segaro* smoke toward the high ceiling.

"Yes, I think everyone had a good time," Drusilla agreed.

"I had no idea," Lord Dudley went on, "that you were well acquainted with young David Boynton."

So that was it! She was about to be lectured for having gone off at length into the garden with David.

But her father surprised her by making no direct reference to the incident. "I hear he's very bright," he said, "a worthy successor to his father and his grandfather."

"He has the quickest, most flexible, and most subtle mind of anyone I've ever known," Drusilla replied, a hint of bravado in her voice.

Her father did not appear to notice. "He has the usual Rakehell and Boynton knack for making money, I must say," he conceded. "I can remember the time when his grandfather was moderately well-to-do. The family was comfortable, to be sure, but they were no wealthier than anyone else in our crowd. Then Charles became active and his son has carried on the tradition, and today the Boyntons are filthy rich. They must control one of the great fortunes in England at the present time."

His daughter made it plain that she wasn't interested in the Boynton wealth. "David is never so crass as to talk about money," she said.

"I'm pleased to hear it." Now was the moment to initiate the real topic that had led Lord Dudley to seek this interview with his daughter. "I'm glad he has manners, but that doesn't surprise me. He did go to all the right schools and received a gentleman's upbringing."

"That's a rather odd thing to say," Drusilla observed.

Her father directed another cloud of smoke toward the ceiling. "Not at all," he said smoothly. "Young Boynton is different from the other young men, you know. Surely you've been aware of the difference."

She considered the remark. "The only thing different about him, to my way of thinking, is that David is by far the most handsome man I know."

Lord Dudley winced inwardly but maintained a calm façade. "That may well be," he said. "I'm no judge of whether or not a young man is or isn't good-looking. I'm more inclined to look beneath the surface."

"What do you mean, Papa?" Her confusion was genuine.

"It isn't accidental," he said emphatically, "that we've fought two major wars against the Middle Kingdom in the course of a single generation. Their thinking, their whole way of life is alien to ours. I understand that their civilization was very old and quite advanced when Britain was conquered by the Romans and was still a land of savages, but we've made up for lost time, so to speak, and today we're infinitely more advanced than the Oriental hordes.''

Drusilla didn't know quite what to reply and nodded uncertainly.

Her father pressed his obvious advantage. "Perhaps this will explain what I mean," he said. "You're on friendly terms with most of the more important members of your generation. I daresay that among your guests last night were not only the leading nobles of the younger generation but also more than a fair sprinkling of future prime ministers and of the board chairmen of major companies, as well."

"I was not thinking of my friends in those terms, but I suppose you're right, Papa," Drusilla conceded.

Lord Dudley took care not to smile or to indicate in any way that he'd achieved the upper hand. "Granted that future leaders of British politics and industry were your guests last night," he said, "can you name any one individual who is as far advanced in his vocation as David Boynton?"

Drusilla thought hard for a few moments, then shook her head.

"The very point that I'm trying to make," Lord Dudley said, "is that he makes a fetish of his business and of his own need for greater and greater success. The Boyntons already have accumulated enough money to live in comfort for generations to come, but you'd never know it from young David Boynton's attitude. He works long hours and as hard as any two-pounds-a-week clerk."

Drusilla was increasingly disconcerted.

"I'm not opposed, naturally, to the needful earning of money," Lord Dudley went on, "but to pile more on more unnecessarily is rather a grubby pastime at best. I've never overheard one of your conversations with young Boynton," he said, deliberately keeping his tone light and conversational, "but I daresay he goes on and on interminably about his business. Am I right?"

"Now that you mention it, Papa," Drusilla replied uncertainly, "he does talk a great deal about ships and shipping."

"It so happens that your mother's family makes up one of the largest wool-manufacturing firms on the face of the earth. But can you tell me, in all honesty, that you've ever heard either of your uncles mention the subject of wool?''

She shook her head and giggled. ''No, Papa. Uncle Fred talks incessantly about salmon fishing and Uncle Todd doesn't seem to talk about anything but the club that he belongs to.''

He raised both hands, then dropped them onto his desk again. ''There you have it!'' he declared. ''David Boynton may be the son of a baronet, who was educated right here in England, but he's an alien! He isn't one of us.''

Drusilla nodded, her eyes saucerlike.

''You're an adult now, my dear,'' Lord Dudley said, ''so I hesitate to give you advice, and I wouldn't presume to dictate to you regarding anyone you consider a friend. But I urge you to think long and hard about your relationship with David Boynton. He *is* Eurasian, so he's different, and no matter what the British patina is that he acquires, he and we are miles apart in our thinking. I certainly wouldn't advise you to give up a friendship with him, but if you don't mind a gratuitous word, you might be wise to let some distance seep between you.''

Again Drusilla nodded, and not speaking, she rose and went off toward her own quarters, thoughtfully tapping her riding crop on the side of her boot.

The Earl of Dudley was well satisfied with his morning's work. He had planted a large and sturdy seed of doubt in his daughter's mind, and he knew her well enough to realize that it would continue to grow. It didn't matter that much of what he had said about David was illogical and unjust. If she was becoming involved in a serious romance with young Boynton, he had succeeded in killing it.

Ruth Boynton accompanied her son to London, and the following morning, at his request, she went with him to the familiar shipyard and mercantile offices in Southwark, directly across the River Thames from the city of London. Here the Rakehell and Boynton empire had grown into a huge complex, as it had in New England. There were yards where wooden sailing ships were built, yards where metal steamships were constructed, and vast acres of warehouses where produce from the Orient and the Caribbean, from all of Europe and South America, were gathered for sale to British merchants.

The summer weather was lovely, and Ruth wanted to walk from the entrance gate, so her son humored her and dismissed the carriage, and they went the rest of the way to the headquarters building on foot.

Ruth could not help noticing that David was remarkably like his father and grandfather. His dark eyes darted here, then there, and he took in everything that was happening in the yard, even though he kept up a steady conversation with his mother. He noted the progress in the construction of a metal steamship and of a handsome wooden clipper ship that was still a mainstay of the firm's business. He saw boxes piled high outside a warehouse, half-covered with heavy canvas tarpaulin, and Ruth well knew that he would soon blister the hide of the subordinate who should have had the merchandise securely placed under cover, rather than leaving it exposed to the elements.

The headquarters building was unchanged and familiarly old-fashioned; Ruth felt at home in it and brightened appreciably as she started up the stairs toward her son's second-floor suite overlooking the Thames. How well she recalled the years that Charles had occupied that office, and the years that it had been his father's before him!

"I appreciate your coming all the way to Southwark with me just to sign some papers, Mama," David said. "I could have brought them to you at home, or even sent them to you at the country place in Sussex for signature."

"Nonsense, my dear," Ruth replied lightly. "You don't know how much I enjoy dropping in here at the yard. I'm flooded with memories, and I find it very pleasant."

"I'm glad, Mama," he replied dutifully, and recalled that she had grown up near the old Rakehell yard in New England, where her own father had been chief carpenter for a generation. She, too, had the family heritage in her bones.

David opened the door to his private suite and stood aside to allow his mother to enter first.

Seated on a high stool in the principal outer room was a pleasantly attractive, blond young woman wearing a prim ankle-length shirtwaist dress. She saw Ruth and immediately smiled. "Hello, Lady Boynton," she called cheerfully. "It's so nice to see you again."

Ruth paused to shake hands with Aileen Christopher, whose title was that of bookkeeper to the chairman of the board, but who, in actuality, was more of a private secretary to David. It was to Aileen's great credit that she had obtained this job, for few vocations were open to women in 1862. Even so, Aileen Christopher, as a bookkeeper, had gone about as high and as far as a woman could progress in any vocation.

Ruth genuinely liked Aileen. She had seen her a number of times when she came down to the shipyard, and they had chatted and even become somewhat close.

As they shook hands, Ruth said, "You're looking well, Miss Christopher. Work seems to agree with you."

"I have no complaints," Aileen replied with a laugh. "As a matter of fact, even if I did, I wouldn't dare voice them. My employer loathes people who complain." She paused, then added shyly, "Good morning, Mr. Boynton."

David was all business. "Morning, Miss Christopher."

"You had several callers while you were away," she said, "and the heads of several departments are eager to see you. I've left the list on your desk."

"Thanks very much," he replied and continued on toward his private office.

Aileen inadvertently followed him with her eyes.

Ruth was thunderstruck. Why hadn't it occurred to her before that, without the slightest doubt, Aileen Christopher was in love with David?

His mother told herself that she should have guessed, but perhaps the development was relatively new and had occurred since she had last visited the office. She was sure of one thing as she followed her son into his private sanctum: He had no idea of the way that Aileen

Christopher felt and seemed to be barely aware of her existence.

He held a visitor's chair for his mother, took some documents from a metal safe, and placed them in front of her, along with a quill pen, a jar of ink, and another of sand. "Would you like some tea, Mama?"

"A cup of tea would be very nice, thank you," she replied. "Must I read these papers or is it enough that I take your word for it that they're in order and require my signature as an officer of the company?"

"I think you can take my word," he replied gravely as he glanced through the notes on his desk. "I was afraid of this," he muttered, then hastened to explain. "There's been a production snag in the schedule for our new steamship, a freighter. If you'll excuse me, Mama, I'll go to the shed and see the supervisor of the project. Miss Christopher will bring you your tea." He raced out of the office again without waiting for a reply.

Ruth calmly began to sign the documents in front of her.

Aileen Christopher stood in the entrance to the office. "Lemon, cream, or sugar, Lady Boynton?" she asked. "I'm terribly sorry, but I don't remember how you drink your tea."

"I'll have it plain, thank you, but I'll only drink it if you'll have a cup with me," Ruth replied on sudden impulse.

Aileen was startled but hastened to comply with the request, and soon came into the inner office with two cups of tea balanced on a small tray. "Mr. Boynton will be dreadfully upset," she said, "if he sees us having a tea party in here."

"Never fear," Ruth replied airily. "He's gone to see about a snag in the production of a new freighter, and if I know him, he'll be there for at least an hour, digging until he finds the root of the problem." She laughed lightly.

Aileen joined in the laugh.

Ruth stole a glance at her. "I'm very grateful to you, Miss Christopher," she said, "for the care and devotion you show to my son."

Aileen was startled. "It—it's my job," she murmured.

"I'm referring to the care you lavish on him beyond the call of duty." Having initiated the subject, Ruth was determined to pursue it.

The flustered young woman turned scarlet and was speechless.

Ruth reached out and patted her on the arm. "I don't mean to embarrass you in the least," Ruth said. "Please believe me, I'm sincere when I say this."

"Oh, I do, Lady Boynton," Aileen replied, trying in vain to recover her aplomb. "It's just that—well—your comment was so unexpected."

"Will it help you to know that I intend to regard this entire conversation as confidential, completely between you and me alone?" Ruth asked.

Aileen nodded and, although still confused and somewhat upset, was nevertheless relieved.

"How long have you loved David?" Ruth asked softly.

Aileen stared down into her tea cup, then raised it to her lips, and even though it was too hot, she managed to swallow a mouthful. "Sometimes," she replied tentatively, "I feel as though I've always loved him, as though I can't remember a time when I haven't."

"If I know David," his mother said, "he has no idea of the way you feel."

Aileen nodded ruefully. "He doesn't have the vaguest notion," she said.

"Does he know you're alive? I don't mean that in an unkindly way."

"To be truthful with you, Lady Boynton," Aileen said, "I'm convinced that most days Mr. Boynton is barely aware of my existence. He's reminded when he wants to see a ledger with the latest financial reports, or when I bring him something to eat on the days when he's too busy to go to his club or keep an appointment, and at times like today when he asks me to make tea for a visitor."

"I'm so sorry," Ruth said. "Your existence can't be easy for you."

"I don't complain," Aileen replied, forcing a smile. "I earn as much as—if not more than—any woman of my class in all of London. I hold a wonderful position with a wonderful man in a fascinating business, and I often tell myself how very fortunate I am.''

Looking at her, Ruth realized the younger woman was even more endowed with real character than she had guessed.

''I realize how foolish it must seem to you, Lady Boynton, that a nobody like me would presume to fall in love with Mr. Boynton. But I didn't do it purposely, it just happened, and the way I see it, as long as he doesn't know, there's no harm done. Ultimately I'll settle down and marry sensibly. Believe me, I have no intention of reaching beyond my station.''

Ruth sipped her own tea and raised an eyebrow. ''And just what do you consider your own station with regard to my son?''

''I'm a nobody, a girl who can be replaced here in this office for one pound, ten shillings a week. Mr. Boynton is the son of a baronet and someday he'll inherit Sir Charles's title. Not to mention the fact that he's already one of the wealthiest men in the British Isles and will become still richer as time goes on.''

''I wonder if you know David's background?'' Ruth spoke with slow deliberation.

Aileen shook her head.

''His mother was named Alice Wong,'' Ruth said. ''She was a prostitute in Canton, and in the days before I married Charles, she had an affair with him. She gave her life to save his, and when Charles discovered David's existence—when the baby was very small—he insisted on bringing him back here. I was hired as a nursemaid for him. That was my first connection with Charles Boynton. I had known the Rakehells, to be sure, because my father had been a carpenter in their yard, and I grew up with Jonathan and with his first wife, Louise, who died when David's cousin Julian was very small. So, as you can see, David has some ordinary people in his own background.''

Aileen stared at her in openmouthed wonder. ''I—I had no idea,'' she said. Then, recovering, she asked curiously, ''Why have you told me all this, Lady Boynton? Why have you confided in me?''

''I'm not too sure,'' Ruth replied slowly. ''I daresay I'm motivated by a desire not to let you become too discouraged. David is strangely vulnerable socially. He's devoted himself so completely to his business that he's had time for little else in his life. So he's far more naive and ingenuous when it comes to women than are most men of his age.''

Aileen continued to stare at her, trying in vain to understand.

"I like you, Miss Christopher, very much," Ruth said, "and I'm sure that Sir Charles would feel as I do if he should come to know you. David would be very fortunate if he fell in love with you and were lucky enough to persuade you to marry him. All I can say is that I'm rooting for you, and if there's anything I can ever do to help your cause with him, please don't hesitate to come to me."

The offer was so generous that Aileen was dazed.

"I may be wrong, and I hope I am," Ruth said, "but David may well need someone with your qualifications to stand beside him in the near future. I hope you won't desert him if he should need you."

"I'd never do that!" Aileen breathed.

"Boyntons and Rakehells," Ruth said with a smile, "seem to enjoy fantastic good luck. It's as though a special guardian angel is hovering over them and swoops down to protect them when they need it most. Perhaps you're what David needs. I wouldn't be at all surprised. So don't become discouraged. Keep your hopes up and trust that everything will work out for the best. I've seen it happen too many times not to trust in the family's good fortune asserting itself, once again, in his favor."

Aileen Christopher nodded slowly, heartened by Lady Boynton's words and bolstered even more by her open approval and support. For the first time ever, her daydreams about David noting and falling in love with her began to assume a more realistic shape.

BOOK II

The military escort supplied by General Tseng provided Jade Rakehell with ample protection on the road from Peking to the port city of Tientsin, ninety miles away. The Taiping rebels created such unsettled conditions that groups of bandits roamed the countryside, even in the immediate neighborhood of the imperial capital, but the presence of the well-trained troops, armed with modern rifles, discouraged even the boldest of the robbers, and Jade reached Tientsin without incident.

Riding to the waterfront, she immediately boarded a coastal junk that flew the familiar Tree of Life banner. That banner was known in every seaport of consequence on earth and signified that the proud vessel that flew it was a Rakehell and Boynton ship.

There were few who knew the history of that banner, however. A generation earlier, Jonathan Rakehell's late wife, Lai-tse lu, had presented him with a pure jade medallion on which was engraved a Chinese Tree of Life. That tree, with three principal branches growing from it, had rightly become a symbol of the company and of the people who were responsible for its operations.

Rakehell and Boynton maintained a large fleet of junks for trade between provinces of the Middle Kingdom, and Jade was made at home immediately as the vessel continued to load bags of wheat that it would transport south to Canton in return for the cotton that had been delivered earlier, when Jade had arrived.

Although this particular junk did not carry any special accommodations for executives of Rakehell and Boynton, the master surrendered his own cabin to his employer, and Jade was very comfortably ensconced in a suite that included a large bed, ample wardrobe space, and an alcove where she could enjoy her meals.

Junks, with their high-sided hulls, might be old-fashioned and clumsy vessels to operate, but they enjoyed a distinct advantage over more modern seagoing craft in that the accommodations were invariably comfortable and often luxurious.

Certainly Jade was no typical female passenger. Attired in the black pajamas habitually worn by sailors and peasants, she joined the ship's master at his command post amidships, and exercising her prerogative as the owner of the vessel, she assumed its command. She had already demonstrated to the satisfaction of the crew that she was thoroughly familiar with both navigation and seamanship, so the sailors obeyed her orders with alacrity, and she sailed the vessel down the long coast of the Middle Kingdom toward Canton.

She stood with the wind streaming through her hair, the junk rising and falling on the swells of the sea, and she came alive, as she did at no other time. All of her cares dropped away, and she worried neither about business affairs nor about the political matters that she had explored and discussed in detail in Peking. She was a Rakehell, which, as people liked to say, meant that she had sea water rather than blood flowing through her veins, and she was completely at home and at ease on board the ship.

Her eyes bright, she was savoring the scent of salt air, which she vastly preferred to the most precious perfumes, as she stood the watch in the command post.

Suddenly her pleasure was interrupted by a call from the crow's nest. "A strange ship has appeared off our port stern," the seaman called.

Jade immediately reached for her glass and studied the junk, which, even at a distance, was obviously far larger than most junks. It was not a vessel of the Imperial Navy, however, and, oddly, it flew no distinguishing flags. "What do you make of it, Wang?" she asked the mate who stood beside her, and handed him her glass.

Wang studied the stranger at some length before he replied. "I don't know," he said. "She seems to be carrying several cannon on her forward deck, and at least two on her aft deck. It's possible she could be a pirate ship."

Jade didn't need to be told that the unsettled conditions that prevailed on land also existed off the coast of Cathay. The presence of robbers and raiders at sea was frequent, and every merchant ship was obliged to protect itself against thieves.

Taking no risks, Jade ordered the junk's two cannon manned and loaded, and also took the precaution of sending for the brace of Colt pistols that she had brought with her from her recent visit to America.

The captain joined her at the command post and had small arms distributed to the entire crew.

Quietly resuming his own command, he ordered new sail added to both of the junk's masts. But the stranger also added sail and easily kept pace with the junk.

"I don't like the look of this," the captain said. "The stranger is acting like a robber on the prowl. I think it would be wise if Rakehell Jade were to go below to her cabin and remain there until the unpleasantness is at an end."

Jade, however, had no intention of missing any action. "Why should I deny myself the pleasure of sending this pirate fleeing?" she demanded. "I shall stay right here!"

The ship's master disagreed but was in no position to argue with her. As the ship's owner, she had every right to do as she pleased.

The bigger ship was also the faster, and she edged closer, then came closer still. Suddenly a black flag was hoisted to her yardarm, identifying her as a pirate, and at almost the same moment, two cannon on her deck roared simultaneously, belching fire and smoke.

The shots, Jade noted calmly, fell short of the target.

A ship as heavy and clumsy as a junk could not be easily maneuvered, so evasive action to avoid the pirate's fire was impossible to achieve. Under the circumstances, all that could be done was to match shot for shot and hope that one's gunners were superior to those of the enemy.

The captain shouted a command, the aft guns were fired, and Jade was chagrined to see that their aim was even worse than that of the enemy.

Soon she had good reason to discover that she had been badly mistaken in her original estimate. The gunnery of the pirate crew was excellent, a second salvo corrected the mistakes of the first, and three heated iron balls landed on the deck of the commercial junk, digging furrows in the hardwood.

The junk's crew fought valiantly but were no match for their adversaries. Watching them in action, Jade realized belatedly that the crews of all Rakehell and Boynton coastal vessels should receive training in naval warfare. But it was too late, by far, to alleviate the current situation.

The pirates outnumbered the crew of the commercial junk by at least two to one, and their firepower was infinitely superior. Jade was mortified as she watched the defenders slowly losing the battle and facing certain defeat.

She refused to surrender without further struggle, however, and when the pirates swarmed aboard the now-crippled junk, brandishing huge double-edged swords and firing everything from crossbows to ancient flintlocks, she planted her feet apart and drew both of her pistols.

Her marksmanship was remarkable, and her aim little short of formidable. Her instructors—her father and Kai, his majordomo, who had been prominent in the Society of Oxen—would have been proud of her. Shooting alternately with her right hand and her left, she made every bullet she fired count, and a half dozen of the invaders were stretched in a semicircle on the deck by the time she had emptied her weapons. She had to pause to reload the pistols, and that was her undoing. A blow from a sword narrowly missed her head and would have decapitated her had the marauder's aim been more accurate. But a savage shove sent her sprawling on the deck, and before the stunned woman could recover from the blow, she felt herself being hauled to her feet.

"In the name of all the sacred dragons that rule the mountains where our ancestors dwell, this is a woman," a pirate said in the rough tongue of Kwangsi Province.

The leader of the band of pirates examined the captive closely. A tall, broad-shouldered man with a barrellike chest, he had the build of the Chinese of the north. His face was broad, he wore his pigtail in a coil at the top of his head so no enemy could catch hold of it, and his eyes were like narrow slits.

Jade returned his stare steadily, and nothing in her demeanor revealed the deep dismay she felt. Her companions, including the captain and the mate of her junk, were lying dead on the deck, and the few members of her crew who were still alive were being hunted and either decapitated or prodded with swords until they toppled overboard into the sea.

The junk itself was being expertly and systematically looted. Its cargo of bags of wheat was being transferred to the larger ship, as were the cannon, sails, and anything else of value that the marauders could find.

The leader of the pirates also spoke the language of Kwangsi. "Tie her hands behind her back," he said. "Then take her to my own cabin and stand guard over her. Let no one approach her."

Jade was privately very much relieved. She had no doubts about the fate that would have awaited her had she been turned over to the bloodthirsty crew of the robber ship.

The crewman tied her hands securely, then grasped her arm and threatened her with a stilettolike dagger. He forced her to cross to the larger junk and took her below to the spacious cabin that the leader occupied. Not bothering to undo the bonds at her wrists, he shoved her inside, then slammed the door and stood guard in the corridor outside it.

With nothing to do but to await her fate, Jade went to one of the large square windows and, by craning her neck, could gain a fair approximation of what was happening above. She was impressed by the efficiency of the corsairs, who swiftly moved the cargo from the Rakehell and Boynton ship and then went on to take whatever else they fancied.

At last they cast off, and the two vessels began to move apart.

A sudden glare filled Jade's vision, and it took her a moment or two to realize that her ship had been set on fire. The fire had been applied strategically to various parts of the vessel, and the dry wood caught hold and flared quickly. Soon there would be no evidence to indicate that such a ship had ever existed and had been robbed on the high seas.

Ultimately, a key was inserted in the lock, the door was opened, and the pirate captain came into the cabin, taking care to close and bolt the door behind him. He sat and, hooking his thumbs in his belt, silently scrutinized his captive.

Jade continued to stand near the windows and made no move, returning his look with a face that was devoid of all expression.

"The clothes and jewels in your boxes on board the ship we've just sent to the bottom indicate that you're a lady of considerable stature," he said. "Who are you?"

She took care to make no reply. It was customary for persons of consequence captured by pirates to be held for ransom, and if this band learned that she was a Rakehell, they would set an exorbitant price on her head.

The leader had not expected a reply and shrugged indifferently. "It doesn't matter in the least," he told her. "No matter who you may be, it will have no effect on the disposition I intend to make of you." He paused and again examined her. "I'm sure you don't need me to tell you what will happen to you if I turn you over to my crew."

"I can imagine," Jade replied in a tight, controlled voice.

"Very well. I shall strike a bargain with you," he said. "We will be at sea for a number of days. You will occupy this cabin, and you'll be unbound, free to move about as you see fit. You'll be given three meals a day, and you'll be supplied with ample fresh water and sea water for washing and cleaning. All I ask in return is that you give me your pledge not to try to escape, because that would be foolhardy. You can go nowhere, and my men are under strict orders to kill you on sight without mercy if you should be apprehended trying to get away."

Thinking rapidly and clearly, she knew he held the upper hand, at least for the moment, and that she had nothing to gain by defying him. On the contrary, she realized that a rebellious attitude well could place her in grave danger. "Very well," she said, "I accept the terms of your bargain. Are there any others?"

"I have only one." He grinned, revealing a gap in the front of his mouth where he had lost several teeth. "When we arrive at our destination, I'll expect you to wear one of your best dresses and to look as pretty as you possibly can. Do you agree?"

Jade thought that his request was odd, to say the least, and shrugged. "Why not?" she said. "Rather than be raped, and mistreated by your crew, I'll do as you ask."

With nothing better to occupy her, Jade followed the progress of the junk by day from the position of the sun, and by night from the positions of the stars. She half expected the pirates to put into one of the many uninhabited islands off the coast of China in the vicinity of the British Crown colony of Hong Kong. But the corsairs surprised her by sailing on through the South China Sea, and after passing close to the new and growing British colony of Singapore, the vessel made its way into the Java Sea.

She was quick to recognize the familiar port of Djakarta when the junk entered it under reduced sail. She had visited the estate of the Fat Dutchman on a number of occasions during his lifetime—and after his death, when his niece, Anna van der Luon, had inherited his business—and she was strongly tempted to break her word to the pirate chief and try to escape. Certainly Madam van der Luon would offer her help and would see to it that she was returned safely to her own home and headquarters in either Hong Kong or Canton.

The leader of the corsairs took no chances, however. After reminding her of her promise to make herself as attractive as possible, he dropped anchor in the outer reaches of the Djakarta harbor and posted strong guards at all strategic points on board his ship. He was anticipating a break on the part of his captive, and he was taking no undue risks.

Meanwhile, Erika von Klausner and Count Pieter Sabov, who had returned to Djakarta a few days earlier from the voyage to the United States, were hurrying to the waterfront from their extensive estate outside the capital of the Netherlands East Indies. Their Indonesian carriage driver was urging the team of matched bays to greater and yet greater speed, and the coach rocked perilously on the rutted road, in constant danger of being overturned.

Erika enjoyed the excitement of the ride and, her eyes shining, clung to the strap on the door of the carriage.

Pieter braced himself against the floorboards as they rode. "I'll grant you that we can ill afford to take the time for this foolish venture," he said, "when we have so many contracts and other documents on our desks after our long absence at sea. But there's no need to kill ourselves, you know."

Erika patted his arm condescendingly with her hand. "Never fear, Pieter. You'll be delivered safe and sound to the docks. I'm in a hurry because the message promised me exclusive rights until sundown, and I don't want to take a chance on anyone else getting in ahead of us."

"We already have fourteen of the most beautiful slave girls in the entire East in our employ," he said. "I honestly don't see why it should be so important to add another."

"For the very simple reason that the Dutchman's clients demand variety," she replied tartly. "That's been a tradition as far back as I can remember. Every year or so there's been a new girl added to the harem who lends a whole sense of excitement and adventure to the enterprise. The people with whom we do business, the British from London and from Hong Kong, the Americans from New England and from San Francisco, the French and the Scandinavians and the Germans and the Italians, as well as the Portuguese, all love the novelty. And so do the Orientals from Saigon and Singapore and Korea."

He shook his head, then admitted with a sigh, "I suppose you're right."

"I know I'm right," Erika replied, her voice brittle. "After all, I was an inmate of that very exclusive bordello for a great many years." Her smile was tight and drawn as she recalled the long period of slavery she had undergone.

Much to Pieter's relief, the carriage delivered them safely to the waterfront, where they were met by a representative from the corsair junk, who escorted them to the ship on board a harbor sampan. There the pirate captain greeted them effusively and welcomed them aboard.

Erika curtly refused his offer of refreshments. "We have come here for a purpose," she said. "You sent me word that you have a slave girl of exquisite beauty to sell. We would like to examine her."

Her words confirmed for the man what he had always heard, that Anna van der Luon was a hard customer to please and satisfy.

Explaining that he thought it best that they examine the girl without her knowledge, he led them to a small chamber that opened off the main deck, and raising his fingers to his lips for silence, he removed a board from the floor.

Erika and Pieter looked down through the opening into the master's cabin, and there they saw Jade, who had kept her word and had dressed for the occasion in a form-fitting Western gown. With it, she wore earrings, a choker necklace, and a huge ring of jade and diamonds, all of which had been her mother's jewelry and which she prized above all other gems in the world for that reason.

Having no idea that she was being observed, Jade moved restlessly about the cabin, occasionally sipping from a tall glass of chilled tea that the captain had thoughtfully provided for her.

Pieter Sabov studied the young woman and was impressed. Certainly she was lovely, but he was troubled by the fact that she didn't resemble a slave in any sense of the word.

Erika von Klausner was ecstatic. She recognized Jade Rakehell instantly, for the young woman had made many trips to the Fat Dutchman's estate. But to make doubly certain that her eyes were not playing tricks on her, Erika scrutinized the captive even more carefully. As if to confirm her belief, she saw that the young woman was wearing the famous set of Rakehell jade jewelry, and that confirmed what she had surmised. Her worst enemy had been delivered into her hands, and she found it difficult to believe her good fortune. She withdrew, trying to appear wooden-faced, and the floorboard was quietly replaced.

The captain led his visitors outdoors again and then turned to them.

"Your message," Erika said, controlling both her appearance and her voice, "indicated that you had a slave girl to sell. I gather that isn't precisely the case, that this is a young woman you planned to sell into slavery."

"There might be a slight technical difference," the corsair leader said with a shrug, "but for all practical purposes, it's the same. The only difference is that you may have a problem instilling the proper discipline into the wench when you first take possession of her, but from what I hear of Madam van der Luon, you will encounter no difficulties on that score."

"I anticipate none," Erika replied grimly. In spite of her attempts to maintain an unruffled façade, her voice shook, there was a gleam in her eyes she could not conceal, and her hands trembled when she moved them.

The pirate leader had no idea why she was affected so deeply by the sight of his captive, but as someone experienced in dealing with human nature, he had no need to know. He was satisfied that Madam van der Luon badly wanted to gain possession of his prisoner.

"What price do you ask for her?" Erika demanded.

The corsair leader instantly trebled the price that he had had in mind. "I want five hundred guilders in gold for her," the pirate chief said.

Pieter was staggered. The sum was the equivalent of a small fortune and represented the profits that one of the company's largest freighters could show from a voyage to Europe and back to the Dutch East Indies.

Erika's face remained expressionless, and she showed no surprise.

"Let me make clear," the corsair leader went on, "that the price includes her jewelry and clothes. I estimate their worth at a minimum of ten guilders."

"I have no use for her clothes," Erika said. "You may dispose of them as you see fit. Pieter, will you be good enough to pay the gentleman his fee?"

Pieter gaped at her in astonishment. Surely she didn't intend to pay that outrageous a sum for possession of a mere slave girl!

"We don't have all day," she said impatiently. "I find this the least appetizing part of the deal, so I'd like to consummate it as rapidly as possible. Please pay the man and be done with it."

Convinced that she had taken leave of her senses, Pieter emptied his purse and gave the pirate chief fifty guilders. "I'm afraid that's all I've carried with me," he said. "I shall have to get the rest from our strongbox at the estate and you shall have it when we take possession of the young woman."

"How soon will that be?" the pirate chieftain demanded.

"I'll need half an hour to drive out to the estate and another half an hour to return," Pieter said. "You may expect me in two hours' time, *meinheer.*"

"When you return to the waterfront with the money, bring four or five of our security guards with you," Erika directed as they got into the carriage, for she intended to return to the estate and wait there. "Be sure that the girl is kept under close watch at all times, and if necessary, keep her bound hand and foot to prevent her escape. Nothing must be allowed to happen to her!"

"Surely you aren't going to pay that criminal's asking price?" Pieter protested.

"Indeed I am!" Erika no longer bothered to hide her delirious joy.

"That's an enormous price to pay for a wench, no matter how beautiful she is," Pieter said.

"The wench, as you've called her," Erika replied in a voice so filled with emotion that she almost choked, "happens to be Jade Rakehell, the daughter of Jonathan Rakehell."

Pieter grew pale beneath his tan. "My God," he murmured. "You're sure?"

"Very sure," she answered triumphantly.

He removed his white tropical hat, the band sweat-soaked from its wear in the tropics, and ran a hand through his blond hair. "I kept quiet in San Francisco," he said, "when you hired the Johnson girl to ruin the life of Julian Rakehell. I thought at the time that you'd made a most peculiar arrangement, but at least it was legal. This situation isn't."

Erika's eyes hardened and she demanded shrilly, "What do you mean by that?"

"Cheng Yu, who has Miss Rakehell in his possession, is notorious as a pirate. It's obvious that he captured her at sea. He'll be hanged in Hong Kong or Singapore, or any other British possession, for daring to sell her into slavery. She's a Rakehell, one of the world's leading heiresses, not the daughter of a poor Balinese peasant who sells her into slavery in order to gain possession of a couple of gold doubloons for the first and only time in his life."

"I've made an agreement with Cheng Yu," Erika replied coldly, "and we shall carry it out."

"We can't, Erika!" he said. "We're going too far! The British will nail our hides to the wall for this if they ever find out," he went on, deeply disturbed, "and the Chinese will be none too pleased, either, considering the favored place that the Rakehells hold with the imperial family."

Her temper flared. "Do what you're told, Pieter, and stop making excuses!" In her exasperation, she reached out and struck him with the back of her open hand, and the large ruby and diamond ring that she wore made a gash in his cheek from which the blood began to flow freely.

The startled Pieter took a handkerchief from his pocket and pressed it to the wound.

"Let this be a lesson to you, and don't argue with me, Pieter," Erika said. "Just because we sleep together now and again doesn't give you special privileges. You say that the British will do this and the Chinese will do that if they find out what we've done. Who will tell them? Only the girl, you, and I know the truth of the situation, and having found myself in the same position she's now in, I can give you my word for it that she is in no position to go to the authorities, regardless of whether they're British, American, or Chinese. So we're safe, perfectly safe, and I'm afforded vengeance beyond my wildest dreams!''

Realizing that Erika was beyond reason, Pieter fell silent as he dabbed at his cheek. It was true that Jade Rakehell could be enslaved, without the world's knowledge and without a protest ever being made. Although it was an appalling prospect, he knew that Erika's bold gamble would succeed.

She herself was so warped by her desire for revenge against the Rakehells that nothing would stop her, and Pieter knew, too, that he was in no position to go to the British or American consuls general and explain the situation to them. His own life had at last turned for the better after years of hand-to-mouth living, and in a short time he would be able to leave Java as a man of means. Perhaps he would become a dashing soldier of fortune, with his own body servant, offering his military expertise to nations who would benefit greatly— and pay him handsomely—for his services. Or perhaps he would buy a ship of his own and become a wealthy trader, plying the seven seas. Whatever the case, he was not yet financially secure enough to set out on his own, and he would do nothing that would antagonize Erika and cut off his present source of income. No, he would best leave well enough alone and let Erika do what she pleased.

While Erika went to her room, he went to the safe for the balance of the money. Meanwhile, the carriage driver obtained fresh horses for the return to the Djakarta waterfront. Pieter took four of the wiry security guards, each of them carrying a murderous *kris*, a short, double-edged sword with a wavy blade that was capable of inflicting great damage on anyone who was struck by it.

The sampan awaited him and his companions, and they were rowed out to the pirate junk without delay. There, Pieter completed the transaction and was taken at once to the cabin where the bored Jade looked up at him inquiringly.

Pieter clicked his heels and bowed as he introduced himself to her. "I have here the various items of jewelry which are your property, and which you are being permitted to take with you," he said, exhibiting the contents of the leather box that he carried under one arm. "Be good enough to accompany me."

Jade looked at him inquiringly. "Where are you taking me, and—"

"Please," he said in embarrassment, "ask me no questions. I am not permitted to give you answers. Let it suffice that your journey is nearing its end, and I wish you all that you wish yourself, although circumstances well may be more difficult for you than you perceive. All I ask of you is that you make no attempt to escape or call attention to yourself in the carriage as we ride. I have an escort of men who would not hesitate to truss and gag you should that be necessary."

She was silent as, her head high, she walked past the pirate chieftain and made her way to the rope ladder that she would use to descend to the waiting sampan.

The corsair leader smiled bloodlessly. He had no idea what might be in store for the wench, but judging by what he had seen of Madam van der Luon, he did not envy the young woman.

The four Malay guards were waiting in the sampan, and when Jade looked at them, she knew that her handsome escort had been speaking the truth. The quartet looked capable of performing any act of violence without a moment's hesitation.

She voluntarily climbed into the waiting carriage, and Pieter took his seat beside her. Two of the Malay guards sat on the jump seat at the rear, and the other two remained with the driver on his seat. Jade noticed the fresh wound on the man's face but decided it would not be polite to inquire how he had acquired it. She wondered if he was Dutch and asked him about his nationality, accordingly, in that language.

He replied politely that he was Russian.

Equally polite, Jade observed that he was far from home.

Somewhat to his own surprise, Pieter found himself telling her about his quarrel with the tsar that had led to his banishment from the court at Saint Petersburg and about his near-starvation as he had wandered through Russia and then the Orient prior to coming to Djakarta.

Jade looked at him eagerly. "I know this is Djakarta," she said, "because I've been here a number of times, and you must be acquainted with the niece of my family's good friend and partner, the Fat Dutchman."

Suddenly he realized he was walking on very thin ice. "I've heard of him," he said.

"And you know his niece, Anna van der Luon?"

There was no escaping the inevitable. "My dear young woman," he said in distress, "I beg you not to ask too many questions."

Jade fell silent but looked at him inquiringly.

"Life here," he said carefully, "is not the same as you once knew it. Much has changed, and there is no explanation—there can be no explanation—for these changes. I realize that I make little sense to you, but for your own good, for the sake of your own welfare, I beg you to be patient and let the forces of nature provide their own explanation of what is and what has been."

As far as Jade was concerned, he was speaking gibberish, but she was convinced of his absolute sincerity. So, even though she didn't know the reasons for maintaining silence, she asked no more questions.

The carriage, she could see, was following a familiar route, going past churches of stone and past wooden, rickety shacks with thatched roofs. There were also solid-looking, pastel-colored homes of three or four stories that looked like those one would see in Amsterdam. Then the carriage turned up the broad, palm-lined avenue, and Jade recognized the entrance to the estate of the Fat Dutchman. The carriage pulled to a halt and was examined by security guards, and Jade was thoroughly bewildered when the vehicle rolled on, turned down a little, unfamiliar driveway, and finally halted in a grove near a clump of buildings that she did not recognize.

She turned to her mentor for an explanation as she climbed out of the carriage, but to her astonishment, she saw him walking rapidly toward the main building, some distance away.

Instantly she was surrounded by several slave girls wearing the usual attire of the estate, floor-length skirts of silk that they wound around their middles and tucked in. They addressed her in several tongues, and she could make out nothing above the babble. Then one spoke to her in Mandarin. "You are to come with us, and we are to minister to you."

Jade accompanied them, and they led her to a building that she had not previously visited on the estate, although she had seen it from a distance. There, to her surprise, they stripped and bathed her, and then rubbed a number of strong scents into her skin. She recognized musk and jasmine, but her attempts to find out the reasons for this unusual attention elicited only storms of giggles from the concubines.

Then, while several of them, treating her like a doll, carefully applied cosmetics to her face and, to her astonishment, rouge to her nipples, others painted her fingernails and toenails with a deep, emerald-colored lacquer.

"Why are you doing all of this?" she demanded.

The Chinese-speaking concubine seemed to misunderstand the question, and perhaps her confusion was deliberate. "The lacquer," she said, "is the same color as your earrings and necklace and ring."

Jade realized they would reveal nothing to her.

Finally, after placing a cluster of pungent white gardenias in her hair, they gave her a length of clinging green silk to use as a skirt and showed her how to wrap it around herself snugly, yet leaving room for her to walk in it.

The truth suddenly dawned on Jade that she was being made up to look like a concubine. Her blood ran cold as the other women took her into an adjoining chamber and triumphantly showed her a full-length mirror in which she could see her reflection. She closely resembled the concubines, and there was little in her appearance that marked her as different from them in any way.

The door was flung open, and one of the girls breathlessly said something in a local dialect, which she then translated into English for the benefit of the newcomer. "Mistress come," she said.

The concubines hastily sank to the floor in a sitting position and touched their foreheads to the floor in gestures of deep obeisance.

Jade, however, continued to stand, and a moment later, a hard-faced blonde stood in the entrance with a deeply worried Pieter Sabov hovering behind her.

Jade's gaze met that of the woman, and although, to the best of her knowledge, they had never before encountered each other, the young woman knew she had never seen such blazing hatred directed toward her.

"My concubines," Erika said harshly, "show me the respect that is my due."

The triple strands of a whip cracked ominously and sang above Jade's shoulders.

In no position to argue, Jade quickly lowered herself to the floor and touched her own forehead to it in a sign of obeisance.

The woman's sigh sounded more like a long hiss of escaping steam.

"Remember your place, girl," Erika told her, "and keep in mind, at all times, that you exist exclusively for my pleasure and that of my guests. Serve us conscientiously, with an imaginative flair, and as you'll learn from your colleagues, you shall enjoy many little benefits and favors. Sulk or, even worse, try to escape, and you shall be made to suffer severely for your temerity. If you've never been beaten across the soles of your feet with sticks of bamboo, I do not recommend the treatment, and I'm sure the girls who have been made to suffer it will tell you it is to be avoided at all costs. Do I make myself clear?"

Choking with rage and humiliation, Jade could only nod.

Again the whip sang close to her ear.

"The customary reply," Erika told her, "is yes, mistress."

"Yes, mistress," Jade said through clenched teeth.

Erika laughed loudly. "You have no idea, Pieter, how much I'm going to enjoy having the new concubine here," she said. "She'll serve my supper tonight, and as we are having a delegation of merchants from Rotterdam to eat with us, she is certain to call attention to herself, so I have no doubt that one of them will choose her as his companion for the night. Girl," she concluded, "you're going to give me much joy." She withdrew, still laughing.

One by one the concubines rose, and two of them helped Jade to her feet, for it would take practice to become accustomed to the uncomfortable position.

"Who is that woman?" she asked the Chinese girl, speaking in Mandarin.

"She is our mistress, Madam Anna van der Luon," the concubine replied.

Something strange was happening, Jade well knew. She had done business frequently with Anna van der Luon, as she had with the woman's uncle, the Fat Dutchman, before her, and she knew, beyond all doubt, that the hard-faced blonde who had mocked her was not Madam van der Luon.

Analyzing her own situation, Jade knew that, for the moment at least, she was helpless. The woman who had insisted on being called "mistress" had not been bluffing, and Jade realized she would be subjected to harsh and severe punishment if she disobeyed orders. For the present, she would have to subject herself to the humiliation of acting as a slave girl and servant, of submitting to the desires of men visitors as a concubine. But under no circumstances would she accept such a lot as permanent.

Perhaps, through unveiling the mystery of the woman who pretended to be Anna van der Luon, she would find the means of escape. One way or another, she was determined to make good her escape and resume her rightful place in the world.

II

The Hotel Pequot was busy New London's leading hostelry, and Alexis Johnson created precisely the stir she had anticipated when she engaged the presidential suite of four rooms. Her wardrobe alone filled one of those chambers.

She occupied a corner-table in the hotel dining room and ate her meals there alone, impressing everyone who saw her with her beauty and regal bearing. She was so considerate of the hired help, so generous in her distribution of gratuities, that the entire staff soon became her enthusiastic admirers.

On her first Sunday in New London, Alexis went to worship services at the local Episcopalian church, which the Rakehell family had attended for generations, and she was discreet if conspicuous. She began to patronize the various merchants of the town and spent money freely, but always what she purchased was in good taste. Inevitably, after she went to church again the following Sunday, the minister and various members of the congregation began to be friendly with her.

Alexis's patience was rewarded on her third Sunday in New London when she heard someone behind her in church say, "Welcome home, Mrs. Rakehell. Did you enjoy your trip to the Dakotas, Jonathan?"

Shifting her position slightly, she examined Jonathan and Elizabeth Rakehell with infinite care, silently sizing them up. Now she was ready to strike.

After the service, she maneuvered in such a way that she was directly in front of them when she left the church, and the minister greeted her before turning to them. As she had anticipated, the clergyman presented her to the Rakehells.

"You have no idea how happy I am to know you," she said, and a deep dimple appeared in one cheek when she smiled. She went on to explain that her hobby was studying clipper ships, but she refrained from mentioning that she had spent weeks reading and rereading the books on the subject that she had purchased in San Francisco and in New York.

Jonathan promptly took the bait. "We've curtailed our output of clipper ships due to the Civil War," he said, "but you're welcome to see the one or two that are in production and being built. Elizabeth, my dear, perhaps you could act as Miss Johnson's guide and take her through the shipyard."

"I'd love to," Elizabeth Rakehell replied.

Alexis chose to react shyly. "I don't want to impose or take advantage of your time," she said timidly.

"You'll be doing neither," Elizabeth told her firmly, and promptly made an engagement with her for the following Tuesday.

Alexis subsequently rejoiced. Her plan was working perfectly.

On the appointed day, she dressed in modest good taste for her tour of the shipyard and surprised her hostess with the variety and complexity of her questions. Most of them were too technical for Elizabeth to answer, and she needed help from the supervisor who was in charge of building the two new clipper ships.

The young woman's luck continued to hold. After they completed the tour, Elizabeth took her to the corner office that Jonathan had occupied since he had succeeded his father as chairman of the board, and there Alexis had an opportunity to display her hard-won knowledge of clipper ships anew.

She discussed clippers, their construction, and their sailing characteristics in such infinite detail that Jonathan was deeply impressed. Rarely had he found a woman who knew so much about the subject that had been responsible for his own great career. It was only natural that his interest in Alexis Johnson grew accordingly.

When Jonathan and Elizabeth displayed natural curiosity regarding her own background, Alexis was ready for them and presented them with a tapestry in which fact and fiction were delicately woven. She was single and had lost both her parents, she said, and strongly hinted, but did not state in so many words, that she was an heiress who had no concern about money. She had come to New London, she explained, because it was the shipbuilding capital of the United States, and she had developed an insatiable curiosity about ships—especially clippers—from her cousin, who was serving in the Union Navy.

Alexis created such a good and deep impression on them that Elizabeth Rakehell invited her to dine with them at the family home on the coming Saturday night.

Alexis, living her role to the hilt, accepted shyly, even while exulting inwardly. Her ruse had succeeded, and she was being accepted socially by the Rakehells!

She would have been even happier had she heard Elizabeth's private remark to her husband after Alexis had left them to return to her hotel. "I like that girl so much!" Elizabeth said. "She's so pretty and obviously so bright."

Jonathan appeared to read her mind and chuckled. "I know what you're thinking," he replied. "She can talk about clipper ships with Julian, so she actually may spark his interest."

"Exactly!" Elizabeth replied. "The only way any woman is going to snag Julian is through her interest in ships, and Alexis Johnson appears to be the most likely candidate we've found yet. I do hope they take to each other."

"Not so fast, madam matchmaker," Jonathan said with a chuckle. "We don't know that much about Miss Johnson."

"She's exceptionally attractive, she has a good mind, and she has the Rakehell mania for ships! As anyone who has married one of the breed knows, those are more than sufficient qualifications to guarantee a happy marriage!"

Alexis continued to read all she could on clipper ships prior to Saturday evening. She also looked for books and magazine articles about steamships, but these vessels were so new that there was very little in print on them. Very well, she decided, she would turn her ignorance to her advantage, and after professing an interest in steamships, she would be in a perfect position to be instructed by a Rakehell on them.

She chose her costume for the Saturday dinner with great care, and the gown of pale green silk that she elected to wear was modest and decorous at first glance, but nevertheless fitted her snugly and showed off her superb figure to good advantage. She applied cosmetics very lightly, using just enough to emphasize her own fine complexion, her large, sensual mouth, and her enormous, sensitive eyes.

After a brief inner debate, she decided not to wear any of her paste jewelry for the occasion, and instead used only the few items of genuine gold and real stones that were in her possession. It was best, by far, to understate rather than overemphasize.

Alexis inadvertently provided a final appropriate touch when she rented a carriage and driver to take her to the Rakehell house at the appointed hour on Saturday evening.

Jonathan Rakehell was apologetic as he greeted her. "It was thoughtless of me," he said, "not to think of how you were going to be transported here. My son would have been delighted to pick you up at your hotel."

"Indeed I would," Julian said, and bowed as he was presented to her.

Alexis was startled when she saw him. She had been aware of the presence of this tall, ruggedly handsome young man with the thoughtful eyes each Sunday in church, but somehow had not connected him with the Rakehell clan, for he had not attended services with his parents the previous Sunday. The realization that he was the object, the goal, of her overall scheme put her project in a new and far more interesting perspective. She wouldn't in the least mind trying to pamper, persuade, and inveigle Julian Rakehell into falling in love with her.

It was Elizabeth's inviolable decree that no business be discussed at the supper table, and Julian, like his father, was careful to obey her order. But the interest of the attractive young female guest in ships and shipping could not be denied, and somehow the order was rescinded. So Julian was free to talk at great length about his favorite subject, clipper ships, and to his delight, Alexis's educated interest in the subject fueled him.

She inquired about steamships, admitting frankly that she knew nothing whatever about them other than the fact that she had been a passenger on board one through Confederate-infested waters of the Atlantic when she had sailed from Panama to New York. Julian devoted the next hour to a discussion in infinite detail of steamships, and he was interrupted only by the questions that Alexis asked.

Somewhat to her own surprise, Alexis was not forced to search her own mind for questions to keep Julian talking. His explanations were so lucid, cogent, and colorful that he stirred her genuine interest, and she naturally thought of dozens of specifics to ask about.

Ultimately, Jonathan cleared his throat and said, "I suggest, Julian, that you invite Miss Johnson to accompany you on a short cruise aboard one of our new steamers. In that way, you can give her an illustrated lecture, so to speak."

"I'm sorry, Papa," Julian said, "and I do beg your forgiveness, Miss Johnson. I'm afraid I get carried away on the subject of ships, and I had no idea that I was devoting so much time to them."

"The fault is mine," Alexis said with a nervous laugh. "I'm afraid I encouraged you with all my questions, but honestly, I never knew that a discussion of ships could be so fascinating."

"In this house," Elizabeth said dryly, "no one ever apologizes for a demonstration of an interest in ships. That's considered as natural as breathing, or sleeping when you're tired, or eating when you're hungry.''

Jonathan and Julian laughed, and Alexis discovered, somewhat to her own surprise, that she joined in spontaneously and wholeheartedly. Her amusement was genuine and, like her interest, was totally unfeigned.

The conversation became more general, and Alexis gleaned, to some extent, what it meant to be a Rakehell in the 1860s. The two men and Elizabeth talked about the influence of the Civil War on trade with Europe and the fact that it had put a stop to all business with the islands of the West Indies, at least temporarily. They discussed the Taiping Rebellion in China, the all-important fluctuations in the price of black pepper in the Dutch East Indies—which, it developed, was the only source of the spice known on earth—and they proved equally knowledgeable about politics in England and France, the German states, and the Low Countries.

As nearly as Alexis could judge, being a Rakehell meant being knowledgeable about economic and human affairs everywhere on earth, and that knowledge was not confined exclusively to the males of the family. The women not only contributed their ideas but were respected for them.

Ultimately, Jonathan said, ''If you and Miss Johnson don't object, Elizabeth, I think we'll forgo the custom of the ladies going their own way for coffee while we stay at the table over glasses of port. It strikes me as rather foolish to indulge in the custom when there are only four of us at the table.''

Elizabeth graciously deferred to the guest.

''I don't mind in the least,'' Alexis said.

''Will it bother you if my father and I smoke *segaros*?'' Julian asked.

She thought of the dance halls and gambling palaces at which she had worked, places where smoke had been heavy in the air and had actually created a hazy atmosphere. ''I don't mind in the least,'' she said. ''In fact, I rather like the odor of a West Indian *segaro*.''

Only once was Alexis forced to dissemble. When Julian offered her a small glass of potent brandy, she hastened to refuse, explaining that the beverage was far too strong and beyond her ability to handle. The truth of the matter was that during her difficult years in and around the gold fields of California, she had often consumed even stronger glasses of cheap whiskey and brandy, which she had been expected to drink with the customers.

The evening passed quickly and pleasantly. Julian began to speak of various adventures he had experienced on visits to China, and Alexis was filled with curiosity about the huge, distant nation, knowing nothing about the subject.

"The next time you come for dinner," Julian said, "we shall have to have a Chinese meal in your honor." He turned to his stepmother. "Do you suppose that could be arranged?"

"With ease and with great pleasure," Elizabeth replied, and exchanged a quick, flickering glance with her husband. Julian, it seemed, was showing more interest in Alexis Johnson than he had displayed in any woman he had met in a very long time.

As the evening drew to a close, Julian insisted on harnessing a light phaeton and driving Alexis back to her hotel. They chatted amicably on the brief ride, and Julian actually appeared reluctant to bid her good night.

Alexis deliberately refrained, however, from inviting him to join her in her suite for a nightcap. The evening had progressed perfectly, and she didn't want to overplay her hand by appearing to be too eager.

Her patience and forbearance were rewarded far sooner than she had anticipated. The following morning when she went to church, Julian approached her as she drew near the entrance, and it was clear to her that he had been waiting outside in the hope of seeing her.

"There's an exceptionally big crowd here this morning," he said. "The place is filled with summer people who've come to the shore from Hartford and from New York. So I thought—that is, if you don't mind—we have ample room for you in our pew and—you'll be more than welcome—"

"Thank you," she said, bringing his stammering to an end, "I'd like very much to sit with you."

So it happened that she sat beside Julian Rakehell in his family pew, and half the congregation began to whisper about the couple.

Another surprise awaited Alexis after the church services came to an end.

"It's a lovely day," Julian told her. "A perfect day for a swim and a beach picnic, if you'd care to join me."

As she graciously accepted the invitation, she knew that her careful plotting had not been in vain. Julian Rakehell definitely was interested in her.

Alexis changed into her bathing costume in one of the many spare bedrooms of the Rakehell mansion, and when she found Julian in the kitchen preparing their picnic, she insisted on joining him and taking charge. She hard boiled eggs, made a salad from leftover potatoes, carved meat and bread for sandwiches, and made a large container of iced tea that they could take out to the beach with them.

She and Julian spent the entire afternoon alone, and much to her amazement, she found it was no chore to talk with him. Not only did thoughts and words come naturally to her lips, but best of all, she found she could be herself. There was no need to dissemble, to pretend to be anything that she was not. She had to avoid any mention of the seamier aspects of her past, of course, but otherwise, she was ebullient and natural in her approach to him.

As the sun sank low in the Connecticut hills behind them, Alexis reluctantly said the time had come when she had to depart.

Displaying far more confidence than he had previously, Julian told her that a new steamship was going out to sea on a brief trial run on Wednesday, and he invited her to accompany him, provided she had nothing better to do. "We'll be at sea for about eight or ten hours," he said, "and as the galley—that is, the kitchen—hasn't been installed on the ship as yet, we're likely to be ravenous when we come ashore. So I thought we could ride over to a splendid little tavern that I know in Groton, across the river, for supper."

Unaccountably, Alexis felt her cheeks growing hot and wondered why she should blush. She recovered sufficiently, however, to accept the invitation with alacrity and to thank him for it.

Julian took her home in the phaeton, and when they arrived at the

Hotel Pequot, he descended in order to hand her to the ground from the carriage.

She smiled at him warmly as she extended her hand. "I honestly don't know when I've enjoyed myself more than I have today," she told him, and there was a ring of sincerity in her voice.

Alone in her suite, Alexis sat down to write to Anna van der Luon and tell her of the progress she was making in what she referred to as her "Rakehell campaign." It was her intention to give Madam van der Luon a detailed report of the various engagements she had had with Julian since she had met him, but instead she wrote sketchily and decided it was sufficient to indicate that she was making considerable progress, that she was doing even better than she had dared to hope.

What bothered Alexis was that for some reason she could not fathom, she felt cheap while she was writing the brief letter. Her reaction bewildered her, and she could not understand why she felt as she did. Certainly Julian Rakehell was very much drawn to her, and she had good cause to anticipate that, barring unforeseen obstacles, the day would come when he would propose marriage to her. So the sum of one hundred thousand dollars that she would be paid was actually within reach and was no longer a mirage.

III

"Although it is summer now in Peking, and the air is constantly hazy and filled with dust," wrote one of the official scribes at the imperial court, "the atmosphere in the Forbidden City is as clear as it will be when the cold weather comes again. The Dowager Empress Yehonala and Prince Kung have achieved a meeting of the minds, and they have agreed to serve as joint regents with no rivalry between them. It is not easy to imagine them acting in concert, but so far, there have been no disagreements between them. The whole palace is excited because they are meeting with the young generals. They have met already with General Tseng Kuo-fan, and this very day, General Li Hung-chang and General Tso Tsung-t'ang are scheduled to come to the palace for a joint meeting with the regents. No one knows what they will discuss, and no one dares to ask."

The atmosphere in the suite where the meeting was to take place was highly informal. Yehonala, wearing a cloth-of-silver cheongsam, and Kung, dressed in the uniform of general in chief of General

Tseng's corps, sat side by side on a broad divan littered with silk cushions. Opposite them, in a chair with three legs of ivory, one a dragon, one a lion, and one a tiger, sat General Tseng, who seemed very much at ease as he sipped a mild glass of clear brown rice wine.

A majordomo announced the arrival of General Li and General Tso, then backed hastily out of the room. The two officers entered and began to drop to the floor, intending to prostrate themselves before the regents in the familiar kowtow, which tradition demanded that everyone in the nation display toward the rulers of the Middle Kingdom.

But Prince Kung instantly raised a hand. "No!" he said sharply. "We'll have none of that!"

"Our subjects will kowtow only at formal audiences," the dowager empress added. "At private meetings among friends, such as this, we are all equals."

The two new arrivals were startled and looked at each other, then glanced at General Tseng for confirmation.

He smiled and nodded. "What the empress has said is so," he told them. "The regents have decided to abolish many of the old rituals that have tied the imperial court with strands of unbreakable silk."

"That is correct," Prince Kung said. "My father, the Tao Kuang Emperor, was the first to see that if the Middle Kingdom is to survive and flourish in the modern world, it must adopt the modern ways. The empress and I are determined that this nation shall enter the modern world quickly and thoroughly."

Yehonala emphasized her coregent's words by rising to her feet and personally pouring glasses of wine for the two newcomers.

The generals were stunned. Never within the memory of anyone living had any official, no matter how high his rank, been served personally by a ruler of Cathay.

"My fellow regent and I," Yehonala said as she resumed her seat, "have decided that the Taiping Rebellion must be smashed for all time, regardless of the cost, the effort, or even the lives that are expended."

"That is correct," Prince Kung declared. "China is like a huge giant that wallows helplessly while being slowly bled to death. The Taiping rebels are draining our lifeblood, and they must be halted. Not only do they occupy large sections of our land, but they deny the authority of the army, kill our tax collectors, and refuse to recognize the Chrysanthemum Throne. Their success encourages the foreign devils, who have so successfully invaded us, and the English and French victories over us have already inspired the Americans and the Imperial Russians to lay claims on us. Also, other nations of the West have been clamoring at the gates of Peking, demanding land and special trade privileges. I admire the West, and in recent talks with the empress, she has admitted that the Middle Kingdom cannot prosper without some guidance from our western friends. But if we are to survive and prosper, we must first become masters in our own house, and first and foremost, we must reestablish the force and majesty of the Chrysanthemum Throne! At last!" he said. "I have prayed for the coming of such a day."

General Li smiled, nodding in approval, and General Tso, ever pragmatic, went directly to the heart of the problem. "I volunteer the services of my corps for such a campaign," he said, "and I'm sure my colleagues do likewise."

General Tseng said, "Of course."

General Li merely nodded curtly, taking it for granted that he was supporting the regents who occupied the throne.

"Our first need," General Tso declared, "is for modern rifles for our foot soldiers and modern cannon for our gunners."

The dowager empress looked smug, and Kung grinned broadly. "We are well aware of those needs and have anticipated them," he said. "I have placed an order for weapons through our friends at Rakehell and Boynton, and I have gone to several other sources, as well, in order to expedite the delivery of adequate arms."

"One of the principal problems with our armies," General Tso said, "has been the rivalries between warlords. In order to avoid mistakes of the past, I will gladly surrender any claims that I might have to the post of commander in chief to General Tseng."

General Li obviously went through an inner struggle before he could volunteer to take second place himself. "I, too, will serve under you," he told General Tseng gruffly.

To their mutual surprise, however, Tseng Kuo-fan shook his head. "The regents have offered me the command of the combined armies of the Middle Kingdom," he said, "and although I am sensitive to the honor they do me, I have refused."

His colleagues looked at him in astonishment.

"Any one of us is competent to lead the armies of Cathay in their present state," Tseng said, "but I believe that something more is needed if we are to meet with the overwhelming success that we seek."

Li and Tso looked at each other in bewilderment.

"Why do you think," Tseng demanded, "that the forces of Great Britain have defeated us so badly in two major wars? Are their soldiers endowed with more courage than the soldiers of the Middle Kingdom? Are the British more willing to risk their lives for the Empress Victoria than our men are willing to die for the emperor? No."

The dowager empress was about to interrupt, but Prince Kung silenced her with a frown. His glance told her to leave this delicate matter in the hands of General Tseng, who would handle it in his own way.

"We have been driven from the field of battle," General Tseng said, "by the soldiers of Great Britain and by the soldiers of France. Only the members of the Society of Oxen have stood up to the foe and held their own in battle. Why? Because they were led by Jonathan Rakehell, who understood and knew how to use the modern arms of the West."

His argument began to make sense to General Tso, who nodded. "I think I see what you mean and are trying to say," he murmured.

Tseng turned to him and then to his other colleague. "Both of you will agree that in order to defeat the foreign devils, we must be led by one who is familiar with their weapons and their techniques. Only such a man must assume the command of our armies."

The doubts that the taciturn General Li felt had not yet been dispelled. "I can see why it would be wise to have a foreigner lead our armies if we were fighting the foreign devils again," he said. "But why must a foreigner lead us against our own people among the Taiping rebels?"

Prince Kung knew it was appropriate for him to intervene. "If a foreigner is likely to win victories over the foreigners," he said, "how much more quickly and thoroughly will he defeat the Taiping rebels?"

General Li was satisfied, and folding his hands in his lap, he grunted in approval. Then, suddenly, he sat bolt upright. "Where is such a foreigner to be found?"

"We are fortunate," General Tseng said, "that there is such a man in Peking at this very moment. He is an American, Frederick T. Ward. He is an American general—"

"He has served in their civil war?" General Tso asked, interrupting.

Tseng shook his head. "No," he replied. "He was second in command of the forces under the famous William Walker in Central America, where he led small numbers of troops to great victory over forces ten and twenty times their number."

"What makes you think that this American would take command of our army for us?" General Tso demanded.

General Tseng shrugged. "I do not know that he would be willing to do this," he said. "I propose that, with your agreement, I meet him and sound him out. If he appears willing, I will arrange a meeting for him with His Highness, Prince Kung, who can decide whether he wishes to entrust his armies to the command of General Ward. But I need your approval first, my colleagues."

"You know this man, and you yourself are willing, not only to serve under him, but to place your own army under his command?" General Tso asked.

General Tseng bowed to indicate that his colleague was correct in his assumption.

"That settles it," General Li said. "If this man, Ward, is good enough for you, he is good enough also for me."

"And for me," General Tso added.

"Arrange a meeting with this American," Prince Kung said crisply, "and learn whether he is willing to serve the Chrysanthemum Throne. If he is, we shall take the next step."

"I will do as you command," General Tseng replied.

"Do not tarry," Kung told him. "In this matter, every day that passes is important to us!"

The home of the United States minister to China was a modest two-story building of gray stone, located directly behind the American legation itself in the American compound in Peking. The minister's home was quiet and the American compound itself was small, for both were reflections of the attitude of Anson Burlingame, who had first been appointed by President Buchanan and, much to the relief and pleasure of the current administration, had accepted reappointment from President Lincoln.

Minister Burlingame made no secret of his pro-Chinese sympathies and his admiration for Chinese accomplishments. He consistently refused to take unfair advantage of the huge weak nation and its people, and he lost no opportunity to promote Chinese interests in Washington.

Burlingame was the host of General Frederick T. Ward, who sat with his feet propped on a delicately wrought Chinese table, drinking Cantonese beer out of a battered tin mug. At first glance, the two men seemed to have little in common. The middle-aged Burlingame was somber and serious, while the much younger Ward, wearing a flamboyant uniform conspicuously lacking in national insignia of any kind, was reckless and seemed to delight in disregarding protocol. The two men were united, however, by their love for China and by their mutually shared conviction that they were in the debt of the Middle Kingdom because of the role played by their government in forcing the late emperor to sign the treaties of Tientsin.

That subject, in fact, was very much on their minds now as they discussed the complex situation in Cathay.

"I reckon this is stupid of me," Ward said, "but I feel guilty—personally responsible—for the fact that America played a role in forcing the helpless Chinese giant to grant territories and trade favors to the West."

Minister Burlingame, sipping a cup of steaming tea, smiled thoughtfully. "I know precisely what you mean, Fred, although I hope you realize that you played no personal part in applying pressure to the late emperor."

"I know all that," Ward replied, "but I still feel that I owe the Chinese a debt."

"So do I," the diplomat admitted, "but I'm afraid there's nothing we can do about it. I'm here to represent the interests of the United States in Cathay, and you'll be on your way home shortly to take up arms for the Union."

"Maybe I will and maybe I won't," General Ward replied with a half smile. "The West Point graduates who are in charge of the army are inclined to look down their noses at a general who gathered his major experience under Walker in Nicaragua. I've been in correspondence with the war department, you know, and although I think I'd have no trouble in squeezing a commission as a colonel in command of a regiment out of them, I regard it as very unlikely that they'll give me a division, a corps, or an entire army with the rank of major general. Unfortunately, I'm so damned independent-minded that I'm afraid I couldn't serve under another general, especially a traditional West Pointer."

Anson Burlingame found it difficult to believe that a man of Ward's temperament, who preferred fighting to anything else in life except breathing, would voluntarily stand aside and let others fight the Civil War. "What will you do, then?" he asked. "How will you occupy your time?"

Ward took a large swallow of his beer and thumped his tin on the table beside him, threatening to mar its delicately inlaid surface. "I may be in luck," he said. "The Chinese government may have work for me."

The minister said nothing and waited for his companion to continue.

"General Tseng invited me to dine at his headquarters yesterday and put on a review for my benefit. It was impressive, I can tell you. He's put together a first-class corps. The British and French would have their hands full with his troops in a new war, and they are not the only Chinese who would give a good account of themselves. The Chinese are subtle," Ward said, "so subtle that it took me longer than you'd believe to realize that General Tseng was sounding me out on my availability. He indicated that General Kung may want me to serve with a new army he's thinking of forming."

Burlingame frowned. "The Chinese generals aren't thinking of throwing the foreigners out of their Peking concessions, I hope," he said. "I don't blame them for wanting to be rid of us, but a show of violence will bring new warships and troops here from the West in almost no time."

"Unfortunately," General Ward said with a grin, "the Chinese don't seem to be thinking in terms of expelling the foreigners, more's the pity. Now that would be a real challenge and I'd love it. What they're thinking of is far more simple. They're hoping to crush the Taiping rebels."

"It strikes me," Burlingame said quietly, "that a new military campaign is the last thing on earth that China needs. She's suffered enough in the recent war, and she needs a time of peace so she can rebuild."

Ward's feet landed on the hardwood floor with a crash. "I disagree," he said firmly. "There can be no real peace in Cathay until the rebels are defeated once and for all. Brigands are everywhere in the land, and as I understand it, they are infesting the seas, too. Taxes are uncollected, and trade and commerce are badly disrupted."

"I'll grant you the truth of everything you claim," the minister replied. "All the same—"

"No!" Ward further threatened the stability of the table beside him by smashing it with his fist. "In order to insure peace for generations to come, it's necessary for the forces of the authorities of Cathay to grind the rebels into the dust. They have no alternative!"

Burlingame's thin shoulders rose and fell. "Much as I hate to admit it," he said, "you may be right, Fred. I'm constitutionally opposed to the use of force, but there comes a time in the course of a nation's history when only force will solve problems which are otherwise insoluble.''

Ward peered at him intently, his pale eyes narrow. ''What do you know about Prince Kung, Anson?''

''I gather it was a sad day for the Middle Kingdom when he failed to inherit the Chrysanthemum Throne. He would have been an exceptionally able emperor in the Tao Kuang tradition.''

Ward nodded slowly. ''That jibes with everything that I've learned about him. He should make a first-rate regent, then.''

''Yes,'' the minister replied, ''if the dowager empress doesn't interfere too much.''

''She's an uncommonly attractive woman,'' Ward said shrewdly. ''How do you estimate her chances of making a muddle of the administration of the regency?''

''If anyone but Kung were her coregent, I'd be inclined to wager on Yehonala making a total mess of things. But the prince is strong-willed and a man of high principle. I think he'll be able to withstand her blandishments. For the sake of the Middle Kingdom's future, I hope so.''

General Ward drained his mug of beer. ''That settles it!'' he said. ''I've been debating with myself whether to call on the prince and learn about his potential offer firsthand. I think I'll do it.''

''Hold on, Fred,'' Burlingame cautioned. ''By going to the prince, you'd be breaking with Chinese tradition. Things simply aren't done that way here. As he's the regent, you wait until he sends for you.''

Ward chuckled. ''Maybe you wait, Anson,'' he said. ''That isn't my nature. I believe I'll waste no time and I'll go straight to the Forbidden City today!''

An hour later, in midafternoon, General Ward presented himself at the palace in the Forbidden City to the astonishment of Prince Kung's servants, aides, and bodyguards. His unorthodox, bold behavior was rewarded, however, when the prince consented to see him immediately.

Kung chose to receive his visitor in the most ''Western'' of the many palace rooms available to him and was seated behind a desk on a stool supporting a cushionlike top. As if the prince divined the visitor's purpose, he had ready a large map on which appeared the cities of Nanking, Soochow, Ningpo, and Anking, all of them in the hands of the Taiping rebels.

Unsure of how to greet the regent, but determined not to kowtow, Ward took refuge in his military status and saluted as he entered the chamber.

Kung instantly put him at ease by rising and extending his hand, Western style, in a handshake.

Ward relaxed and gripped the hand of the broad-shouldered, square-faced young man who looked at him so searchingly.

The prince rang for the inevitable tea, without which no business appeared to be conducted in the Middle Kingdom, and resumed his seat on the stool. "You wish to see me, General Ward," he said genially.

Even in minor matters, Ward refused to be outmaneuvered. "You bet, Your Highness," he said, "but I understand from General Tseng that you've also been eager to see me."

Kung liked his bluntness and responded to it. "I am told," he said, "that we have certain views in common, including a belief about the Taiping rebels."

"I hold," Ward said firmly, "that they must be smashed and their rebellion ended for all time if China is to be a prosperous and peaceful nation."

"Quite so," Kung replied. "How would you achieve this goal?"

"Very simply, Ward said. "I would attack them with the largest force of competent troops I could band together: the corps of General Tseng, the corps of General Li, and the corps of General Tso. I would also hire as many experienced mercenary soldiers as I could round up in Hong Kong and Macao, and I'd pay them well for their services. I'd use the most modern arms that money can buy, and I'd hit the rebels as hard as it's humanly possible for one force to strike another."

Kung was pleased by what he heard. "I have waited a long time to find a military leader with such an attitude," he said.

Ward was not yet finished. "Although my army would be composed exclusively of veterans, plus as many experienced mercenaries as I could hire," he said, "I would still want to put them through a unique course of special training. I'm convinced that new and special military techniques must be devised. Only in this way will we be able to trounce the Taiping rebels and grind them into the dust so thoroughly that the entire nation will be impressed, and any potential future rebels would think long and hard before raising their swords against the throne."

"What do you mean by new and special techniques?" the prince asked.

"By nature," Ward said, "man is compassionate, rather than ruthless. Given his choice, he will avert bloodshed and will take a gentler path. I would want to train my army to deal harshly at all times with the rebels, never showing them mercy, never relenting, never granting them a respite. This will require months of hard work."

Kung nodded thoughtfully. "There are extensive barracks," he said, "in Sungkiang. Would that city be suitable for your training purposes?"

"If you please, Your Highness," Ward replied, "show it to me on the map."

The prince jabbed a finger onto the map spread out before them.

General Ward examined it in silence. "It's close enough to the major cities occupied by the rebel forces for my purposes," he said. "Is it possible for my men to be supplied regularly there?"

Kung nodded. "Of course," he replied. "I give you my solemn word that you shall want for nothing." He drew a deep breath. "Will you accept an imperial commission as a general and take command of the army that you've envisioned?"

Ward drew himself up to his full height, towering above the regent. "I accept the assignment with great pleasure, Your Highness, provided it is understood that I make no promises except that I will do my best to rid the Middle Kingdom of the curse of rebellion that has so blighted the land."

The prince again extended his hand, and they shook hands Western style.

"You will report directly to me," Kung said, "and I will leave instructions with my staff to grant you personal access to me at all times and under all circumstances."

"Thank you," Ward replied, and then added pointedly, "Do I report only to you, Your Highness?"

Kung immediately grasped his meaning. "It would be wise," he said, "if you also took a short time to report to my coregent from time to time," he replied.

"I have no objection," Ward said bluntly, "providing my plans are not subject to the coregent's approval or disapproval, and provided also that I am not required to bed the lady in order to win her approval."

It was clear that he had heard stories about the demands made by the Dowager Empress Yehonala.

The prince hesitated. His relations with his coregent were delicate, but he could not expect the Western military officer to hinder his own operations. "I will convince my fellow regent," he said firmly, "that you must be given a completely free hand in your operations, without interference from me or from her."

General Ward grinned, pleased that the air had been cleared. "That will be a help," he said.

"You will be paid the same salary that is paid to Generals Tseng, Li, and Tso," Kung said, "and you shall have the same personal prerogatives, including a household staff and so forth. Now I think we should discuss your reward after you've defeated the rebels."

Frederick Ward's attitude changed suddenly, and he scowled, his voice becoming metallic as he said, "Not only is such a discussion premature, Your Highness, but it's strictly unnecessary. The total defeat of the rebels will be reward enough in itself. I'll feel that I've repaid the debt that the United States owes China for the concessions that were made to us, and I'll be happy with the results."

Prince Kung marveled at this strange American, the only man he had ever encountered who sought no financial gain or other benefits for himself, but who seemed content with the prospect of accomplishing the mission he was intending to perform.

IV

Julian Rakehell and Alexis Johnson had become inseparable. He dined with her nightly now, sometimes taking her to the mansion on Pequot Avenue and sometimes going to one of the few inns and taverns in the district that served good food.

To the infinite relief of Jonathan and Elizabeth, Julian no longer worked seven days and seven nights a week.

To be sure, he did not completely abandon his strict regimen. The office at the shipyard closed at noon on Saturdays, and it had been Julian's custom to work until all hours on Saturday night. Now, however, he left the yard around four in the afternoon and devoted his evening to Alexis, whom he also joined at church on Sunday, and they made it a practice to go on together from there, most often indulging in a picnic on the private beach behind the Rakehell mansion.

Closemouthed in the usual Rakehell tradition, Julian didn't discuss his romance with anyone. But one evening when he found

Jonathan and Elizabeth reading in the parlor when he returned from dining with Alexis, he could resist no longer the temptation to be frank with them.

Grinning, he poured himself a little brandy in a bell-shaped snifter and sat down opposite them. "Am I interrupting you?" he wanted to know.

"Not in the least," Elizabeth replied quickly as she put down her book, her glance at her husband telling him that she expected him to do the same.

Jonathan was somewhat slower to respond, but he, too, marked his place in his book and placed it on the table beside him.

It was evident that Julian suddenly felt embarrassed. He took his time, first inhaling the aroma of his brandy and then sipping it experimentally before speaking. "I've been wanting to talk with you," he said.

"Good," Elizabeth replied brightly and, convinced that he needed help, added, "We're not in the least surprised."

Julian's attitude was a strange mixture of defiance and bashfulness. "I've grown very fond of Alexis," he announced.

His father nodded gravely and tried to conceal the humor that welled up within him. "So we've noticed," he replied dryly.

"She—doesn't seem to be—avoiding me, either," Julian went on.

His father and stepmother nodded.

He knew as much as any man alive about building and sailing ships, but he was completely naive, virtually still an adolescent in affairs of the heart. "I just thought I'd tell you," he concluded vaguely. "I thought you ought to know."

Jonathan was on the verge of laughing aloud, but Elizabeth's glare silenced him. "Have you proposed to her as yet?" she asked.

Julian shook his head. "It's odd, now that you mention it," he said. "Lately we've started talking in terms of marriage and of making plans, but I've never formally proposed, and Alexis has never formally accepted me. We've sort of taken it for granted that we're going to marry." He smiled at them. "Do you find that strange?"

"Not in the least," Elizabeth replied swiftly and emphatically.

"When two people are in complete harmony and enjoy a meeting of the minds, it's often unnecessary to discuss the obvious."

Julian seemed relieved. "I'm glad to hear it," he said. Then, suddenly, he became tense again. "Well," he demanded, "what do you think? Do you approve or don't you?" He looked first at his father, then at his stepmother.

Elizabeth was the first to reply. "I'm just speaking for myself," she said, "not for your father. But I couldn't be happier. From what I've seen, Alexis is a fine girl, and she seems just right for you. I hope you're as right for her. Goodness known she's accomplished a near-miracle in prying you away from your desk and prolonging your life."

Jonathan chose his words with great care. "I've been very fortunate in my lifetime," he said. "I was too young to know what I was doing when I married your mother, Julian, and she was the same way. Her tragic death spoiled any chance we had of reaching an accommodation, and thereafter, I was lucky enough to marry Lai-tse lu, who was perfect in every way. I thought my happiness was ended when she died, but the fates proved otherwise, and I've been wonderfully happy with Elizabeth for many years now. All I can wish you and Alexis is a measure of the happiness that we've enjoyed."

His wife smiled at him, and their hands met on the center cushion of the sofa on which both were sitting.

"You two," Julian said, "provided me with such a perfect example that I believe I wasn't interested in girls until I found the one who is right for me."

"This calls for a celebration," Jonathan said. "I hope you and Alexis will have dinner with us tomorrow evening. I've been saving some first-quality French champagne for just such an occasion as this."

"I suppose," Elizabeth said with mounting enthusiasm, "that you'll want your sister to attend the wedding, and David—"

"No," Julian replied firmly. "It wouldn't be fair to the business to bring both of them back here so soon after their recent visit. There'll be ample time for Alexis to meet Jade and David after we're married. I'm expected at the London yard on a trip, and I'm overdue for a visit to Hong Kong and Canton.''

Elizabeth laughed helplessly. "Only a Rakehell," she said, "would think of combining a honeymoon with a business trip!''

Jonathan and Julian joined in her laugh, but it was plain that neither of them particularly appreciated the humor of her remark.

She shook her head. "I shall be obliged to have a private discussion with Alexis," she said.

Early the following morning, Julian sat at his desk more than an hour before the office staff arrived and the day crew appeared in the construction yards. To the best of his knowledge he was alone in the building, and as was his custom, he reached for the documents and letters that had accumulated since he had last attacked the mound the previous day. No sooner did he wade into them, however, when he was surprised by a tap at the door.

Before Julian had a chance to call out, the door opened and his cousin, Brad Ellison, stocky and four years his senior, came into the office. Like all Rakehells, Brad had first gone to sea as a small boy and had earned his papers as a ship's master while a Yale College undergraduate. In recent years he had succeeded his late stepfather as commodore of the Rakehell and Boynton fleet, and he was as conscientious and thorough as he was hardworking. His mother now lived by herself in her New London house, and Brad's sister, Judy, had married, to no one's surprise, a man of the sea.

The cousins enjoyed a sense of easy rapport, and Julian grinned at him. "I should have guessed it was either you or Cal, Brad," he said. "The hired help never shows up this early." Brad's brother-in-law, Calvin Clement, the husband of his sister, was chief production supervisor at the yard.

Brad needed no invitation to sit down in a comfortable visitor's chair. "Matter of fact," he said, "I had dinner with Judy and Cal last night, and you were a principal topic of conversation.''

"What a dull evening you must have had," Julian observed, and sat back in his chair, waiting for his cousin to launch into the business matter that had brought him here so early in the morning.

But Brad appeared to be in no hurry. "As a matter of fact," he said, "our talk was anything but dull. We had a long debate, and we examined the subject under a magnifying glass."

Apparently he was leading up to something, and Julian wanted to give him every opportunity to do so. "I didn't know I was that interesting," he replied lightly.

"By yourself, you're not." Brad seemed to be girding himself. "But when you're viewed along with Alexis Johnson, the subject matter becomes much livelier."

Julian lifted an eyebrow but waited patiently. He had the Rakehell knack for drawing people out of a shell.

"I've had one hell of a problem," Brad said. "I presented it to Judy and Cal, and we looked at it from every possible angle. They agreed that I had to take it up with you, that I had no real choice."

"Would you mind telling me what in blazes you're talking about?" Julian demanded.

His cousin raised a large, competent hand. "Give me time," he said. "This isn't easy, and I've got to edge into it in my own way."

"You bet," Julian replied calmly. "My secretary ought to be showing up any minute, and we'll ask her to make some coffee for us."

"I don't think coffee will help much, and it's far too early in the day for the shot of whiskey that I feel like downing," Brad replied. Then, squaring his shoulders, he plunged resolutely into the heart of what he wanted to say. "You may recall," he said, "that before I became grounded as commodore of the fleet, I sailed the seven seas as master of my own ship. I've been just about everywhere on the face of the earth."

"I remember," Julian said, wondering why Brad was so ill at ease.

"About ten years ago," Brad continued, "in the months that followed the discovery of gold in California, I was captain of a clipper ship that put into San Francisco more or less regularly."

Julian again nodded but failed to see the significance of what his cousin was saying.

"San Francisco was a roaring, wide-open town in those days,"

Brad said, forcing a smile, "and that was just right for me because I was a roaring young fellow looking for excitement. During my half dozen visits to port, I must have tried out every saloon, brothel, and gambling casino in the town. It didn't take me too long to find my favorite place. It was elegant—at least I thought at the time it was elegant—and it combined the best features of all of San Francisco's gaudy establishments. I've never forgotten one girl in particular, a perfectly gorgeous redhead, very young, who was a poker dealer and who wore a skintight evening dress of emerald green. I remembered her because she was so very beautiful and so very young. At first I couldn't believe that she was available for other purposes than playing a game of poker with me, and when I found out for certain that she could be taken to one of the bedrooms upstairs, I was too shy to avail myself of the opportunity."

"That's a fascinating background, Brad," Julian said, "but why tell me all this, especially so many years later?"

Ellison clenched his fists and beads of sweat appeared on his forehead. "The young trollop in the green dress," he said, "the poker dealer, was Alexis Johnson."

Julian continued to look at him, his face as rigid as that of an Indian.

It was impossible to know what he was feeling or thinking at that moment.

"I'm sorry as hell, Julian," Brad said. "I thought I recognized her the very first time I saw her with you, and I was sure of it—dead sure—after Uncle Jonathan and Aunt Elizabeth had me over for dinner with the two of you. There's no doubt in my mind that Alexis is the girl I knew in that fancy San Francisco dive."

Julian nodded but remained silent.

His failure to react more strongly made Brad even more nervous and apprehensive. "I've been wrestling with the problem of whether to tell you or not for weeks. To be candid with you, Julian, I kept my mouth shut because I didn't think you and Alexis were heading into a lasting relationship. But it's become pretty obvious to me recently that you're in earnest about each other, so last night I threw the whole problem at Judy and Cal. They felt that family loyalty demanded that I tell you, and I had to agree with them. So there we are, and all I can say is I'm not only sorry you had to be told this, but I'm sorrier still that I had to be the one to break the news to you.''

"I appreciate the difficulties you've faced," Julian said earnestly, "and I'm grateful to you, Brad. You've gone beyond the limits of family loyalty."

Brad Ellison produced a large handkerchief and mopped his face with it. "I don't mind telling you, Julian," he said with a shaky laugh, "that I half expected you to demand that I clear out of here and that I sell you my shares of Rakehell and Boynton stock."

Julian smiled and shook his head. "There's no need for action that drastic," he said. "In fact, I see no need for action of any sort. I'll appreciate it if you'll keep the information you've just given me to yourself, and tell Judy I'll expect the same from her. I don't want Alexis to be embarrassed· by the realization that my cousins are familiar with an aspect of her past that may be somewhat less than savory."

His ability to absorb the startling news with equanimity was astonishing, and Brad couldn't get over that fact. His bewilderment was reflected in his face, and Julian felt compelled to explain further.

"I know her father died unexpectedly and left her penniless and alone after she had joined him in San Francisco," he said. "But she hasn't yet discussed the details of how she managed to survive. I'm certain that if she was forced to work in a brothel for a time, she'll take me into her confidence at an appropriate moment."

Brad didn't know what to say and could only nod.

Julian's eyes reflected his unwavering confidence in the woman he loved. "Alexis and I," he said, "have established a rather extraordinary relationship. I'm quite positive she'll tell me anything she feels I should know."

Brad hauled himself to his feet. "If you don't mind my saying so, Julian," he said, "I'm delighted now to be able to get back to the shipping business!" He returned to his own office, where he promptly buried himself in the scheduling of captains, mates, and crews for the worldwide fleet of Rakehell and Boynton ships.

At noon Brad's austere, balding brother-in-law, Calvin Clement, came into his office. "Unless you have another engagement this noon," he said, "Judy wants to meet us both at the Purple Parrot."

Brad knew that his sister was curious regarding the outcome of his talk with Julian. "You bet," he said, and went with his brother-in-law to the nearby tavern where executives from the yard and ship's captains congregated to eat. The primary advantage of the place was that it had a number of private dining rooms, and Brad Ellison promptly engaged one.

He and Cal ordered bowls of oyster stew, clam fritters, and lobster pie for three. They were sipping their mugs of cold ale when Judy Clement hurriedly joined them.

She bore a far stronger physical similarity to the Rakehells than did her brother, and any stranger would have known at a glance that the attractive young woman was related to Julian Rakehell.

Judy wasted no time on the amenities. "Well?" she demanded as she took the seat that her husband held for her. "Did you speak to Julian, Brad?"

"I certainly did," her brother replied, "and probably lost about ten pounds in the process."

"Don't keep me in suspense!" she demanded. "What did he say; what did he do?"

"He did nothing, and he said very little," Brad replied slowly. "In fact, his reaction amazed me. I'd hit the roof if I found out the woman I loved had supported herself as a whore, but Julian showed that incredible Rakehell self-control and just smiled and nodded the entire time that I broke the news to him."

Judy stared hard at her brother and then sighed softly. "Oh, dear," she murmured, speaking more to herself than to either of the men.

"Julian indicated that he'd guessed that Alexis Johnson's background wasn't all it might have been," Brad continued, "but he also said that he was positive she would reveal anything unsavory to him at the appropriate time."

"I find it difficult," Judy said, "to imagine that any sane woman in her right mind would admit to her future husband that she once had earned her living as an inmate of a brothel."

"I quite agree," Cal said.

Brad shrugged. "I haven't the slightest idea what any woman, including Alexis Johnson, would or wouldn't do. I'm merely reporting to you what Julian did. I don't quite know what I expected, but one thing I didn't anticipate was his good-humored buoyancy."

Judy sighed, and as their waiter appeared just then with their oyster stew, she concentrated her full attention on eating it.

Brad exchanged a blank look with his brother-in-law, then turned to his sister in annoyance. "Well?" he demanded irritably. "I've done all I'm capable of doing, it seems to me. What do I do next?"

"Absolutely nothing," Judy replied. "Julian is a grown man, not a boy, so you can hardly go to Uncle Jonathan and Aunt Elizabeth with your story and ask them to forbid his marriage. You've told him what you know about the background of the girl he intends to marry, and what use he makes of that information—if any—is strictly his business and no one else's."

Brad sprinkled paprika into his oyster stew, taking no solace in the fact that the spice had been imported on board a Rakehell and Boynton ship.

"All we can do," Judy said, "is hope, for Julian's sake and for the sake of the company that depends so much on his maintenance of an even balance, that his judgment is sound and that Alexis Johnson is everything that he appears to believe she is. If he's right about her, I can foresee no serious problem developing. But if he's wrong, then all of us are going to be in serious trouble!"

V

David Boynton grinned at his reflection in the mirror in his private office washroom and had to admit he had never in his life looked more dashing. His dark gray swallow-tailed morning coat fitted him to perfection, his silk cravat matched his pearl-gray waistcoat, and his striped pants had a razorlike crease. He winked, raised one hand in half-salute to himself, and then fished in a waistcoat pocket until he brought out what he was seeking, a huge diamond solitaire ring worth a high-ranking nobleman's ransom.

He had consulted at length with a leading London jeweler and had made his final selection of the ring after examining scores of stones. Never had he seen a more perfect diamond, and he doubted whether his cousin Jade could find him one that was superior in the open markets of Hong Kong or Djakarta.

Certainly the ring was worthy of presentation to the daughter of an earl as an engagement ring. Drusilla Smythe would have good reason to be satisfied when he proposed to her at luncheon today.

Jauntily tapping his hat into place and taking his gold-handled walking stick from his cane holder, he left his office. "I'll be back directly after lunch, Miss Christopher," he said. "I'm expecting no visitors and no crises today, so I may take a bit longer at lunch than usual."

"Very well, Mr. Boynton," Aileen Christopher replied. She knew he had written to Drusilla Smythe, asking the earl's daughter to meet him at a waterfront restaurant not far from the Houses of Parliament, and she had guessed that he intended to propose marriage. So she carefully refrained from looking at him. It was too painful to think of David being married to any other woman.

David walked the short distance from his headquarters building to the small private dock he had established at the yard, and there he descended into the small, steam-powered launch that took him back and forth from London to the yard in Southwark. Ordinarily he took the wheel himself, but he was preoccupied today, and the captain of the launch threaded his way through the busy Thames traffic until he came to the dock alongside the elegant restaurant on the London shore.

Eager to have every detail right, David ordered the vase of flowers on the table replaced and requested that a screen be set up at the end of the table to shield him and his companion from the gaze of other diners.

At last Drusilla appeared, radiant in a summer gown of the finest-spun Chinese cotton, a multicolored fabric from a bolt that David had presented to her as a gift. She looked so lovely that his heart went out to her.

She told him at length about an interminable conversation she had held with her friend, Lady Edwina Warren, and David, not wanting to interrupt, forced himself to listen patiently. He had their champagne served, and their first course, a rich turtle soup, was brought to the table.

Drusilla, scarcely noticing what she ate, continued to chatter about inconsequentials.

At his request, the chef had prepared a dish of chicken and veal cut into small cubes and served with oysters and several vegetables, the whole having been poached lightly in white wine and herbs. The recipe was Chinese, and when Drusilla had eaten the dish on one previous occasion, she had raved about it. David had ordered it for her today as a specialty that would fit in with his proposal, but to his intense disappointment, Drusilla paid no attention to the food on her plate, taking an occasional forkful but scarcely bothering to stop talking long enough to appreciate its subtlety and flavor.

At last David had an opportunity to break in on her monologue. Casting aside the speech he had so carefully prepared and rehearsed, he proposed bluntly and quickly, meanwhile searching in his waist-coat pocket for the ring.

Looking vaguely regretful, Drusilla reached across the table and patted his free hand. "I'm so sorry, David, my dear," she said, "but a marriage between us is impossible. It's out of the question."

Swallowing hard, he located the ring at the precise moment and stared down at it in the palm of his hand.

Drusilla looked at it, too, and her eyes widened, but she spoke firmly. "It's a lovely ring, David, and far too expensive, I'm sure. I have no doubt that the jeweler will take it back and return your money to you."

He hastily stuffed the ring back into his pocket. His world had crumbled and fallen apart very suddenly, and he was so stunned that he didn't know what to say or what to do.

Reaching for a glass of water instead of champagne to moisten his suddenly parched mouth, he drank as he fought for self-control. "I certainly have no desire to offend you, Drusilla," he began.

She looked at him in amusement and laughed her silvery, tinkling laugh. "I'm very flattered, really." She sounded calm, in complete possession of her faculties.

Not until a long time later did the realization finally dawn on David Boynton that Drusilla was totally indifferent to his suffering and that his reaction to her refusal of his proposal of marriage never crossed her mind.

"I was under the impression," he said, "that you returned my affection, but apparently I was mistaken.'' He took a deep breath. ''May I inquire why you seemed to respond to me once, and why you've become so remote now?''

The smile faded slowly from Drusilla's face, and as she looked at him, an expression of resolve came into her eyes. ''Yes,'' she said at last. ''I suppose it's only fair to be honest with you, and I do want to be fair. I did like you very much David—as a matter of fact I'm still quite fond of you,'' she added hurriedly. ''But it simply wouldn't do for me to marry you. In fact, that's the farthest thought from my mind.''

''Why?'' he demanded bluntly.

''If you insist on a reply,'' she said, ''very well. My ancestors were noble lords in this country when William the Conqueror came to England from Normandy in ten sixty-six. I'm proud of my heritage, and I believe I have a right to be. Don't you see?'' she demanded, becoming tense. ''I'd become the laughingstock of everyone I know, and I'm sure my ancestors would turn in their graves if I married someone who was part Chinese.''

The blood in David's veins turned suddenly to ice water. He sat as immovable and as expressionless as a stone Buddha.

Drusilla Smythe had no idea that she had unwittingly restored his equilibrium and ended his suffering. By decrying his ancestry, she had touched the most sensitive chord of his being.

All at once he came to life again. Silently he summoned their waiter and said nothing as he paid their bill. His own main course was untouched, but he had no appetite for food.

After leaving a generous tip, he rose to his feet and bowed to Drusilla. ''You'll forgive me, I'm sure,'' he said, ''but an important meeting awaits me at my office and I must return there at once.'' Not waiting for her reply, he turned away abruptly and made his way out of the restaurant.

The waiter filled Drusilla's glass with champagne.

She had scarcely touched the wine when another exceptionally pretty young woman, wearing a summer gown of light blue silk with a huge floppy-brimmed hat to match, approached the table. ''Don't tell me you've been deserted, Drusilla,'' Lady Edwina Warren said.

Drusilla looked at her friend in astonishment. "What on earth are you doing here, Edwina?" she demanded.

Edwina burst into laughter. "After I learned of your luncheon engagement with David, I simply couldn't resist booking a table for myself and eavesdropping. Gracious, but he left abruptly."

"Do sit down, Edwina, and help me finish this champagne. There's so much of it left that I shall be quite tiddly if I try to drink it all myself."

Lady Edwina Warren promptly sat down in the chair that David had vacated.

She accepted the glass of champagne that an attentive waiter poured for her, and then, making no attempt to conceal her curiosity, asked, "Whatever happened to David Boynton? He raced out of here as though devils were pursuing him, and he looked like he'd just been told of a death in the family."

"I'm afraid," Drusilla said lightly, "I may have upset him a trifle."

Her friend peered at her across the top of her champagne glass, her eyes narrowing.

"He proposed marriage to me, but I turned him down, of course."

Edwina stared at her in unfeigned astonishment. "You rejected a proposal from David? You really did?"

Drusilla nodded. "Oh, I was tempted to accept, mind you," she said. "He offered me the biggest engagement ring I've ever seen. It was so big it was beyond vulgarity. As a matter of fact, it was appropriate for the crown jewels."

"And you actually turned him down?" Edwina was incredulous.

Drusilla giggled. "I couldn't have kept the ring, you know. It simply isn't done."

"Hardly," her friend drawled.

"Don't lose too many tears over David, my dear," Drusilla said lightly. "I've never yet known a broken heart to be a fatal disease."

Edwina sipped her wine, and a slow smile spread across her aristocratic face. "If you want the truth, Drusilla," she said, "I wasn't wasting any sympathy on David. I was feeling terribly sorry for you."

Drusilla blinked at her and, seizing her wineglass, emptied it. "You must be joking," she replied stiffly.

Edwina continued to smile. "I've always thought of you as being an eminently sensible person, as having a head on your shoulders that couldn't be turned or twisted in the wrong direction. But obviously I was mistaken."

"Honestly, Edwina, I don't know what you're talking about!"

"It's almost absurdly simple," Lady Edwina Warren said. "David Boynton happens to be one of the most eligible bachelors in the entire British Empire. He's enormously wealthy. In fact, my father says that his firm controls enough trade and shipping and real estate to make him the equal of the wealthiest tycoons in this country, or anywhere else in the world. Furthermore, in case you haven't noticed it, he's marvelously good-looking. I defy you to name one man in our crowd, married or single, who is his equal in looks or in personality."

"I'll grant you he's handsome," Drusilla replied, "but he is part Chinese, you know."

Edwina became annoyed. "What of it?" she demanded. "What does it matter?"

Drusilla was somewhat taken aback. "Well," she said, "our son would be part Chinese, and I can't quite see his portrait in the Dudley gallery, where the paintings of my ancestors would turn themselves to the wall, if they could, the day that a part-Chinese joined them."

"I had no idea you were so bigoted and shortsighted, Drusilla," Edwina said. "David is as British as you and I. He's going to inherit a baronetcy from his father, he's been educated at the best schools, and he's a complete gentleman in every sense of the word."

Drusilla looked at her crossly. "Why are you leaping to his defense this way?" she asked.

Edwina smiled and pushed back a lock of her auburn hair. "The only reason that there hasn't been a stampede for David is because every girl who knows him figured that he was strictly your property, Drusilla. Since you don't want him, the race will be on, and I can assure you I'm going to be ahead of all the others."

Drusilla swallowed hard. "You want David Boynton—for yourself?"

Edwina laughed harshly. "I certainly do! And I promise you, I'll use every trick I know in order to win him."

Drusilla Smythe looked at her friend obliquely, her mind racing. Perhaps she had been too hasty in accepting her father's attitudes and rejecting David's proposal so quickly and bluntly. The mere fact that Edwina so desperately wanted to be his wife must mean that there was more to him than she had realized. Perhaps she should reconsider and give him another chance. After all, the engagement ring he had offered her was the largest and most brilliant diamond she had ever seen.

VI

The Balinese
woman named Molinda had been absent from Hong Kong for the
better part of a year, but she created an inevitable stir when she came
ashore from the deck of the schooner that had brought her back to
the British Crown colony from her native island. Although she was
in her mid-forties, her figure was supple and slender, that of
someone less than half her years, and there was no hint of gray in
the long blue-black hair that streamed down her back.

She wore a Western-style dress and shoes, as befitted someone
who had served for many years as the Oriental manager of Rakehell
and Boynton, and she carried herself with regal pride, a reminder to
the few who knew that she was the widow of a cousin of the young
boy emperor of the Middle Kingdom.

Molinda was a legend in Hong Kong, and her reappearance on the
waterfront created an immediate stir. The old China hands recalled
that she had started life as a concubine on the estate of the Fat

Dutchman in Java, and that she had appeared out of the blue in Hong Kong to work there for Rakehell and Boynton.

It had been whispered years earlier that she had been the mistress of both Jonathan Rakehell and Charles Boynton, but that theory had been exploded because of her friendliness with their wives. Certain things about her were known: After the death of her husband, she had taken a number of lovers, all of them high-ranking officials and prominent military officers, or leading businessmen. But she had never remarried and had worked indefatigably and without stopping to make Rakehell and Boynton one of the leading forces in the commercial life of the Orient.

For the past few years, ever since she had been succeeded as head of her company's operations in the Orient by Jade Rakehell, whom she had trained, Molinda had traveled. She had made long visits to the home offices in London and in New England, and she had also visited relatives in her native land. Now she had returned to Hong Kong, where she would meet with Jade and advise her on any number of business matters that the younger woman would have questions about.

As the rickshaw pullers at the dock squabbled over which of them was to have the privilege of carrying her, Molinda realized nothing in the colony was changed. Hong Kong was still a fascinating mixture of East and West, of all that was robust and lively, and above all, profitable, in England and in China.

The huge, magnificent harbor, one of the finest in the world, was crowded with ships of every description, from the junks and sampans of the Orient to the newest steamships and superb clippers of the West. Similarly, the streets, overflowing with humanity, reflected the styles of two worlds, as well. There were the business suits of the West, many of them made of white cotton and silk to enable the wearers to live comfortably in the subtropical heat. There were the black pajamas that distinguished the coolies, and the black ankle-length silk robes of the scholars.

How well Molinda recalled a remark of Charles Boynton's that seemed to sum up Hong Kong for her. "Whatever you want in the world is available here," he had said. "Do you want the finest

English or French or American meal? Do you long for a German or a Russian dish? Snap your fingers and you shall have it. Do you want a banquet fit for a mandarin of the first class? Summon a waiter and he will serve it to you."

Charles had been so right, Molinda reflected. Hong Kong was becoming the greatest seaport on earth, a place where trade proliferated and expanded more rapidly than it did anywhere else in the world.

Yes! It was good to be home!

Greeting several acquaintances who welcomed her, Molinda finally selected a rickshaw puller, climbed into the vehicle, and was hauled to her home partway up the Peak, the mountain on which the governor-general's residence and the dwellings of the more important citizens of the colony had been constructed.

The camelias and gardenias, the bougainvillea and jasmine in her front garden provided a riot of colors, and as Molinda dismounted from the rickshaw, she was pleased to note that her herbs in the side garden had been well tended, too.

Teng, her majordomo, was on hand to receive her, and Molinda greeted him warmly.

She listened to his report of the state of her household, and then speaking to him in Cantonese, she asked whether Jade was in residence at her home higher up on the Peak.

Teng shook his head. "Missy Jade," he said, "has not come back to Hong Kong, as yet, from Peking."

Molinda was surprised. "Really? She was due back here at least eight weeks ago, according to a letter I received from her in Bali."

Teng shrugged. "Maybe Missy is busy in Canton."

It was possible that the majordomo was right, but Molinda did not think so. Jade frequently stopped in Canton, staying at the ancestral home that had belonged to her mother, and before her, her grandfather, but there was insufficient business to keep her there for more than a week at the outside. She had to arrange for the export of certain commodities, like tea and cotton, but there was nothing else to keep her there for this long. Well, perhaps there would be a letter or a message of some kind from her at the office.

The following morning after enjoying a delightful dinner and a night in her own bed, Molinda was taken in a rickshaw to the waterfront complex of Rakehell and Boynton warehouses, where she maintained a large office. To her surprise, she found no communication there from Jade, and she became deeply disturbed when she looked in Jade's office and saw mail piled high, unopened, on the desk.

Returning to her own sanctum, she addressed the chief clerk succinctly. "Be good enough," she said, "to send for Lo Fang."

She did not have long to wait. The husky white-haired giant in the simple black pajamas who came into the room had worked for her—as bodyguard, foreman, and majordomo—for more than twenty years, after previously serving the imperial viceroy of Canton.

Molinda was one of the very few outsiders who knew that he had been the head of the all-powerful secret Society of Oxen, and she assumed that he still had connections in the organization, even though he was beyond active age to participate in its functions. Unlike the other Oxen member, Kai, who had joined a Chinese monastery to live out his final years, Lo Fang continued to work for his good friends.

When they greeted each other, their approach was strictly Oriental. Each commented at length on the appearance and obvious good health of the other, and not until these amenities had been performed did Molinda get to the business at hand.

"I sent for you, Lo Fang," she said, "because I didn't know where else to turn. Jade Rakehell was due to return here from Peking at least eight weeks ago. I'm not sure what the business was that took her to the capital—"

Lo Fang smiled slowly and held up a hand, interrupting her. "I know why she went to Peking," he said. "Her business there was connected with the Society." Even in private, he did not mention the Oxen by name.

"Whatever her reason, there's no letter from her awaiting me here, which is most unusual," Molinda said, "and frankly, I'm concerned about her. Can you find out her whereabouts for me?"

"It will be done," the giant replied, and inclined his head.

Molinda dismissed the matter from her mind. She knew that Lo Fang would not fail to carry out his assignment.

In the days that followed, Molinda went regularly to the office in order to attend to the work left undone because of Jade's absence. She labored hard from early morning until long after sundown every evening, and at the end of the week, she had the satisfaction of knowing that she had more or less caught up, that Jade's desk was now cleared.

One evening, when she was wearily finishing her day's chores, she felt rather than saw someone standing before her and looked up to see Lo Fang. As usual, he had entered her office so silently that she hadn't heard a sound.

Unlike most of his compatriots, he wasted no time on ritualistic greetings when he had something of importance to say. "The junk that was carrying Missy Jade from Tientsin to Hong Kong," he said, "was lost at sea. The Coastal Commerce Department had listed it as overdue, and the reason the classification was unchanged and no alarm was given was because of the reluctance of the departmental manager to admit that perhaps something unfortunate had happened to Missy Jade."

Molinda had spent so many years in China that she reacted to bad news as the natives did, and her face expressionless, she inclined her head to indicate that she had heard and absorbed the information that had been imparted to her.

"There were no typhoons or other severe storms during the period that the junk was at sea, even allowing liberally for breakdowns and time for repairs," Lo Fang declared. "So I can only assume that Missy Jade met with foul play."

"Robbers?"

He nodded. "The odds are very great," he said, "that the ship was attacked by pirates. Members of the Society have been alerted in every major coastal city, and I'll be notified immediately if they learn anything of Missy Jade's disposition."

"You don't think she's been killed, then?" Molinda asked, unconsciously growing taut.

The old man shook his head. "It is unlikely. Very unlikely," he said. "I wouldn't give you a copper yuan for the lives of the captain and crew of the junk. But Missy Jade is different. She is young and uncommonly handsome and therefore is worth a very large sum of money to pirates."

Molinda was shocked. "You don't think—they would sell her into bondage?"

"I prefer not to think in such terms," Lo Fang replied crisply, "because we don't know what has become of her and speculation is a waste of time."

"Could you pass the word through the Society," Molinda asked, "that if she has met such an unkind fate, Rakehell and Boynton will pay a very large sum—a fortune, in fact—for her release and safe return?"

"I've had no doubt that such a reward would be offered," Lo Fang said gently, "but it is premature to make such an announcement. First, we must find out, if we can, what has become of her. Then we will consider ways to recover possession of her."

Molinda nodded, warning herself not to be too hasty in such a complicated matter.

"I know how you feel about Missy Jade," Lo Fang said gravely. "I feel the same way. After all, she is the daughter of Missy Lai-tse lu, so you may be certain I will do my very best to recover her unharmed. But I beg you to show patience. This is a mystery that may take many weeks to solve, provided we are fortunate. If we are not, it is possible we may never learn what has become of Missy Jade."

"I know," Molinda replied softly. "I will write to her father, her brother, and her cousin and will tell them the sad news. Then all I can do is to wait and depend on you, Lo Fang."

The old man met her gaze steadily. "You may depend on me, Missy Molinda, in this, as you depended on me for so much in the past. If it is possible to discover what has become of Missy Jade, I swear to you I will learn her whereabouts. If not, at the very least, I will find out the identities of the pirates who captured her, and I will make them pay with their lives for what they have done to her."

BOOK III

I

The days were insufferably endless, but the nights were even worse, and Jade Rakehell taught herself the art of survival. She no longer minded being forced to play the courtesan for the estate's business visitors. Somehow she was able to divorce her inner being from the woman who submitted to the lovemaking of various men, and realizing that she had no choice, that their advances were meaningless to her, she was able to dismiss these unsavory incidents from her mind.

What continued to bother her, however, was the viciously sadistic treatment she still received from the woman who called herself Anna van der Luon. The woman delighted in insisting that Jade wait on her at meals, act as her personal maidservant, and otherwise subject herself to countless whims. Whenever Jade failed to obey an order instantly, or otherwise displeased the woman she was obliged to call "mistress," she received a whiplash across her bare back as a reminder of her subservient position, and her back was perennially sore, always covered with welts.

As if this were not enough, "Anna van der Luon" encouraged the other slave girls to make Jade the butt of their humor, and even though she submitted to them with as good grace as she could muster, she grew tired of having them seize her and daub her fingernails and toenails with vulgar, ridiculous colors, and paint her nipples strange shades of orange and purple and yellow.

She was alone, without friends, and completely helpless; what enabled her to retain her sanity was the strange relationship that she developed with Count Pieter Sabov.

Her fear of being beaten prevented her from initiating conversations with him, and he rarely spoke to her. Nevertheless, he indicated in many small, subtle ways that he sympathized with her plight, and that he wanted to do something to help her.

Jade guessed that he was aware of her real identity and consequently felt sorry for her. Perhaps he sympathized with her because the mistress of the household abused and mistreated her without reason.

He, too, was made to suffer by the woman posing as Anna van der Luon. Ostensibly he was a free man and held a responsible position of honor on her staff. Certainly he was always present at meals when business guests were entertained, and Jade knew that he conferred with these guests on trade matters. But when he was alone with the mistress, he was little better than a male concubine and had no more privileges than did the eunuchs who were kept on the staff for the entertainment of the more depraved visitors. As every girl on the staff well realized, he was forced to submit to the sexual whims of the woman, and she treated him as cavalierly as the concubines themselves were treated.

On two occasions, long red marks on his face and neck revealed that he had been subjected to a fit of ungovernable temper by the woman, who had raked him with her nails. Then he appeared at breakfast one morning with two long, ugly welts on one side of his face, indicating that he'd been struck with a whip. The realization that he, too, was being cruelly mistreated struck Jade forcibly and made up her mind for her: The time had come to act.

She had refrained from using her knowledge of the martial arts to even the score with her tormentor, or to put the concubines in their place. Even with her ability, Jade could not fight them alone. But all that was changed now. The prospect of working with a colleague made her willing to take the risk of being brutally punished by the estate's guards.

Jade stood behind the chair of Anna van der Luon at the breakfast table, waiting to do the woman's slightest bidding. From her vantage point, she gazed steadily at Pieter, her eyes telling him that she knew what he was undergoing and that she sympathized with him.

Whenever the woman's attention was distracted momentarily, Pieter swiftly and boldly returned Jade's gaze, his eyes telling her that he appreciated her feelings and reciprocated them.

All at once, Jade's spirits, which had begun to rise, plunged to the depths again as the woman beckoned to her. "Come here, girl."

Jade approached her tentatively, hesitantly.

"Come closer," Anna van der Luon demanded, and cupped the girl's bare breasts in her hands. She examined them intently, then burst into laughter. "What's this? Indelible purple rouge painted on the nipples? Congratulations, children! You shall be rewarded for your sense of humor and ingenuity."

The promise of a reward, as Jade knew only too well, was a guarantee that she would be subjected to further torment by the concubines. But the worst was still to come.

The woman brutally tweaked, stroked, and pinched Jade's nipples until Jade, unable to tolerate her growing discomfort, wriggled in an attempt to escape from the demanding hands.

Enjoying herself immensely, Erika von Klausner looked up at her in vast amusement. "Unfortunately," she said, "I must go to town for a meeting that will keep me busy all day. But never fear, I shall be back in time for supper, little one, and then I'll spend the evening putting you through your paces, as you deserve." Squeezing her nipples so hard that tears came to Jade's eyes, she left the dining room abruptly.

Jade was free to eat her own breakfast now, but the treatment she had received, plus the threat of an unpleasant evening hanging over her head, robbed her of her appetite, and she listlessly toyed with the tropical fruits on the platter served to her by one of the eunuchs who stood at the bottom of the social order.

She was so miserable that it took her some time to realize that the other concubines and eunuchs had been dismissed by Count Pieter Sabov, who continued to sit opposite her at the table.

He looked at her, his expression unfathomable, until the sound of a carriage moving off down the driveway told him that Anna van der Luon was leaving the estate for her meeting in the town. Then he said very quietly, his voice intense, "I've been abused enough, and I'm certain you feel the same way. I'm leaving here this morning, and I don't intend to return. Do you want to come with me?"

Jade's heart leaped. "Oh, yes!"

"I thought you would want to come," he said somberly. "In fact, I've been counting on it. But there are certain things you must know, and I'll understand if you want to change your mind. Madam is as powerful as she is vindictive, and when she discovers you've escaped, she'll tear the place apart. Never mind what she'll do to me if I'm caught. At the very least, you'll be flayed alive and returned here, and you stand a very good chance of being put to death as a warning to all the concubines to mind their manners."

"I'm willing to take any chance," Jade replied. "Life here has become intolerable."

"Very well," he said briskly, his manner changing. "Now listen carefully. Cover your breasts with a cloth and get a veil for your face. Meet me at my office in a quarter of an hour and I'll see to it that we leave the estate easily. From there on, we'll need the guidance of the saints."

Asking no questions, Jade hastened to do his bidding. She hurried off to her own quarters, where she secured a tiny breastband and a flimsy face veil, coverings that would convince the sentries at the estate gate that she was being taken away on legitimate business. Snatching her mother's jade and diamond jewelry, she donned it hastily, not wanting to leave it behind. Then, as she was making her way toward the exit of the concubines' quarters, she saw two of the other inmates loitering near the entrance. Both were big, rawboned farm girls from Sumatra, and she knew from their expressions that they were intending to torment her anew for their own pleasure. But she had no intention of pausing for them now.

They gaped at her, and the larger of them said, "Well, you didn't like the purple rouge we painted on you. You've covered it up, I see. I suppose we'll have to substitute some other color."

"Get out of my path," Jade said in a low, tense voice.

The smaller of the pair giggled. "Don't be in such a rush. We have all day, and we've planned some lovely surprises for you."

Jade measured her distance from them and suddenly lashed out, leaping high into the air and directing a stiff-legged kick at one, while delivering a hammerlike blow to the other.

The pair, unaccustomed to such a furious reaction from one who had invariably been meek and submissive, sat on the floor and stared at her.

Taking no needless risks, Jade struck out at them again and quickly knocked both of them unconscious. She had never forgotten the advice given her by Lo Fang, one of her instructors in the martial arts: "Do no more than you need to incapacitate a foe. Never strike harder than necessary, but it is better always to use a little too much force, rather than not enough."

Sauntering with feigned unconcern toward the main house, Jade joined Pieter Sabov in his office. She noted at once that he had put on his sword and that he now carried a brace of pistols in his belt.

"Do you have any weapons for me?" she demanded.

He hesitated. "I'm afraid to give you any arms," he said, "because you have no place to conceal them, and I don't want to run the risk of making the sentries at the gate suspicious."

She smiled when she saw a wavy-bladed *kris* in a jar containing a number of knives on the table in his quarters. She, Julian, and David Boynton had been taught by Uncle Charles how to use such a deadly weapon when they were children, and she immediately grasped it by its mother-of-pearl handle. "May I?" she asked and, not waiting for a reply, parted the folds of her long skirt and strapped the knife to the inside of her thigh. When her skirt fell back into place, the weapon was completely concealed from view. "Now I'm ready," she said.

Pieter drew a deep breath. "Let's go," he replied.

Jade adjusted her breastband, pulled the flimsy veil over her eyes and nose, and fell in behind him, a slave girl following a man who enjoyed the status of master.

Pieter had already ordered a small carriage pulled by two horses, and it awaited them in the courtyard. He drove it himself, with Jade seated demurely beside him on the driver's seat.

Pieter halted just inside the gate, where three of the short, dark-skinned guards stared hard, first at him and then at his companion.

Pieter appeared unconcerned and handed them an official-looking document that he had signed and sealed. "I'm delivering this wench to madam's meeting, where she is to be used as bait to persuade a Dutch trader to deal with us."

The sentries grinned at Jade, ogling her, but she pretended to be unaware of their interest and stared stonily through them.

Within moments the carriage had left the estate behind.

"Where are we going?" Jade asked.

"Into Djakarta," Pieter answered grimly, "but we're going to the opposite end of town from madam's meeting. I had no idea she was going to be in town today when I made my arrangements, which I've been working on for weeks. Unfortunately, my preparations, which had to be carefully made, took a great deal of time." He fingered the welts on the side of his face and winced.

Jade's curiosity got the better of her. "What I don't understand," she said, "is why you stayed with her for so long. You've been free to come and go as you please, and I'd have thought that you'd have left long ago."

He smiled ruefully and shook his head. "Obviously," he said, "you've never been on the verge of starvation, not knowing when you were going to eat again. I've been paid handsomely, as the gold coins that are weighing down the money belt around my middle can testify. I've consoled myself with money as I've tolerated abuse and humiliation, although I will admit my situation was never as bad as yours. I'm afraid I waited too long. Now Erika will never forgive me, and she won't be satisfied until my head is severed from my body.''

"Erika?" Jade asked.

He explained that the mistress of the estate was Erika von Klausner, who had murdered Anna van der Luon and had assumed her identity. She hated all Rakehells, holding them responsible for her own years of servitude as a concubine, and that explained her viciousness to Jade.

As she listened in astonishment, it dawned on Jade how far the woman would go when Pieter told her in detail about the plot to have Alexis Johnson win the affections of Julian, marry him, and then embarrass him by exposing her own past.

"The woman is mad and must be stopped," she said.

"First," Pieter reminded her, "we must make good our escape."

"Since we're in this together, and I'm grateful to you for including me," she said, "perhaps you can share your plans with me."

"They're very simple," he said. "We'll leave this carriage in the boatyard in the city, where the horses will be looked after by a boy who will meet us. I've already sent an order to the yard master to release a thirty-foot fishing boat that is a very minor part of the extensive van der Luon fleet. I have spent the last ten days quietly stocking the boat with food and other supplies." He paused and grinned. "This is where you enter the plans. As a Rakehell, you will no doubt recognize some of the seamen who inhabit the waterfront. What I want you to do is find a man who can sail the boat to Hong Kong for us."

Jade burst into unrestrained laughter.

"You won't think it's so funny," he said, glowering at her, "when I tell you I don't know the first thing about sailing. If we don't find a captain, we'll drift aimlessly all over the face of the South China Sea."

"I think it unlikely we'll meet such a fate," she said, sobering with an effort. "I could sail a boat almost before I learned to walk or talk."

He brightened and peered at her. "You're not joking?"

"Hardly," she said. "My name isn't Rakehell for nothing."

Pieter smiled. "To think that I asked you to join me because I wanted you to find a captain for the boat, when you're a fine sailor in your own right!"

"I suggest," Jade said dryly, "that we refrain from congratulating ourselves until we sail safely into Hong Kong harbor beneath the shadow of the Peak."

"You're right," he said, and nodding grimly, he loosened the pistols in his belt as they approached the entrance to the boatyard.

Once inside the entrance, Pieter seemed to know exactly where he was heading. As he drove down one narrow street and then turned into another, Jade saw dozens of seagoing boats at the wooden docks. There were craft of all kinds, including the inevitable junks and sampans of the Orient, old-fashioned schooners and brigs, and several large, handsome clipper ships. She examined the clippers carefully, but looked in vain for the Tree of Life symbol on a flag that would have ended her troubles instantly. None of the ships in the yard was a Rakehell and Boynton vessel.

At last the carriage drew to a halt, and as Pieter helped Jade step to the ground, a small boy appeared out of nowhere and took the reins.

Pieter grinned at him, spoke to him softly in Javanese, and handed him a silver coin, with which the urchin was more than content. The boy promptly drove off.

"Come along," Pieter said, and adjusted his stride to the shorter steps of his companion, who was hampered by her long skirt.

As they made their way along the waterfront, Jade became increasingly uncomfortable. Even though she had acquired a breastband, her seminudity was still startling, and the perfection of her figure and beauty of her face called further attention to her. It seemed as though every seaman in the Dutch East Indies was on the docks that day and was gaping at her.

Pieter was thoroughly aware of the interest she aroused and walked closely beside her to shield her.

Jade tried to concentrate on what she regarded as the real dangers that faced them. Erika von Klausner, she felt certain, once she learned of their disappearance, would leave no stone unturned in her efforts to get them back and silence them. Pieter Sabov was one of the few people on earth who knew her real identity and was aware of the fact that she had murdered the real Anna van der Luon. Under no circumstances would she want him to talk. Also, she wouldn't want it known that she had enslaved and humiliated a Rakehell. That would bring the full wrath of Rakehell and Boynton down on her head, and certainly she realized that Julian and David would be merciless in their treatment of her, would drive her out of business and bankrupt her.

"There's our boat," Pieter said. He pointed to a small craft riding beside the dock about fifty feet ahead, and Jade peered at it with interest. It was a ketch with two masts, and she approved of it instantly. It was sturdy and solid, and although not one of the fastest boats made, it certainly was seaworthy.

Suddenly Jade realized that the wooden walk that separated them from the ketch was blocked by three roughly dressed blond sailors, apparently Dutch, and obviously under the influence of alcohol. They were young and brawny, and it was all too easy to read their minds. They approved heartily of Jade and wanted her for purposes of their own. This goal appeared easy enough to achieve since she was accompanied by only one man, slender, tall, and dressed like a gentleman.

Long accustomed to shipyards, and knowing the men who sailed from them, Jade was sensitive to the nuances of the situation. "We'll be obliged to get rid of them stealthily," she murmured. "A loud altercation or the use of firearms would only call attention to us."

"Right," Pieter replied, "and attention is the last thing on earth that we want or need right now."

The trio spread out across the walk, making it impossible to squeeze past them.

Faced with an emergency, Pieter Sabov did not falter. Not slowing his pace, he reached for his sword, gripping the hilt, and half removed it from its scabbard. "We want no needless trouble from you," he said. "If you're wise, you'll let us pass, and that will be the end of the matter."

The seamen laughed, and their leader, a man with a deep bass voice, seemed particularly amused. "Give us the woman," he said, speaking English with a strong Dutch accent, "and we won't hurt you. In fact, we'll let you go on about your business."

"If you cross us," one of his companions added harshly, "you'll end up at the bottom of the harbor, because we mean to have the woman."

It appeared as though violence could not be avoided, and Jade halted, opened the front of her skirt, and removed the thin, wavy-bladed *kris*.

The seamen gaped at her long, shapely legs, which she momentarily exposed, but their eyes narrowed when they caught sight of the Indonesian knife that she now held in her hand.

"Drop that knife before you get hurt!" the man with the bass voice commanded.

Pieter glanced at Jade, and their eyes met. Hostilities could not be averted, so he drew his sword. "If you can really use that blade," he muttered, "now is the time to prove it."

He held the trio at bay with his sword, and while they hesitated, one of them reached into his hip pocket and produced a wooden club about eight or ten inches long.

Jade took one look at the weapon, and her heart sank. It was one of the ugliest fighting instruments known on the seven seas: The wood was hollowed and filled with lead, and the result was a murderous weapon that sailors used in brawls to kill their opponents. Anyone struck on the head with such a club inevitably died.

Jade, taking no chances, did not hesitate. Balancing on the balls of her feet as she had been taught as a small child, she distributed her weight evenly, then took careful aim and flipped, rather than threw, the *kris* at her target. The secret of one's success in wielding such a weapon lay in accuracy rather than in force. Jade had learned that it was far better to throw the knife easily, almost lightly, rather than try to put all of her muscle into her move.

Even though she had not practiced in the throwing of a knife in some time, she had not lost her skill. Her aim was true, and the blade cut deep into the base of the seaman's throat. His astonishment and pain were mirrored in his eyes as he collapsed to the wooden walk and lay still.

Displaying extraordinary agility and relying on the element of surprise, Jade leaped forward, drew the knife from the dead man's throat, and quickly backed up again to a position of safety, shielded by Pieter.

The young Russian nobleman meantime was doing his share. He lunged at the leader of the trio, and his blade penetrated deep into the man's body. The seaman staggered back, and when Pieter, exerting great effort, withdrew the sword, the man toppled backwards in the harbor.

The water in the vicinity of his body turned scarlet and gradually faded to pink as he sank far below the surface and disappeared from sight.

The third seaman, aware that he was alone now, took to his heels and fled in panic.

Pieter wasted no time. Bending down, he rolled the body of the man Jade had killed into the water and watched as it, too, slowly vanished from sight.

"Come on," he said, "and hurry. The Dutch authorities will raise hell when they discover that two of their merchant marine sailors have been killed. We have no witnesses to what happened, and they're unlikely to take our word for it."

Jade was obliged to pick up her long skirt and run, her bare feet thudding on the wooden planks. She couldn't help noticing that her necessary move had attracted considerable attention. Javanese, Malays, and Dutch fishermen and seamen on a dozen ships were ogling her.

She followed Pieter onto the ketch and felt infinite relief, even though they had a long way to go yet before they would be safe. "Cast off," she told him as she moved to the tiller.

He looked at her blankly.

It would have required too much time and effort to explain, so in her anxiety, she slashed the line that held the ship to the dock with her *kris* and then returned to the tiller. "We're in luck," she said. "The prevailing wind is going out to sea, so all we need is the time to get away and we'll make out all right. Hoist the jib!"

Pieter puzzled for a few moments, then finally understood her order and hoisted the smaller of the two forward sails. Under Jade's direction, he made it fast, and the little craft began to move, with Jade threading a path through the crowded water of the harbor.

"If you please," she said, "go into the cabin and see what you can find that I can use to cover myself. It appears as though every ship in the harbor is going to follow us."

Pieter ducked into the small cabin and reappeared soon, carrying a large cartwheel-shaped hat of straw, a Chinese peasant's headgear, and a smocklike shirt, an outer garment intended to protect a fisherman from the equatorial sun.

The relieved Jade piled her long hair on top of her head and pulled the hat low over her forehead, concealing her face. The rough-textured shirt, although uncomfortable, nevertheless concealed her near-nudity, and she lost her feeling of unpleasant self-consciousness as soon as she had donned it.

Threading a course through the boatyard, and then through the harbor beyond it, was time-consuming because of the vast number of ships and smaller boats that clogged the waters. Never had Jade seen a more crowded harbor, and she had to use all of her skill at the tiller to squeeze her way past countless boats of every description.

While she concentrated on the task, Pieter kept watch behind them and looked out for possible trouble. He knew, as did Jade, that the Dutch authorities kept a close watch on all vessels that came and went from Djakarta, and both of them half expected a customs cutter to hail and stop them.

A frigate of the Dutch navy patrolled the entrance to the harbor, her gun ports open and bristling with cannon, her decks lined with blue-coated marines ready to board any vessel suspected of carrying contraband or breaking the strict trade laws of the Dutch East Indies.

"If there are other smocks and hats on board like the ones you got me, fetch them for yourself," Jade said. "Your clothes and your pale hair are conspicuous, and this is a good time to make ourselves as invisible as possible."

Pieter nodded, went into the cabin again, and reappeared grinning, wearing a similar version of the peasant hat and smock that made up Jade's attire. He took his place again in the prow, and neither of them spoke as they passed within hailing distance of the frigate.

As it happened, however, neither the captain nor any other officer on board the Dutch naval vessel had the slightest interest in the Javanese fishing ketch, which appeared to be manned by two local peasants. The boat was not challenged and passed the frigate without notice.

At last Jade breathed easier. "It begins to look," she said tentatively, "as though we may get away."

Pieter was equally cautious. He grinned, but his tone was tentative as he said, "It may be you're right."

The wind appeared to freshen on the outside of the coral reef that protected the harbor, and the sea became choppy, whitecaps appearing on the water. "Hoist the mainsail, if you please," Jade said.

Pieter obeyed with alacrity, this time having a better understanding of what he was doing, and no sooner was the larger sail raised than the little boat picked up speed appreciably and seemingly darted through the water.

"We'll head due north past Sumatra on our port side and Borneo on our starboard side until we reach the South China Sea off the coast of Indochina," Jade said. "From there, we'll simply sail almost due north past Hainan Island to Hong Kong."

"You make it sound easy," Pieter said.

"It is easy," she replied, "provided all the necessary elements are in place. You say you were very busy procuring supplies. Where are they?"

"In the cabin."

"Here," she said. "Take the tiller while I check them."

"Tell me what to do."

She pointed to the west. "The sun is our guide. Keep it to your port side at all times. You'll find that the tiller is easy enough to handle once you get the hang of it."

He replaced her, and she entered the cramped cabin. The first sight that caught her eye were four water kegs, and she felt infinitely relieved. Water was vital to them, even more important than food, and she knew that, with it, they had a chance of reaching their destination, just as without it their cause was hopeless.

Pieter had been thorough in his accumulation of foodstuffs, and Jade was impressed. There was a bag of polished rice, which the Chinese favored, and another of long-grained, unpolished variety, which the Indonesians preferred. In addition, there were two large sacks of young ripe coconuts and breadfruit, which, although it had to be cooked, also was quite filling. There were two stalks of almost-ripe bananas, and there was a box filled with a pink, juicy-looking fruit, which she didn't recognize. Picking one up and examining it, she became aware of its exotic, perfumed scent. It was plain that it was edible.

Continuing her search, she found whole smoked hams and two large containers of pickled fish. She wasn't particularly fond of the fish, having eaten so much of it when she had traveled on clipper ships as a child, but she knew, all the same, that it was nourishing.

A basket that sat on top of the other food supplies convinced Jade of Pieter's thoroughness and caused her to giggle. It was filled with fresh lemons, and she could only assume that he had read of the disease that attacked sailors whose diet lacked citrus fruits, and he had discovered that lemons or limes prevented the outbreak of such an ailment.

Her spirits much improved, she returned to the deck. "I congratulate you on your industry," she said. "You have enough to eat and drink to see us not only to Hong Kong but probably all the way to San Francisco."

Pieter nodded. "Having known starvation in my life," he said, "I prefer to reduce risks to an absolute minimum."

The snow-covered volcanic peaks that spanned the island of Java from east to west loomed in the distance, and it pleased Jade to see that they were dwindling in size. The crowded harbor had become a small speck on the horizon, and they were leaving the Dutch East Indies behind them.

If their escape attempt succeeded, her nightmare of enslavement by a madwoman was ended. Now all she had to do was to navigate through sea-lanes that were busy with commercial craft—and pirates—and reach Hong Kong, where she could resume her rightful place as head of the Oriental branch of Rakehell and Boynton.

Conscious of the slave girl attire she was wearing, the costume she loathed and, over it, the inexpensive, drab attire of a Chinese fisherman, she could not help thinking that she was far from reassuming her place in the Rakehell and Boynton hierarchy. There were still hundreds of miles to travel, untold and unseen obstacles to be overcome.

II

Not only were the gates of the Middle Kingdom open wide to foreigners under the terms of the Treaties of Tientsin, but the people of China were free to go anywhere they pleased on the face of the earth.

Unscrupulous entrepreneurs, particularly in Great Britain and the United States, saw an opportunity to gain unlimited access to large pools of cheap labor and lost no time taking advantage of the situation. The impoverished masses of China, particularly in Canton and other cities of the overpopulated south, had two supposedly glittering alternatives dangled before their eyes.

They could, if they wished, leave their homes permanently and establish lifelong residence in Britain or in America. Or, if they preferred, they could accept free passage to the West, work there for a number of years, and then return to the Middle Kingdom. Presumably, they would be well-to-do when they came home again.

The gullible poor of China reacted precisely as the planners had hoped and reached for the supposed lifeline, most of them electing to accept free passage to England or America, to work there for a number of years, and then to return home. They applied by the thousands, and their applications were hastily and greedily accepted.

Disillusionment was swift. The emigrants were packed on board what were virtually slave ships under the most crowded conditions, and those who survived the long voyage were systematically subjected to even worse treatment on their arrival.

They were given hard manual labor to perform, the only work they were capable of doing, and in return, they were paid small pittances, far less than any American or Englishman would accept.

By the time the immigrant discovered he had been betrayed, it was too late for him to do anything practical about it. He found himself in a strange land, ignorant of its language and customs, and totally dependent for his food and lodging on those who had brought him so far from his homeland. He was made to understand that he not only had to pay for his keep but was required to earn his return passage to the Middle Kingdom, as well. He floundered, helpless and exploited, and those who were taking advantage of him were free to pursue their own ends as they saw fit.

Humanitarian groups in both the United States and Great Britain organized to meet the challenge. Quickly discovering that it was virtually impossible to halt the tide of Chinese immigration to their countries, they concentrated on trying to alleviate the lot of the bewildered who came to their shores and to provide them with better positions and working conditions.

Concentrating their efforts on San Francisco and London, the principal Chinese points of entry, they met varying degrees of success in their efforts.

In England, no one worked harder to alleviate the living conditions of the Chinese immigrants than did David Boynton. He was appalled by the sacrifices made by Chinese to assuage the greed of those who had brought them so far from home, and he worked tirelessly to help them. The hard work helped to alleviate somewhat the bitter disappointment of being rejected by Drusilla Smythe.

Realizing that unscrupulous promoters were traveling everywhere in China, making extravagant promises they had no intention of keeping, he knew he could not counter their efforts at the source. Therefore, he concentrated on easing the burdens of those who had migrated to England and were disillusioned and disturbed by the harsh fate that awaited them there.

His first step was that of providing a haven for the unfortunates. This he accomplished by utilizing a large estate in Kent, not far from London, that had been left to him when his grandfather died. The manor house was too large, the grounds too extensive for his personal use, but the estate was perfect for its new purpose. Appealing to everyone he knew, David quickly accumulated a group of volunteers to work with him, and his project was under way.

In his enthusiasm, he could not refrain from explaining his salvage operation to his bookkeeper, Aileen Christopher. ''There's ample room at the property to provide housing for two hundred and fifty Chinese, which is the limit. I don't think I could comfortably handle more than that. I've brought in food supplies—sacks of rice, vegetables, and meat—and the guests will attend to their own cooking.''

''May I ask who's paying for the food?'' Aileen inquired.

David seemed surprised. ''Why, I am,'' he said.

''That's very generous.'' She could not conceal her admiration for him.

He seemed somewhat embarrassed. ''I can easily afford it, and they can't. The important thing is to prepare them for life here in England, which is so very different from what they've known in China. A limited number of posts will be available here at the shipyard for them, but I want to make inquiries of everyone I know in industry and commerce to find out who else will open positions to these immigrants and will pay them wages that they deserve.''

''You're planning on sending a number of letters, then,'' she said.

He nodded. ''Why, yes.''

''I'll gladly write them for you, Mr. Boynton, on my own time after working hours.''

Her unexpected generosity surprised him. ''That's very kind of you to offer, Miss Christopher,'' he said, ''but there's no need—''

''I'm volunteering to do what I can because I believe in the principle at stake here,'' Aileen told him. ''Do you have enough people to teach the immigrants the rudiments of English?''

''There are never enough,'' he said with a sigh.

She looked at him, her expression hesitant. ''Well,'' she said, ''I've learned the basics of Cantonese, thanks to the Chinese man you hired for a time last year to help me with our correspondence to some of the major traders in Canton. So I suppose I'd qualify as an instructor, although I don't guarantee my pronunciation.''

He was taken aback. ''You, Miss Christopher?''

''I'll gladly go down to Kent on my day off every week and do what I can,'' she said. ''I'm convinced that everyone who believes in what you're doing should contribute everything possible. These immigrants need all the help and guidance they can get if they're going to acclimate and earn decent livings here.''

''I'll be very pleased to drive you down to Kent myself on your days off, Miss Christopher,'' he said, ''and I'm in your debt.''

''Indeed you're not, Mr. Boynton!''

He desisted and left her office to return to his own. For the rest of the day, however, he kept glancing at her surreptitiously as she worked on her ledgers, and he was still astonished. He hadn't realized it, but his bookkeeper was a remarkable person. Not only that, but she was a very attractive young lady, and he wondered why he had never before taken note of her appearance.

III

Propelled by strong, steady winds that blew from the south, the little ketch cut through the equatorial waters as it headed farther from Java. Jade stayed at the tiller and refused to relinquish her post. She was trying very hard to hold the vessel on course, which was becoming nearly impossible as the winds picked up.

"You haven't rested in hours," Count Pieter Sabov told her. "Let me take the tiller."

She shook her head. "Not now," she said. "Particularly not now. In case you haven't noticed, the weather is getting rougher. I'm not sure that someone who is inexperienced can handle the boat in white water like this."

"I can try," Pieter told her.

She grinned at him, concealing her exhaustion as best she could. "We'll take no needless risks," she said. "So far we've made good our escape, and we don't want to go backwards. Look off to port." She pointed with her head.

He followed her gaze but saw nothing.

"There's an island that I don't recognize off there," she said. "You see it, with the mountain in the middle, rising up toward those clouds overhead?"

At last he spotted the island on the horizon and studied it. "It appears to be a volcano," he said, "probably extinct. What is the place?"

"That's what I was wondering," she said. "I've sailed in these waters countless times between Hong Kong and Java, but I don't recall ever seeing that particular island."

"Perhaps it belongs to the Dutch East Indies chain—"

"I think not," she interrupted. "I'm fairly familiar with the Dutch islands in this neighborhood, as I am with the British islands, and it belongs to neither. I'd guess that it's one of those unidentified Malayan islands that no nation is currently claiming."

As Pieter knew all too well, there were literally thousands of islands in the vicinity; some of them belonged to the Dutch East Indies, others were under the British flag, and still others were claimed by Spain, which governed the Philippine Islands. Of the scores that were unclaimed, some were populated by backward fishermen, the inhabitants of others subsisted on the tropical fruits and vegetables that grew in their lava-rich soil, and still others were deserted, unoccupied by anything but lizards, turtles, and seagulls.

"I, ah, think we'll find out more about the place," Jade said, and her smile slowly faded.

"How so?" Pieter demanded.

She pointed up at the sky with her free hand. "You see those very black, very dense clouds gathering overhead? In case you don't realize it, there's a whale of a storm brewing. I wouldn't in the least be surprised if this develops into a first-class typhoon, and I want to be close enough to that island to put in for shelter there if we need it."

"It's that serious?"

"I hope not," she said, "but I honestly can't judge, and I don't want to take any risks that we can avoid. This is a sturdy boat, but with all due respect to the Dutch, it was built by them and not by natives, who are accustomed to typhoons in the East. So I have no idea how it will stand up under a real battering.''

The sky overhead had indeed turned an ominous black and was filled with deep clouds of dark gray that traveled at remarkably high speeds, propelled by winds of great power and intensity. The entire sea suddenly became alive and was being whipped into a white-capped frenzy as the winds continued to increase.

The little craft began to pitch and rock more violently, rising to the crest of one wave, then dropping rapidly into the trough between it and the next. Occasionally a solid wall of water slapped at the hull, shaking the boat severely and almost knocking the two people inside it off their feet.

Pieter understood the gravity of the situation and marveled at his companion's calm. "What can I do?" he asked.

Her answer was succinct. "I think you'd be wise," she replied, "to lower the sails. I wanted to keep them up as long as possible, but it's growing too dangerous. Besides, we're being swept toward the island as it is."

He noted that the volcanic mountain, with its tropical underbrush on its ascending sides, seemed much closer now than it had been. Working swiftly, he lowered the sails, and struggling to prevent the flapping canvas from getting out of control, he managed to make it secure.

He no sooner completed the task than the rain started to fall. It came down in torrents, making it impossible to see more than a few feet in any direction. The prow was no longer visible from the rear of the deck.

Jade had to raise her voice to make herself heard above the drumfire of the rain. "Are the cabin windows closed—and the door?" she shouted. "Make certain everything is battened down there."

Pieter rose and started to make his way forward to the cabin, and so violent was the storm becoming that he had great difficulty in maintaining his balance. He staggered first to the port rail, then was thrown across the ship to the starboard rail. But eventually he made it to the cabin and there completed the simple task. It was a relief to see that the rain had not entered the interior appreciably and that the foodstuffs he had accumulated were safe.

By the time he returned to the deck, he found Jade standing at the tiller, her feet planted wide apart, her clothes plastered to her body, as she struggled with all her might to keep the ketch on course.

"I . . . need . . . help," she panted.

Pieter joined her, and at her direction, he braced himself, grasped the tiller, and did his best to hold firm. It felt like a living thing under his touch, and it was almost impossible, so strong were the currents, so violent were the still-mounting winds, to keep the little vessel on her course.

They stood together, shoulder to shoulder, fighting the storm, conscious only of the effort they were making and their puniness in trying to combat the wild elements.

The wind whistled and moaned, occasionally raising its voice to a high-pitched crescendo as it howled through the bare rigging of the ketch. The rain fell even harder, and the couple, trying to stand on the slippery, lurching deck, with rivers of water coursing down their heads and into their eyes, forgot how it felt to be on land and dry.

All at once there was a sharp cracking noise, and the tiller handle was loose in the hands of its wielders.

"That's done it," Jade said. "From now on, we're at the complete mercy of the storm."

The couple were plunged into the worst that they had experienced as yet, and the situation was terrifying because it was totally unpredictable.

The ketch bounded and shuddered, first blown in one direction, then, without warning, violently reversing itself as it was subjected to the whims of the winds and water.

Hurled to the deck, then thrown forcibly against the railing, Jade and Pieter soon found it impossible to remain standing. She was the first to recognize the extreme danger that they now faced.

Knowing she lacked the strength and the stamina to make her way into the cabin, she placed her lips close to his ear and shouted, "Can you go inside for a line?"

He looked at her blankly.

"Rope," she screamed. "We need rope. As much of it as you can bring us."

He nodded, then grimly started to make his way forward. Later, trying to remember the incident in full detail, he could recall only snatches. All he knew was that the struggle to reach the cabin was unlike any he had ever experienced before. He opened and shut the door behind him, then picked up a coil of rope, which he wound securely around himself before he ventured into the open again.

When he returned to the deck, he saw that Jade had a huge lump on her forehead over one eye. Obviously she had been knocked to the deck and had been severely bruised.

They worked together, tying the rope securely around their middles and fastening the other end around the base of the mainmast. At last the task was completed, and they were comforted by the knowledge that at least they would not be washed overboard.

Gradually time lost all meaning. Sheer terror gripped both of them, its icy claws tearing at their stomachs, ripping at their brains, and making it impossible for them to think clearly. They had taken on so much water that Jade thought it miraculous that they were still afloat, but somehow the ketch remained intact, although badly battered, and continued to ride and jounce on top of the stormy sea like a buoyant cork.

Never had Jade been so close to death, but suddenly she conquered her fear, and although the storm raged on with unabated fury, a strange sense of inner peace gripped her. Her fate, as she well knew, was no longer hers to determine. She had done her best, and with the able assistance of Pieter Sabov, she had escaped from the prison that Erika von Klausner had created for her. Now the wind and the sea, in the grip of a typhoon, would determine whether she lived or died.

She struggled furiously to regain her feet, but whenever she succeeded, her victory was as brief as it was hollow. Within moments, she lost her balance again and was sent crashing to the deck, smashing first to starboard and then to port.

Only through a miracle, she knew, would she be able to avoid serious broken bones, and she knew that the same was true of Pieter.

He was far stronger and had much greater stamina, but he, too, could not stay on his feet.

Little by little the storm continued to sap their energies and wear them down. Ultimately, they were reduced to a doll-like state and sprawled helplessly on the deck, held there by the length of hemp that they had tied around their middles. They were buffeted, thrown this way and that, but neither responded, and they were more dead than alive, more unconscious than conscious.

At last nature took pity on them, and they truly lost consciousness, drifting off into a deeply troubled, violence-tossed sleep.

The first thought that occurred to Jade when she woke up was that the boat was no longer rocking and seemed to be moving at a slow, tranquil crawl. She opened her eyes, saw that the sky overhead had brightened considerably, and looked around. To her amazement, the extinct volcanic mountain covered with heavy underbrush loomed almost directly overhead, and what was left of the battered ketch appeared to be drawing nearer to the shore, toward a crescent-shaped beach of white sand, the circle on the land delineated by a row of palm trees. The typhoon, almost unbelievably, had completed the job that she herself had started and had guided her and her companion to the safety of the unknown island. Laughing and crying, she took hold of Pieter's shoulders and shook him awake to tell him the good news.

IV

Molinda's letters announcing the unexplained disappearance of Jade Rakehell ripped through the quiet façade of the Rakehell existence in New London with the explosive force of a bombshell. Rakehells were accustomed to act in emergencies and were never immobilized by grief. Jonathan immediately notified Molinda that he would pay handsomely for any information leading to his daughter's recovery, and Julian ordered every Rakehell and Boynton ship that traveled to the Orient to display reward notices accordingly.

Above all, a firm front was maintained. Jonathan and Elizabeth were scheduled to visit friends in Boston for a week, and neither even thought in terms of breaking the engagement.

Julian altered none of his own routines and spent his days at the shipyard as though nothing out of the ordinary had happened. Aside from noting an increase in his correspondence with Molinda, even those employees who were closest to him would have had no idea of what he was suffering.

Julian continued to see Alexis Johnson regularly, too. They had
not set a date for their marriage, nor had they yet discussed Alexis's
past, which had so upset Julian's cousins. But, as Julian believed,
all these things would be settled in their own good time, and he
continued to thank the stars for sending his way a wonderful woman
like Alexis.

Julian showed Alexis Molinda's letter about Jade and told her
what he and his father were doing about the matter, but he did not
mention the subject again. She respected his wishes, so she avoided
the topic, too, but as the days passed, she could see that he was
under a great strain, and her admiration for him increasing, she
decided she would have to bring the whole topic into the open.

One evening when they went to dinner together to a tavern known
for its succulent lobsters, Alexis could not help noticing the deepened
shadows under Julian's eyes and the crow's-feet at the corners of his
lids. Impulsively, without stopping to think, she reached out and laid
a hand over his. "I wish," she said, "that you'd talk to me about
your sister. I know how dreadful you must feel, and it'll be a relief
to you to at least get it out of your system."

He took hold of her hand and held it firmly in his strong fingers,
but smiled and shook his head. "You're sweet and considerate," he
said, "but I'm afraid you don't understand."

"Apparently not," she murmured. "All I know is that when
something is bothering me, it always helps for me to talk it out with
someone who's close to me. I know it doesn't solve any problems,
but just airing my feelings makes me feel better."

"If this were a matter that just concerned me and my feelings,"
he said, "I'd agree with you. But it happens that the subject is my
sister, Jade, and that makes all the difference in the world."

She looked across the table at him, allowing her hand to remain in
his, and waited for him to continue.

"As you've undoubtedly gathered after coming to know my father
and me," Julian said slowly, "Rakehells aren't like other people.
We have our own values, our own standards, our own sense of
what's right and wrong. We're accustomed to doing things our own
way, and when we make mistakes, we pay for them, gladly and

without complaint. This approach has been an inevitable consequence of being born into a family in which each generation has built on the successes of the generation behind it. We're like master architects, creating a pyramid that grows higher and stronger and firmer. Just as I think it can't get any bigger, I'm sure my sons will disagree with me and will prove me wrong, just as I proved my father wrong, and he proved his wrong before him."

"I know what you're saying," Alexis replied, "but I don't see the connection."

"Give me a moment and you will." He interrupted himself long enough to order two glasses of dry sack from their waiter. "Jade is a Rakehell in every sense of the word. In fact," he went on, "she's a very special Rakehell. She belongs to the Orient as much as to the Occident, to the West as well as to the East. She knew from the time she was very small that she would inherit not only a Rakehell fortune but also the house and property of her mother's late father, who was one of the great merchants of Cathay."

Alexis wanted to interrupt to tell him that, if his reminiscences were too painful, there was no need for him to continue. But she could not bring herself to say a word. She had started this, and it was only right that she let him go on.

"From the time she was born," Julian said, "everything in Jade's life was special. She learned the martial arts from a master, and like all Rakehells, she could sail a ship almost before she learned to walk. She was as much at home in Hong Kong and Canton and Peking as she was right here in New London. As a matter of fact, she was equally at ease in England, and like me, she had to attend board of directors meetings from the time that most girls were playing with dolls. It isn't generally known, but before her eighteenth birthday she was admitted to full membership in one of the powerful secret societies of China. She's fearless and resourceful, and above all, she's a Rakehell, which means she has a mind of her own and the will to do whatever she thinks needs to be done under any given circumstances. That's why my own personal concerns don't matter. I can do nothing to help her."

Their drinks came, and Alexis raised her glass of sack. "I'll drink to Jade," she said. "I can't help envying her and wishing I had a brother who admired me so much."

He joined her in the toast but then shook his head. "I've given you a factual account. What I said was not admiration but the truth," he told her. "We have no way of knowing what's become of her, particularly if she's fallen into the hands of brigands, as Molinda has indicated is a strong possibility. I shall assume that she's alive, unless I get irrefutable evidence to the contrary, and if she's alive, then I know that she's coping with whatever situation she finds herself in."

Looking at him as he spoke, recognizing his deep-rooted earnestness, Alexis began to gain some understanding of what he was saying. She knew that Julian was not indulging in rhetoric for the sake of maintaining his own spirits, whistling in the dark, or trying to impress her. He quite literally believed every word that he spoke. Jade was extraordinary, just as he himself was extraordinary, and she would survive whatever difficulties she faced because she had the character and the resilience to overcome obstacles. More than anything else, Alexis had a long glimpse into the sublime faith that the Rakehells had in themselves and in each other. It was a faith based on reason, on proven performance, and it was so great that almost nothing could shake it.

In spite of herself, Alexis found her thoughts turning to the woman she knew as Anna van der Luon, whose strange offer had sent her across the continent of the United States and had resulted in her meeting with Julian Rakehell. She knew her mission had succeeded, that he had fallen in love with her. So far, so good. All she had to do now was to marry him, reveal her background to him, and after she left him, collect the very large sum that was owed to her.

But it was far easier to imagine this course of events than to live through such an experience step by step. In brief, as she looked at Julian sitting across the table from her, she knew that nothing would impel her to go through with the agreement, that under no circumstances would she betray him. She could not allow herself to marry

Julian, to take unfair advantage of his innocence regarding her background.

The truth of the matter was that she had fallen in love with him, as completely as he with her. She found it impossible to bear the thought of the incredulity and disgust he would feel if she told him the truth about herself. No, she could not bring herself to reveal those truths to him. It no longer mattered that she'd been young and had faced certain starvation if she hadn't chosen the only solution open to her. All that was buried in the past, and there it would have to stay.

Julian seemed to admire integrity, above all, in his sister. Very well. Alexis had her own integrity and would live accordingly, even though he did not know it, would not know it, and could not know it.

She had no choice in the matter. In order to be fair to him, fair to the love that they bore each other, she would have to disappear from his life, simply, effectively, and without leaving a trace of her whereabouts. Only in that way could she offer him the protection that he deserved.

V

Shortly after sunrise every morning, lacy white clouds began to gather above the extinct volcanic peak. Their presence attracted still others, and by late morning there were enough clouds that a heavy downpour followed. The rain invariably began suddenly, without prior warning, and the deluge was steady, usually lasting for almost an hour. Then the rain halted again, as abruptly as it had started, the tropical sun came out, and within minutes the ground was dry.

But the regular rainfall, combined with the heat and the brilliant sunlight, performed miracles, and the island was lush and green beyond compare, the most verdant place that the two castaways had ever seen.

They waded ashore in the gentle surf, returning again and again to their badly battered ketch, where they retrieved things of value, including all the wood they could carry. The boat, damaged beyond repair by the typhoon, was breaking up, and they salvaged everything that they could.

The most valuable objects were their weapons and their food supplies, with both their gunpowder and the bags of rice and other staples left out to dry in the sun. One casualty of the storm was that Pieter's money belt had come lose, probably torn away from his body during the violent pitching and tugging when he and Jade were lashed to the boat. The belt was nowhere to be found, and the young couple guessed it had been washed overboard.

As Jade and Pieter rapidly discovered, they were fortunate beyond measure in having landed on this particular island. Food proved to be no problem for them. The jungle that began behind the rim of beach and extended upward to the very lip of the volcanic crater was extensive, and they found, within easy reach, breadfruit trees, coconut palms, and plantain palms. The plantain, like the breadfruit, had to be cooked and peeled before being consumed. There were passion fruits in abundance, as well, and after initial hesitation, they experimented, found the fruit edible, and thereafter added it at once to their diet.

In the shallow waters of the bay, there were vast numbers of crawfish, crabs, and other shellfish, and Pieter discovered that when he tried his hand at fishing, having rigged up a line and hook for himself, he landed large edible fish with firm, delicious flesh.

Inadvertently, the couple also found a supply of meat. Less than twenty-four hours after they had staggered ashore, more dead than alive, they were hoarding their possessions on the hot sands of the beach when a wild boar emerged from the jungle.

Their gunpowder was still damp, making their firearms useless, but Jade had acted without hesitation and had thrown the *kris*, making a perfect strike; the deadly blade landed between the eyes of the beast and it died on the spot.

Knowing the meat would spoil in the intense tropical heat unless they took necessary precautions, they gathered large numbers of coconut husks and built a huge smoking fire. They smoked the carcass of the boar on it, and in that way preserved it sufficiently so that the meat lasted them the better part of a week.

They decided to make their camp on a rocky cliff located behind one end of the beach. The conditions here seemed almost ideal for their purposes. There was a small stream that flowed along the inner ledge of the cliff and that became a torrent during the rains. So it was relatively easy for them to fill several of their wooden tubs and other containers with water, which was vital for the preservation of life.

With a great effort they dragged fallen trees of various sizes from the forest to the cliff, and there, working furiously for day after day, they managed to erect a crude shelter that protected them and their property from the elements, and that they hoped would act as a barrier to any wild animals that might live in the jungle.

Their most pressing problem, as they saw it, was that of learning whether the island was populated and whether the other people living there were friendly or hostile. Until they made such a determination, their movements were circumscribed.

"We'll never know from one day to the next," Pieter said, "when somebody who's after our blood may come popping out of the jungle at us. We've got to find out who else lives in this godforsaken paradise."

Early one morning, after a breakfast of fruit and fish, they started out on a tour of the island, first making a circle of the perimeter and then pushing inland, making their way upward through the jungle to the lip of the volcano. There was ample evidence of animal life in the heavy brush, but they saw no sign of human habitation, no indication that anyone else lived on the island.

Shortly after noon, from the edge of the volcanic crater, they studied every inch of the ground below them, and nowhere could they see any sign of a hut or house or any other dwelling. It was possible, of course, that people might be living in the heart of the thick jungle, but Jade doubted it.

"It doesn't make sense," she said, "to assume that anyone is actually living in the midst of all that jungle growth. There are certain to be snakes and insects there, as well as impossible heat, and I can't imagine anyone living there when they could set up a dwelling in a more comfortable place, as we've done."

"You're right," Pieter said, "but all the same, I prefer to take no risks. I'll cut back and forth through the jungles until I've satisfied myself that no one lives there."

He was as good as his word, and in the days that followed, while Jade busied herself gathering food and preparing it, as well as fixing up their hut, he went through the jungles.

"I'm satisfied," he said at last. "You and I are the only human beings alive on this island."

He made a number of discoveries, however, that they found valuable. For one thing, he learned that one valley, located about a mile or two from their dwelling, was infested with snakes. "I have no idea if they're poisonous," he said, "and I don't intend to find out. They're big, ugly brutes, and I suggest we give them as wide a berth as possible."

From that day onward, they took care to avoid the region they called "Snake Valley."

Other surprises proved to be far more pleasant. They found a long stretch of gull's nests in the dunes facing the water about a half mile from their dwelling, and the discovery promised them a steady source of eggs.

To their delight, they also found that there was a large population of small spotted deer on the island. By this time, their gunpowder had dried, and Pieter proved to be an excellent shot, bringing down two of the animals, each of them weighing at least sixty to seventy pounds.

They smoked the meat over coconut husks, as they had done with the wild boar in order to preserve it, and Jade went to work on the animal skins, going through a long and laborious process of curing them.

Remembering as best she could what she had learned as a small child reading about the curing of hides, she proceeded slowly and carefully, using trial and error. In the main, she was successful, and the intense tropical heat speeded the drying process.

Pieter fashioned two needles for her from bones taken from the tough spine of a fish, and these makeshift tools proved adequate for her purposes, as did the remarkably supple, yet strong, vines that she found in the jungle and used as thread.

What was left of the clothes they had been wearing was very little, the fabrics having been shredded in the typhoon, so Jade confined herself to basics, making a breechcloth for Pieter, a skirt and breastband for herself.

She also recalled from her childhood the plant native to the Philippine Islands that had spread to the Dutch East Indies and was known as abaca. It was more commonly called Manila hemp and was used to make cordage and cloth. The abaca bore a strong resemblance to the common banana palm, except for its fruit, which was inedible. Jade remembered that at maturity the plants were cut down and that long fibers were taken from the overlapping leaves that converged at the base to form a false stem.

The fibers were remarkably strong and long-lasting. Also, as she remembered it, they were resistant to salt water, which would be helpful in their daily existence.

She was pleased to find that the Manila hemp could be woven with great ease, and when Pieter learned the type of trees that she wanted, he cut down enough of them so that she could fashion a long cape for each of them. These they were able to wear in the rain and also as partial protection from the powerful rays of the sun.

The sun bronzed their skin, both of them turning a shade as deep as that of the mahogany trees in the jungle. Its rays transformed Pieter's already blond hair into an almost pure white, and for the first time in her life, Jade's long black hair was blond-streaked. For many days the problems of safety, food, and shelter kept the couple preoccupied, and they had no time or inclination to think of anything else. The task of staying alive and healthy fully occupied them, and they weren't even too aware of the intimacy into which they were thrown. Not until they knew they were secure, that they had enough to eat and drink and that they were protected from the elements, did other thoughts enter their minds.

They fell naturally into certain routines. Pieter spent an hour or more fishing every morning, and while he was occupied, Jade went into the forest and picked enough fruit for their noon and evening meals. When the rain fell, they sat in the hut, listening to the drumfire of heavy raindrops on the broad palm leaves that served as a roof. The sound was so loud that conversation was impossible.

The rain ended very suddenly, the sun blazed in a pale blue, cloudless sky, and the atmosphere was so humid, so heavy, that Jade felt as though she were sitting in a steam bath. "I don't think I can stand this for another minute," she said. "I can scarcely breathe."

"Either we go for a swim or we'll faint," Pieter said.

Without further ado they ran down to the beach, stripped off their abbreviated costumes, and jumped into the waters of the bay. Neither felt any sense of false modesty in the presence of the other. They were living and working in too close daily contact for that, and besides, Pieter had long been accustomed to seeing Jade without a breastband.

They swam for a half hour, taking care not to venture beyond the reefs at the outer rim of the bay that kept out sharks. Smaller, uglier barracuda, each with two rows of sharp teeth in a prominent jaw, were common in the harbor, but as the couple had discovered, barracuda had ample supplies of fish to eat and had no desire to become involved with human beings.

Jade had been an expert swimmer since early childhood, and she moved swiftly, easily, from one end of the crescent-shaped beach to the other, her powerful stroke carrying her smoothly.

Pieter had known only the rudiments of swimming when they had come to the island, but, as he did in all things, he proved an apt pupil and within a short time he had mastered the art. What he lacked in grace he more than made up in strength, and he was able to give a good account of himself, somehow keeping pace with the young woman.

At last they came ashore, breathless, and with Jade in the lead, they ran up to the cliff, where they sat to dry themselves in the sun. She combed her long hair with a comb she had made from a fish spine, then shook her head so the strands of hair would dry, too.

"I've revived," she said.

He ran a hand through his own wet hair, roughly smoothing it into place. "This beach," he said, "is one of the things that make life here worth living."

Her enormous eyes widened. "You know," she said, "I'm afraid I've been taking the beach for granted, which is more than I can say for just about everything else that we've found in this place. We're extremely fortunate, and I well know it, to be so well supplied with food, and even with clothing, such as it is."

"I suppose this is as good a time as any," he said, "to bring up something that I've had very much on my mind."

When he hesitated, she smiled and nodded encouragement.

"I'm afraid," he said, "we may be here for a very long time."

Seemingly unconscious of her nudity, she hooked her hands over one knee and then leaned back. "I've been increasingly aware of that," she said. "We've been here for eleven days, and I haven't caught a single glimpse of a single ship of any kind, anywhere on the horizon."

His smile was thin. "I might have guessed," he said, "that you'd be keeping track of shipping, just as I was. There you have it in a nutshell. I'm afraid our ship was much farther off course than we realized, and we are now on an uninhabited island somewhere north of the Dutch East Indian archipelago. I have no way of knowing whether Great Britain or France or the United States lays claim to this little bit of lush soil. For all I know, it could belong to the tsar."

"I think it far more likely," Jade replied, "that this island belongs to no one. I've observed, in the past—always from the safety of a solid, rapidly moving ship, to be sure—that there are literally dozens of such islands in these waters. If this one belongs to anybody, it's yours and mine—by right of discovery."

He grinned at her. "If we had a flag, we'd be wise to raise it."

She looked up at the leafy crown of a tall, stately royal palm that towered above them in the background. "Do you suppose that you could climb that tree?"

He shrugged and sighed. "Well," he said, "I could try."

"Never mind," she replied. "I'm sure I could do it. I climbed in the rigging on board my father's clipper ships when I was a child, and I'm quite positive I haven't lost the knack."

He stared at her. "May I ask your reason," he inquired politely, "for wanting to climb a seventy-five-foot palm tree?"

"I intend to make a large square cloth of Manila hemp," Jade said, speaking precisely, "and I shall leave it out in the tropical sun until all the colors are bleached from it. Then I plan to lop off the leaves from the top of a royal palm—the tallest one here—and use it as a flagpole. I'll fly the white cloth from it."

"It's a bold plan, and a good one," Pieter said. "But I don't know that it will be effective."

"Neither do I," she replied, "but we have nothing to lose by trying, and everything to gain."

He smiled grimly. "Unless, of course, we should happen to be picked up by a ship that belongs to the fleet of Anna van der Luon."

"I thought of that possibility, too," Jade said. "We know the island sufficiently well that we can always hide in the jungle until we can identify a rescuer and can figure out his intentions."

"It's well worth running the risk," Pieter agreed. "The island is pleasant and life here is anything but difficult, but I'm afraid that if we're here for any length of time we'll stultify."

"Or become subject to tropical rot," Jade said, and laughed aloud.

He blinked at her in obvious surprise.

Jade returned his stare. "Have I done something wrong?"

"On the contrary," he replied. "It just occurrd to me now that this is the first time I've heard you laugh since we began our escape in Java."

"It strikes me," she said, "that I have every reason to laugh. Miraculously I'm healthy and have suffered no broken bones. The greatest miracle of all is that I'm still alive after a horrendous storm in a little boat—the odds against survival were enormous but I survived, as you did. Now I find myself on a tropical island where there's food, where I've been able to get shelter and clothing of sorts, and to the best of my knowledge, I'm relatively safe from enemies—human, animals, and otherwise." She laughed again and shook her hair, which was now almost dry. "Why wouldn't I laugh?

I seem to have just about everything that a person can ask for in life.''

He leaned on one elbow and looked at her intently. ''There's only one thing really missing,'' he said.

''What's that?'' She looked at him, their eyes met, and in sudden confusion she felt her cheeks burning. ''Oh,'' she said, ''I see. I didn't understand.''

''I've tried to be patient,'' Pieter said gently, ''because I've known something of the inner hells that you undoubtedly suffered when Erika forced you to live as a concubine. I've done my best to treat you impersonally, and to be remote—as you've been. But I can tolerate no more. Apparently you don't understand the effect you have on a man. Not only are you incomparably lovely, but you—well, you take my breath away. I'm afraid that, like it or not, I've fallen in love with you, Jade Rakehell.''

She smiled faintly. ''You say you love me. Is that your physical desire speaking or is it really you?''

''As nearly as I can judge,'' he replied soberly, ''it's a very real feeling.''

She inclined her head slightly. ''I must be as honest with you as you've been with me. At the moment, I can't love you or any man. I'm still too bruised after what I underwent at the estate outside Djakarta even to think of love. But I'm very attracted to you, Pieter. You're handsome and forthright and honest, as well as resourceful and a splendid companion. If I had my choice of men I'd want with me on this island and under these circumstances, I'm sure I'd select you.''

He beamed at her. ''Then I have cause to hope.''

Again she laughed aloud. ''I think,'' she said, ''we can progress beyond hope.''

He blinked at her in the blinding sunlight, wanting to be certain he understood her meaning. But the expression in her eyes confirmed that she desired him as much as he desired her, and he reached for her.

But Jade caught hold of his wrist and halted him. ''Wait,'' she said, her voice soft. "There's one point that must be cleared between us. Because we're being sensible and giving in to the animal side of our natures doesn't mean that either of us is making a permanent commitment to the other. I realize it's absurd of me to speak of a permanent commitment when I don't know but what we're going to be on this island for the rest of our days, but I must be honest."

"I understand and I agree," he said. "Neither of us is making a real commitment."

She made no further attempt to stop him, and when she released his hand, she moved closer, voluntarily, as he took her in his arms.

Their lips met, tentatively, experimentally, as their nude bodies came together, and suddenly Jade surprised herself, as well as Pieter, by the intensity and depth of her own desire. She had known that she found him attractive, but she was startled by her desire, which was as great as his.

She had been accustomed to feigning passion during the brief, unsavory period she had been forced to spend as a concubine, but now the tidal wave of her own feelings swept over her, uprooting her. Even as Pieter's hands caressed her, exploring her body, she found she was doing the same to him and was relishing the experience, driving herself to heights of desire that she didn't know were within her.

The dangers, real and imagined, that the young couple had faced together, the enforced intimacy they had enjoyed for so many days, combined to make their mutual tension almost unbearable, and as the pace of their lovemaking increased, their yearning became intolerable.

They forgot time and place, the blazing tropical sun was out of their minds, and they knew only that they wanted each other, that they had to have each other.

Mutual desire enveloped them and they joined, thrusting, striving, each desperately seeking the blessedness of promised relief.

All at once Jade screamed aloud, her fingernails raking Pieter's bare back. At the same instant, he emitted a loud noise, halfway between an involuntary grunt and a low moan. Their thrashing became even more violent, and then slowly both subsided.

Arms and legs entwined, bodies still locked in a tight embrace, they kissed again. Only gradually did they become aware that they were lying on the short grass at the top of the cliff under a fierce equatorial sun.

"Not that it matters," Jade murmured, "but we're drenched with perspiration."

"That's easy enough to cure," he replied. "I suggest we take another swim."

Rising simultaneously to their feet, they ran side by side down to the beach, then dove together into the clean, cool salt water.

As Jade shot far below the surface of the water, then rose gracefully to the top again, she realized she was fulfilled and happy for the first time in a long while. No matter what tribulations might lie ahead, no matter what she had suffered in the past, this time on the island was a time to be remembered and treasured, a time that would stand out in her mind as long as she lived.

VI

Anking was small for a major Chinese city and boasted a population of no more than one hundred thousand persons. But it had an importance far beyond its size, as it was a trade center for the entire valley of the Yangtze River òn which it was located. Now, in the half-light of early evening, four men sat on their shaggy Mongolian ponies on the heights overlooking the city that lay in the valley below them. A group of aides and bodyguards sat their mounts nearby, but they carefully stayed beyond earshot. General Frederick T. Ward, the commander of the expeditionary force, was known to lose his violent temper when he thought that subordinates might be eavesdropping.

The three Chinese corps commanders studied the terrain spread out below them with care, and their attitudes were typical of the officers themselves. General Tseng, the young general to whom Jade Rakehell had pledged the support of the Society of Oxen, was also the deputy commander of the entire army. Tseng was thorough in his survey, missing no detail of the landscape, of the twisting and turning of the broad river, and, above all, of the city of Anking, surrounded by its ancient wall of stone.

General Li, meanwhile, studied the city in order to determine the best point of attack: north, south, east, or west.

General Tso, who lacked the patience of his colleagues, tapped his riding crop impatiently against his saddle and obviously found it difficult to contain himself until the assault began.

"Let me make our position plain, gentlemen," General Ward said, speaking faultless Mandarin. "As you know, the garrison, which consists of five thousand to six thousand enemy troops, according to the best estimates of our agents in Anking, is deployed inside the walls of the city."

"What fascinates me," General Tso said in his deep voice, "is the rebel sentries' seeming lack of concern that our forces are in the area. They must be very confident their troops can hold the city."

"With good cause," General Tseng said. "Keep in mind that we are outnumbered. We can put not quite four thousand fighting men into the field, and we face a foe of almost twice that size."

General Li asked, "Considering those odds, where do we attack?"

General Ward held a light bamboo walking stick in one hand and used it as a pointer. "We might be wise to concentrate our attack in this sector," he said, pointing to a spot about midway around the north side of the walled city.

His subordinates were surprised. "That's the main entrance to the city," General Li said with a note of incredulity in his voice. "You're suggesting that we strike the enemy at the point where he is strongest?"

"Exactly so," Ward replied with a grin. "If we take the enemy by surprise and attack him with spirit, we should be able to gain enough momentum to breach the city walls in that sector. If that happens, the rebel troops will be alarmed, their defenses will be weakened, and the battle will be won in a fraction of the time that it would otherwise take us, and, almost needless to add, we'll suffer far fewer casualties, as well."

There was a long silence, which General Li finally broke. "I must admit that your suggestion, Ward Frederick, is very bold, and if it is effective, it will be enormously successful. If it is not, however . . ." He shrugged and spread his hands in a silent gesture that indicated his feelings far more than if he'd put his thoughts completely into words.

Ward had anticipated opposition and remained cheerful. "Suppose we think about it and discuss it further at dinner," he suggested. Without further ado, he turned his horse away and, gesturing to the troops of the escort, started to ride back to their camp some miles from the city.

The innovations introduced by General Ward in the Imperial Army's style of living defied a tradition that stretched back for many hundreds of years. Officers no longer were attended by their personal servants, nor did they live in pavilionlike tents of multilayered silk, and the common soldiers also had no civilian underlings to cook their meals, wash their clothes, and put up their own pavilions of cotton. Every individual in the army slept in a cramped cotton tent that was about three feet high, and the only difference between officers and enlisted personnel was that each commissioned officer had a whole tent to himself, while subordinates slept two to a tent. Meals were prepared by soldier-cooks, who doubled as fighting men, and were simple, nourishing, and completely lacking in the pretentiousness that had marked the cuisine of the Imperial Army for centuries.

A typical meal served to the highest-ranking general and the lowest conscript, alike, consisted of rice with bits of beef and pork in it, along with whatever vegetable could be obtained from farmers who lived in the vicinity. It was General Ward's theory that an army should subsist on the produce of the country through which it traveled, thus making it unnecessary to carry a long supply train that slowed movements and was subject to enemy attack.

The only difference between the meal consumed by General Ward and his colleagues and that of the rest of the army was that the generals, who drank in moderation, each had a container of brown rice wine to wash down his food. Each used his own personal chopsticks, and they all ate off battered tin plates that were a far cry from the porcelain dishes that had been used for officers of their exalted rank through the ages.

The debate over where to launch the attack had been resolved, with the generals in agreement that a surprise attack against the northern end of the rebel-held city would be the most effective. Now the question remained as to which troops would spearhead the attack.

"My battalion of mercenaries," General Ward said, "numbers men of many nations in its ranks—Americans, Englishmen, Frenchmen, Germans, Imperial Russians. These foreign devils have known fighting everywhere, from the Crimea to the New World. They fear nothing, and they will do exactly as they are instructed, obeying their orders precisely. I plan to use them to launch our drive."

General Tseng smiled and nodded. "There are no troops in all of Asia," he said, "who are better suited for the purpose of committing a furious assault than the battalion of foreign devils. I approve."

"By far the most seasoned Chinese veterans are to be found in General Tseng's corps," Ward continued. "His troops have had experience in battle and have held their own in combat against the British on several occasions, and they are certainly no strangers to the Taiping rebels, whom they have been fighting ever since the Treaties of Tientsin were signed with the Western nations. I propose that the battalion of foreign devils be followed into combat by Tseng's veterans, provided he thinks they are equal to the task."

"They are equal to the task," Tseng said flatly.

"I intend to start the battle with the foreign devils and Tseng's corps," Ward said. "Those are the only troops I shall commit at the outset. After they have breached the city's walls, I hope to bring General Li's and General Tso's corps into the fray. As I see it, your men should be able to pick up their tempo from their comrades who are already fighting."

Li sighed and shrugged. "He whom the regent, Prince Kung, has named as supreme commander of the Imperial Army has made up his mind how he wishes this battle to be fought. I have no real choice, so I submit and will do as I am told."

Tso continued to eat, his chopsticks moving steadily between his plate and his mouth. "I have no argument with General Ward," he said. "I am a fighting man. I am not an orator who competes with scholarly mandarins of the first class."

"Then we are in agreement," Ward said. "I ask you only to have faith in my judgments, to know that I will not ask anything of you that I think you're incapable of doing. Anking is only the first in a series of targets that we must take if the Taiping rebels are to be truly defeated. I would be stupid, indeed, if, through my bad judgment, I lost the first of these battles and had to abandon the war."

There was no way that Li and Tso could ignore or reject such an appeal. Their own futures depended on their cooperation with the American who had been placed above them, and they agreed to accept his tactics and to follow him into battle according to the scheme that he had devised.

According to a hitherto inviolable tradition, the Imperial Army always held a full parade before going into battle, with hundreds of men carrying cymbals, which they crashed, and the entire army shouting invocations to the gods of war, asking them to intervene on behalf of the emperor and his men.

Frederick Ward abolished the tradition, forbidding the use of cymbals and swearing he would have the hide of any man who engaged in chants. He added yet another innovation. Instead of beginning a battle in the late morning, after the early mists had cleared away, he insisted on commencing the operation at daybreak.

This innovation completely bewildered the traditionalists. But the more experienced soldiers of the Imperial Army had to admit that the innovation made sense. Not only would a dawn attack find the enemy completely unprepared for battle, but it was so extraordinary that it was possible that victory would be achieved even more rapidly than the high command dared to hope.

Tents were folded and were stashed, and the entire army, after eating a cold predawn breakfast of rice, meat, and vegetables, moved out and began its descent to the Anking plain. The march was conducted in total silence, the troops having been warned that any man who spoke or made untoward noises would be executed.

General Ward sat on his mount, with his three corps commanders grouped behind him, and the members of the expeditionary force moved past him in single file, with each man being subjected to his intense scrutiny. No detail of a soldier's appearance was too minor to catch his attention, and he devoted the better part of his time to studying their weapons.

Every soldier carried a modern rifle and bayonet similar to those used by the British in the Crimean War and those currently being utilized by the Union Army in the United States. China had been severely defeated in two wars with the West, due mainly to the inadequate training of her men and the hopelees inadequacy of the ancient firearms that the Imperial Army and Navy were forced to use. It was a testament to his genius that General Ward had been able to purchase from western manufacturers many rifles, together with the six-shooter pistols carried by the officers.

Knowing they carried superior weapons on which they could depend made a great difference in the morale of the Imperial Army. Although the troops were somewhat stunned at being called out so early in the morning to do battle, they walked with a confident step, convinced that they could more than hold their own.

Occasionally the line was halted while the commanding general made certain that a bayonet lock was in place or that a rifle was loaded; then the line moved on.

Ward's timing was perfect. The sun was beginning to rise east of Anking and daylight was creeping into the broad valley of the Yangtze when the Imperial Army reached its destination and moved into battle formation. As anticipated, the battalion of hard-bitten mercenaries formed the primary assault corps in the center of the line, with General Tseng's one thousand men moving in directly behind them, ready to follow and give their full support.

The corps of Generals Li and Tso took their places on the flanks, but Ward again emphasized to the commanders that they were not to commit their men to combat without his specific instructions.

A final tradition was broken when the leader of the Imperial Army failed to deliver a long, impassioned harangue to his troops immediately prior to the beginning of the battle. It was Ward's theory that any soldiers who failed to understand why they were being sent into combat were inadequately prepared for a fight and that it was far too late for patriotic speeches.

It was enough that he was in their midst when the mercenaries formed a loose double line, leaving ample space between each man and the soldier who was assigned to the next position.

General Ward rode informally up and down the line, chatting and laughing, joking and making inconsequential small talk with the troops. They were aware of his proximity, they recognized the fact that he was within easy musket range of the sentries who were stationed on the thick stone walls of Anking, and that was more than good enough for the men. They were commanded by a general who took great risks equal to those they took, and they could ask for nothing more.

Those who were observant but had never before fought under the command of Frederick Ward were surprised to notice that he carried neither a pistol, a sword, nor a rifle. His only weapon, if it could be called that, was his light bamboo cane. This was in accordance with one of his theories, to the effect that a senior officer's value lay in the use of his mind, not the accuracy of his aim.

Peering up at the walls through the mists rising from the Yangtze, Frederick Ward could make out the rebel's sentries at intervals along the parapet. They were finishing a long stint of sentinel duty, and they were tired, looking forward to relief and the hot meal and bed that would soon follow.

There was nothing martial in their appearance or military in their attitude. Some wore uniforms, whose tunics were sloppily unbuttoned. Others wore the simple black pajamas of the Chinese masses, their status as soldiers indicated only by ragged armbands. Instead of being alarmed at the presence of the enemy, they lounged on the wall, pausing while making their endless rounds to chat with other sentries with whom they were passing the time more or less pleasantly. Clearly they were supremely confident that the enemy's meager force could never take the city.

Everything was working out precisely as he had planned it, and Frederick Ward grinned slightly as he raised his cane high over his head, then brought it down sharply and pointed it toward the wall.

The double line of mercenaries promptly moved forward in unison at a trot, their bayonets reflecting the filtered light of early morning. The army was in motion and the battle of Anking had begun.

The voice of the battalion commander floated back to the spot where the commanding general was sitting. "Fire at will!" he called.

The crackle of sporadic rifle fire broke the almost eerie silence. The veteran mercenaries were not wasting their bullets and were firing only when sentries offered perfect, irresistible targets. To Ward's intense satisfaction, he saw several sentinels drop to the parapet, and several others toppled off the high level to the ground below.

Taking his nickel-plated watch from his pocket, Ward glanced at it with satisfaction. Only three minutes had passed since the battle had started, and he was already operating well ahead of his own strict schedule.

Scaling ladders were unlimbered and thrown up by the mercenaries, their metal cleats biting into the stone of the walls and holding fast as the troops swiftly mounted them and took possession of the actual parapet. The invasion itself was now well under way.

The troops of General Li and General Tso saw the success that their comrades were achieving with such apparent ease and were anxious to join the fray. But General Ward was not yet ready to commit them to combat.

All at once the massive double gate of Anking slowly creaked open. The mercenaries had gained possession of the gate on the inside and, by opening it, were totally destroying the city's basic defense system.

The men of General Tseng's corps, saved the necessity of climbing the steep walls, poured through the open gate. As the rebel troops were called into action, the tempo of fighting in the city picked up appreciably, and the sound of gunfire increased.

Now was the time to commit the rest of his army, and Ward's bamboo cane jabbed in the direction of Li's corps, then was pointed at Tso's corps. The troops of both units trotted forward, increasing their speed as they approached the open gate, and they, too, burst into the city.

To the surprise and consternation of the headquarters staff, General Ward followed on horseback close behind them. As usual, he paid no attention to his personal safety, even though he was a conspicuous figure, a white man in a well-tailored uniform, with a broad-brimmed, gold-braided hat that could mean only that he was an officer of high standing.

He took in the overall situation at a glance. The rebels, at last, had become aware of their extreme peril, and defenders were pouring into action trying to counter the invaders with their ancient flintlock muskets and with a variety of weapons ranging from spears to hooked swords, all of them unsuitable for modern warfare.

Now was the moment to exert unendurable pressure on the rebels. Instead of using messengers to carry word to his subordinates, Frederick Ward elected to perform that function for himself, and he moved his horse laterally from left to right, from right to left again, pointing his ever-present cane in the direction of the enemy and exhorting his troops, alternately speaking in Mandarin and in Cantonese, to use their rifles freely.

Then he spurred forward, reaching a point in advance of his Chinese units, and found himself in the midst of the mercenary battalion.

"Eat 'em alive, lads!" he roared in English. "Fire at will and make every shot count!" He emphasized his words by waving his walking stick frantically over his head.

The troops of the Taiping rebels broke under the ferocity of the Imperial Army's attack, and no longer able to hold their positions, the disheartened rebel troops began to fall back in disorder.

Sensing that victory was near, the imperial forces needed no urging to redouble the fury of their assault. Soon rebel units of fifty to one hundred men were throwing down their arms and raising their hands in surrender. Then the general in command of the Anking garrison searched frantically for someone to whom he could surrender, and he was vastly relieved when he found General Li and promptly turned over the three thousand remaining members of his force, including his uncommitted reserves, to the Imperialists.

The battle for Anking was ended, and Frederick Ward had won a signal victory, his first of the campaign.

Generals Li and Tso had to conduct a search for him, and finally were told that he and General Tseng could be found in the main square of Anking. The two commanders hurried there and found their colleagues sitting their mounts, oblivious of the crowds of cheering residents, who, freed at last from the domination of the rebels, were welcoming their deliverers. As General Li subsequently wrote in a report that achieved a measure of immortality, Frederick Ward sat in rapt admiration of the curved slate roof of the pagodalike temple of heaven, the religious building that dominated the square.

"That roof, with its lip curling upward," he said, "is a perfect example of Chinese architecture."

Tseng was unable to share his enthusiasm. "I find it attractive," he replied, "but I don't think it's anything out of the ordinary."

"Ah, but it is," Ward insisted. "Don't you see? I've just learned that there's an old Chinese superstition to the effect that evil spirits travel only in straight lines. That's why all roofs are supposedly curved in order to prevent the bad spirits from entering a building."

General Tseng nodded and smiled. "What you've heard is basically true, Ward Frederick," he said. "But I hasten to add that it has been hundreds of years since educated men held the view that evil spirits can be kept out of a building by constructing it with a curved roof. Let us say that such roofs have become traditional in this country, and that as a people who revere tradition, we build houses with curved roofs, regardless of the cause."

"Oh, I understand all that," Ward replied indulgently. "But I find the roof shape fascinating, all the same. The longer I spend time in this country, the more amazed I am by the customs that are practiced here."

Generals Li and Tso exchanged a quick glance. They would come to learn that it was typical of Ward to lose interest in the battle he had fought once he had won it.

The victory achieved by the Imperial Army proved to be unique in several respects. General Ward issued an order to his troops forbidding looting and stating flatly that anyone under his command who disobeyed would be dealt with severely. Three soldiers from General Tso's corps ignored the rule and were caught red-handed looting a small shop that sold rice and other staples. The entire army was summoned to appear in the Temple of Heaven Square, and any civilians for whom standing room could be found were also invited to be present. The entire high command was on hand, and General Ward personally directed the efforts of the executioners, who removed the heads of the three culprits. Thereafter the army engaged in no looting.

Equally extraordinary was the fate of the defeated rebel army. Had precedent been followed, its leaders would have been publiclly executed after being humiliated in front of the people of Anking; the middle level officers would have been placed in cramped cages, where they would have been unable to stand, and would have been turned over to the public for stoning and other mistreatment until they died; and the common soldiers would have lost a hand or a foot in accordance with an ancient Chinese custom.

But Ward abolished all such practices. The commander of the rebels proved recalcitrant and unrepentant, so he was sent off in chains to Nanking to join his superiors. It would be up to them how to punish the commander who was responsible for the loss of a key city. All other officers who wanted to reaffirm their loyalty to the Chrysanthemum Throne were given the opportunity to do so and were welcomed into the Imperial Army without reservation. The same was true of the ordinary soldiers, who were so relieved at not being maimed for life that they became enthusiastic Royalists.

Prince Kung arrived in Anking three days after the victory was achieved and was received by an ordinarily phlegmatic citizenry that went wild when they saw him. Their enthusiasms built to a pitch of near-hysteria, and General Tseng observed that he had never in his life seen anything like it.

Kung ate dinner with Ward and his principal subordinates, and another precedent was smashed when the commander of the Imperial

Army, instead of ordering his cooks to prepare a special meal for the regent, insisted that the usual plain army fare be served.

Kung, both impressed and amused, made no comment about the meal, but he had far more important matters on his mind. "I do not question the authority you exercised when you granted an amnesty to the defeated rebels, General Ward," he said. "I granted you that authority, and your instructions were very clear. But I can't refrain from asking you why you showed them such generosity. I'm sure none of our own generals would have been so kind to them." He looked in turn at each of the subordinate commanders.

General Tseng, as always, was painfully honest. "I would have treated them in the traditional ways of our ancestors," he said, "and I would have been wrong."

General Li nodded emphatically. "I, too, would have shown them no mercy, and I would have been badly mistaken."

General Tso scowled and tapped his bowl with his chopsticks. "I am not certain how I would have acted had I been wearing the uniform of Ward Frederick," he said. "I cannot answer the question until we have had further action against the enemy and the loyalty of our newest troops is put to the real test."

Ward spoke very softly as he always did when he was emotionally aroused. "I realize," he said, "that I have been taking a gamble, but the risk, in my opinion, is small. The rebels have occupied entire provinces and have held much of this territory for many years. They have fed the people with lies and aroused their fears in order to hold their loyalties. The emperor, his generals, and his troops have been painted by them as monsters worse than the most terrible dragons of your mythology. I'm interested in proving—as quickly as possible—that these stories are made up out of whole cloth. I would much prefer to win the allegiance of people by peaceful means, rather than by force of arms, if it is at all possible. The good that will be done by the officers and men who have joined us from the rebel forces is so great there's no way to calculate it."

Prince Kung sat unmoving, his eyelids drooping, as he weighed, digested, and analyzed what he had just been told. "The reason I turned to a foreigner for help," he said, "was that I felt a desperate need for a mind that would rise above the ancient traditions of the Middle Kingdom. Many aristocrats in this country still cling to the old belief that the feet of their daughters are beautiful when they are tiny, and so they bind them with tight cloths from the moment a girl child is born. The result of such folly is that many women are crippled for life because of this absurd belief. It was my wish to free our military from equally crippling views, and I am convinced that we have succeeded. I admit that I find the generous treatment that General Ward has accorded our enemies is very strange and is alien to my entire way of thinking. But I grant him my enthusiastic approval of all that he has done and encourage him to continue to do as he thinks best for Cathay.''

Ward was touched by his unwavering support. ''Your Highness,'' he said, ''I can only repeat what I promised you when you gave me this command. I aim to rid the Middle Kingdom of rebels and return every inch of your territory to your control!''

VII

Alexis Johnson could tolerate no more. Having found that she had fallen head over heels in love with Julian, contrary to her agreement with Anna van der Luon, she was miserable. Her conscience gave her no rest, and totally indifferent to her own fate, concerned only with Julian's welfare, she consequently reached the conclusion that it would be best for him if she vanished from his life. This was her only choice, for she was unable to face him honestly and explain the plot against him and her own role in it.

Knowing nothing of Alexis's suffering or the reasons for it, Julian happily believed they were going to get married. It only remained to propose formally to her and set the date, and as he told his parents at breakfast, he planned to speak with Alexis that very evening.

Jonathan had been waiting for this news. With a meaningful glance at Elizabeth, he said to his son, "Many years ago, Lai-tse lu and I were presented with stunning gifts of great value by the Tao Kuang Emperor of the Middle Kingdom. Those gifts were exquisite large diamond rings of unusual clarity and great brilliance. That which was given to Lai-tse lu I have kept for Jade.'' He swallowed hard, shook his head, and his jaw jutted forward. ''I am still keeping it for her, and when she marries it will be duly presented to her as a gift.''

Julian knew what the effort cost Jonathan because he, too, was deeply concerned about his missing sister. ''Speaking for Jade,'' he said, ''I know how she will appreciate it.''

''The ring that was given to me,'' Jonathan went on, ''has something of a history, too.''

''Your father offered it to me when we were first married, Julian, but I refused it,'' Elizabeth said. ''He'd given me a perfectly lovely engagement ring, and this diamond was just too large and too exquisite.''

''In brief,'' Jonathan said, ''we agreed to keep the ring until such time as you were about to marry, and then to pass it on to you to present to your future bride. I'm delighted that Alexis will be the recipient.''

Julian exhaled slowly. ''I'm overwhelmed,'' he said, ''and I can't possibly find the words to thank you.''

Jonathan nodded. ''Since you're intending to propose tonight,'' he said, ''you'll want the ring. I keep it in the safe in the library, so I'll have it for you when you come home after work.''

Julian shook his head. ''This is foolish of me, perhaps, but I'd rather wait and present her the ring on a separate occasion.''

His father shrugged. ''That's up to you, of course,'' he said. ''Just let me know when you want it, and I'll get it out of the safe for you.''

Even though Julian spent an exceptionally busy day at the shipyard, the hours dragged for him, and the time passed with abysmal slowness. At last the workers on the day shift left, those on the night shift came to work, and the office staff prepared to leave.

The clerks were astonished when they saw Julian preparing to depart at the same time that they did. None of them could remember an occasion when Mr. Rakehell had closed his office for the day this early.

Hurrying home, Julian shaved for the second time that day, changed his clothes, and then drove in a small closed carriage to Alexis's hotel.

He quickly mounted the stairs two at a time to her suite on the top floor and rapped on the outer door. Only after knocking repeatedly and getting no response did he become concerned, and then he went down to notify the clerk on duty at the desk.

The clerk did not appear surprised. "If you please, Mr. Rakehell," he said, "the manager, Mr. Harding, would like a private word with you in his office."

Amos Harding had been dealing with Rakehells all of his vocational life and was well aware of the deference due them as the leading family of the area. "I've been expecting this visit, Julian," he said. "I don't know quite how to tell you this, but Miss Alexis Johnson checked out of the hotel this morning."

Julian blinked at him and swallowed hard. "But that's—that's impossible," he replied. "She had a dinner engagement with me for this evening."

The hotel manager felt sorry for him. "That well may be," he said, "but the fact that she left the hotel this very morning is undeniable."

Julian was still stunned. "Where did she go?"

The confrontation had come even more quickly than the hotel man had anticipated, and he drew in his breath. "I'm sorry, Julian," he said, "but I'm not permitted to reveal that information without the express approval of the guest, and in this case, I was requested by the guest to keep the information confidential."

Rising slowly to his feet, Julian hooked his thumbs in his belt, and when he spoke his voice was conversational, almost gentle. "Three years ago," he said, "when you needed money to carry out the expansion of the hotel you had in mind, my father and I advanced you the money. I'm calling in that loan right now."

The color drained from Harding's face. "You know I can't produce that sum on short notice," he said. "That would drive me into bankruptcy."

Julian shrugged, and his voice hardened. "That can't be helped," he said. "As a matter of fact, calling in the loan is only one step I'll take. As that requires a great deal of time and two or three days will pass before the transaction is completed, I'll invite you to step into the alley behind the hotel with me right now. You'll then have an even more direct choice. Either you'll give me the information I seek, or I'll beat you to a pulp."

Amos Harding surrendered. "Miss Johnson swore me to secrecy. Ah, well," he sighed deeply. "She instructed me to forward her clothing boxes to the Fourteenth Street Hotel in New York City."

"Thanks very much, Amos," Julian said grimly. "Just what is this place? I've never before heard of it."

Harding felt he had already discharged his obligation to the Rakehells, that there was no need for him to explain that the Fourteenth Street was a hostelry of dubious repute, a place that catered to gamblers, ladies of the evening, and others of questionable reputation. "It's one of the newer uptown hotels," he said, hedging. "I've never been there myself."

"It's no matter," Julian replied. "Did Miss Johnson give you any reason for her hasty departure?"

"I'm afraid not," the manager replied regretfully. "She simply paid her bill, ordered her clothing boxes forwarded, and departed very quietly."

"She left no letter for me or any similar communication?"

Harding shook his head. "I'm afraid not, sir."

"I'm grateful for your cooperation, Amos." Julian bowed and took his leave.

He returned to his carriage, nothing in his demeanor indicating that anything out of the ordinary had happened, and drove himself to the restaurant where he had intended to dine with Alexis. His mind continued to function normally, and if anything, it was clearer and sharper than usual. This was one of the most valuable traits that he and Jade had inherited from their father, and he proceeded to analyze the situation in depth, taking into account what he had been told by his cousin Brad about Alexis's past.

Ultimately, he realized that he knew too little to form any hard and fast conclusions. He had too many questions that only Alexis could answer, and it was senseless for him to speculate.

So he left the restaurant and drove straight to the Rakehell mansion, where he found his father and stepmother reading in the library. Facing them, he wasted no words.

"For reasons beyond my capacity to imagine," he said, "Alexis left New London suddenly and unexpectedly this morning and went to New York City. I browbeat the hotel manager until I learned her destination, and I intend to follow her on the early train tomorrow morning. I thought of leaving this evening by ship, but I'll make better time by rail, and I hope to reach her side by noon, at which time I'll endeavor to solve this riddle."

Giving neither Jonathan nor Elizabeth the opportunity to reply, he withdrew and went to his own room.

Shortly before dawn the next morning, Julian boarded the early train bound for New York City. It was made up mostly of sleepers from Boston, and due to the shortage caused by the Civil War, there were no parlor cars available, so Julian was forced to ride in the diner.

In spite of his lack of appetite, he ate a long, leisurely breakfast and then read the newspapers, which were filled with Civil War developments, most of them unfavorable to the Union cause. The war, he was afraid, would last for at least several years, as it would take time for the industrial might of the Union to exert itself and to establish supremacy over the Confederates.

When he at last disembarked from the train at the depot near the Battery, Julian immediately hailed a carriage to take him uptown to the Fourteenth Street Hotel. Long familiar with the community, Julian nevertheless marveled at its continuing, unprecedentedly rapid growth. New York was not only the financial and cultural center of America, but it was the nation's largest seaport, with trade from every corner of the globe centered here, and was also growing rapidly as a manufacturing center.

Fourteenth Street, once a delineating point between New York and the open country above it, now was a major thoroughfare, and it was crowded with carriages and pushcarts, vehicles of every description drawn by everything from teams of horses to single donkeys.

The Broad Way, which ran north and south, was equally heavily laden with traffic, and it took so long for Julian's carriage to reach the Fourteenth Street Hotel that his patience was tried severely.

On sight, he disliked the hard-faced men in pearl-gray swallow-tailed coats with matching high hats, and he didn't think too highly, either, of their escorts, women who wore too heavy makeup and were attired in satin gowns even at midday.

Nevertheless, he pushed through the throngs that did not yield an inch to him in the lobby, and felt a measure of relief when he learned from the desk clerk that Miss Alexis Johnson occupied Suite 408.

A knot of men at the base of a narrow staircase failed to dissolve as he approached, and he was forced to waste some minutes literally squeezing his way past them. Not until later did it dawn on him that they had blocked his path deliberately in order to give confederates an opportunity to get into position to rob him.

As he ultimately mounted the stairs, however, he instinctively took a tighter hold on his walking stick with the gold-knob handle, the only approximation of a weapon that he carried. Certainly he had no premonition of danger; at the most, he felt uneasy in the presence of the flashy, alien characters he had encountered in the hotel.

As Julian reached the fourth-floor landing and turned into the quiet, empty corridor, he suddenly came face to face with a heavyset, bearded man wearing a striped sweater and a knitted cap. The man would have been more at home in the hiring halls for merchant seamen than he was in the corridor of a so-called hotel of stature.

Julian halted abruptly and then became aware that two other men, similarly clad, had appeared and were standing behind him, blocking his retreat to the staircase.

The burly man smiled, revealing two rows of yellowed, uneven teeth, and suddenly he whipped an ugly knife from the scabbard that was hanging from his belt. "No need for ye to get alarmed, mister," he said, his voice almost jovial. "We'll relieve ye of the fat watch that ye carry in your waistcoat pocket, we'll take the greenbacks that are responsible for the unsightly bulge in your wallet pocket, and while we're about it, we'll relieve ye of that cane, too, seein' that it has a gold handle.''

Julian had grown up on the waterfront, where his father had allowed him to fend for himself during seamen's brawls. He was no stranger to violence, but he appeared to be slow-thinking and equally slow-moving as he stared at the robber who confronted him.

"You mean this walking stick?" he asked, and let his hand slide down the length of stout oak toward the foot. Then, before the man could reply, he suddenly sprang into action, swinging the walking stick with all his might and bringing the heavy gold knob crashing into the cheekbone of his startled assailant. "Here you are, m'lad," he said. "You wanted this, and you shall have it."

The ruffian gasped aloud and, dropping his knife, clapped his two hands to his shattered cheekbone.

Still wielding the walking stick like a weapon, Julian rammed its base into the pit of the man's stomach, doubling him over.

"Strange," he murmured. "You said you wanted this, but you seem to have little use for it." He wheeled on the pair behind him. "What was it you two wanted?"

The ruffians, startled by the aggressive bellicosity of their supposed victim, began to back away.

The outraged Julian gave them no chance to escape unscathed, however. Grasping the walking stick by its narrow end, he wielded it furiously like a club, utilizing his knowledge of swordplay, as well.

There was no escape from the heavy gold handle, which struck the pair repeatedly on their heads and faces and which moved so rapidly they could not grasp it.

One of the robbers, who had anticipated an easy time with a frightened victim, quickly lost his appetite for combat and took to his heels.

The odds had been reduced, suddenly and dramatically, and Julian was meeting the only ruffian still on his feet on equal terms. Dropping his walking stick to the floor beside him, Julian moved forward on the balls of his feet, like a boxer, and lashed out suddenly with a succession of left jabs and right hooks that drove his opponent against the nearest wall.

Still incensed, his anger unabated, although his mind remained cool, Julian continued to pummel the man unmercifully, his fists driving into his body from the pit of his stomach to his shoulders, and rocking his face with punishing blows. The victim had looked soft, as befitted a gentleman, but he was hard-muscled from his years at sea and from his incessant current inspections of ships being built, and his opponent was literally incapable of fighting back.

The door to Suite 408 opened, and Alexis Johnson, who had heard sounds of a commotion and had decided to investigate, peered out into the corridor. She was wearing a dressing gown, her face was totally devoid of cosmetics, and her hair was hanging in loose waves down her back.

Julian saw her before she recognized him and, snatching up his walking stick, he walked quickly toward her.

She saw him and appeared to have half a mind to retreat into her suite and shut the door.

But Julian was too quick for her and stepped into the open doorway. "I appear to have bloodied my knuckles somewhat," he said. "May I trouble you for a basin of water to wash my hands in?"

She closed the door and sighed, her shoulders slumping. "How did you find me?" she murmured.

He didn't intend to reveal that Amos Harding had done him a favor. "If you don't mind, may I have that water, please?"

"Of course." She busied herself fetching a basin and pouring water into it, and then handed him a bar of soap and a towel.

He nodded his thanks, his smile impersonal, scrubbed his hands, and then dried them on the towel.

Her face as pale as her off-white robe, Alexis watched him wearily. "You're all right, I gather?" she asked in a half mutter. "You weren't hurt?"

"I'm perfectly fine," he replied grimly. "Among other questions that I'll want answered is why you chose to come to such a disreputable hotel as this."

There was no way she could tell him that she had learned of it because it was a familiar establishment in the circles in which she had traveled, and that she had known of nothing of any better stature.

"If you please," she said, speaking so softly he could barely hear her, "I'd like to finish dressing, if you don't mind."

He had no intention of losing sight of her, of perhaps having her give him the slip while ostensibly going off into the bedroom from the sitting room to change her clothes. "You may sit down," he thundered, pointing at an easy chair with his walking stick.

Alexis meekly sat.

"Now, then," he demanded, "what have you to say for yourself?"

She drew a long, tremulous breath. "I—I scarcely know where to begin."

"Never mind," he said curtly. "I'll start. I had a dinner engagement with you last night, at which time I intended to propose to you and to set our marriage date. Having had no such opportunity, due to forces beyond my control, I've traveled approximately one hundred and fifty miles in search of you in order to repeat to you as emphatically as I'm capable of doing that I love you."

Alexis tugged nervously at the tassel on the belt of her robe. Leaning forward in the easy chair, she looked miserable as she said, "I know you love me, and I know we both thought we were going to get married. I ran away because I love you, too, and I—I just couldn't marry you."

He stared at her in astonishment, completely bewildered. "What in the devil are you talking about?"

"You—you don't understand," she wailed.

"I'm afraid I don't, and I'm becoming more confused with each passing moment. So we'll stop and review our joint situation from the beginning. I love you. That is a fact. You tell me that you love me; we'll assume that is also a fact. As two people who love each other, we'll marry and presumably we'll live happily ever after. That's a conjecture, but it's based on fact."

Alexis tried in vain to blink back the tears that welled up in her eyes. "But that's the whole point," she cried miserably. "We wouldn't live happily ever after. We couldn't!"

Julian's self-control was monumental. Seemingly completely calm, he sat back in his chair and folded his hands. "May I ask your reasons for that remarkable conclusion?" he asked quietly.

It was useless to dissemble, impossible to evade any longer, and Alexis found the whole truth spilling out of her, beginning with the visit she had received from the woman who had called herself Anna van der Luon.

As Julian listened, his bewilderment grew. "I find it very strange," he said at last, interrupting her, "that Anna van der Luon should try to trap me and embarrass me. The Rakehells have done business with her and with her uncle before her for many years, and we've considered them among the best friends and trading partners we have anywhere on earth. However, we'll let that pass for now. Please go on."

Alexis took a deep breath. "She offered me the huge sum of one hundred thousand dollars if I would entice you into proposing marriage to me, and then, after I became your wife, I was to reveal my background to you. By then it would be too late, and the good name of Rakehell would be ruined forever." Unable to meet his gaze, she stared miserably down at the floor.

"You came very close to having your plan succeed," he said. "What caused you to abandon it just as you were about to win?"

"Why must you be so thickheaded?" she cried, her temper flaring. "I've already told you that I love you! I didn't plan on that!"

"I see." He pressed his fingertips together and stared at her over his hands. "What was so horrible in your background?" He knew what Brad had told him, but he had to hear it from Alexis herself.

She was in agony. "Must I tell you?"

"What was it?" he demanded, his manner unyielding.

The last of the young woman's reserves crumbled. "I was brought up as a lady in Philadelphia," she said, again unable to return his gaze. "My father had gone west because he was convinced he was going to become very rich when gold was found in California. He sent for me after my mother died, and soon after I was reunited with him in San Francisco, he passed away, too. So I was left with nothing but my—natural assets. I used them for a number of years, and I was highly successful at it, as a number of gentlemen who live to this day in the San Francisco area can testify. You're probably already acquainted with a number of them, since they're shipowners and bankers and commercial traders.''

Julian pulled himself slowly to his feet and looked down at her. ''You haven't killed anyone? You've never committed murder?''

''Certainly not,'' she answered indignantly, in a choking voice.

''You've never robbed a bank or committed any other major crime?''

''No! Of course not!''

He continued to regard her steadily. ''I know of no law,'' he said, ''no man-made rule, no convention of society, that gives me the right to condemn you for earning a living in the only way that was open to you. I'm fortunate because I've never faced starvation, but I've known a great many people who have, and I've seen how desperate they can become.'' He paused for a long time, and she looked up at him.

In her misery, Alexis was unable to read the expression in his eyes.

Julian reached down, caught hold of her shoulders, and pulled her to her feet. ''I've had hell's own time finding you and catching up with you,'' he said. ''So there's something that I must know before you slip away again. Will you marry me?''

His words released a dam and the tears came.

He embraced her, and she returned his kiss fervently, but still she continued to weep. Finally he held her at arm's length. ''I've asked you a civil question,'' he said. ''The least you can do is to answer me.''

''You're—sure you want to marry me—knowing what I've been?''

He simulated great exasperation. ''Will you or will you not do me the honor of becoming my wife?''

''I will, darling, with all my heart,'' she replied, and when he kissed her again, the flow of tears miraculously stopped.

By early afternoon, the young couple were comfortably ensconced in parlor car seats for the return railroad journey to New London. Julian spoke firmly but gently. ''You're not taking up residence again in the hotel," he said. "You're coming home with me—where you belong, and my parents will act as chaperons for you until we're safely married. I don't intend to let you out of my sight again!"

Still in something of a daze, Alexis returned his smile. The developments of the day had been so rapid, so unexpected, that it was hard for her to accept them. She was very sure of one thing: Julian's love for her was so great that her past no longer mattered. He fully intended to marry her, regardless of her background, and she could begin to live in the present, for the future, regardless of what she once had been.

They ate a light meal of soup and sandwiches in the dining car, and although neither of them mentioned the strange agreement that had led to their meeting in the first place, Julian was severely troubled by it. He examined the matter from every conceivable angle but, finding no satisfactory solution, he relegated the problem temporarily to a corner of his mind.

Jonathan and Elizabeth Rakehell reacted exactly as Julian had expected and welcomed Alexis with open arms, insisting that she make her home with them, effective immediately, and taking charge of all wedding arrangements.

Alexis and Julian offered no explanation to the older couple for the reasons that the young woman had disappeared from New London, forcing Julian to follow her, and Jonathan and Elizabeth asked no questions. Elizabeth, however, realizing that Alexis had undergone an ordeal that had exhausted her, quietly insisted that her guest go to bed immediately after supper.

She escorted Alexis to her quarters, leaving father and son alone in the dining room. Julian poured two glasses of port. "Let's take these into the library," he said. "There's a perplexing business problem that I want to discuss with you."

Jonathan made no comment as he followed his son to the library.

"Alexis would be mortified if she knew I'd mentioned this to you, Papa," Julian said, "so I'll rely on your discretion. She had an offer from an old associate of ours that I can't, for the life of me, understand." He proceeded to outline, in full detail, the deal—as he understood it—that Alexis had made with the woman known as Anna van der Luon.

Jonathan concentrated on what he was hearing, and although he frowned from time to time, he did not interrupt.

"What I can't understand," Julian said, "is why Anna should have chosen such a strange revenge against me. If we had offended her in some business matter, why didn't she simply make trade arrangements with another company?"

"You or David—you, in particular—never had a falling-out with Anna van der Luon?"

"Never," Julian replied flatly.

"This scheme sounds to me," Jonathan said slowly, "like a vindictive plan of a woman who's been slighted or jilted. Are you quite certain that you never rejected Anna van der Luon romantically?"

"I'm quite positive of it," Julian replied emphatically. "I've always enjoyed very pleasant, but strictly impersonal, relations with Anna."

Jonathan's perplexity increased. "I find this very odd indeed," he said. "You don't suppose that some outside party, perhaps someone who'd stand to benefit by a rift between us and the Dutchman's company, went to Alexis posing as Anna van der Luon?"

"I thought of that," Julian said, "so I questioned Alexis about the woman's appearance. She sounds like Anna."

Jonathan sighed. "This is too bad. We owe the solvency of Rakehell and Boynton to the Fat Dutchman, who saved our hides by obtaining several shiploads of pepper for us one time, just before the Dutch government put a freeze on the exportation of pepper from the Indies. We did very well with that arrangement, thanks to the Dutchman's generosity, and it saved us from bankruptcy. Since that day, we've exchanged so many favors that I can't begin to enumerate them all."

"If Jade was at work in her Hong Kong office, I'd ask her to investigate the matter for me," Julian said. "But, as she isn't there, my hands are tied."

"Not necessarily," his father replied. "Molinda will be in charge in the East until Jade returns to duty, and I assure you, she's thoroughly competent to deal with the problem.''

"I'll write to her first thing tomorrow morning and ask her to make discreet inquiries," Julian said. "Whatever's responsible won't influence my relationship with Alexis in any way. We've gone beyond that, thank goodness. But there's more to this problem than meets the eye, and I'd very much like to get to the bottom of the mystery."

VIII

Aileen Christopher was satisfied and told herself she could ask for little more in life. She saw David Boynton daily, working beside him seven days a week and frequently continuing until late in the evening, writing letters for him, meeting with prospective employers, attending to the many details associated with bringing the Chinese into England. She and David were growing close, and Aileen reflected that her good fortune was staggering, and that she should not be greedy and wish for a still closer relationship.

They left the office together at noon on Saturdays, and David drove them himself in one of the Boynton carriages to the country estate that he had transformed into a hostel for immigrant Chinese. There they worked side by side, and the volunteers who made up the staff took it for granted that Aileen would be close to David as he made his rounds, inspecting the premises, interrogating the Chinese guests in their own language, interviewing newly arrived immigrants, and giving instructions to the staff who were training the Chinese newcomers. They became accustomed to seeing her quietly taking notes as he issued orders, and later they cheerfully accepted their share of responsibility as she distributed his wishes to the entire staff.

Aileen and David even conducted English classes for the Chinese, and the volunteers marveled at the stamina that Aileen displayed as she maintained the blistering pace that David set. They knew that he, like his father before him, could call on seemingly inexhaustible reserves of energy that enabled him to work at a rapid pace for hour after hour without tiring. But they were startled when they saw Aileen keeping step with him.

So many details demanded David and Aileen's attention after an absence of almost a week that they rarely paused for something to eat until midnight, or later, on Saturday nights. On Sunday morning, they resumed their labors early and could be found anywhere and everywhere on the property throughout the day and long evening.

In spite of the grueling pace, however, Aileen always looked fresh and rested when she and David departed for their week's work in London before dawn on Monday morning.

David invariably took a number of the hostel's problems back to London with him and worked on them after his responsibilities for the operations of Rakehell and Boynton came to an end for the day. He went out and met with factory owners and labor organizers, to see about finding jobs for the Chinese immigrants, and he went about recruiting additional staff to train the newcomers at the house in Kent. In these matters, too, he came to rely on Aileen for assistance, and she made no complaint when he utilized her services until nine or ten o'clock in the evening.

David felt obligated to take her out for a late supper on these occasions, and always chose one of London's better dining places.

Aileen, who had never before eaten in such elegant establishments, learned to accept her presence in them with aplomb. But she secretly didn't care where they went or what they ate. It was enough for her that David had chosen her as his companion, and that they were dining together.

Although they now spent most of their waking hours together, their basic relationship remained unchanged. Aileen continued to address her employer as "Mr. Boynton," and he was careful to call her "Miss Christopher" at all times, too.

Aileen found it difficult to prevent herself from indulging in daydreams. She had come to know David much better and understood him accordingly, sympathizing with his moods and grasping the subtle changes in his mercurial temperament even before he himself became aware of them. It was all too easy to imagine herself married to him, although she knew, deep down, that there was virtually no chance she would be lifted so far above her present humble station.

One Saturday, she and David arrived at the estate shortly after noon and were immediately inundated with problems. Forty newcomers from China had arrived at the estate during the week and were finding their adjustment to life in England difficult.

David promptly called a meeting of the group and, after listening to their complaints, delivered a pungent address to them. They expected too much, he told them in blunt Cantonese, and those who were dissatisfied with their treatment at the hostel were free to return to London, where they were certain to be exploited by unscrupulous employers.

Everyone at the hostel, he told them, was expected to work for the common good. Suddenly he jabbed a finger in the direction of Aileen, who sat beside him, trying as best she could to make out the meaning of his speech in the Chinese dialect.

"Look well at this woman, you who do not like the food that is served to you and who complain that your mattresses are too hard. Note her well! She is poor and must earn her own way in the world, but she believes in what we are trying to do at this hostel, and so she gives freely of her time and her efforts on your behalf. She gives up her days of rest for you, and often she works late at night to help you. Can you face her, and as you thank her for her efforts on your behalf, can you assure her that you are doing your part to become accustomed to life in this country and to do your share for yourself?"

Aileen was able to make out enough of the gist of what he was saying to feel uncomfortable and embarrassed.

David's words had the desired effect, and the immigrants, ashamed of themselves, promptly clamored for tasks to prove they understood and were willing to reform their ways.

Several, who had been farmers in the Middle Kingdom, were assigned to work in the vegetable gardens, where they would help to alleviate the perennial food shortages at the hostel. Others were assigned to duties in the kitchen, and the tallest and strongest were reserved for a labor pool that was utilized whenever brawn was required. The group broke up gradually, with the immigrants drifting off to take up their new assignments.

David breathed more easily and turned to Aileen with a worried smile. "So much for that crisis," he said. "What's next on the agenda?"

As she studied a list they had made out in London, a rider approached them, the dust of the road still thick on his boots.

"Mr. Boynton?" the man inquired politely. "Forgive the interruption, sir, but I've just arrived. I carry a letter for you that's marked 'Urgent.'"

A glance at the horseman's uniform was sufficient to tell Aileen that he wore the livery of the house of Dudley. He handed David a scented, mauve-colored envelope that bore the Dudley seal, too, and the young woman stiffened.

David instantly grew tense, and although his eyes gleamed as he tore open the envelope and read the contents, it was impossible for Aileen to know what he was thinking.

"I'm so sorry," he told her, "but something totally unexpected has just come up. Can you do without my presence for the rest of the evening?"

It would have been a simple matter to find adequate excuses, to tell him that his presence at the estate was mandatory. But Aileen merely smiled and replied crisply, "We'll manage."

"Good," he said. "I have a long ride ahead of me tonight. I'll try to be back here in time for breakfast in the morning, and then we'll make up for lost time." He nodded impersonally, and putting the letter into an inside coat pocket, he hurried away.

Aileen's spirits drooped. She felt certain that the communication had been sent by the Earl of Dudley's daughter, Drusilla Smythe, whom she herself had mistakenly dismissed as a potential serious rival for David's affections. Obviously Drusilla was not yet finished with him. He had just said that he had a ride of several hours ahead of him, so that undoubtedly meant that he was going off to the Dudley estate. She wondered what possibly could have arisen to cause him to abandon his beloved hostel, and although she couldn't guess the answer, she felt certain it did not improve her own slender, remote chances.

All at once life lost its savor for Aileen Christopher. She struggled in vain to overcome her feelings, and she went about her business with her customary vigor, determined that the Chinese immigrants who were depending on her would not suffer because of negligence on her part. Nevertheless, the hours dragged.

At midnight, several of the volunteers, aware that she had spent the evening alone, joined her in the kitchen for something to eat, but in spite of her efforts to maintain appearances, she had no appetite and the food tasted like dry sawdust in her mouth.

All she could think was that Drusilla Smythe had crooked her little finger, beckoning David, and that he had gone flying to her.

It was heartbreaking and painful to watch a daydream die.

BOOK IV

I

Drusilla Smythe knew she was being inconsistent, but she no longer cared. It had taken some time for the truth to sink in, that her so-called friend, Edwina Warren, had not been joking when she had said, "If you don't want David Boynton, I want him!" Furthermore, she knew that Edwina had twice invited David to social functions, and that he had refused because he had been busy on some project or other at an estate he owned in the country.

Edwina's attitude had forced Drusilla to reconsider David as a suitor, and she couldn't help but regard him in a better light now. Certainly Edwina had been right when she had called him handsome. In fact, Drusilla had compared him with every other man she knew, and she was forced to admit that even the best-looking of them failed to live up to the standards set by David. Actually, his appearance counted for less than did his attitude. He was dashing and socially imperturbable, and that was more than she could say for the bulk of the stodgy males of her acquaintance.

There could be no doubt, either, that David was one of the wealthiest bachelors—by far—in all of Great Britain. His fortune exceeded that of most dukes and marquesses, and his funds were greater than those of any three or four of the wealthier young men that she knew. Edwina had been quite right when she had said that the woman whom David married would emerge as a social power in England equal to none. His parents appeared to be quiet people who lived modestly, but his wife, especially if she, Drusilla, became his wife, could create quite a stir. Her jewels could equal Queen Victoria's, and she could blaze a path that would be the envy of everyone who knew her.

Her father was still opposed to David on the grounds that he was part Chinese, but she refused to worry about Papa's attitude. After all, he was a realist; the Dudleys might be one of the oldest and most distinguished families in Great Britain, but their fortune had dwindled appreciably, and in these times when new millionaires were appearing on the social scene every year and it was becoming more and more difficult to maintain appearances, she had no doubt that Papa—in time—would learn to appreciate the value of a son-in-law whose purse was unlimited. In fact, Drusilla felt that with her to guide David, a gift of cash made at the right time, with the appropriate delicacy, would placate Papa sufficiently to win his enthusiastic support of a son-in-law who happened to be Eurasian.

Still sure of the power she could exert over David, Drusilla had planned her move with great care. She had no sooner arrived at the Dudley country estate than she dispatched a messenger with the letter that she had written previously. In it she had merely told David that she wanted to see him, as soon as he could join her, on a matter of the utmost mutual interest, and to ensure that he responded favorably to her summons, she had closed the communication by sending him her love.

Certain he would obey her summons, she had dressed for the evening in a glittering cloth-of-silver gown that had strained the family's financial resources but was well worth the expense because it so enhanced her pale beauty.

She had carefully planned the intimate supper that she would serve him, and had conferred at length with the cook. She had called on the butler for his knowledge in selecting the wines that would go with the meal, and everything in the family living quarters reflected her taste. Masses of fresh-cut flowers stood in vases strategically scattered around the room, and although the weather was still warm, a small aromatic wood fire glowed in the hearth.

The thunder of a rapidly approaching horse's hoofs caused her to glance at the clock that stood on a mantel, and she smiled in self-satisfaction. David had lost no time in coming to her and had, in fact, arrived a half hour earlier than she had expected him. Fortunately, she was ready.

She sat in a thronelike chair with a tapestry cover and appeared to be taking her ease as he was ushered into the room.

Drusilla rose slowly, gracefully to her feet and extended both hands to him. "How good of you to come all this distance," she murmured huskily.

David had not seen her since the day she had rejected his proposal of marriage, and he suffered a severe wrench. She was even lovelier than he remembered her.

"You look radiant," he told her.

She contrived to blush as she thanked him.

The butler entered with a bottle of wine, and Drusilla took it from him and poured it herself for her guest.

She seemed to be in no great hurry to tell him the reason she had summoned him to the Dudley estate. Whatever the problem, it did not appear to be quite as urgent as she had indicated in her note. However, David preferred to be a gentleman and to say nothing on the matter, instead waiting for her to bring up the subject.

When the butler announced that dinner was served, Drusilla clung to David's arm as they walked to the dining room, and he had the uncomfortable feeling that she was flirting outrageously with him.

He was somewhat surprised to discover that they were alone at the table, which he had not anticipated, but he had no chance to bring up that subject. Drusilla chatted amiably, lightly, talking about nothing, and as a guest, he was obliged to keep pace with her.

To his dismay, the main course was roasted pheasant, a dish that he never touched. Years earlier as a boy he had built feeders for pheasants, both at his parents' country place and at the house in Kent that his grandfather had left him, and they were still in use. He regarded the pheasant as a noble, handsome bird, and as a matter of principle he would not, and indeed could not, eat one.

Drusilla, however, was too busy chatting to notice that he left most of the food on his plate untasted.

Not until their dessert of fresh strawberries was served and glasses of champagne were poured to accompany it did Drusilla finally acknowledge that this was no ordinary social occasion.

"I had a reason—a very good reason—for writing to you, David," she said at last.

He made no attempt to conceal his relief. "I'm glad to hear it," he told her. "I didn't enjoy a hard three-hour ride across the countryside to get here tonight, and I'm not looking forward to an equally long ride home."

"You're welcome to spend the night here," she said quickly.

"That's kind of you, but I'm afraid it's impossible." David offered no explanation, feeling there was no way that he could tell her that his work for the immigrant Chinese had to take precedence over whatever the problem was that she had in mind.

She was sufficiently sensitive to realize that she was losing touch with him, so she hastened to make amends. "David," she said breathlessly, her eyes fixed on his. "I have a confession to make to you. I made a mistake, a dreadful error, when you did me the honor of proposing marriage to me and I rejected your offer. I don't know how else to say this to you."

He smiled faintly but remained remote. "That's pleasant to hear," he said, "and it's very generous of you to make such an admission." He smiled again, then sipped his wine.

Drusilla was privately dismayed. According to the scenario she had written, this was the moment he should have jumped to his feet, come to her, and swept her into his arms. Instead, he remained seated and his behavior was cool and controlled, to say the least.

"I—I felt I had to tell you," she murmured.

"Thank you," he inclined his head and waited for her to continue.

His failure to react as she had anticipated completely confused her, and she began to lose control of the situation.

Again David smiled a little. "Does your father agree that you erred?" he inquired politely.

His question so took her aback that she blurted out the truth before she could stop herself. "I—I haven't discussed you with Papa!"

"Oh? I was wondering whether I'd see him this evening."

She shifted uncomfortably in her seat, which felt unaccountably hard. "He and Mama were required to go to Windsor Castle to attend Queen Victoria this weekend."

"I see." David took a deep breath. "May I ask if you would have invited me here had your parents been in residence this weekend?"

She was trapped and realized it, so her temper flared. "I don't think that's a very fair question at all!" she cried.

"In the light of our last discussion," David said, "I'm inclined to think it's most appropriate. On the basis of what you have told me previously, I gathered that Lord Dudley did not consider me an appropriate suitor for the hand of his daughter because my mother— unfortunately, in his opinion—was Chinese. Under the circumstances, I believe I have a right to ask whether he's changed his mind, and, if so, what has caused the change.

The girl was perplexed by the total lack of hostility in his attitude. He spoke calmly, matter-of-factly, without showing feelings of any kind, and she didn't quite know how to react. "I've had no occasion to discuss you with Papa," she said, "but when I do, I'm confident that he will change his mind completely about you, as I have."

Again he sipped his wine. "May I ask, then, what caused you to entertain a change of mind?"

She could hardly tell him that she had been goaded by Lady Edwina Warren's outspoken interest in him. "Let's just say," she replied archly, "that I exercised a lady's privilege and changed my mind."

David's mind raced, his powers of analysis undisturbed. He knew Drusilla was being far less than candid with him, that her coy response to his question was evasive and in no way truthful. He realized, too, that she had brought him here under false pretenses, hinting at an emergency that did not exist. Everything in the house, from her gown to her carefully arranged hair, from the intimacy of their dining arrangements to the variety of wines that had been served, led him to the inescapable conclusion that she had been setting a trap for him, making it virtually mandatory that he renew his proposal.

Oddly, it occurred to him that he no longer loved Drusilla Smythe. Yes, she was very pretty, and her breeding enabled her to exude a certain measure of charm, but he saw her now in a light that had been impossible weeks earlier before he had launched into his plans for his hostel for the immigrant Chinese. Drusilla had no knowledge of his world—the real world, in which people suffered and went hungry, were lonely and upset and needed help. He had been completely mistaken when he had imagined himself enamored of her, and he told himself he should be grateful that she had turned him down and had avoided a catastrophe for both of them.

"I wonder," he said carefully, "if you're familiar with the Book of Ecclesiastes in the Old Testament? As I recall it, the prophet wrote,

> To every thing there is a season, and a time to every purpose under the heaven:
> A time to be born, and a time to die; a time to plant, and a time to pluck up that which is planted;
> A time to kill, and a time to heal; a time to break down, and a time to build up."

Drusilla stared at him in wonder, not comprehending a word of what he was trying to tell her.

"There was a time," David said, choosing his words with great care, "when you and I might have married and established a successful marital relationship. But that time has passed, as I'm sure you'll agree when you think it over, as I have. I bear you no ill will and will always think of you with affection. I hope you'll regard me in the same way." Not wanting to prolong the painful scene, he rose, bowed, and hastily left the dining room.

Drusilla Smythe sat unmoving in a stunned silence, unable to believe that David Boynton had actually dared to reject her offer to renew their romance and to marry him.

The impudence of the damned part-Chinese!

Not until she heard his horse galloping off down the road did Drusilla arouse herself from her reverie. Then she stood and systematically began to wreak havoc, smashing every glass, every vase, every dish, every bottle that she could reach.

David rode hard along the quiet country roads and narrow lanes in the half-light cast by the moon. He galloped in half-hour spurts, resting his mount at a slow canter and then spurring to a faster pace once more.

His blunt declaration to Drusilla, breaking off relations with her, had cleared his mind, and he marveled at the improvement and at the simplicity of his feelings. His emotions had been clouded, but now he knew precisely where he stood.

Until tonight, he had continued to imagine himself in love with Drusilla, but he had been the victim of an illusion based on his past feelings. Tonight she had been so crude in her treatment of him, her motives had been revealed so blatantly, that the mist had evaporated before his eyes, and he knew he was cured of her for all time.

Even more important, he belatedly realized what he should have known all along, that he'd been taking Aileen Christopher for granted. Here was a lovely, charming woman, admittedly only a bookkeeper, who nevertheless had given unstintingly and uncomplainingly of her own time and effort for a cause in which she believed. He'd been spending his days and most of his evenings with a woman who was a gem without price, and he had been too myopic to recognize it.

Now—provided he wasn't too late—he was at last in a position to right a grievous wrong.

In his anxiety, he pushed himself and his mount to the edge of exhaustion.

It was a little after two in the morning, and David felt infinite relief as he reached the crest of a hill and saw his estate spread out ahead of him in the moonlight. Only then did he look at his watch and realize that he had returned in the record time of two and a half hours. He rode direct to the stable, where he unsaddled his mount, and after hastily watering and feeding the animal, he hurried to the main house.

Entering the manor house by a side door, he bounded up the rear stairs to the second floor, two at a time, and scarcely aware of what he was doing, he went straight to Aileen Christopher's room and pounded on the door.

Aileen had not slept at all since retiring an hour or two earlier, and startled by the knocking on the door, she sat up in bed. "Who's there?" she called, brushing her long hair away from her face.

"It's David!" a hoarse voice outside the door declared. "I've got to see you at once!"

Thoroughly alarmed, she donned her slippers, pulled on her flannel dressing gown, and after making it secure, went to the door and opened it.

With the dust of the road coating his face and hands, boots and clothes, David looked gaunt and forlorn.

Aileen raised a hand to her throat. "What's wrong?" she demanded anxiously.

"It isn't appropriate for me to go into your bedchamber," he told her. "All the same, I must speak to you."

"Very well," she said, and led him downstairs to the kitchen. There, simmering on the stove, was a huge kettle of tea, which was kept there night and day for the convenience of the Chinese immigrants.

"I'd like a cup of tea," she said, "and from the way you look, you could stand one yourself."

David nodded nervously, and while she poured two cups, carefully adding a slice of lemon to his, knowing that he liked it, he paced the kitchen slapping at his boot with his riding crop.

Knowing she looked far from her best, Aileen wished she had had time to at least comb her hair and put on a little lip rouge before seeing him.

She sat at the kitchen table and gestured to an empty place opposite her. "I think you could sit and talk at the same time," she said, sipping her tea.

David chose to remain standing, however, and glared at her across the table, his feet planted apart. "I love you," he said, speaking so roughly that his declaration sounded like an accusation.

Half convinced she was dreaming, the stunned Aileen drew her breath in sharply.

"I am a blithering idiot, the biggest damned fool in the entire British Empire," David went on in the same tone. "We've been working side by side for day after day for weeks on end, and I failed to recognize what should have been as plain to me as the nose on my face." He glowered at her, scowling as he roared, "I love you!"

"I—I heard you," she replied faintly.

The words tumbling out rapidly, he told her how he had responded to Drusilla Smythe's invitation and had gone to the Earl of Dudley's country house earlier that evening, only to have his eyes opened at last to the truth about his own feelings.

Aileen was numb, and her mind whirled so rapidly that she couldn't think straight. "Sit down and drink your tea before it gets cold," she ordered automatically.

He obeyed without thinking, sank into the chair opposite her, and gulped his tea.

Then he glared at her again and demanded, "Will you or will you not marry me?"

By now she was sure she was dreaming, but nevertheless she managed to answer, "Oh, I will, David, gladly."

They looked across the table at each other, both of them gradually becoming aware of the commitment they had just made. David grinned, Aileen giggled, and all at once both of them were whooping with laughter. He leaped to his feet and came around the table, and she rose to meet him, melting into his arms.

They embraced and kissed, each of them certain that this was right, that they had found each other, and that they were establishing a relationship that was both solid and lasting.

"This calls for a celebration," he said at last. "I think we'll take tomorrow off and go to my parents' place to tell them our news."

Early the next morning they were on the road, with David driving the team of two horses that was pulling the light carriage, while a radiant Aileen sat close beside him. They knew each other so well that, although this was the first time they had ever had a truly intimate conversation, both felt as though they had been betrothed for a very long time.

"Unless it's inconvenient for you, or you have some reason to wait," David said, "I'd like to be married immediately, as soon as possible."

"As you know," she said, "I've been alone in the world without a family, so I have no need to wait."

"Good!" He smiled and nodded emphatically. Then he went on to explain that he was scheduled to leave on a voyage to the New London headquarters of the company in ten days, and that if they married in the meantime, she could accompany him and they could utilize the journey as a honeymoon.

"Isn't a trip to the United States rather dangerous when the Americans are at war with each other?" Aileen asked.

He shook his head. "Not in the least," he said. "One of the advantages of our company is that the ship on which we'll travel will fly the British flag, and both the Union and the Confederacy will respect it."

When the young couple arrived at the country home of the older Boyntons, Charles and Ruth were surprised to see them, but one glance at the radiant young faces of the pair who slipped from the carriage told them all they needed to know.

Ruth promptly hurried forward and embraced Aileen. "I'm so happy for both of you," she said.

Sir Charles gripped his son's hand and claimed his right to kiss the bride-to-be. "You're finally showing some sense, son," he said, "and judging from what I've seen of Aileen, you'll be as fortunate as I was in my choice of a wife."

Learning that the young couple wanted to marry in the immediate future, Ruth took charge and would tolerate no opposition. She wrote a note to the vicar of the local church, who had known David since he'd been a child. The communication was delivered by messenger, the vicar called that same day, and arrangements were made for the wedding to be held the following Saturday.

Ruth also arranged to go into London early on Monday morning with David and Aileen and said she would take charge of buying the bride's trousseau.

"I have work to do at the office," Aileen protested.

"We have a company rule that prohibits wives from working for their husbands," David told her with a grin. "It looks as though I'll have to promote one of those assistants you've been breaking in."

As they went into the house, Ruth hurried off to the kitchen to give instructions to the cook for a festive noon dinner. By the time she returned to the parlor, Charles was opening a bottle of champagne in honor of the occasion.

Toasting each other, drinking their champagne, David now presented to Aileen the diamond engagement ring he had bought for Drusilla and had not returned.

"I didn't know I'd be giving this to you when I bought it," the young man told Aileen truthfully, "but I think it was probably destined to happen. And there is no one on earth I'd rather give it to."

Aileen gasped. "It's gorgeous!"

"It's all of that, and more," Ruth said.

Aileen hesitated to take it from David.

He looked at her. "Well, do you like it?" he asked softly.

"Do I! But no, I can't take it! It's too much!" Aileen was breathless.

David, smiling, caught hold of Aileen's left hand and slipped the ring onto the fourth finger. "How's that for a good omen?" he demanded. "It's a perfect fit!"

The young couple spent the rest of the day in a daze, to which their mutual excitement, the champagne they consumed, and their lack of sleep the night before all contributed. That night they retired early.

Early on Monday morning, the young couple drove to London with Ruth, who took full charge of operations. She established headquarters at the Boynton mansion in Belgravia, where, in Ruth's absence, the stunned Aileen would become mistress of the house in another week. Ruth took her future daughter-in-law on a two day clothes-buying spree and bought her a wardrobe befitting a Boynton bride.

"As time goes on," Ruth said, "you'll make whatever changes you feel are necessary in the Belgravia house. But there's no need to rush any of that. I think you'll find everything is more than adequate for the present."

The dazed Aileen could only nod. Her tiny London flat consisted of an infinitesimal living room, an even smaller bedchamber, and a cramped kitchen. But she was suddenly being transformed into the mistress of a home that had at least thirty-six rooms.

"There may be forty, actually," Ruth told her with a laugh. "It depends on how you count them."

The realization dawned slowly on Aileen that she was not just marrying David, whom she loved, but was becoming a Boynton, with all of the pomp and power that such an act entailed. She and David would have been happy to have had no one but his parents present at the wedding ceremony, but Ruth would not hear of it.

"We have business associates, and social friends, who would be mortally insulted if they weren't in attendance," she said. "We've got to invite them."

Every newspaper in London printed a story about the coming marriage, which would be held in Sussex, of the new head of the British branch of Rakehell and Boynton. Aileen felt as though she were sleepwalking, and the sensation became more pronounced as the week advanced. She gazed in wonder at the dazzling ring on her left hand, she stared in awe at the racks filled with her new clothes, and she worried, secretly, how she could ever remember the names of the dozen or more servants in the Belgravia mansion, whose mistress she was to become when Ruth was in residence in the country.

The wedding gifts that arrived in large numbers at the house in Belgravia and at the elder Boyntons' country place all week were so grand, so expensive, that they numbed Aileen's mind. There were presents of crystal and silver and gold, there were rare laces and thick rugs from the Orient, presents of sandalwood and of teak and of mahogany that shone like mirrors. Not the least of the gifts was a handsome silver bowl sent by Queen Victoria, a lifelong friend of the bridegroom's parents.

Aileen was further inundated by invitations from everybody who was anybody in London, ranging from dinners and suppers to balls and musicales and assemblies. Society, it appeared, was eager to judge the Boynton bride for itself. Fortunately, the trip that David and Aileen were making gave her a respite for some weeks, but her future mother-in-law had to act as her guide for the period that preceded, and a complicated set of markings indicated which invitations were to be accepted, which were to be refused, and which were to be tentatively approved.

At last Saturday came. The church in Sussex was crowded with more than seventy-five persons, all of them people of prominence who had come down from London.

Aileen, dressed in a white gown, stood at the back of the church with one hand on Sir Charles Boynton's arm as she waited for the music that would signal their march down the aisle to the altar. Chills raced up and down her spine, and her hands and feet felt like icicles as she saw those seated in the church turning around and looking at her. She had become the center of attention for some of the wealthiest and most powerful men and women in the entire British Empire, and she was afraid her knees would give way.

Then the church organ started, Sir Charles smiled and nodded, and Aileen took a deep breath as she grasped his arm and started down the aisle with him, planting one foot in front of the other.

After she had traveled about half the distance to the altar, she suddenly saw David standing there waiting for her. He was pale and obviously nervous, but he was composed and, as always, had his emotions well under control. Their eyes met, and he lowered one lid in a slow, solemn wink.

Only by exercising supreme self-discipline was it possible for Aileen to avoid disgracing herself by giggling aloud. Instead she smiled at David, and there were many in the congregation who swore they had never seen a more radiant bride.

When she joined David at the altar and they stood side by side, their shoulders brushing, a great sense of calm swept over Aileen. All at once she was at peace; more than that, she felt a sense of intense, almost fierce, joy, unlike anything she had ever experienced. A miracle beyond credence truly was taking place: She was being united in marriage for as long as she lived with the man she had loved for so long and who now loved her. She could ask for nothing more in life.

The ceremony ended with David's kiss, but the dream went on. At the reception held in the garden of his parents' country home, she accepted the well-wishes of the mighty and the wealthy, and replied automatically to scores of people whom she had known by name only.

Toasts without number to the bride and groom were consumed, and Aileen was then served a meal she was too excited and nervous to eat. Then she danced, first with David, then with his father, then with at least a score of other men. She was rescued by her mother-in-law, who beckoned to her and, taking her upstairs, helped her change into a smart traveling costume.

Aileen couldn't remember sneaking away from the party, but she was never able to forget her feeling of immeasurable relief when she and David at last were alone in their carriage on the road to London.

Oddly, the tensions of the day crept into the carriage with them. Both found it strangely difficult to converse freely, and the words would not come with ease. Aileen could tell that David was constrained, and she was stricken with a peculiar shyness that made it impossible for her to respond in more than monosyllables.

This mood persisted when they reached the house in Belgravia, where the entire staff had congregated and embarrassed the couple by applauding. Smiling weakly and murmuring their thanks, the couple escaped to their private suite.

There Aileen went into the dressing room—now her private sanctum—and changed into the most attractive of the negligees that she and Ruth had purchased during the week. She wiped smudges of makeup from the corners of her eyes, daubed fresh lip rouge on her mouth, and forced herself to return to their sitting room, where David, now clad in a silk dressing gown, awaited her.

"After what we've been through today," he told her with a laugh, "I think we can survive anything."

She sank into a chair and gratefully accepted the glass of chilled champagne that he handed her. "I still can't believe it," she murmured.

"What can't you believe?"

"That you and I are married."

He raised his glass to her in a silent salute. "Our marriage was essential," he said. "I wanted you, and I wasn't going to allow anything on earth to stand in my way of having you. But I respected you too much to have an affair with you. So, everything considered, I found it absolutely necessary to propose."

She couldn't help giggling. "Darling," she said, "for one of the most prominent businessmen in England, you do speak utter rubbish."

David gestured toward the sideboard. "What can I serve you, Mrs. Boynton? I can offer you cold sliced chicken, or cold joint of beef. We also have several hot delicacies, including creamed oysters—"

"I don't care for any of them just now," she interrupted.

He looked mildly surprised. "I'm not particularly hungry myself," he said, "but the staff has gone to so much trouble for us that we really should eat something."

"We'll have ample time to eat—later," she said, quietly but firmly.

He looked at her blankly.

She drained her glass and extended it, silently asking for more champagne.

David refilled the glass for her.

She sipped it, then looked pensively at the bubbles rising in a steady stream to the top. "You know," she said softly, "I've loved you for a very long time, since you were gadding about with high society ladies and I was nothing but a nameless little bookkeeper on your staff. All that is changed now. I'm Mrs. David Boynton, if you please, and I expect to be treated accordingly—" Suddenly she broke off and laughed. "Especially by Mr. David Boynton."

David failed to comprehend and stared at her in puzzlement as he sipped his champagne.

With deliberation, she drained her glass, rose slowly to her feet, and faced him. "In the world from which I come," she said, "a ceremony isn't an end in itself, it's only a beginning. And a marriage isn't a real marriage until it has been consummated." She couldn't help blushing as she spoke.

David hurriedly put down his own glass, and as he leaped to his feet, color burned in his cheeks, too.

"Make love to me, darling," she murmured. "I've waited long enough."

"Yes, my darling," he replied as he swept her off her feet and started to carry her toward their bedchamber, "anything to oblige a lady."

Aileen started to speak, but his ardent kiss stopped her.

The ice was broken and neither needed urging to cast aside all restraints. They wanted each other, and that desire took precedence over everything else in their lives.

Quickly overcoming the initial shock of embarrassment, they undressed each other and kissed and caressed without self-consciousness. Eager and curious, they explored each other with lips and tongues, hands and fingers.

When they could tolerate no more, they were united. They drove relentlessly toward a climax, miraculously finding release together.

Then, limp but euphoric, they continued to cling to each other.

"I never knew that an experience could be like this," David muttered.

"I knew," Aileen replied dreamily. "I knew from the very first moment I realized I loved you that we'd make love like this."

He was silent for a moment, and then his grip on her warm, vibrant body tightened. "I'm just beginning to realize,' he said, "how very perspicacious and wise you are, Mrs. Boynton. Perhaps someday I'll be fortunate enough to realize how lucky I am to have you for a wife."

II

The *Jessica B*, named for the late Lady Boynton, was one of a number of vessels in the Rakehell and Boynton fleet known as sister ships. This development—building ships to identical specifications—followed a policy established by the Cunard Line, and all other shipowners quickly followed suit. Built as a combined passenger vessel and freighter, she weighed an impressive three thousand tons and had steampowered screw engines, which drove four-bladed propellers. In addition, she was outfitted with five masts, which carried more than six thousand square yards of canvas to assure her of additional speed when the winds were favorable. Basically, however, she depended on coal, rather than on the direct forces of nature, for propulsion.

The quarters available to passengers on board steamships were far more cramped and infinitely less sumptuous and attractive than they were on the wooden clipper ships. But as Rakehell and Boynton had discovered, there was no lack of demand for cabin space, because an iron ship propelled by steam was able to hold to an exact schedule, no matter what the weather.

Aileen Boynton, who had visited various of the company's ships in port but had never traveled in one, was delighted, however, with the quarters that she and her husband occupied on board the *Jessica B*. As one of the owners of the ship, David was given the only suite available to passengers, and his bride marveled at the sitting room and bedroom.

The larger cabin was the drawing room, which boasted two portholes and was fifteen feet long and equally wide. The sofa and chairs were comfortable, and the dining table, where the couple could eat their meals when they chose not to join the other passengers in the saloon, was fashioned of solid oak. The sleeping chamber was dominated by a real double bed, and there was even a private bathroom, which had a sink with running water, and a compact bathtub.

"This is like traveling in a snug little house of our very own," Aileen said when she first saw the suite.

David didn't want to disillusion her or spoil her pleasure, so he refrained from mentioning that their leather clothing boxes had to be stored elsewhere than in their quarters, and that there was insufficient space for them to entertain any guests at dinner, had they wished to do so.

The *Jessica B* was piloted by tugs through the crowded water of the Thames, where ships of all descriptions were coming and going, and when she reached the English Channel, she ran into an initial patch of foul weather. Aileen promptly demonstrated that she was a true Boynton. She required only a short time to gain her sea legs, and suffering no ill effects from the squall, she donned a rainhat and coat and stood with her husband on the bridge of the vessel, watching the *Jessica B*'s prow slicing through the waves that washed over her foredeck.

The voyage, as David had hoped, became a perfect honeymoon experience for him and for his bride. They joined the other passengers in the saloon for a light meal at noon, but usually had breakfast and dinner alone in their suite. They spent hours each day walking the long wooden decks of the ship, and each day David took Aileen to the bridge, where he gave her a lesson in celestial navigation. A high point in their voyage was the day when she actually took the helm and steered the *Jessica B*.

Encountering fair weather on the better part of his voyage, the ship's captain had no difficulty in maintaining his assigned schedule. On the morning of the fifteenth day of the voyage, the *Jessica B* rounded Montauk Point, at the eastern end of Long Island, and as she headed toward the estuary of the Thames River in New London, she fired the traditional salute of three small cannon shots that heralded the approach of a Rakehell and Boynton ship.

A reply of three shots boomed from the shipyard, and as the vessel was maneuvered into her berth by a tug, David, who stood on the deck with one arm around his wife's shoulders, removed his hat and waved it. "There's Julian!" he shouted.

Aileen stared at the tall, good-looking man who stood alone on the dock. "Surely he doesn't meet every company ship that puts into port," she said.

"Certainly not," her husband told her with a laugh. "He knew I was on board."

She was completely mystified. "How?" she demanded.

David pointed to the Tree of Life banner flying from the yardarm. "When putting into port in New London," he said, "we only keep the company pennant in place when one of us is on board."

Minutes later the couple went ashore, and when Julian was presented to Aileen, he greeted her with a kiss. "There are certain advantages to being a member of this family," he told her.

They went directly to the Rakehell mansion, where the honeymooners received a warm welcome from Jonathan and Elizabeth, and where they were introduced to Alexis. Then, leaving the women to get acquainted, David accompanied Julian back to his office at the shipyard. It was an old Rakehell and Boynton family custom to waste no time before discussing urgent matters of international concern.

The cousins discussed highlights of both the American and British ends of the business. Their earlier dispute about conducting business in the Orient had been resolved, and they were in full agreement now to step up production and shipping schedules on the British side of the Atlantic, while the American branch of the company outfitted ships for the Civil War.

Then David said tentatively, "If there'd been any news of Jade, I'm sure you'd have mentioned it before this."

Julian nodded somberly. "I'm afraid she's vanished without a trace—so far," he said. "I heard from Molinda the other day to the effect that she's trying to locate Jade through the Society of Oxen, but an investigation of that sort takes time."

David hooked his thumbs in his waistcoat and bit his lower lip. "The outlook isn't very hopeful, I'm afraid. On the other hand, I've never known anyone more resourceful than Jade, and she has a will to survive that puts you and me both to shame. I refuse to abandon hope for her."

"So do I," Julian replied. "I'm convinced that she'll turn up sooner or later."

"In your last letter," David said, "you mentioned that you had a problem you didn't want to discuss in writing."

"Quite so," Julian replied with a frown. "It concerns Alexis."

"Aunt Elizabeth told me that Aileen and I are just in time for your wedding, which delights me," David said.

"It makes us very happy, too," Julian told him. "You'll stand up at the altar with me?"

"Indeed I will! Nothing would make me happier."

"Good." Julian took a deep breath and then, swearing his cousin to secrecy, told him in detail about the plot concocted by Anna van der Luon.

David was astonished. "That doesn't sound at all like Anna."

"That's exactly what my father said," Julian told him. "Both of you know her better than I do, but just from where I stand myself, I couldn't picture her plotting against me."

"To the best of my knowledge," David replied slowly, "she has no reason to be vindictive, no reason to seek your downfall or to embarrass you."

"If she has any cause for vengeance against me, I don't know it either," Julian said flatly.

David rose to his feet and began to roam his cousin's office. Long accustomed to shipboard living, he thought better on his feet than when seated. "What are you doing about it?" he demanded.

"I've written to Molinda in confidence," Julian said, "asking her to investigate fully."

"That's fair enough—for a start," David told him, and stared out the window for a time. "I don't know where you are planning to go on your honeymoon," he continued, "but I think the time is fast approaching when you and I should be making a joint trip to the Orient, and, of course, taking our brides with us."

Julian knew his cousin had more in mind than honeymoons. "Oh?"

"I'm convinced," David said forcibly, "that we'll gain the best and fastest results if we take personal charge of the search for Jade."

"You're right!" Julian concurred at once. "Certainly it's worth the effort to try."

That night at the end of supper when the ladies withdrew from the table, the cousins discussed their plan over glasses of port with Jonathan Rakehell. He immediately gave them his unqualified approval. "It's been my lifelong experience," he said, "that you do far better for yourself than you do through someone else. I have no idea what may have become of Jade, but our chances of locating her are vastly improved if you lads take charge of the search."

The wedding of Alexis Johnson and Julian Rakehell was celebrated with due pomp and was called by the local press the leading event of the social season. Alexis had hoped she and Julian could be married quietly in the presence of only a few guests, but Aileen Boynton laughingly disabused her of the idea. "As I learned last month," she said, "Rakehells and Boyntons don't sneak silently to the altar. They march there with trumpets blaring and drums playing a loud tattoo. You and I don't just marry husbands, Alexis. We're wedded to an empire!"

The young women became excited when they learned they would be traveling to Cathay in the immediate future. They bombarded Julian and David with questions, asked Elizabeth what to take with them in the way of wardrobes, and leaped from subject to subject with dizzying speed. Looking at the young people and listening to them, Jonathan was glad for their enthusiasm, though he missed his daughter more than ever.

Jonathan's conviction that the future of the company was in good hands grew and solidified when Julian married Alexis. David acted as his cousin's best man, Aileen served as matron of honor, and the two couples, standing together in the receiving line at the reception that followed at the Rakehell mansion, were typical of all that is good in the younger generation. "I'm convinced," Jonathan said privately to Elizabeth, "that the company's future is as bright as its past."

One of the most famous of the Rakehell and Boynton ships was the *Lai-tse lu,* which Jonathan had built more than two decades earlier for his late Chinese wife. Because of the wartime shortage of shipping, the renowned clipper had been pressed into service, carrying cargo between coastal ports, and, as she was making a thirty-six hour voyage from New London to Philadelphia, then returning to her home port immediately after discharging her cargo, Julian availed himself of the opportunity to engage the owner's cabin for himself and his bride for a short holiday prior to the voyage to Cathay. The Boyntons would remain at the Rakehell mansion on Pequot Avenue.

The young people who had attended the wedding and reception escorted the couple to the company wharf en masse, and showered them with rice as they raced aboard the proud, elegantly appointed sailing ship.

The bride and groom stood arm in arm on the aft deck, waving to their relatives and friends as the clipper, her sails slowly filling, silently left her berth and began her quiet, swift voyage through Long Island Sound into the open Atlantic.

Only when the figures on shore receded and became too small to be recognized did Alexis sigh and smile up at her husband.

"I'm giddy," she said, "and it isn't from drinking champagne."

"Isn't it strange?" Julian replied. "I feel exactly the same way." Taking her elbow, he guided her firmly to their large, flower-filled cabin.

Once the cabin door closed behind them, they turned to each other with one accord, embracing and kissing hungrily. Certainly Alexis knew that, with her background, it would be thoroughly inappropriate for her to play the role of a blushing bride. And Julian certainly did not expect it of her.

Alexis was not coy, and Julian did not treat her as though she were either fragile or virginal. Both had long awaited this day; they had long wanted each other and intended to wait no more. Their lovemaking was as intense as it was forthright.

Understanding the values and joys of dalliance, they took their time in mutual arousal, and their pace was leisurely until, suddenly, in the grip of deep passion, they could control themselves no longer and their desire became explosive.

They achieved only partial release and had to make love twice more before they achieved satiation. Then, clad in matching silk Chinese dressing gowns that had been one of Elizabeth's wedding presents to them, they lay in bed and sipped and slowly savored the bottle of wine that Julian had just opened.

Alexis put a hand on her husband's thigh. "If I'm honest with you," she wanted to know, "will you be equally truthful with me?"

"That's the only way I'll ever be," he replied.

She hesitated briefly, then spoke a trifle too rapidly. "What were you thinking just now, when we were making love?" she demanded.

Julian hoisted himself to one elbow, took a long swallow of his wine, and looked her full in the face. "You won't find this very complimentary, I'm afraid," Julian replied, "but I couldn't help wondering whether you were—well—simulating passion, or whether your feelings were genuine."

"I knew you had to be thinking such thoughts," she replied. "It was inevitable in view of the life I've led."

"I swear to you," he said, "that I didn't intend to disparage you in any way."

Alexis put two fingers over his mouth to silence him. "Never mind," she said. "I understand, and I don't blame you in the least. In fact, you deserve an answer."

He caught hold of her hand. "I'll be perfectly satisfied if we drop the subject for all time."

"Not at all," she replied, and her face became serious, her emerald-green eyes grew enormous as she responded slowly. "I've gone to bed with more men than I care to remember," she said, "than I'm capable of remembering. They all run together in my mind, and the experience was completely unsavory. I felt nothing with any of them, and I simulated passion with all of them. Because it was expected of me. Because I would have failed to give them their money's worth had I not seemed to come alive. But that has not been my experience with you, dear Julian. Just now, with you, I found release for the first time in my entire life, and now I know the meaning of true love, the difference between the real and the counterfeit."

Julian nodded but made no reply.

Alexis sipped her wine and sounded apologetic as she said, "I had to say it once to you, but I won't repeat it ever again."

Julian turned to her, his face set in stern lines. "You've said far more than was necessary, far more than I ever expected to hear," he told her. "Well, I'm just going to say something to you once, and then I'm never going to mention it again, either. To be as honest as I can, I don't give a damn about your past. I don't care what you were, or how many men you knew, or what your relations with them might have been, or how you reacted to any of them. What's important to me is what you are. You're my wife. That—and nothing else—matters to me."

Even those who knew Julian and Alexis best marveled at the rapport that they achieved immediately after their marriage. They had a sense of mutual understanding, a sensitivity to each other's moods that most married couples took years to develop.

After a brief preliminary holiday of three days' duration, the couple returned to New London, and Julian promptly plunged into work with his cousin. David worked equally hard so they could clean their respective slates before leaving for the Orient.

"Do whatever is necessary to find Jade," Jonathan told them before they departed. "Offer as large a reward as you think needed, and hire as many people as you deem necessary."

The two couples set sail from New London on board one of the older vessels in the British Rakehell and Boynton fleet, a clipper ship that Jonathan had built many years earlier. They would be sailing through waters controlled by the Confederate Navy, so it was necessary to travel under the British ensign. They took the clipper as far as the Isthmus of Panama and then debarked, crossing from the Atlantic to the Pacific coast through the thick Panamanian jungle on a railroad that had been built to accommodate the thousands of travelers who used the route during the California Gold Rush.

In the Pacific, they were picked up by one of the newer long-range vessels that belonged to Julian's fleet, a steamship that used paddle wheels and a screw engine, and also was equipped with sails for the voyage of thousands of miles that would end in Hong Kong.

There were thirty-eight other passengers on board the *Sarah R*, named for Jonathan's stepmother, and Alexis and Aileen learned rapidly, through necessity, what was expected of Rakehell and Boynton wives. They had no complaint, however. They were spending every moment of every day with their husbands, and the voyage across the boundless Pacific was truly a honeymoon to be savored.

III

Clad in a breastband and skirt made of animal skins, Jade stood beneath the intense tropical sun and leaned on the long handle of her homemade broom as she stared out across the placid blue waters of the sea. The steady glare of the sun on the water made her eyes smart, but she blinked them rapidly and continued to concentrate on an island that stood in the distance. She could plainly see two outrigger canoes, each of them manned by eight or ten half-naked men, putting out to sea.

There was nothing out of the ordinary about this phenomenon. She and Pieter had seen the same sight every day for weeks. As nearly as they could make out, the canoes were attached to fishing nets, which they dragged through the water, and the daily catches were used by the inhabitants of the distant island as basic food supplies.

A mystery that bewildered the castaways was the undeniable fact that their considerable efforts to attract the attention of the natives had failed and continued to fail. The couple had put up the flag, attached to the royal palm tree, and they had built huge bonfires, one after another, on a high bluff looking out to sea. Although it was impossible to believe that the men in the outrigger canoes could remain unaware of the flames or the flag, they paid no heed to them and did not row toward the volcanic island on which the castaways lived.

Telling herself that after so many failures she should not expect anything more, Jade tried in vain to conquer her feeling of deep disappointment. Knowing the natives of the area, and being familiar with their superstitions, she had reasoned that the inhabitants of the distant place were well aware of the signals being sent from the volcanic island but chose to ignore them deliberately because of a belief that evil spirits lived on the island and might harm them if they drew near it.

Pieter hadn't known any more than Jade herself had known whether her estimate was accurate. He had to admit, however, that her reasoning was logical. "What's important," he stressed, "is that there are other human beings nearby who can take us off this island, and we've got to attract their attention in one way or another."

Watching the two outrigger canoes fading into insignificance in the distance, Jade swallowed her disappointment. When Pieter returned to the cliff from a hunting foray, they would go for a swim. Then, perhaps, they could make love on the beach. Jade badly wanted to be loved and held now.

Her bare feet felt heavy as she made her way back to their hut, on which they had worked and which was now far more solid and secure in keeping out the elements. She went inside and began to sweep, and then froze.

Coiled up inside the entrance was a greenish-brown glittering serpent, its long body at least six inches in diameter. It had raised its head, and two tiny eyes regarded her closely. Her heart sank when she saw that it was a cobra, and that its hood had opened, presaging an attack.

Instantly, instinctively, Jade covered her eyes with her hands. Cobras, she had been taught as a child, were able to spray venom from their fangs into the eyes of their victims, blinding them, and were capable of spraying accurately for distances of ten feet, sometimes even farther. Afraid to use the *kris* that protruded from the top of her skirt for fear that she'd be totally helpless if she missed, she used the only weapon at her command, the broom that she still held in her hand.

Shielding her eyes, she jabbed repeatedly at the cobra, which reluctantly moved inch by inch out of the hut into the open.

The serpent's tail switched back and forth ominously, a sure sign that it was deeply annoyed. But Jade could not stop now and continued to prod and push with the broom until the creature was completely outside the hut. This enabled her to slip into the open, too, and she felt greatly relieved. Now, at least, she was no longer cornered and had a fighting chance to save herself.

Squinting, her eyes half closed, she drew the Malaysian knife and continued to wield the broom. She would have only one chance to strike, she knew, and if she missed, she would be in serious trouble.

She jabbed hard with the broom, and the dried palm fronds that made up the bristles penetrated the snake's skin, causing it to raise its head several feet from the ground. It had opened its hood wide, and its long, supple tongue flicked venomously. It was waiting for the right moment to attack its tormentor.

Jade reminded herself that skill rather than strength was the secret of wielding a throwing knife, and resisting the impulse to hurl the *kris* with all her might, she lobbed it instead at the target that held its head upraised and relatively immobile.

The wavy blade appeared to ease itself into the cobra's head, directly between the eyes.

The snake's head drooped, dropping to the ground, and its entire body shuddered spastically, continuing to thrash after the serpent was dead.

The knife had fallen into the dust of the ground, but Jade continued to take no chances; even though the cobra was dead, she pushed it clear of the blade before she stooped and picked up the *kris*. Then, but only then, a reaction set in and she leaned against a coconut palm, shuddering, her flesh crawling.

At that juncture, Pieter appeared on the scene. "Well, those damned natives continue to avoid us," he said irritably, then broke off suddenly and stared first at the dead snake, then at Jade. "Good Lord," he murmured, and took the knife from her. "We'll make sure there's no venom on this before you put it next to your skin again."

She smiled at him wanly. "There are moments," she told him, "when I find this island to be anything but paradise."

"I know what you mean," he replied, and although he tried to be cheerful, he could not conceal the underlying bitterness of his tone. Then, taking the broom, he swept the dead cobra off the cliff. He dipped the knife into the stream, holding it for some time in the running water, and then carefully wiped the blade dry on a broad-leafed banana palm. "Here you are," he told her. "Come along."

"Where are we going?"

He led her to the narrow path he had made that took them to the higher point on the cliff, where they had lighted their bonfires. "I want to show you something."

Her adventure with the snake forgotten, she followed him willingly until they reached a small stand of trees some feet behind the edge of the precipice.

"We've talked about these trees," he said. "We can't identify them. All we know is that the young ones are very supple and can be bent all the way down to the ground."

She nodded, trying to conceal her impatience. He was thorough, as always, but she wished he would establish the point he was trying to make. However, it was wrong of her to show irritation; she supposed that they were bound to grate on one another's nerves.

Pieter illustrated what he meant by walking to one of the young trees, which stood seven to eight feet high. Bending its trunk, he brought its top all the way to the ground. When he released it, the tree made a whistling sound as it snapped upright again.

"It has occurred to me," he said, "that we have half a dozen perfect catapults at hand. If we were to prepare a bundle of dried coconut leaves that will burn furiously, we could attach it to one of these trees, and when we see the canoes again, we can catapult a flaming brand high into the sky.''

"I see what you mean," Jade replied thoughtfully. "It's a sound idea!"

"Whether the top of the tree will be burned and make it useful only for one catapult remains to be seen," he said, "but I'm willing to prepare two of them and hold the other four in reserve against the day when we might see another ship somewhere out there."

"It strikes me," she said slowly, "that we have everything to gain and nothing to lose."

Although the sun stood directly overhead now, when the blistering heat of the day was at its worst, they were sufficiently acclimated to the tropical atmosphere that they paid no attention to the weather and went to work with a vengeance to prepare the flares they would send skyward.

They gathered large bundles of dried leaves and other flammable material, which they tied together and made secure with vines. Their only real problem was in finding a place where these flares would remain dry, and they finally found a nearby overhanging ledge and were able to place the bundles beneath it, where the tropical rains would leave the material untouched.

The task completed, they knew they could enjoy the reward to which they looked forward, a lazy swim in the bay, followed by leisurely lovemaking on the beach.

Suddenly, however, they were startled by a sound like that of thunder, and they looked at each other uncertainly. As always, a few clouds drifted above the crest of the volcanic peak, but otherwise the sky was clear. There was no sign of a rainstorm anywhere within view.

"Do you suppose it's possible . . ." Pieter asked, never finishing his sentence.

Jade laughed briefly and shook her head in wonder. "I'd say it's more than likely that the volcano is less extinct than we believed."

Her words were punctuated by another, more prolonged rumbling sound.

Their swim and lovemaking at least momentarily forgotten, they started up through the jungle toward the peak. In spite of their concern and hurry, they had learned enough of the island's ways to take no unnecessary risks. The jungle was an alien place where the unwary could lose their lives within moments.

Pieter, who was in the lead, carried his cocked rifle, ready for immediate use, and a pistol hung in a holster from the belt he wore over his loincloth. Jade, who followed close behind him, gripped her *kris* in one hand and kept a watchful eye for the foes of humans who lurked everywhere in the tropical wilderness. Her experience with the hooded cobra was still vividly fresh in her mind, and she well knew that there were other, equally deadly snakes in the vicinity.

Equally dangerous were such insects as scorpions and centipedes, whose sting could be fatal, and her gaze darted constantly to the ground ahead as she ran barefooted through the jungle.

Ultimately, the vegetation thinned, and the ground ahead rose more sharply toward the peak. The climb became harder, and both Jade and Pieter were breathless, their faces and bodies glistening with perspiration by the time they finally reached the summit.

The soles of their feet had been toughened by their style of living, but they nevertheless winced as they made their way over the rough, jagged rocks of lava toward the lip of the volcano.

Reaching it, they were confronted by a wall of thick stone that stood about chest-high, and instinctively they held hands as they peered down into the large crater of the volcano.

They found themselves staring into a vast pit, perhaps seventy-five feet deep and many hundreds of feet long. At the center of the crater's interior was a surface that was earth-brown, and that, the one previous time they had examined it, had looked solid and unmoving. Now, to their mutual astonishment, it had come alive and resembled the contents of a pot of liquid that was boiling slowly. The surface of the volcano's interior moved slightly, gently, and occasionally a huge dark bubble swelled and then fell again.

Occasional wisps of smoke rose from the crater, dissipating by the time they emerged from the opening at the top, but the young couple could feel the heat being generated and realized that there was great ferment in progress beneath the surface.

"We were wrong," Jade said in a hushed voice, "when we thought the volcano was extinct. It's very much alive."

"With a force building up within it," Pieter said, "it's certain to erupt. But there's no way of knowing whether that will happen in a day or in five years."

She faced him thoughtfully. "What we need to know," she said, "is how dangerous that eruption can be. I'd hate to be in the path of lava flow, and our belongings, such as they are, would be totally destroyed, too."

"With luck and the application of a little common sense," Pieter said, "perhaps we can trace the direction that a flow of lava takes."

"How in the world can we do that?" she demanded, her enormous eyes wide.

He pointed to a low, jagged portion of the crater wall. "The last time there was an eruption," he said, "no matter how many years ago it happened, I'd say the lava overflowed the lip of the crater there. You'll notice that the ground outside it for a distance of several hundred feet is somewhat higher than the jungle on either side of it."

Jade saw what he meant and nodded. "You think, then, that the hot lava flowed down toward the sea in that direction, away from the area where we've built our hut?"

"Exactly," he said, "if my reasoning is accurate."

"We may find out—eventually," Jade said, and shrugged. All at once she straightened, standing erect, and her smile faded. "In the meantime, I'm not going to worry about it. We live from moment to moment on this island. By exercising vigilance, we have managed to preserve our lives from one day to the next, but there's always a chance that our guard will slip, that a foe of mankind will succeed in snuffing us out, either on land or in the water. I've learned to enjoy each moment—everything we experience—for its own sake, never looking ahead to what might happen next, any more than I allow myself to look back at the past."

"You're right," Pieter replied somberly. "We face too many imponderables. To dwell on them is to invite madness."

As if to accentuate his words, a faint rumble sounded within the crater, and the broken ground below their feet trembled.

They started down toward the sea again, following the path they had taken on their ascent. The threat of an active volcano sobered them, and they drew near to each other, each of them seeking comfort and strength from the other. Pieter slid an arm around Jade's waist, and she did the same to him. They walked silently, side by side, keeping a vigilant watch for the ever-present, hidden enemies of mankind. At first glance, they seemed to have been cast away in paradise, in a place where the climate was so benign they needed little in the way of shelter and clothing, a place where food was plentiful and could be procured with little effort. But they knew better—they knew they were lucky to be alive.

The volcano remained quiet, and in spite of themselves, Jade and Pieter found that their spirits improved.

That afternoon, Pieter speared a large fish with firm white flesh, which Jade grilled, preparing it with plantain that she fried in a small quantity of wild boar fat. After they ate their fill, they made love and then went for a long, languorous swim.

They stretched out on the hard-packed sand of the beach, where the sun dried them, and they drifted between consciousness and sleep. Pieter's laugh broke the silence. "Sometimes I wonder," he said, "whether this life has spoiled us for existence in the real world. I wonder how we'd act if we returned to civilization and went back to work."

"We'd manage, I think," Jade replied with a yawn. "Lifelong habits aren't easy to lose." What she really wondered was whether their romance would survive a return to civilization, but she made no mention of the conjecture.

There was no doubt in her mind that Pieter loved her, that he was sincere in his devotion to her, but it occurred to her that he might be less attached to her if other women were available and he were given a choice. Perhaps she was being unfair to him, but the kernel of doubt remained.

She felt even less sure of her own feelings for him. Not only had she never been in love with anyone before, but her experience as a concubine on the estate of the Fat Dutchman in Djakarta had soured her on all men. Certainly she realized that their proximity and their mutual isolation were primary factors in making Pieter attractive to her, and she wondered, idly, whether he would fade from her consciousness if they were suddenly thrust into the busy world of Hong Kong.

As Jade well knew, however, it was useless to speculate. No amount of conjecture could substitute for reality, and for the present, at least, life on this island was the only reality that she and Pieter knew.

Suddenly Pieter sat upright, his sharp exclamation interrupting her reverie. "Look," he said. "The natives are putting out to sea again in their outrigger canoes."

Jade focused on the island in the distance and saw two canoes heading slowly out of the inner lagoon into the open waters of the sea. She hastily donned her breastband and skirt, snatched up her *kris,* and followed Pieter, who was sprinting toward the promontory above.

They had prepared themselves earlier in the event of just such an occurrence, and each of them knew precisely what to do. While Jade hastily and busily kindled a fire, Pieter tied a bundle of flammable refuse to the top of one of the supple young trees. As soon as he saw that she held a burning brand in one hand, he exerted all of his strength and bent the tree down to the ground.

Jade carefully set fire to the refuse.

The moment the bundle began to smoke and burn, Pieter released the tree, which sprang back to its natural position and sent the bundle, which had been loosely attached to it, soaring high into the air.

The couple watched it in silence for a moment as the torch made a wide arc high overhead and then plummeted gracefully into the sea.

"Unless those natives are blind," Pieter said, "they couldn't help but see our fireworks exhibition. Let's give them another."

They repeated their previous exercise and sent another flare soaring high into the sky.

"They saw our signals, Pieter, and they're responding!" Jade's voice was thick with suppressed excitement.

"You're right," he replied. "The outriggers are heading this way."

In something of a daze, they watched the two canoes shooting rapidly through the calm blue waters of the sea.

As the craft drew closer, the couple could see that their surmise had been correct: The outriggers were manned by small, wiry, dark-skinned men, typical native Malays. In all, there were eighteen oarsmen, nine in each canoe, and, like Pieter, wearing only loincloths. On the seats of their fragile craft were weapons, and, from a distance, Jade could see spears, bows, and arrows.

In spite of herself, she felt a twinge of uneasiness.

In their eagerness to be rescued from the island on which they'd been cast away, the thought had not occurred to them that the occupants of the outriggers might be other than friendly.

"I'd feel safer if we were armed," Jade murmured.

"You're right," Pieter told her. "Wait here for me and keep yourself concealed behind the trees. We won't reveal ourselves until we know whether these men are friendly or hostile."

She waited anxiously while Pieter hurried off to their dwelling on the lower portion of the cliff. In the meantime, the two canoes, traveling with deceptive speed, drew still closer to their sanctuary.

She felt somewhat relieved when she saw Pieter dash into their hut only to emerge moments later carrying their weapons, his rifle and the two pistols.

These firearms, along with her *kris*, formed their only arsenal, and her concern grew when she saw how many men there were in the outriggers. Perhaps, she thought, he also should have brought the spears they used for fishing. With so many potential enemies approaching, they needed every weapon they could gather.

Pieter suddenly materialized beside her and handed her a pistol, together with a leather bag containing ammunition and gunpowder. "We'll stay right here for the present," he said, "making sure we keep ourselves concealed. There's no need for us to become panicky and run until we learn the intentions of these men."

"Why should they attack us?" she asked somewhat plaintively. "We haven't threatened them, and we mean them no harm."

He shrugged. "We represent an unknown element to them," he said, "and they're primitive people, so they prefer to take no risks." He crouched low in the high, thick grass.

Jade followed his example, and from her vantage point, she watched the outriggers sweep up onto the beach. Their occupants leaped ashore and, obviously accustomed to working together, picked up the boats and carried them still higher onto the sand, out of reach of the gentle waves that lapped at the shore.

Then, to her dismay, she saw them return to the boats for their spears and their bows and arrows.

The Malays gathered in a group; then, occasionally pointing toward the high cliff above, they conversed in low tones. One of them saw the two pairs of footprints in the sand leading away from the beach, and Jade's heart sank still lower. She and Pieter surely had been discovered now.

The men spread out, notching their arrows into their bows and taking firm grasps on the shafts of their spears. There no longer could be the slightest doubt of their intentions. It was clear that they intended to hunt down and kill the couple who had left the footsteps.

An experienced soldier, Pieter knew not only that he and Jade were badly outnumbered but that they held a position that would be exceptionally difficult to defend. The tall grass and a few scattered trees provided the only shelter, making it essential that they escape to a position among bigger boulders and rocks where they could hide and, he hoped, pick off their foes one at a time.

He beckoned and darted off toward the interior.

Running rapidly, silently, Jade followed him, her *kris* in one hand, a pistol gripped in the other. She was afraid that if the Malays discovered the dwelling she and Pieter had built so laboriously, they would loot it, taking cooking utensils, tools, sewing instruments, and other valuables necessary to sustain life in this remote place. But the danger was so immediate, so grave, that she could not allow herself to dwell on the threat to mere property.

Familiarity with the terrain made it possible for Pieter to set a blistering pace, and for Jade to keep up with him. As he ran, taking care to remain under cover, he turned occasionally and grinned at her.

She smiled at him in return, encouraging him, just as he was trying to sustain her.

Eventually they came to high ground, where the jungle thinned and huge boulders littered the steep hillside. Here they halted, and Jade wiped perspiration from her eyes, blinking away the moisture so she could see more clearly.

They peered cautiously from behind the boulder and caught occasional glimpses of the intruders, who had spread out in a long, thin line and were advancing slowly, with the utmost caution, through the heaviest part of the jungle.

Pieter put his lips close to Jade's ear and spoke so softly that she had to strain in order to hear him. "Don't fire until I give you the signal," he told her. "I'm going to hold off as long as possible, so we'll have the best targets available. And when you shoot, make every bullet count. There are too many of them for us to bring all of them down, but if we can kill or wound enough of them, perhaps the others will become discouraged and leave."

She nodded, agreeing with his strategy. The supreme irony of their situation was that they had created the unnecessary dilemma themselves. Had they not gone to such ingenious lengths to signal to the natives, their presence on the island would have remained undiscovered.

The Malays continued to advance and steadily moved closer.

Discovering that her trigger hand was perspiring, Jade blew on her fingers in order to dry them. She knew now how soldiers felt in the tense moments immediately preceding the outbreak of a battle.

Suddenly a low rumble sounded, deeper and more sustained than thunder, and the ground underfoot shook violently.

The volcano had chosen this moment to speak.

One of the Malays stood erect, no longer bothering to conceal himself in a half-crouch, and began to shout, his screams rising above the thunder of the volcano.

Jade had picked up an understanding of his tongue from the concubines at the estate of the Fat Dutchman, and it was not too difficult to make out the meaning of his words.

"Those who say that evil spirits dwell on this island are right!" he screamed. "We were wrong to come here! The spirits lured us here and now they would destroy us!"

Making no attempt to conceal himself, he turned and fled toward lower ground.

His panic sparked a similar reaction in his companions, and they needed no urging to follow his example. Within moments, the entire band raced down the mountainside, crashing through the foliage of the jungle in a desperate attempt to reach the safety of their outriggers.

The thunder of the volcano increased, blotting out all other sounds. At the same moment, a mighty plume of thick, oily smoke shot high into the air, obliterating the sun and turning the day into darkest night. The air became acrid, as though the entire jungle had been engulfed in a huge forest fire, and gray ashes fell like a blizzard of snow, making it impossible to see and difficult to breathe.

Jade twisted around and peered, as best she could, at the top of the mountain behind her. What she saw was a spectacle so awesome, so terrifying, that she never forgot it. Gasping, she gripped Pieter's arm, her nails digging into his flesh.

Together the couple stared at the unrestrained power released by the infuriated forces of nature. Soaring thousands of feet skyward were huge dark clouds, which scattered a thick coating of ashes everywhere. Directly below this cover glowed a fiery inferno that made the young couple think that the entire interior of the earth was ablaze. Searing flames—their centers an intense, hot blue, their outer edges an ugly, deep orange—soared hundreds of feet into the air from the crater of the volcano and, mirrored by the clouds above them, seemed to threaten the entire island with immediate destruction. In addition, huge showers of countless sparks shot into the air and scattered everywhere, starting fires in dry places on the slopes below.

In the meantime, the roar became still louder, and the earth rocked terrifyingly.

Pieter had to shout at the top of his voice to make himself heard. "We've got to get down to the sea! If we're trapped in the lava flow, we'll be burned to cinders!"

Catching hold of Jade's hand, he began to run as though possessed by demons. The absurd thought occurred to Jade that, with his head, face, and body covered by a thick coating of ash, he resembled a being from another world. Not until later did it occur to her that she, too, was smeared from head to toe with the thick, sticky volcanic ashes.

The ashes were so thick and heavy they entered the noses and mouths of the couple, interfering with their breathing and depriving them of needed oxygen. Their lashes became coated with ash, and they had to wipe their eyes repeatedly so they could see.

Gasping and stumbling, half running at the same time that she was being dragged, Jade used all of her strength, all of her stamina, all of her willpower, to escape the furious wrath of the volcano.

The natives who had come in search of her and her companion were forgotten. Never had she known such untamed, wild violence. Never had she been so frightened. At the same time, however, her mind continued to function clearly.

She knew that the lava, which would gush from the volcano, would flow down the mountainside with a speed far greater than any that she and Pieter could attain. So she had to assume that he had judged correctly, that he was leading her in a direction opposite that which the lava flow was taking.

Nevertheless, the heat engendered by the eruption was intense. It pressed against Jades's back like a solid wall and made her think that the forest behind her was on fire. Occasionally she had to turn and look back in order to reassure herself that the flames were not ready to swoop down on her.

Suddenly her foot caught in a hidden tree root, causing her to lose her balance, and she sprawled headlong onto the ash-covered ground.

Giving in to her terror and pain for the first time, she screamed aloud.

Pieter proved equal to the crisis. First snatching the *kris*, which had fallen to the ground, he placed it securely in his own belt. Then he lifted Jade bodily in his arms, and cradling her gently but firmly, he resumed his flight.

An excruciating pain in her ankle told Jade that she could run no farther that day herself.

"Put me down, Pieter!" she told him, sobbing. "You can't escape if you've got to carry me, too. Put me down and save yourself!"

Pieter Sabov paid no attention to her demands and continued to make his way down the slope, showing surprising speed and agility in spite of the heavy burden he was carrying.

"Leave me to fend for myself," she told him. "It's better that one of us lives, so I beg you, save yourself!"

He bared his teeth in a painful grimace, and his bloodshot eyes glowered at her.

She knew, then, that he would not waste precious breath replying to her protests. His actions alone were making it infinitely plain that he had no intention of obeying her injunction. Curling her arms around his neck, she clung to him, and tears dampened her cheeks.

Struggling with all of his might, fighting for breath with every step he took, Pieter continued to flee the volcano. The nightmare seemed endless.

Afraid he would weaken and collapse at any moment, Jade was shaken by spasms of pain and was ever conscious of the fury of the forces of nature overhead and behind her. She lost all consciousness of the passage of time, which was nature's way of protecting her, perhaps, and miraculously, she realized that Pieter was leaning against a tree outside their hut which was somehow intact.

He placed her on the ground, propping her back against a tree, and then, shaking off his weariness, he dropped a bucket into the stream beside their hut. He pulled up the bucket and then astonished Jade by throwing the contents onto the palm fronds of the dwelling's roof.

Not until he repeated the gesture, filling a second bucket of water and disposing of it in the same way, did Jade finally understand. He was deliberately wetting the roof of their house so that sparks dropping from the volcano above them would not set fire to it and destroy what there was of their home and belongings.

"Let me help," she said, and ignoring his protest, she filled the bucket a third time. "I don't have to stand in order to do this," she said, and somehow hauled the bucket out of the stream, where Pieter emptied the contents onto the roof.

They spent the time filling more bucketloads of water than they could count and drenching the roof of their hut repeatedly. Jade's arms ached and felt as though they were being torn from their sockets, but Pieter's foresight paid handsome dividends, and the house was spared from the ravages of the volcanic eruption.

"I thank the Almighty that I was right," he told her. "The lava is flowing down the other side of the mountain and is building up a new clifflike barrier there."

Suddenly, inexplicably, he laughed hoarsely and pointed out to sea.

Jade followed the direction of his finger and a giggle welled up within her. In the strange halflight created by the glow of the volcano's fire, she could just make out the two outrigger canoes of the Malays being paddled rapidly away from the accursed island where the natives had made the mistake of offending the gods by landing.

"You and I seem to lead charmed lives," she told him.

"Indeed we do," he said, and in spite of his exhaustion, he kissed her.

Then he returned to his duties, ignoring the ache in his body. Leaving Jade with the *kris* and a pistol to protect herself, he went off in search of animals driven into the vicinity by the fire that burned as the lava advanced on the far side of the island.

As he anticipated, he enjoyed good fortune and brought down a wild boar and two small tropical deer. These he carried back to their dwelling area one by one and desisted from further hunting only because he was so tired that Jade ordered him to stop.

Still sitting, she cut up the carcasses while he built a fire of fresh palm leaves that emitted thick smoke, and they began to smoke the meat.

By the time these tasks were finished, the volcanic eruption had come to an end, halting as abruptly as it had started. The rumbling noise ceased, and an almost eerie quiet seemed to envelop the entire island. Although there was still a fog of volcanic ash, the sun managed to penetrate it, at least to some extent, and semidaylight gradually returned.

Jade's throat felt parched, and a great thirst seized her. She discovered that Pieter felt the same way, but they faced a problem when they realized that the stream that ran adjacent to their dwelling from the mountaintop above had become a muddy, opaque brown. Jade solved the dilemma by filling a bucket with water, then straining it through a cloth as she poured it into a second bucket. After the water was transferred no fewer than a dozen times, it became sufficiently clear to be potable.

Pieter examined Jade's ankle, prodding gently and moving her foot first in one direction then in another. "You twisted it," he said, "and that caused a considerable swelling. But as nearly as I can determine, you broke no bones."

"Thank goodness for that," she replied.

"I recall that when I had a similar accident some years ago," he said, "the doctor prescribed soaking my ankle in a salt water solution. So I'd say that the best place for you right now is in the ocean."

She looked down at her arms and body, then grimaced. "I don't believe," she said, "that a long swim will do me any harm. I've never been so filthy in all my life."

"Neither have I," he replied. "But if you're going to be clean, you give me no choice, so I'll have to swim, too." He picked her up, carried her down to the beach, and slowly made his way into the water.

Ordinarily, the water of the bay was placid, but thanks to the volcanic upheaval, the surface was riffled by miniature whitecaps. However, the water was clear and clean, the strong currents having dispersed all the ash resulting from the eruption.

Pieter deposited her gently, and Jade was overjoyed to discover that she could float easily, without effort and without undue strain on her sore ankle. Her companion went back to their hut, returning with two coconut shells filled with soft soap made from the coconut meat.

They soaped themselves and washed their hair repeatedly and, floating and swimming lazily, managed to rinse away the grime that had rained down on them from the skies. The water of the lagoon, heated by the lava that had flowed into it at its far end, was much warmer than usual. Jade remained immersed for as long a period as she could tolerate, and then made her way ashore reluctantly, supported by Pieter when she reached the shallows and had to walk.

Then she sat on the beach, and Pieter strengthened her ankle by bandaging it with a strip of cloth. Feeling clean and refreshed, Jade studied her surroundings and was surprised. The shape of the volcanic crater that loomed above them in the background had changed somewhat, but it had become peaceful again, and only a few wisps of smoke still rose from it. The remnant of a forest fire still flickered in the jungle on the far side of the island, but otherwise the peaceful tropical atmosphere was restored.

Pieter took in the scene and became thoughtful. "We're fortunate beyond measure," he said, "to be alive and to have suffered no serious damage. Our belongings are miraculously intact, and the fire didn't reach the trees that supply us with bananas and coconuts and breadfruit. So we'll continue to eat. There's game still in the jungle, and there are fish without number in the sea." He smiled and shook his head. "We even have the volcano to thank for saving us from the natives who would have given us a very rude reception, had they found us. I have an idea they had the fright of their lives and won't be returning here for a long time."

"Even the flowers are intact," Jade said, and pointed to a bush that was loaded with fragrant, white gardenia blossoms, some of them covered with ash.

Sensing that she was depressed, Pieter went to the bush and picked the largest of the flowers, blew off the ashes, and handed it to her with a flourish.

She tried hard to smile as she put it in her hair, where the contrast of the white against the sun-streaked blue-black strands was startling. "It's almost as though the volcano didn't erupt," she said softly.

Pieter failed to grasp her meaning and looked at her in obvious perplexity.

"I'm grateful to the Almighty for preserving us," she told him," "but our basic situation really hasn't changed. We're still prisoners here, trapped in a paradise from which there's no escape, caught in a web where any moment could be our last. I don't mean to sound discouraged, but we face years of this life without a change."

IV

Erika von Klausner had been in a foul mood ever since the escape of Jade Rakehell and Count Pieter Sabov. She had notified her representatives in Hong Kong, Singapore, and the many offices she maintained throughout the Dutch East Indies that she would offer a reward for any information gleaned regarding the errant couple, but she received no word on them.

Her business associates remained unaware of her mood, because she allowed nothing to impair her good relations with them. Similarly, the guards on the estate and the female concubines also escaped her wrath, because she recalled all too vividly how she herself had been mistreated when she had been in the unfortunate position in which the girls currently found themselves.

The four young eunuchs of the household staff, who masqueraded as women, were forced to bear the brunt of her bad temper. She summoned them to her private quarters every night, and there she subjected them to humiliation, pain, and degradation. She delighted in biting them, scratching them, and pulling their long hair, and when these activities gave her no relief, she became even more violent in her lovemaking, pinching their breasts, jabbing knives into their buttocks, and ultimately beating them with a leather whip until they fled hysterically from her presence.

As the weeks became months, her rage gradually subsided, and ultimately, having heard not one word about the fate of Jade and Pieter, she concluded they had died in a storm at sea.

This belief gave her a measure of satisfaction, although she took the precaution of continuing to offer a reward to the subordinates who manned her various offices for information on the fugitive pair, or for their capture.

The bulk of the business she had taken over from the late Anna van der Luon consisted mainly of deals for the spices that were grown in Java. Her predecessor, it was true, had established trading relations with merchants from Canton, but Erika wished to increase her business with the Middle Kingdom.

After making a thorough study of the current trade situation with Cathay, Erika was forced to conclude that there was nothing she could do to break the hold of Rakehell and Boynton or of the other British and American companies that had a stranglehold on business dealings with the Middle Kingdom. All of these companies were eminently fair in their dealings with the Chinese, and her representative in Peking wrote to her that Prince Kung, the regent who was in charge of commercial relations, had no desire to make changes or to substitute a new company for one with which he was already doing business.

Accustomed to dealing boldly with business as well as personal problems, Erika decided on a daring maneuver: She would set up a deal with the Nanking rebels! Wanting to assure herself of a warm, open reception, she investigated the rebel leadership and soon discovered that H'ung Hsiu-ch'üan, the nominal leader of the rebels, was in actuality a mystic who lived with his head in the clouds. The active head of the Taiping rebels was Yang Hsiu-ch'ing, their military general and principal commercial strategist.

So she wrote a carefully worded letter to Yang, suggesting a meeting that would be mutually beneficial.

Yang Hsiu-ch'ing replied promptly and with equal caution. He would welcome a visit, he said, from Madam van der Luon Anna at her earliest convenience.

Erika took personal charge of planning every aspect of the voyage. She decided to make the journey through the South China Sea to the city of Nanking on the Yangtze River on board a clipper ship that had been built for the Fat Dutchman by Rakehell and Boynton. As it was by far the fastest vessel in her fleet, she knew it could outrun any pirates or vessels of the Imperial Navy she might encounter on the high seas.

Preferring to take no unnecessary risks, and mindful of the fate that had befallen Jade Rakehell, she assigned twenty of her rugged Malay guards to act as escorts. Certainly that would give her the strength to beat off any possible pirate attacks.

No detail of the journey was too small to capture her full attention. As a gift for H'ung she chose an ancient life-size ivory statue of Confucius, yellow with age, and for Yang she took a sword with a multijeweled hilt from the Fat Dutchman's extensive armory.

She chose her wardrobe with infinite care, and to the dismay of her young eunuchs, she selected two of them to accompany her as lady's maids, as well as sexual partners.

The voyage proved uneventful. Erika occupied the master suite, and amusing herself with the eunuchs, she made infrequent appearances on deck or in the dining saloon.

South of Hong Kong, the clipper encountered the first of several British frigates of the Royal Navy whose path would cross hers, and as she moved farther north, two United States Navy gunboats were sighted. The Dutch flag that flew from the clipper's yardarm was a guarantee of her good intentions, however, and she remained unmolested, none of the captains of the navy ships suspecting Erika von Klausner's real purpose in making her voyage.

The clipper reached Hangchow Bay, the entrance to the broad estuary of the Yangtze-Kiang River, shortly before sundown one evening, and at dusk they began the final stage of the voyage, heading inland up the broad, twisting river.

Twenty-four hours later the ship approached Nanking, and the walls of the inner city, which towered more than twenty feet above the ground of the ancient capital of the Middle Kingdom, were plainly visible from the deck of the ship.

Erika, who had worn men's attire on the better part of the voyage, had elected to make herself as feminine as possible when she met Yang. She had been endowed with a rare beauty as a girl and was still strikingly attractive when she chose to bother; she had spent the entire day primping, with the aide of the eunuchs, and the results were impressive.

As the clipper ship moved into the berth assigned to her, Erika came on deck, and the men of the Taiping rebel shore patrol couldn't help gaping at her. Her blond hair gleamed in the dying rays of the sun, aided by a fresh application that morning of blond dye and lemon juice. She was dressed in an elaborate Western-style gown of rich ivory-colored silk, with an off-the-shoulder bodice and a huge hoopskirt that she managed with practiced ease.

Behind her came the two eunuchs, similarly gowned, carrying the gifts for H'ung and Yang. The trio was surrounded by Erika's Malay guards, each of them carrying a long *kris* with a naked blade, and every eye was on the blond woman who carried herself with the grace of an empress as she went ashore.

Sedan chairs, each of them carried by four husky men in embroidered livery, were provided for Erika and her two companions, who the Taiping rebels had every good reason to assume were also women. With her own troops still acting as an escort, the chairs were borne inland and were carried to the Great Palace that had been the home of emperors of the Middle Kingdom for hundreds of years.

The interior of the palace, second only to that in the Forbidden City in Peking, was dazzling, and the two eunuchs, one a native of Java and the other a Balinese, sat in their sedan chairs with deliberately downcast eyes, afraid they would show their awe if they looked at the marble statues, at the mosaic tiles of gold and silver, at the copper, and precious jewels that decorated the walls.

At last they came to a huge audience chamber, where a hard-bitten senior officer of the Taiping rebels insisted that the Malays remain outside. Only a trusted few, he said, were permitted to carry arms in the presence of H'ung and the chief of his field forces.

Erika nodded, almost imperceptibly, and the escort remained outside the audience chamber. At the far end of the room, on a throne of magnificent carved jade on a raised dais, sat H'ung Hsiu-ch'üan. White-haired, with a long white wispy beard, H'ung wore the simple black silk robe of a mandarin of the first class, and certainly bore more of a resemblance to a scholar than to the leader of the largest and most successful rebellion in the history of the Middle Kingdom. Two dozen burly pikemen stood ceremonial guard duty, and there were any number of men in the audience chamber, some in civilian clothes, some in the brown uniforms of the rebel forces. All of them stared at the new arrivals being borne in triumph in the sedan chairs, but H'ung showed no interest whatsoever in them.

He glanced first at Erika, then at her companions, and returned to his reverie, looking absently into space.

A far more dynamic figure was Yang Hsiu-ch'ing, a husky, broad-shouldered man in his late forties, who stood on the dais in a gold-encrusted brown uniform of Western cut, tapping a riding crop against his high polished boots. He glanced at the eunuchs, whom he assumed to be women, and then concentrated on Erika, his gaze piercing.

Her instinct unerring, she returned his interest and favored him with a dazzling smile. Then the sedan chair bearers halted and lowered their burdens to the floor.

Acting in unison, the trio performed a maneuver they had practiced earlier in the day, dipping low in a curtsy, then touching their foreheads to the floor. Then the eunuchs returned quickly to their sedan chairs, one of them having presented the ivory statue of Confucius to H'ung while the other gave the jeweled sword to Yang.

That ended the ceremony. H'ung seemed mildly pleased with the gift he had received, while Yang examined the jeweled hilt of his sword with shrewd, calculating eyes.

He gestured abruptly, then stalked out of the chamber, and Erika followed him without a moment's hesitation.

He led her to a small room that obviously had been prepared in advance for their meeting. Incense, sweet-smelling and thick, burned in several pots, and Yang lowered himself to a mound of silk cushions, then indicated to his guest that she was to do the same.

Erika gracefully lowered herself to the cushions.

The rebel leader clapped his hands twice, and servants came into the room. One carried a tray containing tea in tiny, fragrant cups, a second bore exquisitely formed glasses, with a magnificent container filled with rice wine, while a third offered mother-of-pearl inlaid pipes, which were filled with opium.

Erika chose tea, and General Yang calmly followed her example. She had the feeling that had she elected to drink wine or to smoke a pipe full of opium, he would have done the same.

"Welcome to Nanking," he said, breaking the silence.

"I am overwhelmed by Your Excellency's hospitality," Erika replied, flirting with him subtly, expertly.

Yang was enjoying himself. Leaning indolently on one elbow, he examined her at length and then said, "The fame of Madam van der Luon has preceded her here. She is known not only throughout our realm, but also in the portions of the Middle Kingdom still loyal to the old dynasty, as a trader without equal. But I was totally unprepared to entertain a lady of such great beauty."

"I am flattered," Erika replied, inclining her head graciously, "but Your Excellency is not alone in being surprised. I did not expect the conqueror of the Manchu dynasty to be so young, so virile, and so handsome."

They looked at each other. Both of them knew that if they were able to strike a bargain acceptable to both sides in their negotiations, they would seal the agreement by spending the night together. That knowledge tended to remove much of the tension from the air.

Yang absently rubbed his fingers on the jewels in the hilt of the sword that Erika had presented to him as a gift. "I was much intrigued by the letter I received from Madam van der Luon," he said.

"I am intrigued by Your Excellency's accomplishment," she replied. "You've captured many cities from the Manchus and you hold vast territory. There your people not only grow the food they need for survival but they also raise tea and cotton, herbs of many kinds, and even that most rare of products, opium. But nothing grown in the territories that pay allegiance to H'ung Hsiu-ch'üan is to be found in the markets of the world."

Yang pounded a cushion in frustration, and his voice was harsh as he replied. "I am not to blame for that sorry state of affairs," he said, "nor are my people. The fault is that of the foreign devils who curry favor with the Manchu regents in Peking. The merchants and traders of England and the United States, of France and Portugal and Imperial Russia, will have no traffic with those to whom they refer so contemptuously as the Taiping rebels. Our tea and cotton rot in warehouses. Our spices remain untouched, and even our precious opium is shunned."

"So I have heard," Erika replied sympathetically.

"Occasionally," he said angrily, "a merchant of courage has come to us and has offered to buy our goods in trade. He has dared to brave the blockade of our ports that the navies of the West have established, but his act of courage has been in vain. His ships are halted on the high seas, and our merchandise is removed and burned."

"Your Excellency," Erika said calmly, "has told me only that which I already know. I wonder if the thought has struck you that the only merchants who have attempted to break the naval blockade established by the Western powers have been small, independent operators."

"To be sure," Yang said bitterly. "The major traders, those who are the proprietors of large fleets, are too timid to deal with those who oppose the Manchu dynasty."

Erika drew in her breath and then said quietly, "There is one major shipping company that dares to challenge the blockade. There is one company that actually welcomes such a challenge."

He peered at her intently, his eyes boring into her. "Are you familiar with our movement?" he demanded. "Do you know the principles for which we stand? Do you sympathize with our attempts to rid the Middle Kingdom of the curse of the Manchus?''

Erika shook her head. ''I must deal with you honestly, Your Excellency, and I tell you in all candor that I'm a trader, not a politician. I engage in the business of selling goods for profit, and I daresay I can find a lucrative market for your tea, cotton, silks, and spices, and your opium, as well.''

''Why will you deal with us, when the other major merchants turn their backs to us?'' he demanded.

Erika smiled. ''Like General Yang,'' she said, ''I am driven by a boundless ambition. I have a broader vision, let us say, than my more timid colleagues possess. I can envision the day when the Taiping rebels, their treasury filled with gold that my trade will bring them, will buy armaments, and fresh recruits will flock to their cause. They will drive the Manchu regents from the Chrysanthemum Throne of the Middle Kingdom, and all Cathay will pay tribute to H'ung Hsiu-ch'üan. His deputy, Yang Hsiu-ch'ing, will be in charge of all aspects of life in this land, and in gratitude for what my company has contributed to the great victories he will achieve, he will grant me the sole and exclusive rights to trade with China.''

His puffy eyelids narrowed. ''The vision of Madam van der Luon,'' he murmured, ''is truly remarkable.''

''On the contrary, Your Excellency,'' Erika told him forcefully. ''It is eminently practical. It is based on the most simple and elementary of equations. I will help you if you will help me, and both of us will prosper.''

As he thought about what she said to him, he ordered a servant to fill their glasses from the carafe of rice wine, and then he thrust a glass at her. ''Only a fool,'' he said, ''would fail to understand the principles of what you have said to me. But there is one thing that I fail to understand. In order to prosper you must carry the merchandise that I would sell to you to the marketplaces of the world. Is that not so?''

She sipped her wine, certain that he had risen to the bait, and again she flirted with him over the rim of her glass. ''Of course,'' she replied.

"Then tell me this, if you please, Madam van der Luon," he said, raising his voice. "How do your merchant vessels avoid the powerful warships of the Western nations? How do you stop your vessels from being halted on the high seas and searched, and your merchandise confiscated?"

Erika had anticipated just such a question and was ready with an answer. But she could not prevent herself from laughing merrily; all men were fools, and the powerful and widely feared General Yang of the Taiping rebels certainly was no exception.

"Ordinarily," she said, "I don't discuss my operations with anyone, but, in this instance, I will gladly tell Your Excellency the secret. In all, I have approximately forty ships in my fleet. If you and I reach an agreement, I will send all forty of them to Nanking or to any other seaport under your control. They will come singly and in pairs, a few at a time, and will all be gathered together simultaneously in your port. There they will be loaded with silks and cottons, with tea and herbs and opium. They will take dishes and ornaments of porcelain and jewelry of jade. Everything, in brief, that the world is eager to obtain from the Middle Kingdom."

She had his full attention now and he nodded, totally absorbed in her recital.

"When all of my vessels are loaded," Erika said dramatically, lowering her voice to a hoarse whisper, "they will set sail at the same time. All of them will leave port together and put out to sea together. Once they reach the open waters they will scatter. No Western power maintains a tight blockade of the coast of Cathay. The French and the Russians and the Portuguese simply don't have enough ships for the purpose. The British maintain only a limited fleet in the Orient, and the Americans have—at best—a handful of gunboats in these waters because their navy is too busily engaged in their Civil War at home."

"I begin to see," Yang murmured.

"My vessels," she continued, "will fly the Dutch flag, as is their right. Holland is at peace with every power in the West and enjoys great respect as a trading partner. My own company is highly respected, largely because we provide the nations of the West with pepper and other spices that are in great demand everywhere. So I promise you, the officers commanding the warships will think long and hard before they order a Dutch merchant vessel to halt for an inspection. No nation wants to incur the ill will of Holland.''

''That is clever of you. Marvelously clever,'' Yang said. ''But surely, after you have disposed of the merchandise, what you have done will become common knowledge, and the navies of the Western powers will learn they've been tricked.''

Again she laughed, and then she shrugged prettily. ''There's no doubt that the Western nations will learn that my fleet broke their blockade of the ports controlled by the Taiping rebels,'' she replied. ''But that is a matter of supreme indifference to me. By that time the merchandise carried by my forty ships will have earned vast sums of money. Your treasury, Your Excellency, will be filled to overflowing with gold and silver.''

His eyes gleamed appreciatively.

''I must admit,'' she added lightly, ''that I will have earned a considerable fortune for myself, as well. But, I repeat, this maneuver is only the beginning. With the funds that will be earned for your cause, you'll be able to buy large numbers of modern rifles and other weapons that your soldiers need. When the word spreads that your troops will carry arms that are the equal of the weapons carried by your enemies, you'll be deluged with offers from recruits who are eager to serve with you.''

Yang grinned broadly and again pounded the cushions, this time joyfully. ''You're right,'' he said. ''You're absolutely right! We'll have all the recruits we want and need!''

''As your forces progress,'' she said, ''as you drive the armies of the Manchus from more cities and more open countryside, you will have still more goods to trade, and under the terms of our bargain, I will become your sole agent in selling this merchandise.''

''So you shall,'' Yang told her, and ordered the servant to refill their glasses. ''Our warehouses already are filled to overflowing with bales of silk and cotton, with boxes of tea and of various herbs and spices,'' he went on. ''As to the casks of opium, I will take personal responsibility for transferring them to the warehouses in time to be taken on board the ships of your fleet.''

"We understand each other perfectly," Erika said. "The next step is to prepare our agreement." She was wasting no time in making certain that the exclusive rights she sought would belong only to her.

Yang summoned a scribe, who wrote the agreement that the rebel leader dictated to him onto a tablet of wax. Occasionally Erika interrupted to interject a word or a phrase, and Yang invariably was agreeable to the changes that she made.

She realized, to be sure, that the contract was being inscribed in Chinese, which she could neither read nor understand. Unwilling to admit her ignorance, she was tempted to bluff a knowledge of the written Chinese language, but decided that the agreement was too important to take the chance. She was banking everything on a move that, if it succeeded, would double her wealth.

When Yang finished his dictation and the scribe completed his task, he handed the wax tablet to Erika.

"Let my Javanese serving maid be sent to me," she said.

The eunuch, badly frightened, entered the room hesitantly, afraid he would be subjected to physical abuse and ridicule. Nevertheless, he showed the results of his rigorous training and curtsied deeply.

"You read and write Chinese, do you not?" Erika demanded brusquely.

The eunuch was so relieved that he giggled. "Indeed I do, mistress," he murmured.

Erika thrust the wax tablet at him. "Then translate this."

The eunuch spread his full skirt, then translated the document aloud in a high-pitched voice.

Listening carefully, Erika knew that neither Yang nor the scribe had tried to fool her. The contract was precisely what it had purported to be.

The eunuch and the scribe were dismissed, and Yang, again re-filled their glasses with rice wine.

Erika's eyes met his, and she became brazen in her flirtation.

He moved nearer to her on the mound of cushions. "Our cause will prosper, and so will you," he said. "This calls for a celebration."

"I prefer to think of it as sealing our bargain," Erika told him, and slowly, suggestively, she began to unbutton her gown.

BOOK V

I

Inexplicably, the eruption of the volcano had changed the island's weather pattern, and rain now fell early in the morning, shortly after dawn. Often the downpour was heavy, lasting long after sunrise.

Jade and Pieter adjusted easily to the situation. They continued to awake at daybreak, but instead of arising they reached for each other and fell asleep again, listening to the rain pattering on the roof of their hut as they embraced.

Otherwise, the volcanic eruption proved to be no more than a minor inconvenience. Indeed, hunting proved to be somewhat easier, due to a reduction in the size of the jungle and the fact that animals had been driven from their lairs. Jade's ankle healed, and she gradually was able to resume her normal activities, no worse for her experience.

Only in one aspect of their lives did the eruption have a lasting significance. Neither Jade nor Pieter forgot their close escape from the natives who had come in search of them, and they abandoned all efforts to attract the attention of the outrigger canoes that put out to sea from their neighboring island. They no longer discussed the possibility of being rescued, and quietly abandoned their efforts to attract the attention of travelers who might come within sight.

They continued to cling to the hope that they would someday be taken off the island that had become their prison, but they no longer mentioned the subject to each other and clung to their hopes in private.

So they were totally unprepared for the developments that took place one morning when they least expected new drama in their lives. The day began like any other since the volcano had erupted, with a steady, heavy rain that continued for several hours after sunrise. They slept late, took their time making love, and then had a breakfast of bananas and slices of a sweet-sour fruit whose name they did not know.

"The rain has finally stopped," Jade said, peering up at the sky through the entrance opening. "I think I'll go for a swim before I attend to any chores."

"Go ahead," Pieter told her. "I'll join you in the water in a moment."

She left the hut, intending to go down to the beach via the path they had made on the side of the cliff. But she stopped, looked down at the bay, and in an agonized voice, called softly, "Pieter!"

Recognizing the extreme urgency of her tone, he hastily joined her.

She pointed down at the bay, so upset and excited she could not speak.

He was equally stunned. In the shallow waters of the inner edge of the bay a two-masted sloop about forty feet in length had dropped anchor.

She was so startled, she could not think straight. "What flag is that?" she whispered, pointing to the pennant flying from the ship's yardarm.

He peered at the ensign. "It's the flag of Sweden."

As they stared in wonder, a white-haired, white-bearded man, wearing spectacles, emerged from the cabin onto the deck. Dressed for the tropics in lightweight trousers and an open-throated shirt, he peered for some moments at the volcanic crater and then called into the cabin.

He was soon joined by two other men similarly attired, one of them middle-aged; the other, obviously the operator of the boat because he wore a seaman's hat, was young. All three looked up at the volcano, conferring earnestly, and the middle-aged man made copious notes in a notebook that he carried. Then, while the old man collected what appeared to be instruments of various kinds, his companions lowered a dinghy into the water and soon all three were rowing toward the shore.

"They're carrying no firearms, which is encouraging," Pieter said. "Come along, I appoint you and me as a reception committee to greet them."

"One moment." Jade looked at herself, then at him, and giggled. Then, without saying another word, she ducked back into the hut and donned her skirt and breastband, Pieter followed her, flushing beneath his tan as he, too, put on his loincloth.

He picked up his rifle and a pistol, handed Jade the other pistol and her *kris,* and then started off on the trail into the jungle.

They concealed themselves behind an impenetrable bamboo thicket and waited. When they heard the trio approaching, Pieter stepped into the open and addressed the men, first in his native Russian, then in French.

They were too startled to reply.

Jade followed her companion into the open and spoke to them in English. "Who are you?" she demanded. "And what brings you to this island?"

The men were incredulous and gaped openmouthed at the half-naked Eurasian woman and the blond young man, both of them burned a deep mahogany color by the sun.

Ultimately the new arrivals recovered their poise sufficiently to introduce themselves. The old man was Professor Anton Irmgaard, chairman of the Department of Biology at Uppsala University. He was enjoying a year's sabbatical leave and had come to Singapore to study the insects, birds, and animals of the Malay jungle. While there, he had heard reports of the eruption of the volcano on the island and had formed a small expedition in order to study its effects.

Jade warned Pieter with a glance to say no more about their situation than was necessary.

Pieter introduced Jade and himself, diplomatically citing Hong Kong as their home, and explained briefly that they had been cast away on the island when their ship had foundered in a fierce tropical storm.

"How long have you been here?" the old man asked.

Jade had been meticulous in keeping her records. "We have been on this island for six months and four days," she said, and promptly invited the trio to inspect the dwelling that she and Pieter had erected.

Awed by the ingenuity of the hardworking couple, the professor and his companions assured the castaways of passage back to Singapore, as soon as their expedition was done. The professor and his men inspected the property at length; then, while Pieter led them to the volcano, Jade remained behind and prepared a dinner of fresh broiled fish, fried plantains, breadfruit, and wild melons.

The men returned as she was completing her preparations, and the captain of the boat rowed himself out in the dinghy for eating utensils and plates. He also came ashore with several large bottles of beer, the first alcoholic beverage that the castaways had tasted in more than a half year.

Professor Irmgaard, anxious to learn all he could about the volcanic explosion and its aftermath, questioned the couple in infinite detail on their experience, and by the time they finished telling him all that he wanted to know, it was too late for him to go out into the field again. So he postponed his visit to the opposite side of the island until the next day.

The visitors insisted on providing supper, and they ate a meal that consisted of a thick vegetable soup, "bully beef" similar to the staple utilized in the British navy, and loaves of bread baked three days earlier, which they served with large helpings of butter and jam.

Jade and Pieter had become so accustomed to their own simple, healthful fare that, as they confessed to each other later, they far preferred it to the so-called meals of civilization.

Not until they retired to their hut for the night, however, did they raise the subject that was uppermost in their minds.

"Well," Pieter said, "pretty soon we'll be returned to civilization, if you can call Singapore civilized."

"You can," Jade replied, "and what's more, it's far more civilized than Djakarta. Under no circumstances would I want to land in Djakarta and take the risk of falling into the hands of Erika von Klausner again."

"Nor would I," Pieter said with a tight smile. "I can only hope we've seen the last of her. But we do have some practical problems to face. All I know about Singapore is that the British have established a colony there, and that it has been growing quite rapidly because it stands at a crossroads for sea trade. But I'm afraid you and I will be destitute there."

Jade grinned and shook her head. "Not exactly destitute," she said. "The name of Rakehell still carries a great deal of weight, and I'm sure we can get appropriate quarters, and that tailors and dressmakers will make us some suitable clothes on credit. There's almost sure to be a Rakehell and Boynton ship or two in the harbor, so we can get passage to Hong Kong with very little difficulty."

"You make it sound very simple," Pieter said.

"It is simple," she replied.

He realized that the woman who had been his willing mistress for the past half year was not the same person as the one who was a principal in the powerful Rakehell clan, and he guessed that there would be major changes taking place in their relationship. But this was not the time to speak of such matters. It was necessary first to go to Singapore, and then worry about their future.

Singapore, an equatorial island with a magnificent deep-water harbor and dense tropical jungles, was separated from the southern tip of the Malay Peninsula by the narrow Johore Strait. The harbor was located at the southern end of the island, which faced the Singapore

Strait, a waterway that was rapidly becoming one of the crossroads of the world. To the northeast lay Hong Kong, the vast domain of the Middle Kingdom, and the Dutch East Indies. Directly to the west stood the subcontinent of India. Not yet a British Crown colony, Singapore was administered as part of India.

Still overshadowed by the spectacular commercial growth of Hong kong, Singapore nevertheless gave promise of the greatness it would ultimately achieve. It was said that the total population of the island had numbered fewer than two hundred people when the colony had been founded fewer than forty-five years earlier in 1819 by Sir Thomas Raffles. Now there were already more than one hundred thousand occupants, most of them Chinese and Malays.

Jade, wearing a borrowed shirt and trousers, stood in the prow of the Swedish scientists' boat with Pieter, similarly clad, and pointed out for Pieter's benefit the sights of the Singapore waterfront as they approached the city. "The docks are over there," she said, pointing to the left, "and they stretch out for a very great distance. In Hong Kong they're crowded together, but here they spread out for miles."

Shading his eyes from the rays of the equatorial sun, Pieter studied the ships within sight, the many junks and schooners, clippers and old-fashioned brigs, as well as many steamships of iron that were replacing the older sailing vessels. "I don't suppose," he said, "you can see whether there are any Rakehell and Boynton ships in port?"

She laughed and shook her head. "It's highly unlikely that we'll see any of them on the route we're taking into port," she said. "Usually our cargo ships utilize dock space that's about a mile and a half or more off to our port side. So I think we'll be wise if we hold to our original plan. We'll get quarters at a hotel, have some clothes made, and then we can start searching for one of our ships."

He grinned. "I suppose I'd feel a lot better if we had ample funds of our own. But you know Singapore—which I admittedly don't—so I'll leave matters here in your hands."

As the boat slowly approached the dock, the couple turned and went to the cabin to thank the professor for enabling them to leave their island paradise-prison.

"Not at all," he told them. "I'm in your debt, really. The information you've given me on the volcanic eruption is priceless, and the guide work that you did, showing me where the damage was done, and to what extent, will enrich mankind's knowledge of volcanoes."

A few minutes later the young couple left the boat and walked barefooted away from the waterfront, with Jade acting as the guide. "This is a far rougher frontier town than Hong Kong," she told Pieter. "There's almost no respectable veneer to society here, as yet. We've thought of opening a permanent office here, but so far there's been no real need for it. Our captains come here and do their own bargaining, and so far they've fared very well. The coming of steamships into their own has speeded trade for Singapore enormously, and I can foresee the day when it will become necessary to open an office. But as it stands at present, I'd have trouble finding a respectable businessman who'd consent to act as our manager here, and under no circumstances could he keep a family with him. I think it'll be another decade or two before Singapore becomes truly civilized."

Pieter nodded thoughtfully and walked somewhat closer to her as he took a fresh grip on his rifle.

They passed huge warehouses and tiny shops, innumerable eating stalls and occasional restaurants, and many taverns crowded with the seamen of a dozen nations.

"I've never walked the streets of this city without an escort, I must admit," Jade said. "I'm afraid it would be far too dangerous."

Pieter chuckled wryly. "I've noted the way most of the men we pass stare at you," he said, "and I think you are very wise. I'd be apprehensive, too, if I were you."

Jade couldn't help giggling. "The neighborhood improves somewhat when we get away from the waterfront," she said. "At least I don't have to grip my *kris* for dear life and be ready for a battle royal at any moment."

Pieter saw no improvement in the atmosphere as they left the waterfront, but kept his views to himself.

"The inns of Singapore are not of the highest quality," Jade said, "largely because this was originally a city without women, and the few who were here were in great demand as courtesans. So the standards adopted by the inns have remained rather elastic. We've habitually made our headquarters at one of the better ones, the Queen Victoria, although I admit to you that it leaves something to be desired."

"The prospect of sleeping in a real bed again is quite good enough for me," Pieter told her.

After walking a short distance farther, they came to the Queen Victoria Inn, and there Jade asked the middle-aged man behind the desk if he would be good enough to summon the manager, Mr. Ching.

After a brief wait, an elderly Chinese man, wearing spectacles, appeared from an inner room. "I am Jade Rakehell," the young woman told him. "You may recall me from my last visit here about two or two and a half years ago. This is Mr. Sabov, my friend and associate."

The manager bowed respectfully.

"I'm temporarily without funds," Jade told him, "but I assume that I can arrange to stay here on credit."

"Of course, Miss Rakehell," he murmured.

"We'll require the immediate service of tailors and dressmakers, haberdashers and bootmakers," she went on. "Is it possible for me to arrange to advance them money through you?"

"Naturally, Miss Rakehell," Ching told her. "You have unlimited credit at the Queen Victoria Inn."

Pieter was impressed by the power of the Rakehell name. What had an even greater effect on him, and surprised him considerably, was the fact that the manager personally escorted them to a suite that consisted of a small sitting room and a large bedchamber dominated by an enormous old-fashioned four-poster feather bed.

The man took his leave of the couple after arranging to send the clothes-makers to the suite at once.

"The influence of the Rakehell name is certainly great here," Pieter said, raising an eyebrow once he and Jade were alone. "But I must say I'm somewhat stunned by the fact that he automatically assumed we'd be using one bedroom.''

She laughed. "I told you that Singapore is a rough town, Pieter, and I meant it quite literally. I'm sure there's no innkeeper in Singapore who would have given us separate rooms had we come to him looking like a pair of ragamuffins and carrying no luggage of any kind. The hotel men of this city jump to certain conclusions, and usually they're quite right.''

Within less than a half hour, the tradespeople began to arrive at the suite, and soon the former castaways were immersed in the details of arranging for their first real wardrobe in many months.

Meanwhile, Mr. Ching also had a visitor. No sooner did he return to his office than he sent a messenger speeding to the waterfront with a letter that he had written and carefully sealed, and he admitted his guest, a nondescript-looking Chinese, with whom he exchanged a curt nod.

Then he carefully closed the door and addressed the new arrival in a low tone.

"I sent for you," he said, "because I claim the reward that Madam van der Luon has offered for information on the fugitives from her estate. I have the honor and pleasure of informing you that Rakehell Jade and the man named Sabov are quartered under my roof at this very moment.''

His guest stared at him. "You are sure, Ching?''

The manager nodded complacently. "I am very sure," he said. "I recognize the young woman from her previous visits, as well as the descriptions that Anna van der Luon issued. The only difference is that both she and the young man have very dark skins. They appear to have spent much time in the sun.''

"If your information proves correct," his visitor told him, "you shall have the reward at once.''

"In gold, if you please," Ching replied, "and remember I can tolerate no violence under the roof of the Queen Victoria Inn. You'll have to wait until they leave here to go elsewhere for a meal or on an errand, or whatever they intend to do, and then take whatever action you plan against them. As long as I get the money that is promised in the reward, and you don't violate the hospitality of my inn, I don't care what you do to Rakehell Jade and Sabov.''

The Pacific
Ocean was as gentle as its name. The sea remained flat under a
bright blue sky that was reflected in the water, and high, lazy clouds
drifted overhead. The steamship made her way through southern
waters, and the temperature was mild, benign.

Alexis Rakehell, wearing a light summer dress, and her bridegroom,
clad in a cotton suit, stood at the ship's fantail, watching the wake
created by the churning paddle wheels at the sides of the boat.

Ordinarily sensitive to the nuances of weather, the couple had a
far more serious matter on their minds and concentrated their full
attention on it.

"I realize my request is probably quite childish," Alexis said,
"but the scheme concocted by Anna van der Luon to discredit and
embarrass you was so vicious that something inside me demands
justice. How I'd love to confront her as your wife and have her learn
from you that you know my background and that you don't care!"

Her hand rested on the deck rail, and Julian covered it with his.

"I know precisely how you feel, honey," he said, "and I don't blame you in the least. In fact, I'm not only proud of you, but I'd like the vindication of thumbing my nose at the woman, too. But I'm afraid we've got to be sensible."

"Why isn't it sensible to be honest with her?" Alexis asked. "That's what I don't understand."

"Life in the East," he said slowly, "isn't lived by the same rules that prevail in our part of the world. We place a high value on the dignity and the stature of an idividual. Those things count for very little in the part of the world to which we're traveling. In fact, life itself is very cheap and is easily shrugged off."

Alexis turned and looked at him in astonishment. "Are you saying," she demanded, speaking slowly and distinctly, "that we'd be in actual physical danger if we went to Djakarta and confronted Anna van der Luon?"

Julian shrugged. "I'd hesitate," he said, "to claim flatly that Madam van der Luon would be that coldly unscrupulous, but it wouldn't surprise me in the least. Her uncle, the Fat Dutchman, was a law unto himself, and he lived like an Oriental potentate. He had the power of life and death over his subjects."

"That's absolutely unbelievable," the wide-eyed Alexis said, shaking her head.

Her husband smiled without humor. "In a nutshell," he said, "that's the East. If you and I were to go by ourselves to her estate outside Djakarta, there's no way of predicting what might happen to us. She could hold us captive, she could have us killed, or she could do anything else that she wished. I don't understand the reasons that she's become my enemy, but I don't wish to hand myself into her power. That is foolhardy."

She studied him intently and saw that he meant every word. "It's hard to believe that we live in the second half of the nineteenth century, a supposedly civilized time," she breathed.

"You begin to grasp the way life is lived in the Orient," he told her.

"Suppose we let David and Aileen in on our secret and took them with us?'' she said. ''Certainly Madam van der Luon wouldn't dare to harm all four of us.''

''I'd hate to take that risk,'' he replied. ''Actually, we'd be safe only if we were escorted by a strong contingent of United States Marines that kept their rifles loaded at all times.''

''I see,'' she murmured.

''We'll go to Hong Kong,'' he said, ''where we'll see what Molinda has been able to discover for us. If I know her, she's also put the Society of Oxen on Anna van der Luon's trail, and we'll find out what they've learned. On the basis of the information that they give us, we'll know how to proceed. I'm every bit as anxious as you are to obtain vindication in this matter, but I'm not going to jeopardize our safety. I urge you to develop the Oriental trait of patience. In the East it's the most powerful of weapons and it invariably stands one in good stead.''

III

Jade looked at her reflection in the bedroom mirror at the Queen Victoria Inn, and for the first time in a year, she was satisfied with her appearance. At last she felt properly dressed in a snug-fitting Chinese cheongsam, with its high mandarin collar and its skirt slit high on both thighs to allow freedom of movement. On her feet were black high-heeled slippers, and for the first time since she had been a castaway, she wore the precious jade jewelry that had belonged to her mother.

Pieter, lounging in a white tropical suit, couldn't help laughing. "It's been so long since we've worn civilized clothes," he said, "that I scarcely recognize either of us."

"We can go now to look for one of my company's ships without shame," she said. "Are we ready?"

He immediately rose and moved to the door. "I've been waiting for some time."

"One moment," Jade replied and, pulling up her skirt, fastened her *kris* to the upper part of one thigh with two thongs of rawhide.

"We're still in Singapore," she said. "I strongly urge you to carry your pistols. They won't show under that loose-fitting jacket, and at least you'll be armed."

He shrugged and put on his belt, from which the two pistols were suspended. "Should I take my rifle, too?"

She considered the question. "I think it would be wiser to leave the rifle here," she said. "We don't want to call undue attention to ourselves and cause a needless fight with lawless elements. There's enough of that sort of thing that happens in this town in any event."

He nodded, and they left the suite together. "It's good to be getting outdoors again," he said. "We've already spent forty-eight hours in this place."

She nodded and peered out the window. "At least the weather is nice," she said. "Singapore can be a perfectly miserable place when the rain comes. The deluges here are even worse than they were on our own island."

They walked together out into the street, and Jade slipped a hand through Pieter's arm. The street was deserted, and she remembered belatedly that the residents of Singapore did not venture out of doors at noon, when the sun stood directly overhead.

They turned the corner, and suddenly, out of nowhere, they were assaulted by three men, all of them nondescript Chinese. They had no idea, of course, that the trio were in the employ of Erika von Klausner, posing as Anna van der Luon.

Jade reacted instinctively, her long training in the martial arts standing her in good stead. One of the men lunged at her, while the other two directed their attentions to Pieter, and she did not hesitate.

Using a sharp chopping motion, she struck the man a blow on the neck with the side of a hand that had been hardened by months of toil as a castaway. He halted, the blow stunning him, and she followed through with a vicious sideways kick that caught him in the pit of the stomach and doubled him over.

As he gasped for breath, she drove two fingers into his eyes, then hit him again with the side of her hand, this time striking him in the Adam's apple.

Blinded and rendered helpless by the woman's expert attack, her assailant staggered beyond her reach, then took to his heels and fled.

Jade turned, intending to render what assistance she could to Pieter, and discovered that he needed no help. One of his attackers was running off down the street as rapidly as his spindly legs would carry him, and the other, caught in the young Russian's grasp, was being subjected to brutal punishment. Pieter, his expression fierce, bore him to the ground and, grasping him by the neck, banged his head repeatedly against the hard earth. The eyes of the Chinese were glazed, his flailings became increasingly feeble, and he gradually lost consciousness.

Pieter immediately turned to Jade and assured himself that she was unharmed. "What do you suppose is the meaning of this?" he asked.

"I don't know," she replied quickly, "but I don't think this was any ordinary robbery. Look there, down the street."

He followed the direction in which she pointed and saw that the attacker who had fled from Pieter's wrath was reporting to two other Chinese, who had appeared in the distance. He was speaking rapidly, gesticulating and pointing.

"Come along," Jade said, and turned back in the direction from which they had come.

Pieter hastily followed her around the corner.

"They'll assume we've gone back to the hotel and will come there looking for us," Jade said. "So we'll fool them and buy ourselves a little extra time." Instead of heading back into the Queen Victoria Inn, she continued to hurry off down the street.

"Where are you heading?" Pieter asked.

"I—I'm not sure," she said, "but I know one thing. We've got to shake off the men who are following us."

"You know Singapore and I don't," he told her, "so you're in charge."

They walked rapidly but refrained from breaking into a run in order not to become conspicuous. Jade glanced back over her shoulder with seeming casualness and saw that the Chinese who had fled and the two others who had met him were following the couple at a safe distance. Her one idea now was to reach a part of town where the streets were sufficiently crowded so that they could lose their pursuers.

The only part of Singapore that fitted her urgent need of the moment was the district near the waterfront, where the saloons and brothels were located. She headed in that direction, consoling herself with the thought that at least she and Pieter would be that much nearer to the dock areas, where they were going to search for a Rakehell and Boynton vessel.

It was not difficult to find the area, but an unexpected complication soon developed when individual seamen wandering in and out of bars or loitering on the streets stared hungrily at the extremely attractive Eurasian woman, whose appearance was far more striking than that of any of the streetwalkers loitering in doorways or sauntering in and out of taverns.

Pieter instinctively moved closer to Jade and put an arm around her shoulders to shield her.

They continued to make their way through the maze of Singapore's narrow streets and alleyways, turning left at one corner and right at the next. But as occasional glances over their shoulders told them all too emphatically, their pursuers remained doggedly behind them.

"I don't know who those men may be or what they want with us, but they're persistent," Jade said. "Too persistent. We've got to get rid of them."

"We were fortunate in our skirmish because we took them by surprise," Pieter said. "But I don't want you to take the risk of becoming embroiled in another fight."

"I can look after myself," she replied.

"I have no doubt of that," he told her. "But all the same, I see no need to take unnecessary risks. Surely there must be constables in this benighted community to whom we can appeal for protection."

Jade laughed sourly and shook her head. "The constables here report directly to the governor-general of India," she said, "and unfortunately, since we're hundreds of miles from Delhi, any constables we encounter are going to pay precious little attention to our complaints. They're going to assume that we're engaged in a sailor's squabble or that we're in some sort of an argument between seamen and local tradespeople. They'll wash their hands of us. That's one of the failings of Singapore, I'm afraid.''

''The jungle was more hospitable to us,'' he replied.

Suddenly a hard-faced Chinese girl, heavily made up and wearing a skin-tight cheongsam, called out to Jade in a rough Chinese dialect from the doorway in which she was leaning. ''The customers from that tavern are in my territory, woman!'' she shouted. ''Go someplace else!''

Jade replied instantly and unhesitatingly in the Cantonese dialect. ''I'll go where I please, when I please,'' she said, and pulled up her skirt to reveal the *kris* strapped to her thigh. ''And if you don't like it, I'll carve out your heart and eat it for supper!''

The startled trollop promptly hurried off down the street.

''What was that all about?'' Pieter wanted to know.

''It doesn't matter,'' Jade said, ''but she did give me an idea, and I think I know how to get rid of our pursuers now.'' She looked over her shoulder. ''We've lost them for the moment, but they'll catch up. But before they do, we'll go into the tavern.''

Before he could protest, she had opened the swinging door and walked into a place which reeked of sour whiskey, bad gin, and stale tobacco. There were a dozen roughly attired seamen in the room drinking, three of them involved with Chinese streetwalkers, who were sitting on their laps and allowing themselves to be fondled. Over a door at the far end was a sign crudely printed in English:

ROOMS—ONE SHILLING

''Stand where you can keep watch out the window without being seen,'' Jade instructed her companion. ''Don't worry about me. I'll rejoin you shortly, after our pursuers have gone.''

Pieter guessed her intention and started to protest.

She cut him short. ''I'll be fine,'' she said. ''I can look after myself. And this is no time to act like ladies and gentlemen.'' She moved away from him quickly and stood near the bar, boldly letting her gaze move up and down the line of sailors who were drinking there.

A seaman, who appeared cleaner than the others, caught her eye. He had reddish-brown hair and a beard to match, and was wearing a high-necked sweater and dark trousers. Short and stocky, he peered intently at Jade over the rim of his glass of cheap whiskey. She knew that if she was any judge, she could handle this man, and she smiled at him encouragingly.

To Pieter's horror, the sailor wiped his mouth on his sleeve, rose from his bar stool, and sauntered across the room to where Jade stood. "Do you want a tot o' whiskey, or a beer maybe?" he asked her in a Cockney accent.

Still smiling steadily, Jade shook her head. "I never drink when I'm working," she said. "I have other ways to amuse myself."

He inched somewhat closer to her, sucking in his breath. "You want to go upstairs with me?"

She tried to ignore his yellow, uneven teeth. "It's possible," she replied. "It depends on your generosity."

"How would ten bob suit you?" the sailor asked.

Jade had no idea what fees the streetwalkers of Singapore commanded, but she knew that ten shillings was absurdly low. Besides, she had found the loophole on which her plan depended. She could see Pieter frowning, ready to leap to her defense, and she shook her head almost imperceptibly. This was a situation she felt certain she could handle. "Double the ten bob," she told the seaman, "and you'll be coming closer to my language."

He was stunned by her seeming audacity. "A pound! You must really think you're something special!"

"There's one way you can find out for certain," she replied.

"Come along," he told her gruffly, and his arm swept around her.

Ignoring Pieter's alarm, Jade allowed herself to be led through the door at the rear end of the bar, and slowly mounted the stairs, with the seaman close beside her. She made no objection when his hand slid to her buttocks, which he grasped tightly with his fingers.

An aged Chinese crone appeared near the landing and extended a withered claw.

The sailor removed a purse, fished a coin from it, and dropped it into her hand.

Ignoring him, the old woman addressed Jade. "Take any room you please," she said, speaking in the Cantonese dialect. "We're not very busy this time of day."

"Thank you. The man has been drinking, I think," Jade said. "What do I do if he becomes unruly?"

The woman revealed her gums when her thin lips parted in a smile. "Just call for Wing Ho," the woman replied with a wheezing cackle. "The girls who come here call him the dragon slayer because he has taught good manners to so many drunken English sailors."

Jade joined in the laugh as she started down the hall, and seeing an open door on the right side, which overlooked the street on which she and Pieter had been walking, she entered the chamber.

The sailor was close behind her, and he closed the door, then bolted it. "What was so funny?" he demanded.

Her shrug indicated that her exchange with the old woman had been of no consequence. "You and I," she said, stationing herself near the window where she could watch the street below, "have a little financial matter still to be settled."

"There's girls aplenty in the East End o' London what begs for me favors," he said, "and wouldn't dream o' chargin' me a ha'penny."

Approaching her, he reached for her breasts and began to caress them through the thin fabric of her dress.

Stalling for time, Jade allowed him to do what he pleased. If she had judged the passage of time correctly, the three men who had been following her and Pieter should be passing on the street at any moment.

The sailor felt her nipples harden beneath his touch and was encouraged. "Maybe you'll believe me now, luv," he said, "when I tell ye I'm somebody special."

Ah! The trio walked warily down the opposite side of the street, and Jade studied them carefully, committing each of their faces to memory. She would not forget them when she saw them again.

The seaman was becoming bolder and more insistent in his ministrations. "I'd be the last to deprive you of a living," he said, "so I'll pay you ten bob, just like I offered you downstairs."

The trio below passed from view, and Jade became aware of the foul breath of the man who was pawing her. He had outlived his usefulness to her, and she acted accordingly.

Brushing his hands aside playfully but firmly, Jade took a single step backward. "We start discussing my fee at one pound," she said. "The longer we talk, the higher the price goes."

His eyes narrowed, and a surly, unpleasant note came into his voice. "I don't let no woman in England tell me what to do and how to spend my money, and I'm damned if I'm going to take orders from a chink."

He thought his firmness had won a victory when she bent down and raised her skirt to reveal her smooth, solid thighs. He assumed she was engaging in a deliberately provocative gesture, and he was stunned when he saw that she had an ugly Malay *kris* gripped in one hand.

"You have precisely three choices," Jade told him, her voice suddenly hard and metallic. "If you wish, I will call for assistance, and I'm sure the Chinese gentleman who will reply will resent your use of the word 'chink.' We regard it as an insult, you know. Your second choice is to take your chance with me and try to subdue me. I give you due warning that I'm thoroughly familiar with this knife, and that I won't hesitate to use it. Your third choice is to remove your ugly person from my sight permanently and instantly."

He continued to gape at her, the realization slowly dawning on him that this aroused creature meant what she said and was dangerous.

"I could carve the word 'chink' on your forehead as a permanent memento of this little encounter," Jade said, her eyes bright. "Think of the stories you could tell to all the ladies in London's East End who love you. You'd be enormously popular with the tales you could tell them." She began to advance on him slowly.

It occurred belatedly to the sailor that this young woman was inexplicably spoiling for a fight. Although he was heavier, she stood half a head taller than he, and even if he managed to disarm her, he knew that she could inflict severe damage with her tapering blood-red nails. Furthermore, he had heard stories about the strong-arm man employed by this particular establishment and wanted no encounter with him. He began to edge toward the door, out of reach of this strange young woman, whose movements were so stealthy and graceful that she reminded him of a panther.

He backed into the door, hastily unbolted it, and then ran out into the corridor, stumbling as he made his way rapidly down the stairs. He wanted to escape from this she-devil as soon as he possibly could.

Jade followed him into the hallway, and not until she heard the old crone's wheezing cackle did she realize that she still gripped the Malay knife in her hand. "The foreign devil ran away," the old woman said, "as though the ghosts of his own ancestors were chasing him. And you have not even soiled your knife with his blood."

The remark gave Jade an idea. So far she had maneuvered nimbly, but she and Pieter were not yet truly safe. "Perhaps you will tell Wing Ho that I would like to exchange some words with him. And perhaps, also, you could fetch for me a friend who awaits me in the bar." She described Pieter Sabov briefly.

A worried Pieter bolted up the stairs moments before Wing Ho arrived on the scene. "Are you all right?" he asked. "I've been worried—"

"Of course," she assured him. "I got rid of the sailor easily. But listen, Pieter. We got rid of the three men following us—for now. But they'll be back, perhaps with others. We need help, Pieter. We can't manage this situation by ourselves, and we've got to trust someone. I think I've found the man."

No sooner did she utter the words than Wing Ho appeared on the scene. He was tall and broad-shouldered, like a Chinese northerner, and bore scant resemblance to the slight, slender Cantonese who were in the majority of the natives of the Middle Kingdom who traveled abroad.

Opening and closing his hands, Wing Ho looked first at the Eurasian woman, then at the white man who stood near her. This was no ordinary streetwalker, and no ordinary customer, he concluded. For one thing, the woman's jewelry was worth a fortune, and her cheongsam was expensive. For another, he noted, both she and the man were heavily suntanned, so he assumed that the seeming coincidence was not accidental and that they had known each other previously.

Jade was taking the long chance that the strong-arm man in an establishment such as this might well be a member of an overseas branch of the Society of Oxen. Certainly she had nothing to lose by trying.

She addressed him in the Mandarin language and spoke slowly and deliberately. "On the road to Chungking, which lies in the western part of the Middle Kingdom, one can see the great mountains that tower above the valleys below. In the mists that surround those peaks live the most ferocious dragons ever known to man."

Wing Ho blinked at her in surprise but nevertheless was quick to pick up the narrative, also in Mandarin. "He who occupies the Chrysanthemum Throne could not eat and could not sleep because the dragons had sworn an oath that they would consume him alive."

"But they did not take into account the lowly oxen of the Middle Kingdom," Jade said.

The burly strong-arm man grinned at her. "Oxen gathered by the hundreds and by the thousands, and together they marched up into the mountains."

"There they encountered the dragons and overcame them by their courage and the sheer weight of their numbers," Jade said, concluding the litany.

She and the man stared at each other and then exchanged two formal bows, which they followed with a formal embrace.

Pieter understood nothing of what had been said, nor did he realize that they had been going through a strict ritual of identifying a fellow member of the Society of Oxen.

"Do you understand English?" Jade asked the man in Cantonese.

He nodded his head. "Enough to warn drunken sailors to behave themselves," he replied, still speaking Cantonese, however.

"My friend and I," Jade said, "are fleeing from enemies who seek our lives. The reasons they wish to capture and kill us we do not know. At the moment, we are without funds, and we seek a certain ship at the docks that will carry us to safety in Hong Kong. But between this place and the docks are numerous foes who seek our death."

Wing Ho's response was prompt and emphatic. "You have only to command your brother and I will come to your aid," he announced.

Jade formally bowed her head in thanks. "We do not know where the ship that we seek is berthed," she said, "and we shall be obliged to search the docks for it. Can you help us to reach that section of the waterfront in safety, and to gain the time for us to conduct our search?"

Wing Ho was lost in thought for a moment, obviously figuring out ways to help the couple before he gave them an unqualified promise. "What arms do you carry?" he wanted to know.

Jade raised her skirt to show him the Malay *kris* and added, "My friend has two loaded pistols, which he can fire with accuracy."

The strong-arm man walked hurriedly down the corridor and returned a few moments later carrying an innocuous-looking walking stick with a heavy bulbous head.

Pieter was not impressed. "I'm not sure how much damage can be inflicted with a club if we become involved in a nasty fight," he said.

Jade had recognized the walking stick at once and smiled. "Show my friend your weapon, Wing Ho," she said.

The Chinese man grasped the cane by the head and the body and tugged gently. The walking stick came apart, and in one hand he held a wickedly pointed double-edged sword of great sharpness.

Pieter laughed aloud. "That's more like it!" he said, and grinned at Wing Ho.

The strong-arm man smiled at him in return, and they needed no language to seal their bond of friendship. They were about to launch on a hazardous expedition together, and each of them knew that he could rely on the other.

"First," Wing Ho said, "we will go from the town of Singapore into the jungle of the interior. We will emerge from it at a section that lies closest to the docks. In that way, you'll be exposed to the view of passersby as little as possible."

Jade nodded in approval.

"It may be," the burly Chinese man added, a gleam appearing in his dark eyes, "that we can lure some of your foes into the jungle behind us. Then we can treat them as the Oxen treated the dragons, who were the foes of the Celestial Emperor."

His plan delighted Jade, who hastened to explain to Pieter.

He, however, remained dubious. "Aren't we asking unnecessarily for trouble?" he asked.

"We are not!" There was no time, Jade felt, to explain to him in detail the philosophy of the Society of Oxen, who always took the initiative when possible, always assumed the offensive, and forced their enemies to defend themselves rather than attack.

The trio made their way through the tavern onto the street. Jade walked in the middle, between the two men, and for the moment, at least, she felt reasonably secure.

Wing Ho set the pace as he headed farther inland, and he dawdled deliberately, hoping that they would encounter the enemies who had followed them.

At last the ruse proved successful. Heading in the opposite direction were two men whom Jade instantly recognized as a pair who had been recruited to follow her and Pieter. She took the arms of her companions and squeezed them to indicate that foes were approaching.

Neither Wing Ho nor Pieter Sabov revealed that he had been alerted. But the Chinese man grasped his walking stick in such a way that he could remove the wicked blade from its sheath instantly, and Pieter's right hand stole to the pistol that he carried under his loose-fitting jacket.

The two Chinese men heading in the opposite direction gave no sign, either, that they had come face to face with their quarry. They passed the trio, their faces stonelike, their attention ostensibly directed elsewhere. They soon reversed themselves, however, and after walking only a short distance in the opposite direction, they fell in behind the strolling trio.

Jade glanced casually over her shoulder and then announced, first in Cantonese and then in English, "They've taken the bait."

We are the bait, Pieter thought, but refrained from expressing the thought aloud.

After a time the pursuers were joined by a third man, and shortly thereafter by two others. One was Chinese and the others were Malays.

"The dragons are gathering," Wing Ho announced with a tight smile.

Little by little, almost imperceptibly, Wing Ho increased his gait until he and his companions were walking at a very rapid pace. Their pursuers, not wanting to appear too obvious, fell farther behind, and that was enough to satisfy the Chinese strong-arm man, who was merely trying to put distance between the two parties rather than evade the enemy.

"Do you know the jungle?" he asked. "You are familiar with it?"

"Neither of us has ever been in the Singapore jungle," Jade said. "But we lived on the edge of a jungle for a half year, so we know what to expect."

Wing Ho nodded. "Good," he said. "Shortly we will enter the jungle. You will notice that there are very large bamboo thickets to the right and to the left. Both of you will hurry and conceal yourselves behind the thicket that lies to the right."

Jade hastened to translate his words into English for Pieter's benefit.

"I will go behind the thicket to the left," Wing Ho went on, and Jade continued to translate. "Our enemies are far enough behind us. They will not be certain which path we have taken. They will divide up. Some will go to the right and others to the left. It is important that we separate them, because when they stand together, they form a superior force."

When his words were translated for Pieter, the young Russian nodded emphatic agreement. The strategy being outlined by Wing Ho was sound.

"Do not use firearms," the Chinese said. "If it is at all possible, dispose of our foes silently."

Again Pieter agreed, but Jade became perplexed. "Why shouldn't we use pistols?" she demanded.

"Silence," Wing Ho explained, "increases a sense of mystery. If the enemy is killed in quiet, one by one, those who survive—who have not yet been attacked—will become frightened and will be much more inclined to flee from the scene and run for their lives."

At last Jade understood. "If some of them run away," she said, "the odds will be more nearly even."

Wing Ho nodded. "Exactly so."

"Ask him," Pieter said, "in the event most of the enemy follow the thicket that goes to the left, would he be able to handle them alone?"

The Chinese man did not deign to answer in words. When Jade translated the question for him, he looked at Pieter, grinned, and lowered one eyelid in a broad wink. Of far greater importance, however, was his quietly confident attitude.

Jade knew that his self-confidence was not misplaced. Any self-respecting member of the Society of Oxen was capable of fighting a number of enemies simultaneously.

The houses of wood and the huts of mud with thatched roofs that lined the dirt road became more sparse, with greater distances between them, and the road itself was almost obliterated by weeds that sprang up everywhere.

"Soon we will be in the jungle," Wing Ho said softly. "Be prepared to run quickly so you will be ready to receive the enemies when they come upon you."

Jade translated his words, then paused and removed her high-heeled slippers. Breaking off a vine that wound its way around a nearby tree, she tied the heels together and carried them around her neck. The soles of her feet were still rock-hard, and she could move far more easily with bare feet in the increasingly thick foliage.

The trio entered the jungle abruptly. One moment they were flooded with sunshine, and the next they were enveloped in a world that was dark and dense and strangely muggy. They could peer ahead only a few yards, and the quiet was so intense that when the foliage off to their right rustled slightly, indicating the presence of a small animal that was taking itself elsewhere to avoid contact with the humans, the sound it made was much magnified.

Wing Ho pointed, and to the right and left loomed enormous bamboo thickets. They towered high overhead, blotting out other vines, plants, and creepers, and they were so thick and so dense that it seemed, at a glance, that they could not be penetrated. Wing Ho darted off to the left, waving a hand in cheerful farewell, and Pieter, following his example, went off to the right, with Jade close behind him.

The jungle foliage overhead was so thick that it formed a near-roof, and it was so dark below that the young couple, walking as quickly as they dared in an alien atmosphere where they might encounter a snake or a wild beast at any moment, had to grope their way. Their goal was to walk around the bamboo thicket and conceal themselves behind it.

Soon they discovered that the bamboo thicket suddenly jutted out to the right and then turned back to the left. By following it around, they discovered they had come to a perfect hiding place. Pieter noted that by looking back through the outer edge of the thicket, he could make out the approach of anyone who might be coming behind them. So they could prepare a reception for their pursuers.

He pointed to the see-through portion of the thicket, and when Jade looked for herself and realized what he meant, she nodded quickly. He had found the perfect place for them to halt and make their stand.

Jade bent down and removed her *kris* from its hiding place beneath her skirt. She knew that it would be unwise to utilize her skills at knife-throwing in the coming fight. She had no other weapon and therefore, would be obliged to keep the knife in order to stay armed. As she pondered the problem, Pieter took the knife from her, smiling apologetically, and cut himself a thirty-inch length of a thin but sturdy vine before giving the knife back to her.

He wound the ends of the vine around his hands, and all at once Jade understood. He had made himself a garrote, an ingenious and lethal weapon that he could loop over the head of a foe and tighten around a man's neck, choking him to death quickly and efficiently. He stood now looking through the bamboo thicket to see when a foe was approaching.

Jade instantly knew the part that she was to play. She moved several feet down the thicket and faced the direction from which a foe would come. It would be her role to make herself plainly visible, then to hold an enemy at bay while Pieter sneaked up behind him and permanently incapacitated him. Gripping her *kris* tightly by the handle, she braced herself and waited the opening of hostilities.

She did not have long to wait. Pieter signaled her that one man was approaching.

A moment later, a wiry Malay pursuer rounded the thicket and came into view. Like Jade, he carried a *kris* in one hand. He halted abruptly when he saw her, and grinned, but his smile faded rapidly when he saw that she, too, was armed.

Feigning fear that she was far from feeling, Jade took several slow backward steps.

The Malay instantly recovered his poise and self-confidence. Thinking he faced only the woman, who was obviously afraid of him, he advanced toward her, his *kris* held at shoulder height. With luck, he would be able to take her captive without harming her.

Her expression did not change as she watched Pieter creep up behind the man and drop his noose over the pursuer's head.

Quickly drawing the garrote taut, Pieter placed one knee in the small of the man's back in order to increase the pressure he was exerting.

A half-smile never left Jade's lips as she watched the Malay die.

Pieter, who had known her as a courageous and high-spirited companion, as a lively, loving mistress, realized for the first time that she had a quality that undoubtedly distinguished Rakehells from ordinary mortals. When necessary, she could be coldly ruthless.

Bending down and rolling the man's body with his hands until it was almost completely covered by the heavy foliage on the floor of the jungle, Pieter resumed his place and continued to wait.

In spite of the fact that, so far, the operation had gone smoothly, Jade couldn't help feeling apprehensive. There was always the chance that she would not fare as well against the next opponent. She knew, nevertheless, that Pieter was right. It was virtually impossible to imagine that the enemy had sent only one of the pursuers off to the right of the bamboo thicket.

So she took her place again and braced herself when Pieter again signaled to her. This time a slender Chinese came into view and halted abruptly when he caught sight of her.

He gestured menacingly with a short curved sword, but the gesture failed to have the desired effect, possibly because it looked so out of place in the jungle.

"Surrender, Rakehell Jade," he said in Cantonese, "and I won't be obliged to harm you."

Even though she should have faced the situation with equanimity, Jade was stunned. It was one thing to suspect that these foes who were searching for her might know her identity, but it was a far different matter to be addressed by name in the heart of a jungle located in alien Singapore.

Before she could reply, however, Pieter struck again, looping the garrote over the head of the Chinese man and drawing it taut around his neck. The little man was surprisingly strong and put up such a spirited resistance, wriggling, kicking, and flailing, that Jade thought she would have to intervene. Before she could drive her *kris* into him, however, his struggle ceased abruptly and he went limp, his sightless eyes almost bulging from his head.

"We'll take the chance that there's another one in the vicinity who'll appear," Pieter said. "Let's be on our way." Holding the vine with one hand, he started off again, taking the lead as they continued to work their way around the bamboo thicket.

At last they approached the end of the thicket, and Pieter, hearing someone else moving through the underbrush off to their left, held up a warning hand. Then he recognized Wing Ho and relaxed.

The Chinese strong-arm man communicated with him in sign language, and grinned as he held up two fingers.

Pieter responded by raising two of his own.

"This means," Jade murmured in English, "that only one of our pursuers still survives."

"That's one too many," Pieter said as he fell in behind the young woman, who was walking single file behind Wing Ho.

Her sense of direction, part of her Rakehell inheritance, enabled her to realize that their guide was making a wide swing to the left and was at last turning back in the direction of Singapore. She assumed that he would lead them out of the forest somewhere in the dock area, where they could begin their search in earnest for a Rakehell and Boynton ship.

Suddenly Wing Ho demonstrated to Jade and Pieter that their hearing in the jungle was less acute than his. He paused, then doubled back and ran at a furious pace before lunging forward in a bruising tackle.

Pieter and Jade followed quickly and were astonished to find that he was sitting on a struggling young Chinese who obviously had been following them.

Jade recognized the man as one of the pursuers she had seen from the second floor of the tavern. "Don't kill him, Wing Ho," she said. "It is better that he lives. If he's wise, he will give us information that will be helpful to us."

The captive looked up at her and spat in disgust.

Her eyes became cold, devoid of expression, and even before she spoke, Pieter felt sorry for the captive.

She issued her instructions, first in Cantonese, then in English. "Tie the man's hands behind his back," she said. "Then spread his legs far apart and attach each of his ankles to a stake that you'll drive into the ground. In that way, there is no chance that he will escape or that he will do us any harm."

Pieter and Wing Ho obeyed her instructions to the letter, and took the further precaution of disarming the man, removing an ugly curved knife with a forklike point at one end from the back of his belt and taking an old but serviceable pistol from beneath his voluminous shirt.

Jade, aware that the prisoner was watching her closely, showed no sign of emotion as her companions rendered the man harmless and tied him securely.

When they were done, she moved closer and stood directly above the captive. "There are two things we wish to know," she said. "First, who hired you to follow my friend and me and to attack us, and second, how many men are there in your master's employ?''

The prisoner's eyes glittered with hatred, and he spat again.

Wing Ho would have struck the man, but Jade caught his arm and prevented him from acting. Instead, she looked calmly at the captive. "I shall give you one more chance to answer my questions promptly and with civility," she said. "And I feel it my duty to warn you that if you fail to cooperate with us, you shall have ample cause to regret it."

The man remained silent, clamping his teeth together as he glared insolently up at her.

Jade reacted instantly. Removing the *kris* from beneath her skirt and wielding it expertly, she slashed at the man's trousers in a single sweeping motion. Then, reaching down with her other hand, she tugged and he was exposed from the waist down, the entire lower portion of his body becoming unclad.

Suddenly he felt cold metal against his skin, and the point of the *kris* exerted pressure on him.

"There's a woman in Java named Anna van der Luon," Jade said pleasantly. "Perhaps you've heard of her. She pays an exorbitant price for eunuchs whom she dresses as women and uses for her own pleasure. I see no reason why we should go empty-handed after all the trouble we have been caused today, so I shall deprive you of your manhood here and now. You are young and slender, and it will be a simple matter for Madam van der Luon to transform you into one of her pretty little serving maids."

The pressure of the *kris* became more intense.

The prisoner lost his courage and stared in horror at the woman above him who was coolly wielding the knife. Her actions, combined with her expression, told him that she would have no hesitation in emasculating him.

"Don't do it, I beg you!" he cried. "I'll tell you everything you want to know!"

The pressure of Jade's *kris* remained unrelenting. "Talk!" she commanded. "Who is paying you and the others to molest my friend and me?"

He was so terrified that he babbled, the words spilling out rapidly in a steady stream. "It's the very woman you mentioned, the rich Dutch trader in Java, Madam van der Luon," he said. "We have had orders for months that you and the Russian were to be captured alive and sent back to Java. We never expected to see either of you, but Ching, the manager of the Queen Victoria Inn, notified us that you had truly come, and we have been lying in wait for you to appear for two days."

"Why did Ching turn against us?" Jade demanded bitterly.

"For the same reason that my companions and I have been trying to capture you," the captive said. "Madam van der Luon has endless wealth, and she is willing to spend it all to gain possession of you and the blond Russian."

The girl translated what she had just learned from Cantonese into English for Pieter's sake, adding sourly, "We should have known not to trust the manager of the inn. We were remiss."

Giving him no chance to reply, she turned back to the prisoner. "How many men are waiting in the dock area of Singapore to capture us if we should appear there?"

"There are four or five," the miserable captive replied. "No more than six. But I cannot tell you for certain. Only the paymaster could tell you that, and I don't know his name or where to reach him. He has been very careful that we learn nothing about his identity or his movements. I swear to you that I've told you the truth—all of it! I've told you everything I know!"

The pressure of the *kris* was eased. "Very well," Jade said. "To the best of my knowledge, you've been truthful, so your life and your manhood will be spared. But all in Singapore who serve Anna van der Luon must learn quickly that there is a power in this colony greater than hers. Let all who would obey her orders tremble when they hear the name of Rakehell!" Acting swiftly, with a single slash she removed the man's queue of long braided hair that hung down his back, and then she used her knife on the clothing that still clung to his ankles. Then she set him free with a few more swift strokes of the *kris*.

The prisoner saw his long hair, the symbol of his masculinity, lying on the floor of the jungle, and at the same time he realized that he was completely naked below the waist. Trembling, near hysteria, he covered his face with his hands. "How can I go back to Singapore looking like this?" he sobbed. "The whole city will laugh at me and mock me."

"You will go there," Jade replied coldly, "because your only alternative is to remain in the jungle, where you'll be killed by wild animals or a vicious snake. When the people of the city pause in their laughter, make certain you tell them to beware the name of Rakehell." She gestured to her companions, and they walked off with her, leaving the miserable former pursuer to face his unhappy future alone.

Jade put their recent pursuer out of her mind as she concentrated on the problems that faced them now.

Pieter, marveling at her calm as he walked beside her, could not help wondering whether she would have carried out her threat to emasculate the foe if he had continued to refuse her the information that she had demanded from him.

Wing Ho peered hard at Jade. "So you are a member of the Rakehell shipping family," he said.

She inclined her head slightly. "I don't deny it."

"I should have guessed," he replied with a smile. "You are wise to be cautious, of course, but your caution could have cost us time and effort and could have created many complications for us. Yours are the ships, are they not, that fly a flag on which is painted the Tree of Life?"

"They are our ships," Jade admitted.

"That makes our task far simpler," the strong-arm man said. "I happen to know where one such ship is docked at the present time, and I can lead you to it."

Jade was sheepish as she translated his remarks for Pieter. Her failure to identify herself, which had been a cautious move on her part, had inadvertently added to the problems that they faced.

"There are probably no more than six of our enemies at large in the dock area of Singapore," Wing Ho said, "but we have a very great natural advantage over them. They know their comrades followed us into the jungle, and they anticipate that we have been either killed or captured. They do not expect us to appear suddenly out of the jungle in the vicinity of the Rakehell ship. So we will be in actual danger for only a very short distance as we come out of the jungle and go through the city streets.''

''How far is a very short distance?'' Jade wanted to know.

''No more than six or eight city squares,'' Wing Ho answered casually. ''After what we have done separately in the jungle, it should not prove too difficult for us to act in concert now, if we must.''

Jade kept her misgivings to herself. She glanced at Pieter, who also appeared unconcerned, and she could only assume that he took the attitude expressed by the strong-arm man at face value. She could not share their optimism, however. Anything could happen on city streets, particularly in a community where the constabulary was conspicuous by its absence and by its refusal to intervene in brawls and other personal disputes.

She decided to reduce risks as best she could, and kept her *kris* tightly gripped in her hand. It was ready for instant use, and she steeled herself, knowing she could not hesitate if she had to utilize it.

They emerged from the jungle, and as Jade looked down the dirt road that served as a street directly ahead, she understood why Wing Ho had been so unconcerned. They were in a district of enormous warehouses, huge one-story structures of stone and jungle hardwood, each of which occupied at least half of a square block.

Of primary importance was the indisputable fact that the street was deserted. Jade breathed more easily.

Wing Ho began to move more rapidly. In fact, he set such a fast pace that Jade was relieved she had not donned her shoes again, but continued to carry them suspended by the vine around her neck.

She couldn't help counting each time they passed an intersection. We've gone one block, she thought. Two blocks. Three blocks. Four blocks.

Pieter was the first to become aware of impending danger. ''Watch out!'' he called. ''Off to the left!''

In the narrow lane between two warehouses, four men, all of them

Chinese, emerged into the open intersection. All were armed with curved swords that ended in a forked prong, typical of a blade used in Cathay centuries earlier, and they rushed the trio.

Jade did not hesitate and threw her *kris* at the man who was leading the enemy. Her aim was true, and the lethal blade penetrated the left side of his chest.

He uttered a choked scream, flinging his hands high in the air, and collapsed in a heap in the dust of the road.

Pieter, too, reacted at once, and snapped a shot with one of his pistols. His aim was accurate, the ball penetrating the head of the foe between the eyes, and the man pitched forward without a sound and sprawled head down in the street.

Wing Ho's walking stick was transformed into a sword, and the strong-arm man advanced boldly, wasting not a moment as he attacked the third of the quartet.

The startled thug made a feeble attempt to protect himself and raised his own curved blade. But Wing Ho knocked it aside with such force that it clattered to the ground, and then he impaled the enemy on the point of his sword.

The entire engagement had lasted only a few seconds, and three of the four attackers were sprawled on the ground.

The surviving member of the quartet lost all desire for a fight and, turning, fled in the direction from which he and his companions had come.

But Pieter raised his second pistol, took careful aim, and squeezed the trigger. Almost simultaneously, the fleeing Chinese screamed, staggered into the wall of the warehouse beside which he was running, and collapsed onto the ground.

Wing Ho raced forward, scooped up the swords of the three enemies who had been felled in the immediate vicinity, and, removing the *kris* from the body of the man Jade had killed, wiped the blade clean on the back of his shirt. Presenting the wavy blade to the young woman with a flourish, and handing her one of the curved swords as well, he grinned at her. "You may want this for a souvenir," he said as they quickly resumed their walk toward the waterfront.

"I hope," she replied, "that I'll have no need for it today."

Pieter had had his fill of fighting, too, for the day, but he remained alert. At least two men in the pay of Erika von Klausner were still at large, so the danger was not yet ended.

As they approached the docks, Jade scanned the yardarms of the ships she saw tied up at the wharves. All at once she made out the familiar Tree of Life pennant and breathed a sigh of infinite relief. "Providence is favoring us at last," she said.

As the trio drew nearer to the vessel, they saw it was a large three-masted schooner, a commodious old-fashioned sailing ship that could carry surprisingly large amounts of cargo. Two crew members, both of them Chinese, were standing sentry duty near a gangplank that extended from the deck of the ship to the wharf, and some distance behind them on the quarterdeck, Jade saw a fair-haired young man wearing the insignia of a second mate.

"Ahoy, Mr. Kimball!" she called.

As the mate sauntered from the quarterdeck to the rail of the main deck, he wondered how the heavily tanned Eurasian woman with sun-streaked hair knew his name. To the best of his knowledge, he had never seen her before.

Jade's relief was so great that a giggle rose up within her and exploded. "Don't tell me I've changed so much that you fail to recognize me, Mr. Kimball," she said.

The mate stared at her for a long moment, then suddenly galvanized into action. "Bo's'n's mate!" he shouted. "Come here on the double, and pipe the owner aboard!"

"We'll dispense with formalities, Mr. Kimball," Jade told him. "It will be quite enough if we can board the ship."

Kimball extended a hand to her and helped her across the gangplank. She was closely followed by Pieter, and Wing Ho brought up the rear.

Kimball stared in openmouthed astonishment at the arms that the new arrivals carried.

Standing on the deck of a Rakehell and Boynton ship was like entering her own home in Hong Kong, or her ancestral dwelling in Canton, and Jade felt totally safe, totally secure for the first time since she had been captured by the pirates in the South China Sea so long ago. All the same, there were certain precautions to be taken. "Who is your captain, Mr. Kimball?" she asked.

"Captain Allen, ma'am. Harry Allen. He's gone ashore to arrange for the final shipment of the cargo we're picking up here, and he ought to be back shortly."

"What is that cargo?" Jade persisted.

"Mahogany and teakwood from the jungles of Malaysia, ma'am," he replied.

"When will it be delivered?"

"Sometime this afternoon." He anticipated her next question. "We should be loaded to capacity by this evening, and we should be able to weigh anchor no later than the midnight tide."

The sooner they left Singapore, Jade thought, the happier she would be. "What's your destination, Mr. Kimball?"

"Hong Kong, ma'am," the mate replied. "This is our last scheduled stop before we head for home."

"Better and better. Do you have accommodations for two of us?"

Kimball couldn't help laughing. "I wouldn't worry about that if I were you, Miss Rakehell," he said. "You will have space if the first mate and I have to pitch tents on the aft deck."

His frankness caused her to smile. It had been a long time since she had been treated with the deference to which Rakehells were accustomed. "There's one other matter that I feel it necessary to mention, Mr. Kimball. We have some opponents in Singapore who are anxious to prevent our departure from this colony. In fact, if they learn we're on board this schooner, it wouldn't surprise me if they tried to damage the ship in order to prevent its departure. At the very least, they well might try to board it in order to drag us off."

Wing Ho demonstrated that although he could not speak much English, he understood the language without difficulty. Addressing Jade in Cantonese, he intervened quietly. "There is no need for Rakehell Jade to worry about the safety of her ship or her person," he said flatly. "Her brothers in the Society of Oxen will attend to her welfare and that of her property."

She felt as though the last great weight had been lifted from her.

She could ask for nothing more than the protection of the local branch of the Society of Oxen. No matter how many hirelings of Erika von Klausner might try to kidnap her or damage her ship, she knew she could rely totally on her fellow members of the secret society.

They were interrupted by the arrival of Captain Allen, a bluff, hearty Englishman who had spent the better part of two decades in the service of the Oriental division of Rakehell and Boynton. Learning that Jade and Pieter had eaten nothing since their early breakfast that day, he insisted they accompany him to his cabin for a meal.

They did, and Wing Ho quietly took his leave; he said nothing about his destination, and Jade wisely asked him no questions.

The ship's master had known that Jade had disappeared and had been the object of a thorough manhunt by the company that had lasted for a number of months. He was curious about what had become of her, but she made it plain that she had no intention of telling her story at the present time.

"There are some matters to be settled," she said, "before I'll be in a position to discuss the events that have taken place over the past months."

"Of course," the captain murmured, and his nod told her that he considered the subject closed.

"There is one thing that you can do for me," she said. "I'll need about twenty guineas from your safe in company funds to settle a hotel bill here."

Captain Allen went to his safe and took out the sum she had requested. "Are you sure that's all you will need?"

"Quite sure."

"You'll be going ashore, then, to pay your hotel bill and bring your belongings to the ship, Miss Rakehell?"

Jade smiled and shook her head emphatically. "No power on earth," she said, "is strong enough to compel me to set foot in Singapore again. The errand will be attended to by friends—the same friends who are going to prevent our foes from boarding your ship or doing harm to it between now and the time we sail."

Had the speaker been anyone but his employer, Captain Allen would have bombarded him with questions. Under the circumstances, however, he had to content himself with accepting Jade Rakehell's statement at face value.

When they finished eating a meal of locally caught fish cooked with curry, peppers, and other hot spices, washing down the meal with schooners of ale, they went back on deck again and found that Wing Ho had returned, bringing a number of silently efficient comrades with him. Two had stationed themselves on the dock near the gangplank, and two others had taken up duty at the deck end of the gangplank. At least a half dozen others ranged along the dock to prevent any sabotage against the ship. Timbers were being loaded, and in the open hatches of the hold, crew members were identified for Wing Ho by Mr. Kimball, who vouched for the authenticity of each of them.

Wing Ho seemed to be everywhere, keeping watch for the approach of possible foes, checking on the loading of the cargo, and keeping the members of the Society of Oxen constantly notified that, so far at least, all was well. He saw Jade and Pieter the moment they appeared on deck and immediately went to them.

Jade took in the scene and was well satisfied. "I must commend you on your efficiency, Wing Ho," she said, "and my thanks to the brethren."

Pieter, who knew nothing about the existence of the Society of Oxen or of Jade's connection with it, was astonished by her seemingly endless contacts in Singapore, a town where she claimed to have known no one. Rakehells, it seemed, were even more influential than he had imagined.

Wing Ho was unhappy. "You can see anyone approaching the ship on shore from here," he said, "and similarly, anyone on shore can see you. I think you would be wise to stay under cover until darkness provides you with a secure blanket."

Jade had suffered enough to have learned caution. "Very well," she said. "I'll go below and so will my companion. But there is one final favor I must ask of you. Even though it was Mr. Ching of the Queen Victoria Inn who betrayed our presence here, we are indebted to him for our lodging, our meals, and the clothing that we bought through the credit that he extended to us. Is it possible for you to arrange to have him paid, and I think you know what I mean when I say 'paid?' ''

The burly Wing Ho chuckled. ''I shall, ah, pay your debts myself,'' he said. He patted his seemingly innocent walking stick to emphasize his words.

Jade was satisfied, and so was Pieter, when she repeated the gist of the conversation to him.

Even though the afternoon heat was stifling, the couple retired to the cabin they would occupy and remained under cover there for the rest of the day. They took turns staring out at the wharf, but nothing untoward happened to arouse their suspicions or alarms, and the daylight hours passed slowly.

When night came and stars filled the equatorial sky, the couple went on deck again, and Captain Allen told them the loading of cargo had gone more smoothly than he had anticipated, and he would be ready to sail in approximately two hours' time.

As they absorbed that information, they saw Wing Ho approaching the ship along the wharf, followed by two much younger men carrying a clothing box. It was apparent at a glance that he had succeeded in his mission. Jade was also overjoyed after lacking clothing for so long. She had been made unhappy by the thought that she might have to leave some of her new belongings behind.

Wing Ho came on board and refused to discuss what had happened at the inn.

Jade guessed, however, from his expression, and his words confirmed her belief.

''Never again,'' he said, ''will Ching betray those who make their home in his hostel. Never again will he allow his greed to endanger their lives.''

Jade felt certain that the manager of the inn had suffered a sudden, violent end, but she could not grieve for him.

Farewells with Wing Ho were brief. Jade tried to thank him for his great help in making it possible for her and Pieter to escape from Erika von Klausner, but he cut her short. ''Those who are members of the Society," he said, "swear in the names of the ancestors they worship that they will come to the aid of each other in time of need. Rakehell Jade and her friend had such a need, and I was able to be of assistance to them."

"You haven't heard the last of me," Jade told him. "I never forget friendships and favors." She fully intended, after she reached Hong Kong, to speed the establishment of an office for the company in Singapore, and the first person she would hire would be Wing Ho.

Embarrassed by unaccustomed praise, the tall Chinese said his farewells and took his leave.

But the young couple he left behind on the deck could not help but notice that he nevertheless remained in the vicinity, lingering on the wharf and wandering constantly from the guard post of one of his associates to that of the next. He was taking no chances, and he intended to make certain that they remained unharmed in Singapore.

Captain Allen invited them to join him for supper, but Jade demurred. She was too nervous, too apprehensive, and would not become calm again until the schooner reached the open sea.

"If you don't mind, Captain," she said, "I'd rather wait until after we leave the harbor."

"Of course." He assumed that her attitude reflected a long-standing Rakehell custom, and did not insist.

Somehow the time passed. Whenever Jade or Pieter caught sight of a stranger approaching the ship on the dock, they quickly retreated to the shadows on the far side of the deck and remained there until the stranger departed.

Then, at last, the harbor pilot boarded the vessel, the ropes were cast off, the sails were hoisted, and the schooner began to nudge her way through the heavy traffic of the busy Singapore harbor.

When they reached the entrance to the harbor, the graceful vessel paused long enough for the pilot to transfer to a small boat that would take him ashore. Then additional sail was put on, and soon the rhythmic rolling and pitching of the schooner told Jade that they had reached the Strait of Singapore and were heading eastward toward the South China Sea.

"We're safe at last," she murmured to Pieter, who stood beside her at the port rail looking at the lights of the colony off to their left.

"We've had more than our share of adventure and danger," he replied. "I hope they've come to an end."

Jade astonished him by laughing. "It's strange, but in retrospect, at least, I enjoyed most of the experiences that we've had. I'm afraid my father is right when he says that Rakehells thrive on adventure!"

IV

The Rakehells and Boyntons decided to stop in Peking before visiting Molinda in Hong Kong. It would be politic to pay their respects to the regents first, giving them gifts and explaining their mission to Cathay.

Julian and David, together with their wives, left their steamship at Tientsin, and the vessel immediately sailed for Canton in order to discharge its valuable cargo of trading goods as soon as possible. The two young couples were provided with horses and were given a full military escort for their ninety-mile journey to Peking.

Alexis Rakehell and Aileen Boynton were fascinated by the sights and sounds and smells of all they encountered. Nothing in the West was like the Middle Kingdom, and they were completely caught in its spell. Their sense of wonder increased after they reached the Forbidden City in Peking and went to the house adjoining the imperial palace that had been given to Jonathan by the emperor and was regarded as his property and that of his descendants for all time.

The women were intrigued by the chairs of carved stone, the

three-legged tables, the piles of cushions that were used in place of furniture, the inlaid mosaics that decorated the walls, and the magnificent marble-tiled floors that were so different from anything they had ever known in America or in England.

Then a messenger appeared, summoning the Westerners to appear before the regents in a private audience. Alexis and Aileen, thrilled at the opportunity of actually meeting these important people face to face, discussed with their husbands what they would wear and what they would say and do when they met the regents.

"I suggest you dress modestly but well," Julian said, "as though you'd been asked to lunch by Mrs. Lincoln at the White House, or to tea with Queen Victoria at Windsor Castle. I suggest you curtsy when you see David and me bow to the regents, and otherwise be your natural, charming selves."

"And if you're going to change," David added, "you'd better hurry. The imperial messenger will be coming for us at any time, and once he arrives we can't keep him waiting."

Alexis and Aileen immediately went to their respective bedrooms and hurriedly began to dress. Alexis, who knew how to dress for a special occasion and how to make a favorable impression, selected the outfits she and Aileen would wear. Their husbands, meanwhile, checked to make sure they had the gifts that they were presenting to the regents, and they sat down to await the arrival of the imperial courier.

The cousins were delighted when they were joined by their wives, who had changed into similar long-sleeved, floor-length gowns of pale silk, Alexis's gown a lime green, which emphasized her fiery-colored hair, and Aileen's gown a pale blue to match her eyes and complement her blond hair. Both men stood and bowed, Julian exclaiming he had never seen Alexis looking lovelier. David uttered no words as he walked over to where his wife stood and took her hands. The look in his eyes expressed his feelings.

Then the imperial aide, a young officer attired in the yellow uniform of the household guards, arrived. To the surprise of the women, he led the two couples through their own garden to a door set in a high wall opposite their house.

"This was a very private way of entering the palace that my father often used," Julian explained. "He was summoned to appear before the emperor often, and by using this entrance he avoided members of the court. No one but the emperor and his sister even knew that he was in the palace."

They saw precisely what he meant when the door opened onto another door in the palace wall, and they found themselves inside a mammoth building.

They were led down broad marble corridors filled with breathtaking objects of art. There were exquisite porcelain vases that stood seven and eight feet high, statues of men and half-human, half-animal figures in jade and marble, enormous utensils of gold and of silver, and occasional chairs of carved stone, inlaid with rubies, emeralds, and other precious stones.

Alexis wanted to pause to examine some of these treasures, but her husband kept a firm grip on her elbow and propelled her in the wake of their escort.

They came at last to a high-ceilinged chamber that, at first glance, looked barren. There were several mounds of cushions on the floors but no other furniture was evident, and the walls were bare except for a superb Gobelin tapestry that had been a gift to one of the Manchu emperors by Napoleon I of France, and it was so large it covered almost all of one wall. Fittingly, it showed Napoleon seated on a horse reviewing his cavalry.

The escort vanished, and the two couples were left alone.

"I didn't know quite what to expect," Aileen said in bewilderment, "but it wasn't this!"

David smiled at her and squeezed her hand. Then all four of the visitors turned toward an inner door that slid open. The dowager empress and Prince Kung entered the room.

Yehonala, as always, wore a cheongsam that appeared to be plastered to her flawless, superb figure. Her face, however, on which cosmetics were heavy, looked more like a caricature and resembled the masklike makeup worn by the characters in the Chinese operas that the two couples would see during the remainder of their visit to Peking.

Prince Kung, genial as always, was attired in the uniform of a general of the Imperial Army. He was smiling broadly. The alliance he had forged with Yehonala had exceeded all his hopes, and she deferred to him in all things, dispelling his fears of possible treachery on her part. The successes achieved by Kung's and General Ward's Ever-Victorious Army against the Taiping rebels caused the prince to gain great stature in the eyes of the beautiful coregent, and she dared not cross him, for the sake of her own future and that of her child, who would one day be emperor.

Julian and David bowed, and the two young women obediently dipped to the floor in deep curtsies.

Yehonala studied the makeup and dress of the two attractive young Western women. Though she had been subdued by Prince Kung and had learned her place, she still retained enough vanity to be highly jealous of her guests. She would have allowed them to remain in their curtsies indefinitely had it not been for Prince Kung, who said, "Please rise, and please make yourselves at home." He surprised his guests by speaking to them in English that was only slightly accented.

The prince sat on a mound of cushions, and at an almost imperceptible nod from David, Aileen and Alexis followed his example. The two young men, however, remained standing.

"Your Majesty," David said, "I have the honor to present you with a gift from Her Majesty, Queen Victoria of England, who hopes you will regard this token as a sign of her friendship for you and for the people of the Middle Kingdom." He handed her a box fashioned of heavy carved gold.

The natural avarice that was so much a part of Yehonala's nature showed in her eyes as she reached out and grasped the box. Then she opened it and gasped aloud.

Nestling on a velvet cushion inside the container was a magnificent diamond, the size of a walnut, to which was attached a chain of thin gold. The multifaceted gem gleamed and sparkled in the pale Peking light that streamed in through the windows, and it was obvious, even to those who knew little about jewels, that this was no ordinary diamond. It was, in fact, a virtually perfect stone and was destined to become a centerpiece among the crown jewels of Cathay.

Yehonala snapped her fingers loudly, and a servant came into the room and kowtowed. The dowager empress demanded a mirror, and while it was being fetched, she looped the chain around her neck and looked down at the diamond in admiration. Barely remembering her good manners, she addressed David in Mandarin and asked him to convey her thanks to her "dear sister, Victoria of England."

The servant came in with a mirror, and all further conversation was suspended for some minutes while Yehonala admired herself wearing the precious gem.

"Your Highness," Julian said, noting that Prince Kung was becoming extremely restless, "I'm privileged to present you with a gift from President Abraham Lincoln of the United States, who has stressed that this is not a personal present from him to you but a gift from all the American people, through him, to all the people of Cathay, through you."

Prince Kung unwrapped a scroll and opened it with extreme care.

"That, Your Highness, is an original early version of our Declaration of Independence, written in the hand of its author, Thomas Jefferson. It is a precious heirloom of our American heritage."

Prince Kung beamed. "It is I who am privileged to be the recipient of this precious memento of the great President Jefferson," he said, still speaking in English. "I shall treasure it always and shall take steps to have it placed on exhibit so that it may be viewed by all the people of Cathay." He was too polite to mention that his subjects knew neither the identity of Thomas Jefferson nor the significance of the Declaration of Independence.

Julian knew, however, that it was a wise and timely gift. China was just being opened to the West, and that meant that the ideas and philosophies of the West were going to be introduced for the first time into what had been a totally closed society for thousands of years. The day would come, he thought, when Thomas Jefferson and the principles for which he stood would be recognized, admired, and emulated by the people of China.

The dowager empress stopped admiring her reflection long enough to present Alexis and Aileen with pairs of long, magnificently wrought jade earrings. She made a point, too, of telling David that she would respond to Queen Victoria's gift with a gift of her own in return through the Middle Kingdom's minister to Great Britain. Obviously she wanted time to find some way to equal Victoria's dazzling gift to her.

Prince Kung lost no time in launching a discussion of trade with the active heads of Rakehell and Boynton. He explained that China was emerging from centuries of isolation into the modern world and had a great need for books and machinery, for medical supplies, and for technological advances of all kinds.

Julian replied that he and his cousin were well aware of the needs of the Middle Kingdom, as his father and uncle had been before them, and were doing their best to fill those needs.

Kung became even more blunt. "We also have an ever-present need for modern weapons—rifles and artillery pieces—and the ammunition that is necessary for them," the regent said. "Our armies are in constant combat with the Taiping rebels, and I am pleased to say that your American General Ward, who leads my forces, has captured Anking and is planning soon to attack Ningpo. To accomplish this feat, he has an urgent need for additional arms."

"I must defer to my cousin, Your Highness," Julian said. "Unfortunately, my country, also, is engaged in a terrible civil war, and the Union needs all the arms that are produced by our munitions factories."

David promptly assured the regent that the ordnance plants of England would be pleased to fulfill the requirements of the Middle Kingdom.

Prince Kung was delighted. "If you don't mind, gentlemen, I'll call in General Ward, who happens to be in Peking at present, following the fall of Anking, so you can pass this good news on to him yourselves." Without waiting for a reply, he summoned a servant to whom he gave instructions.

After a wait of only a few minutes, the sliding door opened again and Frederick Ward came into the room, exuding his own brand of energy. He saluted the regents, shook hands enthusiastically with

Julian and David, and only with Aileen and Alexis did he exhibit uncharacteristic shyness.

"If you gentlemen will provide me with adequate numbers of modern rifles and at least twenty to thirty howitzers," he said, "I'll be in a position to guarantee His Highness that Ningpo will be taken from the rebels."

Prince Kung's laugh was jovial. "Then the city is as good as in our hands," he said. "Mr. Rakehell and Mr. Boynton have already assured me that they'll supply us with whatever weapons and munitions you need, General."

Ward scowled at the young shipping magnates. "How soon can you get me the arms I need?"

David was not intimidated by his attitude. "That depends on the specific nature of your needs," he said. "We may have to send all the way to England for some items, while others are readily available in our warehouses in Calcutta and on the island of Ceylon. Give me your list, General, and I'll go over it item by item with you and tell you precisely how long a wait you'll have for each order."

As one who made almost a fetish out of organization, General Ward was impressed. "Mr. Boynton, Mr. Rakehell," he said, "as you may know, our recruiting problems are at an end, thanks to the victory, we've been achieved over the Taiping rebels. We have more volunteers now than we can possibly train and use. Our one serious lack is in the realm of senior officers, those who have managerial experience. Obviously, both of you have had ample experience, so I'd be pleased to offer you lieutenant-colonelcies if you'd care to join me. Think it over, if you will."

To the surprise of her husband, Alexis Rakehell replied before he had an opportunity to speak. "I'm sorry, General," she said with quiet emphasis, "but it would be impossible for Julian to accept a commission from you. For your information, he volunteered for a post in the Union Army, but President Lincoln personally ordered him to retract it, saying that he's far too valuable to the Union cause doing what he's doing with the company.

"The same is true of David. Together, he and Julian aren't mere executives of the company. They *are* Rakehell and Boynton. Their efforts on behalf of the Middle Kingdom are so great they can't possibly be measured. So, with all due respect, General Ward, both of them must decline your generous offer of commissions!''

Her outspoken candor delighted Ward, who grinned at her. "Forgive my presumption, Mrs. Rakehell," he said. "I stand corrected."

Julian and David had two long sessions with General Ward and then met once again with Prince Kung before they and their wives left Peking and headed back to Tientsin, accompanied by a strong military escort. Their steamship having left earlier in order to deliver its cargo as soon as possible, and no other Rakehell and Boynton ships available at the moment, the regents arranged for them to have the use of an imperial junk to carry them to Canton.

Aileen, whose middle-class background had prepared her for nothing like this, was awed by the living conditions in the cabins. With Alexis, David, and Julian in tow, she inspected the oversized double beds, complete with silk sheets, the divans on which cushions were piled high, and the full-length marble bathtubs. She shook her head in wonder. "This," Aileen said, "is what I call real luxury!"

Even Alexis, who was far more worldly-wise, was greatly impressed. "For the first time," she said, "I begin to understand what the phrase 'fit for a king' really means. I never dreamed that a ship could be like this."

"Imperial junks," Julian explained, "are intended for only one purpose, the transporting of emperors and members of their families. They carry no cargo, and they're not expected to make money."

"As a matter of fact," David added, "I'd hate to estimate the burden that's imposed on the imperial treasury every time one of these superior junks puts to sea."

The ever-practical Aileen had the final word. "Well," she said, "we have no idea when we may ever ride in one again, so we may as well enjoy ourselves."

The two young couples, temporarily free of all responsibilities, proceeded to enjoy themselves to the hilt. The food prepared by a chef who worked in the kitchens of Prince Kung was delicious and varied, and the scenery, as the junk sailed from Tientsin through the Gulf of Pohai into the Yellow Sea, where it stayed close to the shores of Shantung Province, afforded fascinating glimpses of the countryside.

It did not surprise Julian and David that the clumsy-looking junk, with its high poop, prominent stem, and battened lugsails, proved eminently seaworthy, rocking and pitching very little, even in rough weather. It was as seaworthy in every way as any Rakehell and Boynton ship.

The days were pleasant and uneventful, blending into each other so smoothly that it was difficult to keep count of the passage of time. The others agreed with Alexis, who said that the voyage was an extension of her honeymoon.

Then, suddenly, the idyll was rudely interrupted.

One evening at sunset a war junk, its decks loaded with cannon, a huge eye painted on its prow to ward off evil spirits, appeared off the imperial junk's port bow and forced it to halt.

Heavily armed men in ragged green uniforms, each with a red band of cloth around his upper left arm, poured on board the imperial junk and announced that they were taking possession of it in the name of the Taiping rebels.

The master of the imperial junk and his crew offered the boarders no resistance, and the capture was effected swiftly and without violence.

Julian and David were armed with pistols, as they always were when traveling in the East, but they hesitated to use their weapons against so many. In any event, the intruders took great pains to treat the four Westerners with studied courtesy, though they took the guns away from the men.

They headed for shore, and no sooner did they land than Mongolian ponies were provided for David and for Julian, and sedan chairs carried by teams of four brawny coolies each were made available to the two women. Other coolies were provided to carry their clothing boxes, and Julian waited until they were on the road, surrounded by a strong escort of men in motley uniforms, before he spoke freely to David.

"I can't help wondering," he said, "whether this raid was staged for the exclusive purpose of taking us as prisoners."

"The same thought had crossed my mind rather forcibly," David said. "In the first place, the captain and his crew put up no resistance whatever. It was as though they had been expecting the raid and knew they'd be well treated."

"More than well treated," Julian said. "They've stayed on board their junk, and for all we know, they're free to sail wherever they please. It strikes me that perhaps they were paid in order to betray us."

"Then," David went on, his eyes narrowing, "when they brought us ashore, it couldn't be accidental that they had horses for you and me and sedan chairs waiting for our wives. What puzzles me is why would the rebels bother?"

"The answer may be very simple and typical of the Middle Kingdom," Julian said thoughtfully. "Keep in mind that General Ward has been pushing the rebels quite hard, and they badly need men, arms, and ammunitions. H'ung Hsiu-ch'üan undoubtedly believes that they'll be forthcoming in some mystical way. But Yang Hsiu-ch'ing certainly knows better. I have the uncomfortable feeling that Yang intends to hold us for ransom and will send notices to our offices in Canton and Hong Kong that we'll be set free if he receives payment of a million silver yuan for each of us—or whatever the sum is that he thinks he can get."

"Damnation," David said. "You're probably right. I wish we hadn't surrendered our pistols so readily. Maybe we can steal them back again from the officer who took them."

Julian shook his head. "This is no time for heroics or false posturing," he said. "Never forget that the Taiping rebels are in a desperate situation. They've held a large strip of territory under their absolute control for more than ten years, but their revolution, instead of spreading, is being more and more contained."

"So their spies in Peking saw an opportunity to hold up a pair of wealthy Western traders and their wives," David said bitterly. "And we unwittingly walked into their trap. I resent it, and I'll be damned if I'm going to sit still and be pushed around. If there's one thing

I've always hated about this country, it's the callous attitude of the unprincipled toward decent people."

"For the present," Julian told him, "we will do absolutely nothing that could create any trouble for us or put our wives in jeopardy of any sort. Our escort is obviously under orders to treat us kindly, and I want to do nothing to cause them to become unpleasant or tough. I'd hate to be thrown into a bamboo cage where I couldn't stand upright or stretch, and I'm sure you feel the same way. And far more important than what happens to us, I don't want to see Alexis and Aileen humiliated or mistreated in any way."

"It isn't like you," David said, "to submit meekly to injustice, Julian."

His cousin smiled at him. "What gives you the strange idea that I'm submitting?" he demanded. "We'll move gently, one step at a time. First, we'll see where they're taking us and what their intentions toward us may be. Then we can consider the steps we'll take to free ourselves from this absurd bondage."

The party made its way across the open countryside, occasionally following a dusty, seldom-used country road, the rest of the time going across unmarked fields. In the distance, the foreign captives could see farmers working with oxen or water buffaloes in the rice paddies, and occasionally they caught glimpses of women in the huge-brimmed coolie hats and black pajamas of the peasants as they weeded in their small gardens.

"I have no idea of where we are," Julian confessed, and tried to find out by asking the commander of the convoy. The officer, however, appeared to be under strict instructions not to communicate with his prisoners. He smiled politely but vaguely, and made no reply.

Shortly before dusk the procession halted, and all at once a group of pavilions and tents sprang up in the midst of the agricultural countryside.

Three of the pavilions, which were exceptionally large and commodious, were made of double layers of thin but tightly woven silk. The commander reserved one for his own use, and the others were assigned to the Rakehells and the Boyntons.

To the surprise of David and of Julian, the two couples were also provided with bedrolls of cotton with silk exteriors, and in addition they were given a number of cushions. "We really can't complain about our treatment," David said, and the others had to agree.

Cooking fires were started and, to the astonishment of the women, who were unaccustomed to the ways of the Middle Kingdom, a delicious meal was prepared within a very short time. They were served with bite-sized chunks of beef and pork, which had been cooked over charcoals and anointed with a pungent but delicate sauce. With the meat they ate stir-fried vegetables, which appeared to have been cooked very quickly and tasted amazingly fresh. Aileen and Alexis found themselves unable to identify the majority of the vegetables that they ate. They had to agree, however, that in spite of the circumstances, the meal was very pleasant.

With their supper they were served large quantities of tea, and when they first tasted it, David was deeply impressed. "This is no ordinary tea," he said. "If the memory in my taste buds is correct, this is the same type that is served at banquets given by the highest-caste mandarins."

"I think you're right," Julian agreed. "Well, it's certainly clear that we're being accorded the treatment given to members of the nobility, and they don't want any harm to come to us."

Breakfast, prepared early the following morning, consisted of leftover rice and vegetables from the previous night's supper, together with more tea. Then, without further ado, the march was resumed.

The terrain remained flat, looking much as it had the previous day, and Julian and David tried in vain to figure for themselves where they were being taken.

"The route we're taking," Julian said, "has been laid out very cleverly. You'll notice that we haven't come through any cities or even any smaller towns of consequence."

"The same thought has crossed my mind," David replied. "We've been no place that we could identify, and I can't believe that that's anything but deliberate. It isn't easy to lay out such a route in a country as populous as the Middle Kingdom."

On the third day of their journey, their location began to be clarified when they came to the bank of an exceptionally broad river that appeared to be at least three-quarters of a mile in width. Its color was a muddy brownish green, and Julian began to piece their whereabouts together.

"I know of only one river in all of China with this stream's particular characteristics, David," he said. "This must be the Yangtze."

David's mind raced. "In that event," he said, "we're undoubtedly being taken to Nanking."

"That makes sense," Julian replied, "a great deal of sense. Nanking is the headquarters of the rebels, which means that we've been abducted on the orders of Yang or of someone close to him in their hierarchy."

"It's as I thought," David said harshly. "We're going to be held for ransom."

Julian nodded.

"It's one of the oldest methods in China for raising money," his cousin told him. "Remember, countless warlords have resorted to kidnapping for ransom when they were low on funds. I'm afraid that we shall have to resist rather strenuously. I'm sure Yang has a fairly good idea of the size of our company and of the business that we do in the Orient. He's certain to hold out for a huge ransom, and I'll be damned if we're going to see the company go bankrupt in order to win our personal freedom."

Ultimately, they came to Nanking, where the harbor was crowded with ships, including several clippers that Julian felt certain he recognized. He had no opportunity, however, to investigate in depth because his captors moved inland from the waterfront and took care to avoid the harbor district.

At last they came to a setting that resembled a smaller version of Peking's Forbidden City. After passing through a gate set in a massive stone wall, their escorts were relieved by troops carrying modern rifles, and the four foreigners were taken to the old imperial palace.

A smartly uniformed young officer who identified himself as an aide to Yang Hsiu-ch'ing appeared on the scene and escorted the two couples to a suite of rooms on the second floor of the palace overlooking the formal gardens that stood at the rear.

The suite, which consisted of a sitting room and dining room, two bedchambers, and separate dressing rooms for each of the ladies, was marvelously comfortable. There were wide, soft divans for sleeping, cushioned three-legged stools, each of them big enough to hold at least two persons, for sitting, and there were a half dozen serving maids assigned to attend to the wishes of General Yang's "guests."

After eating a sumptuous meal, Alexis who was leaning back on a large, cushioned stool, shook her head in wonder. "I feel like an honored visitor, not like a prisoner!" she exclaimed.

Her husband's smile was bleak. "I'm afraid," he said, "our circumstances may be altered for the worse after we have a confrontation with our hosts."

They did not have to wait long for a crisis to develop. Almost immediately after they finished their meal, the aide to Yang returned and addressed them in Mandarin. "I have been instructed by General Yang," he said, "to request that you write to the headquarters of your company in Hong Kong. You will request them to send you the sum of eighteen million silver yuan. Five million for each of the gentlemen, and four million for each of the ladies."

David laughed loudly in shocked disbelief.

Julian, however, remained sober-faced, his expression and manner unchanging. "General Yang," he said to the aide, "appears to be laboring under a strange misapprehension. The funds of Rakehell and Boynton are not unlimited. Eighteen million yuan is a sum so enormous that it would take our associates in Hong Kong at least one year to collect such a sum, and to turn it over to the Taiping rebels would destroy our company and reduce us to the status of paupers."

The aide was in no way impressed. "General Yang," he said, "anticipated that you would react as you have done. He begs to remind you that he has received you in comfort and style. But all of that can be changed very quickly. The worst of our enemies are held in the old imperial prison on the river, and I solemnly warn you, gentlemen, because I have seen the place myself. Do not allow yourselves to be incarcerated there. The cells are partly under water, and living conditions are unfit for humans. As to the ladies," he continued, and paused delicately, "let me only say that the brothels that General Yang maintains for our troops are always in need of recruits."

David sprang to his feet, his fists clenched.

Julian maintained his self-control and was relieved that neither Alexis nor Aileen understood a word of what was being said. "Perhaps General Yang," he said casually, "will be amenable to reason and will be willing to accept a somewhat lesser ransom."

"Perhaps," the aide agreed.

The cousins, both of them experienced Cathay traders, knew that they were letting themselves in for a series of interminable bargaining sessions with the military head of the Taiping rebels, sessions that might drag on for many weeks before they could strike a mutually agreeable sum that they could ask the Hong Kong office to send as ransom.

The aide withdrew, and a glowering David, his fists clenched, said to his cousin, "We're in trouble far more serious than I imagined. What do we do now?"

"For the moment," Julian replied calmly, "we do nothing. The next move isn't ours. It's General Yang's."

Erika von Klausner looked out the high windows of the sitting room of her suite in the old imperial palace in Nanking, and as she gazed at the ships of her merchant fleet gathered in the harbor, she felt a surge of wild elation. Her plan was working perfectly, and soon, when the vessels discharged their cargo, she would be wealthy beyond her wildest dreams. Her clippers and schooners, brigs and junks, all of them flying the Dutch flag, as was their right, had sailed up the Yangtze River in ones and twos over a period of several days. As she had received the reports of their captains, she realized that her good fortune was holding and that she apparently had nothing to fear. Almost none of the ships had encountered any warships, British or American, European or Chinese.

As she intended to tell General Yang this very night, she anticipated no serious problem when the ships left the Nanking harbor. Though the voyage might be prolonged because of the need to avoid other ships, every last one of her ships would reach its destination in safety and would be carrying a cargo worth a fortune.

She went to her dressing room to primp before going on to join General Yang at his apartment in the palace. Pausing to study her reflection in the mirror, she had reason to feel satisfied. Although she was in her forties, she was as attractive as she had ever been, and her years on the Fat Dutchman's estate had done her no harm. As a matter of fact, she had good reason to believe that General Yang was enamored of her, and that, too, gratified her.

Keeping a close watch on the time in order to make sure she was prompt, Erika finally went through the maze of the palace corridors to General Yang's private quarters, which occupied one entire wing overlooking the harbor on the Yangtze to the north and the palace gardens to the south.

General Yang was pacing the length of his sitting room, his face like a thundercloud when Erika entered, and he barely noticed her presence, which he failed to acknowledge. Even one far less sensitive than she would have been aware that he was upset by something.

She did her best automatically to improve his mood. "My dear," she said, "our scheme is working to perfection. You shall soon have the sinews of war you need to defeat the imperial forces for all time."

He did not favor her with a reply and merely grunted. It was a waste of time to pretend that everything was normal.

"What's wrong?" she demanded sharply.

He did not reply in words but instead took her to the rear of the room and pointed out the window into the garden, where she saw two couples wandering down the formal walks and peering at the miniature gardens laid out with meticulous care by gardeners trained in the ancient traditions of Cathay.

"My people went to a great deal of trouble to capture those four," Yang said. "I was certain they'd bring huge sums in ransom money that would enable me to buy the services of more military recruits.

But now—may their ancestors disown them—they're balking at my terms. You know something of the world and its ways. What do you think a Rakehell and a Boynton are worth in ransom money?''

Chills raced up and down Erika's spine, and she found it so hard to breathe that she could scarcely speak. ''You hold Julian Rakehell and David Boynton as captives?'' she asked incredulously.

Yang nodded in obvious dissatisfaction. ''Yes, and their wives, for all the good it does me.''

Erika peered harder at the two couples below, who were unaware of her scrutiny. She recognized both Julian and David, having seen them at the Fat Dutchman's estate when she had still been a helpless concubine there. But it was the sight of Alexis Johnson that caused her pulse to pound. This was the woman she had hired to entrap Julian Rakehell and destroy his reputation. Instead, she had married him and—obviously—had kept her own past secret. She had deliberately crossed Erika's will in order to get him for herself and enjoy the benefits of being a Rakehell wife.

Her eyes narrowing, Erika felt hatred flowing through her. She would show them! She would make them suffer! It would be justice at its very best if she could transform Alexis Johnson Rakehell and young Boynton's wife into concubines on her estate. As for Julian Rakehell and David Boynton—well, she would be in no rush to decide their fate. How she would relish mulling the question of how to dispose of them best!

''I didn't answer you immediately, Yang,'' she said, ''because I was pondering the problem. I'll pay you the sum of ten million yuan in silver if you'll put all four of them into my custody.''

The rebel general made no attempt to conceal his surprise. ''What will you do with them?'' he wanted to know.

''Believe me, I have use~ for them,'' she replied.

''In that case,'' he told ~r smoothly, ''you surely can pay more than ten million silver yuan.''

She was startled, realizing instantly that he was trying to take advantage of her desire to gain control of the prisoners for herself. ''I've already offered you a great fortune,'' she said. ''I can afford no more.''

He detected the eagerness in her voice and shrugged. "Suppose we discuss the matter over supper," he suggested.

They bickered and bargained for hours as they consumed an elaborate seven-course meal. Neither paid any attention to the servants who waited on them, and General Yang's spirits rose immeasureably. He had a potential customer for his captives now, and if he couldn't persuade young Rakehell to pay the ransom demand himself, perhaps he could talk this foolish woman into giving him eighteen million silver yuan for them.

V

Alexis, tired after the long journey to Nanking and knowing nothing of the swiftly gathering crisis, dropped off into a dreamless sleep. But Julian was too tense, too distraught, and sleep would not come. He went into the living room of the suite and peered with unseeing eyes out at the garden. It had become clear to him since the aide to General Yang had made his exorbitant demand that he and David would have to take steps to restore their freedom in the immediate future. But he was uncertain how to begin.

They had no friends or supporters in the hierarchy of the Taiping rebels. On the contrary, they had never dealt with the insurrectionists in any way and knew no one in Nanking.

Julian pondered the problem, his mind going in circles, and he was so deeply immersed in thought that, at first, he failed to hear the faint tapping at the door of the sitting room. The tapping sounded again, and he went to the door and opened it a crack, wishing that he had a pistol or at the very least, a throwing knife.

A liveried servant, an insignificant man of about thirty years of age, nodded and slipped into the room before Julian could stop him. "Rakehell Julian," the man said in a low, intense voice, "you and those who are near to you are in grave danger."

Julian was startled. "What do you mean?" he asked.

"You must take immediate steps to put Nanking behind you," the manservant continued. "You must act now. By morning it will be too late."

Before Julian could reply, the door into one of the adjoining chambers opened, and David came in, having been aroused from his slumber by the murmur of voices in the drawing room. Blinking sleep from his eyes, he absorbed the situation quickly and knew that something serious was happening.

For his benefit, the servant repeated what he had just told Julian.

David's quick, agile mind began to function. "What makes our situation so precarious?" he demanded.

"The woman from Djakarta," the man said, "who is now in Nanking with her many ships, and who is known as van der Luon Anna, has offered General Yang ten million yuan in silver if he will give her possession of Rakehell and Boynton and their wives. General Yang has demanded eighteen million, and they are bickering. But sooner or later, before the night ends, they are bound to reach an agreement. By dawn armed men will come to this apartment, and you and your wives will be taken forcibly on board one of van der Luon Anna's ships and will be taken off to Djakarta."

Julian was startled, astonished to find that the niece of the Fat Dutchman again was seeking vengeance against him for reasons unknown.

David was quick to recognize the threat and immediately decided that the solution of the riddle would have to await a more propitious moment. The man who had brought the warning was right, and it was essential that they depart at once. But how they could leave the closely guarded palace was another matter. "Let us assume," he said, "that you've spoken the truth to us. How do we escape from Nanking?"

The man turned to him, his expression inscrutable. "Put your trust in me," he said.

"Not so fast," Julian told him. "Why should we? How do we know that you aren't leading us into another trap?"

The man did not reply in words. Reaching into a pocket, he withdrew a small smooth chip of polished marble about the size of a man's thumbnail. On the face of it were scratched crude representations of the heads of a pair of oxen.

Julian had once been shown a similar talisman in great confidence by his sister, shortly after Jade had been accepted into membership in the Society of Oxen. He began to understand now.

"Your sister," the man told him, "is one of our number. Your father served us well and faithfully at great risk to his own life when we opposed the British twenty years ago. It is our duty to help those who are related to faithful members of our organization."

Julian exchanged a swift glance with David, and together they arrived at an immediate decision. "Lead and we will follow," Julian said. "Tell us what to do and we will do it."

"Fetch your women," the man said, "and let them cover their hair with cloths so that they can be less readily identified as foreigners. Leave this apartment in silence, and go to the left when you reach the corridor outside."

"One moment," David protested, "Our weapons were confiscated when we were taken prisoner. We have no means of defending ourselves."

A smile lighted the man's face for an instant, and then he sobered again. "Your first need," he said, "is for stealth. Make sure that neither you nor your women make any sound as you go down the long hallway. In due time, when it becomes necessary for you to carry weapons because the danger of conflict threatens, you'll be supplied with arms." Not waiting for a reply, he let himself out of the suite, and the outer door closed silently behind him.

This was not a time to pause, to speculate, to wonder about the many questions that crowded into their minds. They hurried off to their respective bedchambers, where they awakened their wives and briefly explained the situation to them.

Alexis and Aileen proved themselves equal to the sudden emergency and dressed hastily, making sure that they covered their heads with shawls. Then, carrying their high-heeled slippers in their hands in order to avoid creating audible footsteps on the marble floors of the corridor, they accompanied their husbands into the hallway. They started off to the left, as they had been instructed, and went in single file, with Julian in the lead and David bringing up the rear.

The corridor was almost totally dark. The windows on either side let in only a faint outdoor light. No oil lamps or candles burned in the wall holders, and no lights showed under the doors of other rooms that they passed. Groping his way and proceeding very slowly, Julian realized that the darkness was not accidental. Ordinarily, he assumed, oil lamps would have been burning in the hallway, but tonight they had been extinguished by the thorough members of the Society of Oxen, who forgot no details.

Suddenly a wiry hand clamped Julian's wrist. He peered as best he could through the gloom and dimly made out a figure dressed in black.

Alexis's faint gasp alerted him to the fact that she, too, had been accosted by an escort. He could only assume that David and Aileen had received a similar treatment.

Certainly he offered no protest as he followed his guide down the very long corridor. They came to a flight of steps, which they descended slowly, painstakingly, to make sure that none of the escaping quartet stumbled and injured an arm or a leg.

A further surprise was in store. A door was opened, and the four young people found themselves in a large room apparently located on the first floor of the mammoth old imperial palace. There was no artificial illumination in the chamber, but in the faint night light that came in through the windows, the newcomers could see several men and women in the place.

What was significant beyond all else, Julian realized, was the fact that a virtual headquarters had been established by the Society of Oxen under the very noses of the leaders of the Taiping rebellion. A cell of some sort existed in the very place where the rebels planned the military moves and administered the territory they had won.

Strong hands grasped Julian's shoulders and sat him on a low stool. He gathered from tugs and pulls that he was being requested to remove his upper garments. He obeyed without question.

He assumed that Alexis and Aileen were being subjected to a similar treatment, having been conducted by two women behind some lacquer screens. David was seated on another stool, receiving the same treatment as his cousin.

An oillike substance that smelled of walnuts was smeared on Julian's face and neck, arms and hands, and torso. At the same time, another thicker oil was worked into his hair.

Only when he was handed trousers and an upper garment of black cotton, along with a pair of sturdy black boots, did Julian understand. His guess was confirmed when his own wife and Aileen Boynton reappeared, both of them resembling Chinese women—provided that one did not examine them too closely. He, too, was being roughly disguised as a Chinese man, as was David.

Julian grinned at Alexis in the half-light, but neither of them spoke, and the continuing silence was eerie. Then a man pressed a long double-edged dagger with a slender blade and balanced hilt into Julian's right hand, and his relief was infinite. At last he was armed and could act in self-defense if it became necessary!

A tall, husky man, also dressed all in black, whose size and build indicated that he was a native of one of the Middle Kingdom's northern provinces, emerged from the shadows and beckoned abruptly.

The four foreigners immediately went to him, and the women were separated from their husbands and were placed in the care of several competent-looking Chinese women, who followed the tall man out into the dark corridor again.

The men followed, and Julian found himself next to David, who was also armed with a dagger that could be either thrown or used in hand.

They emerged into the open; behind them stood the old imperial palace, while directly ahead was the high stone wall that surrounded the complex of buildings. Julian and David were led to an archway, where a rebel officer armed with a sword and several sentries carrying old-fashioned matchlock muskets were stationed.

All turned their backs to the group and stared off into space as the cousins and their escorts passed throught the gate.

Julian caught sight of his wife and Aileen in the group of women some yards ahead of them and felt another surge of relief. At the very least, through means that he found incomprehensible and beyond understanding, they were now clear of the palace.

He soon discovered, however, that they were not yet out of danger. They walked quickly through the silent, deserted streets of Nanking, most residents having retired hours earlier, and eventually they came to a large open square dominated by a huge pagodalike structure of stone and marble, obviously a house of worship of some sort.

Suddenly a dozen or more Taiping rebel soldiers in dark green uniforms emerged from the shadows at the side of the temple. All were well armed, and they were commanded by an officer who carried a long curved sword.

Julian noted at once that the group of women up ahead were undisturbed. They kept going and were shepherded down a narrow street at the far side of the temple by the burly leader of the Society of Oxen unit.

Taking stock of the situation, Julian knew that in addition to himself and David, his group had two escorts; they were outnumbered by the rebel troops by at least three to one.

But the Society of Oxen member who was in charge did not hesitate. "Attack!" he said softly but distinctly in curt Cantonese. He suited action to words by drawing a straight sword with a double forklike point and charging directly at the rebel officer.

Julian did not hesitate but immediately threw his own knife at a soldier in the first row of the enemy force.

David did the same, and they were gratified to discover that their years of training with the Indonesian weapons continued to stand them in good stead. The two soldiers dropped to the ground, and although it was not possible to determine as yet whether they were killed or wounded, it was obvious that they were out of combat.

The officer, too, went down under the furious charge of his assailant. The fourth member of the group upheld his own honor by dashing forward and slashing wildly with a similar sword. Another of the rebel soldiers toppled to the ground, and two others, panicking, took to their heels and fled.

The technique of fighting with the Indonesian knives had been drilled into Julian and David as children, and they reacted instinctively now, dashing forward and retrieving their knives. Julian saw at a glance that the man at whom he had thrown his blade was dead, so he quickly picked up the soldier's rifle and looked around for another enemy with whom he could engage in combat.

He needed no one to tell him not to fire the rifle. He knew that the sound of gunfire at this time of night would awaken a great many people in Nanking and would complicate the escape effort. But the bayonet attached to the rifle was useful and dangerous, and he lunged at another of the rebel soldiers, who had struck a defensive posture.

One of the escorts lunged at the same man from the opposite side, and the soldier had had enough of combat for one night. Dropping his rifle, he fled from the square, running as though all the dragons of antiquity had descended from the mountains and were pursuing him.

The fight ended as abruptly as it had started. The rebel officer and three of his subordinates lay sprawled on the ground, and the formation of the survivors had been broken by the ferocity of the attack by Julian, David, and their two accomplished escorts.

Within moments the entire square was empty of rebels, except for the still bodies of the four who had been killed. Before proceeding on their way, however, the escorts carefully picked up and carried with them several of the rifles and bayonets that had been dropped by the fleeing soldiers.

The escorts led Julian and David to the same narrow street down which their wives had gone, and they followed it for a considerable distance. They walked rapidly, not slowing their pace until they came to a district of two-story middle-class houses, most of them occupied by minor government functionaries in the employ of the Taiping rebels, officials in the shipping industry, and educators.

To Julian's untutored eye, one house looked exactly like another.

But the escorts stopped at one of these dwellings and tapped out an intricate signal on the door set in the garden wall.

The door opened silently, and the four men were admitted to the interior of the house, which they found to be a beehive of activity behind the heavy drapes of silk that covered the windows. The tall, heavyset leader was present, and the escorts reported to him in detail about the encounter with the rebel soldiers.

He listened carefully, then nodded blandly to Julian and David. "Our confidence in you was not misplaced, I'm glad to say." Having complimented them, he turned to inspect the captured weapons. "These will be useful," he said, "but we will leave them behind here. It will be too great a risk to carry them on our present expedition. The guards at the city gates are certain to be at least doubled and trebled, and the sight of one of these rifles would be enough to expose our entire plan."

He watched the rifles being carried off to another part of the house, and then gestured to Julian and David to go into an adjoining room.

They did as they were bidden and saw two young Chinese women, both exceptionally attractive, both wearing cheongsams, who were sitting on three-legged stools. One was submitting patiently to the plaiting of her long black hair into a single braid down her back, while the other was being attended by a young woman who was applying cosmetics to her face, apparently paying particular attention to her eyes and cheekbones.

Julian gaped in amazement as he finally recognized his wife and Aileen.

"I'm not surprised that you didn't know me," Alexis said with a laugh. "I scarcely recognize myself."

The two new arrivals were ordered to sit, too, and the women went to work on them at once, first attaching long queues of hair to the backs of their heads, and thereafter, applying cosmetics to their eyes in order to give them an Oriental slant.

A wispy beard was glued to David's face, and Aileen found the sight so ludicrous that she giggled helplessly. He was given an ankle-length scholar's gown of black silk to wear and was handed a large leather-bound volume to carry. Opening it, he found it was hollow inside and was intended as a hiding place for the throwing knife that he could no longer reach beneath his scholar's gown.

Julian's disguise was far less elaborate. He continued to wear the same clothes he had been supplied for his departure from the imperial palace, and nothing was done to alter his appearance other than to give him the false hairpiece and apply cosmetics to the outer corners of his eyes.

When all four of the Westerners had been prepared, the tall Society of Oxen leader came and inspected each of them briefly, in turn. He nodded and seemed satisfied. "Be good enough," he said, addressing himself to David, "to translate what I say into a tongue that your wives will understand."

David began to speak rapidly in English.

"In order to leave Nanking successfully," the man said, "we must resort to very considerable subterfuge. The gates are well guarded, particularly now, with prisoners of General Yang's having escaped and some of his own soldiers having been killed this very night. Special care will be taken to make sure that only authorized persons leave the city." He opened his voluminous cape and revealed that he was attired in the uniform of a high-ranking general of the Taiping rebels. "I am leaving Nanking," he said, "in the guise of General Yang's deputy." He gestured toward the two young women. "These ladies are far too attractive for them to escape notice from the guards at the gates. Therefore, we will take advantage of a natural situation and will use it to its fullest extent. They will pose as my official concubines."

The women could only blink when David had translated his words.

"It is urgently important," he continued, "that they act their roles convincingly, showing the fervor expected of a Chinese concubine who depends on her lord and master for all that she is and all that she has in this world."

Alexis knew what was expected of her and nodded confidently. There was no question in her mind regarding her ability to playact the role that she was being called on to assume.

Aileen, however, looked blank and was bewildered. "Forgive my stupidity," she said, "but what does he mean?"

David translated for the leader, who minced no words. "You will do and say nothing," he told her, "until I become aware of your presence. When that happens, you will flirt with me. You will pretend I am your husband, and you will try to ensnare me with your body."

Aileen's cheeks reddened beneath the walnut stain that covered them.

"You, Boynton David," the Society of Oxen chieftain said, "will pose as a scholar who is attached to my retinue. You will say and do nothing, and you will act as befits a mandarin of the first class whose head is in the clouds and whose feet do not descend far enough to touch the earth."

David smiled and nodded. He had known many such scholars in Canton and in Peking, and he looked forward to the opportunity to behave like them. At the same time, however, he wanted to take no needless risks. "Is it possible," he wanted to know, "to supply me with more than one throwing knife in the event that trouble develops and I should need to rely on weapons?"

"By all means," the leader replied, and ordered an aide to bring David several more of the delicately balanced knives.

"You, Rakehell Julian," the leader said flatly, "are the most difficult member of your party to disguise. Therefore, you will become a sedan chair bearer for my concubines. You will take your place at the left rear of the chair, and you will keep your head downcast at all times. Under no circumstances do you want the guards at the gate to look at your eyes. They would be startled by the appearance of the first hazel-eyed Chinese they have ever seen."

His joke relieved the growing tension somewhat, and everyone laughed. But Alexis became thoughtful. "Aileen has blue eyes, and mine are green," she said. "Won't we be noticed?"

A concerned David repeated the question in Cantonese.

The Society of Oxen chieftain was blunt, as he always was. "You, madam," he said, "have other prominent attributes. By calling attention to them in the right way, we can hope to cause the guards to ignore the color of your eyes."

His manner changed abruptly, and he beckoned. "Come," he said. "The time grows short and we must eat before we depart. It may be many hours before we have another opportunity to put food in our bellies."

They followed him into another chamber, where each of them was handed a bowl and a pair of chopsticks. Then, silent attendants went from person to person, passing rice and mounds of bite-sized meat and fish, as well as more vegetables than Aileen and Alexis knew were grown in Cathay. Aileen, who had learned to use chopsticks when working with the Chinese immigrants, handled them adeptly, but Alexis was clumsy, and in spite of Julian's efforts to help her, she was forced to hold her bowl close to her mouth and, holding her chopsticks together, shoveled in the food.

The different approach of the two women to the meal they were served was completely opposite to their overall attitude, however. Alexis regarded the whole experience they were undergoing as a fascinating challenge, and she rose to it, determined to carry out her part to the best of her ability. Aileen, far less worldly and lacking in experience, was frightened.

The leader of the Society of Oxen, who had taken great care not to mention his name, was conscious of the differences in the attitudes that the two young women displayed, and he made mental notes accordingly.

The meal was consumed quickly, the servers insisting on refilling the bowls before they would allow any person making the journey to stop eating. At last the entire group moved to a courtyard, and there, further surprises were in store. A donkey was provided for David, and he took his place next to a similar mount ridden by a Buddhist priest in a flowing saffron robe. A study of the priest's attire revealed several suspicious bulges around the middle, and David knew at once that his companion was no more a Buddhist priest than he himself was a scholar.

As Julian emerged into the courtyard close behind Alexis, the

Society of Oxen chieftain halted him with a gesture and handed him a Colt six-shooter pistol. "You are familiar with this weapon, Rakehell Julian," he said, "and I have no doubt that you are well able to use it should the need arise."

Julian thanked him and put the pistol into his belt, concealing it beneath the voluminous upper garment of black that he wore.

"I'll be close to you at all times," he told his wife and Aileen, "and David will be only a few yards away."

The women nodded silently, and he encouraged them with a broad grin that he was far from feeling before they disappeared into the sedan chair and closed the door behind them.

Three burly chair bearers appeared on the scene and exchanged hearty claps on the back with Julian, whom they were welcoming into their fold. Ranging on either side of the chair, they hoisted it into the air, and each of them rested it on a shoulder seemingly without effort. Julian was surprised that the chair containing Alexis and Aileen wasn't heavier than it was.

The "general" mounted a spirited Mongolian pony, and as he led the group out of the courtyard, a final surprise was revealed. An honor guard of thirty troops, all of them smartly uniformed, mounted, and carrying rifles and sabers, was waiting and fell into line, surrounding the priest, the scholar, the sedan chair, and its bearers.

Julian was impressed by the size of the Society of Oxen force and the care that had gone into the planning for this operation. There were enough men in the detail, all of them heavily armed, to face almost any emergency and to give a good account of themselves in the event that trouble erupted. In the past, he had heard only snatches about the exploits of the Oxen, but now he could truly begin to appreciate them and could understand how, when it had been necessary, they had been able to rule entire provinces until the Imperial Army had been able to establish order in a given area.

The sky grew increasingly lighter as the detail made its way through the streets of the city, and pedestrians who were beginning to appear in appreciable numbers scurried out of the path of the mounted men.

Julian, who was making the discovery that the task of a sedan chair bearer required great stamina as well as strength, nevertheless retained a sharp interest in his surroundings. Watching the reaction of the passersby to the presence of the ostensible general of the Taiping rebels and the members of his armed escort, he came to the conclusion that the citizens of Nanking were anything but fond of the rebels who had taken their city. Perhaps when General Ward attacked the garrison he would find that he had more sympathizers inside the walls than he believed possible.

At last, after spending more than a quarter of an hour traversing the city, the detail saw the high stone wall that surrounded Nanking looming ahead. The general immediately began playacting, and his pony actually pranced as he approached the gate where a score or more of troops were on guard.

An officer of medium rank, followed by two younger juniors, appeared out of the guardhouse set in the wall and, approaching the general's horse, kowtowed before him, making their obeisance in the dirt of the road.

Julian was dumbfounded, finding it hard to believe that any military organization, particularly that of the Taiping rebels, would cling to such an outmoded, ancient tradition.

The general behaved as though he long had been accustomed to such groveling tributes. Dismounting from his horse, he ordered the officers to rise again, and he walked forward to meet them.

The trio bowed before him.

He returned their bow and then said loudly, "Since I wrote the regulations governing the conduct of people leaving Nanking, I know what's expected of me. There," he went on, waving expansively, "sit a priest and a scholar who are members of my suite. They accompany me on all of my trips into the countryside, and, as you can see," he went on with a booming chuckle, "they are the most dangerous of subversives. Both of them are secretly in the employ of the regents of Peking, and they're plotting to overthrow the armies of General Yang."

The three officers and the soldiers under their command laughed dutifully at his somewhat warped sense of humor.

He beamed at them. "In the chair," he said, "are other constant

companions whose services are of a somewhat different nature.''
Turning toward the sedan chair, he called loudly, ''Women! Come
forward!''

Julian's blood froze. In spite of the precise, careful planning, the
Society of Oxen chieftain had made a grave and major error. Alexis
knew not a word of the Cantonese dialect and Aileen had only a
rudimentary knowledge of the language, having worked with the
Chinese in England. Neither woman, however, would be able to
respond to a barrage of questions from the rebel officers. Making the
best he could of an awkward situation, Julian flung open the door of
the sedan chair and said softly, ''The general is calling you. Play
your roles well.''

Alexis, the first to appear, playacted superbly. Ostensibly smoothing
her cheongsam, she ran her hands over her body in a slow-moving
erotic gesture, and then she took tiny, mincing steps as she walked
toward the general, her hips swaying.

The attention of every officer and man of the wall sentry guard
was riveted on her, and even the Society of Oxen members posing as
soldiers couldn't help staring at her, too.

Her performance so far, Julian thought, was perfect.

Aileen, who followed her into the open, was far less self-assured,
and her self-consciousness was obvious as she, too, moved forward.

The general slid his heavy hands around the waists of the women
and pulled them closer to him. ''I suppose,'' he boomed, ''you'll
want to question these dangerous concubines.''

Reacting as though she understood him, Alexis emitted a prolonged,
high-pitched giggle.

Encouraged by her reaction, the Society of Oxen leader dared to
carry his playacting a step farther. His hands became busy as he
caressed the breasts and stroked the buttocks and thighs of the two
supposed courtesans.

Alexis reacted precisely as a genuine concubine would have done:
Simulating intense pleasure, she leaned against the general and favored him with a dazzling smile, all the while making certain, to be
sure, that the three officers of the guard did not see her eyes.

Aileen was startled and embarrassed by the man's crude, unexpected ministrations, and she wriggled in his grasp, trying to break away from him.

Watching the scene closely, Julian wanted to shout to his cousin's wife not to act like a prude and spoil everything.

But the general had judged Aileen's temperament correctly and acted accordingly. Twisting her head toward him, he planted a long, hard kiss full on her mouth. When he released his pressure slightly, he pinched her playfully on the buttocks, slapped her, and pointed to the sedan chair. "For someone of my age," he said with a chuckle, "you're far too eager at this time of the day. Go back and sit down."

The members of the wall guard laughed dutifully again at his supposed humor.

Alexis knew the moment had come to take the bulk of attention from the other woman, so she, too, began to saunter back to the sedan chair, deliberately wriggling her buttocks and again causing every man present to gape at her.

After she had followed Aileen into the confines of the closed chair, Julian responded to a signal from the general and slammed the door behind her. Then he and the other bearers picked up the chair and hoisted it onto their shoulders once more.

The Society of Oxen chieftain quickly remounted his Mongolian pony, knowing full well that the men stationed at the gate had completely forgotten their mission of inspecting each of the persons who was leaving Nanking. Thoughts of lovely, seductive concubines filled their heads, and by the time they recovered, the detail would be long gone. The Oxen general shouted an order, and his entire party was on the move again. Within moments the wall of Nanking was left behind, and they had reached the relative safety of the open countryside.

BOOK VI

I

Jade Rakehell's return to the British Crown colony of Hong Kong created a sensation. As the ship that carried her maneuvered into its appointed space at the extensive docks of the Rakehell and Boynton complex, many employees, from executives to dock workers, were gathering below.

Since learning the news of Jade's disappearance, Lo Fang had worked tirelessly with the Society of Oxen to learn her whereabouts. It was only when Wing Ho in Singapore met up with Jade and Pieter that word was sent back to Lo Fang, and this news traveled to Hong Kong faster than the ship carrying the twosome.

The closely packed ranks of the workers parted to permit Molinda, escorted by Lo Fang, passage to the gangplank that was being lowered. Count Pieter Sabov, standing beside the radiant young woman on the deck, couldn't help noting that the elegant middle-aged Molinda, dressed like Jade in a cheongsam, had a figure that was almost as perfect as that of the far younger woman.

The company workers—among them British subjects and Americans, Malays and Dutch, as well as numerous Chinese—cheered when Jade came ashore and embraced Molinda fiercely. Their roars of approval grew louder when Lo Fang lifted her off the ground and enveloped her in a bear hug.

Pieter, who was presented to the couple, felt increasingly ill at ease. Molinda's wise eyes seemed to bore into him, weighing, evaluating, and measuring, and Lo Fang's expression indicated his belief that no man was good enough to be Jade's lover.

Before the crowd thinned sufficiently for Jade to depart, she had to shake the hands of scores of workers and accept their good wishes. She was deeply touched by their sincerity, and realizing for the first time the degree of regard in which she was held, she had to blink back the tears. As she would subsequently confess, the moment was one of the most emotional of her life.

At last she and Pieter escaped to the executive offices, where Jade discovered to her delight that Molinda had performed wonders during the year she had been away. Her desk was clear, and there were no problems that required immediate attention. "It's almost as though I've never been gone!" she cried.

Molinda smiled gently. "Not precisely," she said, "but our mutual stories can wait. It will take a day or two to assemble your staff and open your house again, so until that time, I insist that you and Count Sabov stay with me. Lo Fang, you'll come to dinner this evening, too, and we'll make it a real celebration."

Demonstrating the rigid self-control that had marked her whole career, Molinda curbed her curiosity and waited until the evening meal to satisfy it. In the meantime, she had to conduct her young guests to her house, and then arrange with her cook for a festive welcoming meal.

The meal they ate that night was one of the most memorable that Pieter had ever encountered. As nearly as he could recall it later, the appetizers included hard-boiled egg served with minced ginger root and soy sauce, tiny Chinese sausages, shredded chicken with cucumber and hot mustard, and dried jellyfish served with white turnips and Chinese parsley in vinegar, sugar, and sesame oil.

There followed a bewildering variety of main dishes. Among them were pork and fish squares, which were prepared with smoked ham, soy sauce, eggs, and flour, and were deep-fried in oil. Also deep-fried were small squares of roast pork, crab meat, and bamboo shoots. They also had one of Jade's favorites, wine-simmered roast duck cooked with tangerine peel and cloves of star anise.

Pieter recalled other exotic dishes unlike any he had ever before encountered. Principal among them was a deep-fried, marinated sweet-and-pungent carp, served with red dates, ginger roots, water chestnuts, bamboo shoots, bacon, lettuce, and parsley. There were vegetables too numerous to mention, and the meal ended with the serving of a traditional pork and mustard cabbage soup, for which Pieter had no room. Jade, however, managed to empty her bowl.

As the young couple ate, happily gorging themselves, Jade told the story of what had happened to her since her capture by pirates after leaving Tientsin on board the junk. Pieter filled in details from his point of view after she reached Djakarta in her narrative, and together they did their best to explain the unique existence they had lived as castaways on the volcanic island. The meal was finished by the time they concluded their tale with an account of what had befallen them in Singapore.

Molinda and Lo Fang exchanged long, significant looks. "You're both fortunate to be alive," the woman said.

"Hereafter," Lo Fang added, "we shall reduce risks to a minimum and you shall be guarded at all times by unseen brethren of the Oxen."

"Only a few days ago," Molinda went on, "Lo Fang learned through sources of his own that the woman who is posing as Anna van der Luon actually put the Fat Dutchman's niece to death and assumed her place. She is Erika von Klausner."

She gave Jade and Pieter no opportunity to explain that they already knew at least a part of Erika's story.

"She is a German noblewoman, an adventuress who was sent to the Orient by Hamburg shipping interests," Molinda explained. "She set her cap for Jonathan Rakehell, and when he failed to propose to her, she lost her reason. She became the total enemy of the Rakehells and the Boyntons. She especially hated me, mistakenly holding me responsible for Jonathan's lack of interest in her, and she almost succeeded in a plot to murder me. I was the Dutchman's protégée after serving on his estate as a concubine, and he was very fond of me. So the attempt to kill me harmed Erika immeasurably because the Dutchman had his own odd and warped sense of justice. He forced her to become a concubine on his estate as a punishment, and she lived there for many years as a slave girl. Perhaps now you can see why she hated you, Jade, and why she also loathed your brother.''

''I know nothing about any feud with Julian. I've been away a long time,'' the girl said.

''So you have.'' Molinda hastily filled Jade in on the details of the marriage of Julian and Alexis, and also of David Boynton's marriage to Aileen Christopher. ''Had you reappeared as recently as five days ago, I would have been forced to tell you that your brother and cousin and their wives were kidnapped by General Yang, the military leader of the Taiping rebels, who intended to hold them for ransom. But Erika von Klausner, still posing as Anna van der Luon, was in Nanking and tried to gain possession of the prisoners. It was necessary for the Oxen to intervene.''

Lo Fang allowed himself the luxury of a slight smile. ''The former captives,'' he said, ''are safe and in good health. The brethren managed to extricate them from Nanking, and they are now traveling southward to meet the Ever-Victorious Army of the American General Ward.''

''Where is his army located?'' Jade asked eagerly.

Lo Fang shrugged. ''All I can tell you,'' he replied, ''is that it is in the field, and I presume it is encamped somewhere south of the city of Shanghai.''

Jade looked down at her hot, steaming tea, her expression dreamy. ''If you please, Lo Fang,'' she said, ''be good enough to inform the Grand Master of the Oxen that I shall be making a formal application to him for guides and a protective escort to take me to the army of General Ward. I've been separated from my brother and my cousin for long enough, and I can think of no meeting place more fitting than the bivouac of the troops who are going to destroy the Taiping rebels and bring peace, at last, to the Middle Kingdom, which has had more than its share of turmoil and upset in recent years. Also, when I was in Peking last, I promised General Tseng and Prince Kung my full support in the fight against the rebels. Now I intend to give it by bringing him the supplies he needs to fight the war.''

Lo Fang turned to Pieter and addressed him deferentially in broken English. ''You go with Missy Jade to visit army, to see brother and cousin?''

Pieter hesitated for a moment, uncertain what to reply.

Jade answered for him, however, and her manner was positive. ''Of course he'll come with me,'' she said. ''We go everywhere together!''

Molinda saw the confusion in Pieter Sabov's eyes and thought she detected a hint of anguish, as well. It was easy enough for a woman of her experience to put herself in his shoes and to understand the complexities of his thinking. He had known Jade first as a concubine on the estate of the Fat Dutchman, and then as his only associate on an island where they lived in constant danger. Now, after another harrowing experience in Singapore, he found himself suddenly in Jade's own world, a world in which she was a personage who wielded enormous power and influence, a woman of great wealth and standing, a member of the secret Society of Oxen, and virtually a princess in her own right.

Pieter's status, however, was much diminished. Instead of being the ''man of the family'' on whom Jade depended for food, shelter, and safety, he was reduced to a minor, secondary role. Inasmuch as he had lost favor with the tsar of Russia, his title had become meaningless, and it was obvious that he had no independent means on which he could live. The money he had acquired on the estate of the Fat Dutchman's niece would seem paltry compared to the fortunes of the Rakehell family. Thus, instead of Jade's needing him, the tables had been turned abruptly, and he was totally dependent on her.

Molinda wondered whether she would be wise to discuss the

matter with her protégée. The root of the problem, she knew, lay in the fact that Jade had become so intimate with Pieter over such an extended period of time that she had reached the point where she took their relationship for granted, and she did not stop to think of the adjustments that her return to civilization required of him.

After pondering, weighing the question from every angle, Molinda finally determined to leave well enough alone.

Jade and Pieter had forged their close relationship with no help from her, and whether they became still closer or were wrenched apart by the restoration of her status was a matter that in no way concerned the older woman. Regardless of what she herself felt, she had to allow them the freedom to work out their own destinies.

II

Sunkiang was
a small, old-fashioned Chinese city surrounded by the customary
high wall. It lay in the heart of an agricultural district where tea and
rice were grown, and where the cultivation of silkworms had
become a high art. It was in this city that General Frederick Ward
had, at the suggestion of Prince Kung, trained his troops for the
battles against the Taiping rebels.

The peace of Sunkiang had been shattered when General Ward
first made the city his headquarters. He and his generals had moved
into the large house that the imperial governor thoughtfully but
hastily vacated, and the people of the town braced themselves for the
presence of the troops.

To their astonishment, however, the soldiers were models of
decorum, and even the regiment of foreign mercenaries behaved
impeccably. The young ladies of Sunkiang remained unmolested;
there was no looting of shops and no terrorization of the citizens. In

fact, even the brothels were inspected, and only those that met Ward's almost impossibly high standards were opened to his men.

Now as General Ward returned to the Ever-Victorious Army from Peking, the high command waited for the battle of Ningpo, where the rebels would next be attacked. General Ward relaxed from time to time, playing a game of Mah-Jongg, somewhat similar to dominoes and played with one hundred and forty-four ivory slabs, or counters. He had been taught the popular Chinese game by General Tseng, and General Li and Tso also were Mah-Jongg enthusiasts.

General Ward was irritated because he lost consistently to his colleagues, and his spirit was so competitive that he could not tolerate the situation. So he taught the three Chinese generals to play poker, and their love of gaming made them widely enthusiastic over the American pastime.

One evening after dinner they were playing poker, and General Ward, chewing on a long, unlighted cigar, was pleased because by far the largest number of chips sat directly in front of him. He scowled, however, when the game was interrupted by the arrival of his aide-de-camp, who was under strict orders that nothing was sufficiently important to interrupt a poker game.

"I'm sorry, General," he said, "but a lady is here to see you, Eurasian, young, and exceptionally pretty. She appears to be someone of standing because she was accompanied by an escort of about forty men, all of them heavily armed with the latest weapons and many of them carrying crates. There's also a man traveling with her, a Russian count, if I understood them correctly—"

"Who is she?" Ward demanded bluntly.

"She says she's a Miss Rakehell and—"

"Show her in," Ward roared. "Don't keep her waiting!"

A smiling General Tseng was already on his feet.

"Keep all of your cards, gentlemen, and remember I have the deal," General Ward told his companions. "We'll continue our game in due time."

Jade came into the room, greeted Frederick Ward warmly, and bowed to Generals Tseng, Li, and Tso. She was acquainted with the latter two but did not know them well; with Tseng, of course, she was well acquainted, though this was not the time or the place for any intimacies.

Pieter was presented, General Ward's aide was sent for a bottle of mild rice wine, and the poker game appeared to have been ended for the night.

Jade answered the questions of the curious generals, giving them an abbreviated version of what had happened to her during the year she had been missing. She was delighted to learn that her brother and cousin were expected any day.

To their great pleasure she told the generals of the arms and ammunition she had brought with her from Hong Kong. Then she inquired about the progress of the war.

Frederick Ward appeared to be concentrating on studying Pieter Sabov surreptitiously, so General Tseng replied to her question.

"If we hold to our schedule," he said, "and there's no reason we shouldn't, the rebels will be crushed by spring. We have three cities still to take—Ningpo, Soochow, and—after they fall—Nanking should drop into our hands like a ripe plum."

"Count," Frederick Ward said abruptly to Pieter, "you look like a military man. Am I correct?"

A fleeting, sad smile crossed Pieter's face. "I was," he said. "I had the honor to serve as second in command of a battalion of cavalry until I fell out of favor with the tsar."

"What was the battalion's designation?" Ward demanded.

"First Tatar."

The general raised an eyebrow and stared at the younger man with growing respect. "Obviously you can ride."

"Tolerably well," Pieter admitted.

"You're a marksman with both a rifle and a pistol, and what's more, you can handle a cavalry saber superbly."

Pieter was embarrassed by the unexpected recital of his military qualifications. "I suppose you might say I'm a fair enough shot," he said. "As to a saber, I believe I grew up with one in my hand."

"On top of everything else," the general went on, "you must have strong command capabilities. It couldn't have been easy to control as wild a gang as the Tatars."

Pieter flushed beneath his heavy tan and could only nod.

Ward whirled around to face Jade and jabbed a finger in her direction. "Do you vouch for this man?"

"Of course! Without qualification," she replied firmly.

Ward turned to Tseng and gave him a significant look. "We may have fulfilled our greatest need. Count," He declared abruptly, turning back to Pieter, "what would you say if I were to offer you command of our volunteer regiment that calls itself the Foreign Devils? They're all combat veterans who know how to ride and shoot, and they're men of several nationalities. There are Englishmen and Americans in the unit, Frenchmen, Portuguese, and Germans. You'll even find a handful of fellow Russians who found the ways of the tsar too dictatorial for their tastes."

Pieter stared at him. "I find it very hard, General, to answer hypothetical questions, particularly when details are lacking."

General Ward liked the younger man's style and became even more enthusiastic. "I'm prepared to offer you a full colonelcy in the Imperial Army. You'll be paid one thousand silver yuan per month, and you'll get an equal sum for expenses. If you want to make a lifelong career of the army, I'm reasonably sure that General Tseng would be delighted to have you serving with him."

"That's correct," Tseng declared. "I would be honored to continue your commission as a colonel, Count Sabov, and I assume that, in due course, you would rise to the rank of general."

Pieter appeared to be dazed by the offer. "How long a time would you give me to reply, General Ward?" he asked.

"You and Miss Rakehell will be our guests here in Sunkiang," the American replied, "so I'll give you until the time tomorrow morning that we finish breakfast. That's when I'll make my customary inspection of my troops, and if you accept, I'll swear you in immediately and take you along to your regiment."

"Thank you, General." In a quiet, subtle way, Pieter took charge of the situation. "If you'll forgive us, gentlemen, I need to discuss this matter with Miss Rakehell." He took Jade's arm, bowed to each of the four generals in turn, and then withdrew with her.

Behind them they could hear Ward's voice. "I have the deal, and I'm raising all of you five yuan. How many cards do you want?"

The waiting aide-de-camp diplomatically showed the young couple to adjoining bedchambers on an upper floor.

Pieter peered out of the windows and then walked unannounced into the bedroom where Jade had unpacked her bags and changed from her traveling attire. "There's a garden below," he said. "Let's go down there."

She nodded and accompanied him. There was no need for words because she realized their relationship was moving swiftly toward a climactic resolution of the problems that had plagued it.

For a time they wandered aimlessly in the gardens, which were not particularly well tended, and when they came to a stone bench, Pieter spread a handkerchief on it so Jade would have a place to sit. "I'm not certain where to begin," he said, "except to tell you that when we left our island I more or less expected that we'd be spending the rest of our lives together. In brief, I took it for granted that we'd be married."

Jade started to interrupt.

He held up a hand to silence her. "Please," he said, "this isn't easy, so let me finish what I have to say. When we reached Singapore, I began to sense your very special place in the world, and when we arrived in Hong Kong, the knowledge swept over me like a tidal wave. Now I realize how ridiculous it would be for me, a nobody, a refugee from his homeland, with no prospects for gainful employment, to ask one of the greatest heiresses on earth to marry me. I'm sure you can appreciate that my mind and my spirit have been whirling, and I'm not sure where I stand. All I know for certain is that I love you, and I hope that you reciprocate my love."

Usually coolly controlled, Jade found it impossible to reply unemotionally. "You came into my life," she said, "at a time when I most needed a friend, when I was desperate for help. Not once did you fail me, and when we began to live together it was a natural extension of our feelings for each other. I've been with you so much that I have become very fond of you, Pieter, but I honestly don't know whether I love you. I need time to sort out my feelings, and time to think. I—I've taken it for granted that you'd enter the company in a high executive position. I haven't mentioned the idea to you because I wanted to discuss it with my brother and my cousin first, but I have no doubt they'll approve."

"I'm not at all certain that I approve," he said dryly. "I don't enjoy the prospect of being known as Jade Rakehell's lover, whom she felt she had to take into her company."

She gestured impatiently. "What do you care what jealous people say about us? There's bound to be gossip." She saw his expression and became penitent. "I'm sorry, Pieter. I'll try harder to see this situation through your eyes."

"Thank you," he said. "I was trained to be a soldier, and I've spent the better part of my life in uniform. So General Ward's unexpected offer appeals to me enormously."

"Of course it does," she murmured.

"There's no doubt in my mind that I would perform well as the commander of a cavalry regiment of Europeans and Americans. Not only would I be doing what I know best, but I'd be performing a useful function, helping the imperial forces to win a war against the Taiping rebels and then, afterwards, to keep the peace." He twisted toward her on the bench and put his hands on her shoulders as he looked hard at her. "What do *you* think I ought to do, Jade?"

She sighed and regarded him steadily. "I think that you'd be far happier as a colonel in the army than you'd be as an executive at Rakehell and Boynton. Am I right?"

Pieter nodded slowly. "Yes," he said, "you're correct. Because I believe that each of us has a destiny to fulfill, and by becoming an officer again I can lead the life I was intended to lead. But I must attach one condition to this stand. Would you be prejudiced against me in any way if I accepted a commission from General Ward?"

"Oh, no," she replied quickly.

"I understand your need to get your bearings, to know what you feel and what you think and where you stand," he said. "I won't be impatient, and I'm willing to give you all the time you may need and want to find yourself. Rest assured that I'll repeat my proposal of marriage from time to time, and I shall live in hope that one day you'll give me an affirmative answer.''

He was being so generous, so sweet, that she reacted by curling her arms around his neck and kissing him. When they drew apart, she said, ''You deserve a wife who puts you first in her life, Pieter, ahead of everything else. And that includes the business of being a Rakehell. I'll consent to marry you only if I'm certain in my own mind and heart that you'll always be first there. It's what you deserve, and I won't permit you to settle for less.''

They embraced and kissed again, and then with one accord they went upstairs, where they went to the same bedroom and spent the night together, regardless of the impression the act might create on Frederick Ward and the Chinese generals.

The following morning, when they went down to breakfast arm in arm, they saw General Ward in action when Pieter said to him, ''I've reached my decision, sir. I've made up my mind to join you.''

His breakfast forgotten for the moment, Ward began to bellow orders.

Before Pieter quite knew what was happening to him, various underlings appeared with portions of the uniform that he was obliged to don, and when he was fully dressed in it, General Ward, taking no chances that he might change his mind, ordered him to raise his right hand and repeat the oath of office. Only when he was duly sworn in to the Imperial Army as a colonel was he allowed to sit and eat his breakfast.

To Jade's amusement, he had no opportunity to enjoy the meal, however. Frederick Ward glanced repeatedly at his watch and drummed his fingers on the table.

Recognizing his impatience, Pieter announced his readiness to be presented to his regiment.

Within moments he, Ward, and the three Chinese generals departed, leaving Jade sitting alone at the breakfast table. She was by no means unhappy, however, and she smiled as she thought of the eager expression she had seen on Pieter's face as he had gone off with his new commanding general.

Pieter did not return for twelve hours, and Jade didn't see him again until she was dressing for dinner that evening. Then he came into her bedchamber, dusty, obviously tired and hungry, but bubbling with enthusiasm.

"My regiment," he said, "has the opportunity to become something unique in the military annals of Cathay. Every last trooper in the unit is a veteran of combat, a soldier who understands discipline and does what he's told. What's more, all of them ride like demons! I put them to the test this afternoon, jumping their horses over fences and across gullies, and without exception, they passed with flying colors."

"If I know you," Jade said, "you set the example for them by performing the tests first."

He nodded a trifle sheepishly. "Well," he said, "they had to be shown what to do, after all."

He couldn't understand why she laughed so heartily.

At dinner that night, General Ward, still delighted by his acquisiton of a new commander for his regiment of mercenaries, told the couple the news for which Jade had been waiting: Her brother, her cousin, and their wives would arrive late the following afternoon in Sunkiang.

She found it difficult to sleep that night, and the following day the hours dragged slowly. A surprise awaited her in midafternoon when Pieter came to the house at the head of a column almost five hundred strong. He and his regiment, he announced, would escort her out of the city to meet her relatives. He had a mare for her, and he also provided her with a sidesaddle that enabled her to wear her cheongsam.

Then with the Foreign Devils riding four abreast behind her, she headed for the city gates that faced to the north with Pieter on her right and the regimental standard-bearer on her left. A trumpeter sounded a call, and the city gates were opened as the regiment approached.

Jade eagerly scanned the horizon as she searched for her approaching relatives.

All at once she caught sight of the large party moving across the open countryside. After reaching territory safely held by imperial forces, the Rakehells and Boyntons had been able to wash off the temporary dyes from their hair and skin, and Jade instantly recognized her brother.

She urged her horse to greater speed, riding as rapidly as she could sidesaddle, and when she drew nearer, she raised a hand in greeting.

Julian and David responded, both of them grinning broadly, and as the two groups drew nearer to each other, Jade realized that the wives of her brother and her cousin, whom she had yet to meet, were concealed in a large sedan chair caried by four sturdy bearers.

Dismounting before Pieter could come to her assistance, she raced forward on foot, covering the last yards that separated her from her loved ones.

Julian and David grasped each other's wrists, using both hands to make a crude seat, and when Jade drew near they hoisted her into the air. As she slid her arms around their necks to steady herself, all three laughed hilariously. There were tears in Jade's eyes, too, as the trio went through the motions of a greeting ritual they had observed since earliest childhood.

Alexis and Aileen emerged from the sedan chair and looked in stunned amazement at the horseplay. Pieter Sabov, too, was startled by the behavior of the three heads of the vast Rakehell and Boynton enterprises.

"Put me down!" Jade demanded, kicking her heels frantically as the two men swung her higher and higher off the ground.

"You know the formula," Julian told her. "Say it!"

"Oh, all right," she replied with a sigh. "Julian is stronger than I am and David is smarter. Does that satisfy you?"

"Completely," David replied as they released her.

With her feet once more safely on the ground, Jade looked at each of them in turn. "I lied," she said equably. "I didn't mean a word of it." Then she threw her arms around them in turn, exchanging hugs and kisses. All three were laughing, but their eyes were moist.

Eventually Julian and David recovered sufficiently to present their wives to Jade, and she in turn introduced Pieter to her relatives.

Herself very attractive, Alexis believed Jade was one of the most beautiful women she had ever seen. Aileen, enjoying the family warmth of the reunion, shared Alexis's feeling. "I've never seen anyone quite like her," she said. "I have an idea that she's unique in all the world!"

Jade greeted the burly Society of Oxen leader who had been responsible for the escape of his charges from Nanking, and it was obvious from her greeting that she was well acquainted with him.

All of them mounted their horses again for the ride into Sunkiang, and everyone was speaking simultaneously, making it impossible to understand a word of the babble. "As president of the company," Julian said, raising his voice, "I demand that you be recognized by the chair before you gain the floor."

"Never mind all that," Jade replied rudely. "How are Papa and Elizabeth?"

"They were in the best of health when we last saw them," Alexis told her," and they'll certainly be wild with joy when they learn that you're safe."

"I wrote to them the day that Pieter and I reached Hong Kong," Jade said, "and my note went off early the following morning on board a steamer that was making a direct run across the Pacific to San Francisco. They should be getting my letter before too long."

When they reached Sunkiang, they discovered that General Ward, as thoughtful as ever, had provided them with a private dining room for their family reunion. There, over a long, leisurely supper, they exchanged news of what had happened during the year they had been separated.

Alexis and Julian were particularly interested in the accounts of Erika von Klausner, who had been masquerading as Anna van der Luon, and David listened intently to that part of Jade's and Pieter's tale, too.

"Now I understand," Julian said, "why we were in such mortal danger when we encountered her in Nanking. We're eternally in the debt of your Society of Oxen for helping us to escape from the vengeance of the woman."

"We haven't seen the last of her," Jade said, casting a momentary pall on the group. "I don't know how or when she'll appear again in our lives, but rest assured she will."

All three of the young women made conscious efforts to become better acquainted, and as the evening progressed, they became increasingly relaxed in one another's company. Pieter Sabov felt uncomfortable, regarding himself as an outsider, something of an intruder. But Julian and David went to great lengths to put him at his ease, and their wives, too, were conscious of their obligations as Rakehells and Boyntons and did their best to include him in the family group.

That night Jade slept with Pieter for the last time prior to her departure in the morning. She had stopped at the ancestral estate in Canton on her northward journey to Sunkiang to pray at the tombs of her mother and grandfather, and now she was heading directly for Hong Kong, anxious—as were Julian and David—to take personal control of the company's affairs again.

"Dear Pieter," she said gently, "we've walked a long, tortuous path together, and you shall be ever-present in my thoughts during this period of our separation."

"I hardly need to tell you," he replied, "that you'll be in my mind and in my heart every moment of every day."

Jade clung to him. "I must confess to you," she said, "that I find just the thought of our separation so painful that I already miss you dreadfully. But I mustn't complain. I know it's right for you to pursue your own vocation, and you're in the right place. I wish you every success, and I know you'll have it. By the time this campaign ends, I'm sure you'll be promoted to the rank of general."

"What concerns me is you," he replied, "not my military career."

"Seeing Julian and David again has helped me to gain a proper perspective," Jade told him. "I can see myself and my future far more clearly than I could before, and I can promise you, Pieter, that whenever you come for me, I'll be waiting for you."

III

As always, the port of Ningpo, located near the mouth of Hangchow Bay in northeastern Chekiang Province, was busy. The ancient walled city, virtually unknown in the West, was a vital key in the domestic trade of the Middle Kingdom. Textiles, tea, and a variety of agricultural products moved in and out of the port on barges and junks in a steady flow, and the Taiping rebels, recognizing the importance of Ningpo to their cause, had established a strong garrison there.

General Frederick Ward and Colonel Pieter Sabov sat on their horses, shielded by the double ring of hills that surrounded Ningpo, and looked down in silence as they studied the city. They paid virtually no attention to the sampans, junks, and barges that crowded the river; instead they concentrated their full attention on the height of the wall and the breadth of the plain that extended into the open countryside beyond it.

"Well, what do you think, Sabov?" Ward demanded.

Pieter tugged at the stiff visor of the cap that shielded his eyes from the rays of the late morning sun. "As I see the situation, General," he replied slowly, "we're in for a hard fight, no matter what tactics we employ."

The general chuckled mirthlessly. "No question about that. The latest information from the spies we've sent into the city indicates that the garrison has a total strength of at least ten thousand, and the most combatants we can muster are fewer than six thousand. Regardless of what we do, we're bound to be outnumbered approximately two to one."

"The difference in numbers," Pieter said thoughtfully, "doesn't worry me unduly. From what I've read of the Opium War and of the more recent foreign war, the Europeans were badly outnumbered, but by using superior strategy and superior weapons, not to mention vastly superior leadership, they won every battle. I don't see why we shouldn't repeat that record."

Ward grinned bloodlessly. "All right," he said. "We have fifty-five hundred men waiting in these hills for orders. What will we tell them to do?"

Pieter stared down at Ningpo again. "I'll grant you, General," he said, "that the odds are tilted a little more in the direction of the Taiping rebels this time. They have fifteen hundred horsemen, so in sheer numbers their cavalry is three times the size of my regiment. But what stands in our favor is that it needs to be employed if it's going to be effective."

The general had a glimmer of what the younger officer had in mind. "Go on," he said.

"You've beaten the rebels sufficiently often for them to exercise great caution when they face you. That means they've got to be lured into battle. My idea is very simple. I knock on the city gates of Ningpo with my regiment. The bulk of the army will remain concealed. The rebels will see five hundred mounted men gathered in the plain outside their wall, and the target will look especially attractive because the regiment is composed completely of pale-skinned foreign devils. I'm hoping they'll send their entire brigade of cavalry out to crush us once and for all and to administer a devastating defeat to us."

"What then?" Ward demanded.

"Somehow—and this is the trickiest part of the entire operation—I must maneuver my troops in such a way that I place them between their own cavalry and the city walls. Their high command watching the battle from the heights of the walls becomes convinced that if they attack me from the rear they'll have me surrounded and can destroy my entire regiment. So they send their foot troops on a sally into the plains beyond the walls, as well."

Ward, who had been scowling, suddenly brightened. "Aha!" he said. "Now I see what you have in mind. The moment the rebel infantry is committed to combat, the bulk of our army makes its appearance, swoops down from the hills on the double, and engages the enemy in full combat."

"That's my plan, sir," Pieter said.

Frederick Ward's fingers drummed a tattoo on his saddle. "It might work," he said, speaking aloud to himself.

"I'm sure it would," Pieter told him. "As you know far better than I, sir, without special training, Chinese troops don't act, they react."

"You've summarized them in a nutshell, Colonel," Ward said vigorously. "What you're suggesting is that when I move out of the hills with the corps of my three Chinese generals, I strike as hard and as quickly as I can."

"Correct, sir."

"You've assigned yourself one mighty rough task, Sabov," the general told him. "While you're waiting for me to march out of the hills and engage the enemy in combat, you're forced to hold off the rebel cavalry and, at the same time, immobilize their infantry. Yet you can't overpower either force because they'll race back inside the gates, and after they slam them shut, they can hide behind their walls again and our whole tactical plan will be washed away."

"That's a very fair estimate of my assignment, General," Pieter said calmly.

"Do you think you can carry it off successfully?" Ward demanded.

Pieter remained calm and unflustered. "If I didn't, General, I wouldn't have suggested the entire scheme."

Suddenly a broad grin split Frederick Ward's face. "By God! It *will* work!'' he exclaimed. ''We'll do it!'' Without further ado, he turned and galloped back to his army's bivouac area, with Pieter close behind him.

Immediately after they reached headquarters, they met with Generals Tseng, Li, and Tso and the officers of their respective staffs. Everyone present agreed that the plan was sound, on condition that the Foreign Devils regiment perform the arduous task assigned to it.

Immediately after the meeting was dismissed, Pieter, who was cheerful and unworried about the outcome, assembled his entire unit and explained what he had in mind.

He had planned on ending his talk on an inspirational note, but that proved unnecessary. Once the battle-hardened mercenaries understood what was expected of them, they cheered. Here, at last, was a chance for them to prove their mettle.

Word of the overall plan for the impending battle spread quickly through the ranks of the Ever-Victorious Army, and General Ward, afraid that some unseen, unknown enemy espionage agent might be lurking in his camp and might carry word of the scheme to the rebels, decided to attack immediately.

Within moments part of the army was on the move, with the three Chinese corps remaining hidden from the vision of those below in Ningpo behind the crests of the hills to the west of the city.

The commanding general and his immediate surbordinates solemnly shook hands with Pieter. ''May the best of good fortune attend you, Sabov,'' Ward said. ''If you carry out this maneuver successfully, you'll win a permanent place for yourself in the military annals of the Middle Kingdom.''

Pieter rode to the head of his waiting column and there gave the order to his regimental bugler. ''Advance!'' he called.

The Foreign Devils appeared at the crest of the hills and rode at a slow canter in strict formation down toward the walls of Ningpo.

Rebel officers lined the ancient thick walls of Ningpo, studying the approaching Foreign Devils through their glasses, and as Pieter watched them conferring excitedly, he chuckled quietly. The enemy, he thought, was already nibbling at the bait.

Holding up a hand to indicate a lessening in the rate of march, he reduced his own horse's gait to a stately walk. Five hundred men behind him did the same thing.

Pieter well realized that the decision on when the battle would be joined was no longer in his hands. The leader of the Ningpo garrison would determine the initial success or failure of his ambitious scheme.

When Pieter and his vanguard reached a point about a quarter of a mile from the plain, approximately one-half mile from the actual walls of Ningpo, the gates slowly opened and the defending cavalry began to swarm into the open.

Pieter was elated. His scheme was working! As he watched the ever-increasing numbers of the enemy riders appearing on the plain and heading toward the hills, however, he suffered doubts for the first time. He had not realized how large a force fifteen hundred cavalry-men constituted, and the Taiping rebels, at least from a distance, looked fiercely martial beneath their banners flying from bamboo poles, with the ornamental ribbons on their old-fashioned lances fluttering as they increased their speed to a gallop.

He was encouraged when he saw the entire enemy column veering to the left. Obviously the rebel cavalry commander had decided on a tactic of attacking him obliquely, rather than head on. "Wheel to the right!" he called.

His bugler promptly sounded the battle call, and the crisp, clear notes floated on the soft breeze of an autumn afternoon in Cathay.

The highly trained regiment obeyed instantly, and the entire column swung to the right as they left the hills and reached the flat plain that stretched to the city gates.

It appeared to the high command of the Taiping rebels on the heights of the Ningpo wall that these despised foreigners, representatives of the hated Frederick Ward, were taking an evasive action in an attempt to avoid battle.

Vastly encouraged and seeing an opportunity to strike a decisive blow in the initial phase of the combat, the high command ordered its infantry to join in pursuit of the enemy horsemen.

Pieter felt a sense of deep satisfaction. The foe had taken the bait.

He bided his time, waiting while regiment after regiment of semi-uniformed rebel foot soldiers poured through the gates of the city into the open. Some were clad in uniforms of the rebel forces, while others wore only armbands as identification. Most important of all, Pieter noted that the majority were armed with hopelessly old-fashioned breech-loading muskets, rather than modern rifles. He suspected that the majority were untrained volunteers, attracted to the rebel cause by the mysticism of H'ung Hsiu-chüan, and that they would be easy enough to scatter when the appropriate moment came.

That moment had not yet come, however, and until it did, he chose to ignore the infantry, regarding them as rabble.

The rebel cavalry constituted the only real danger, and he half-stood in his saddle as he rode, inspecting the enemy horsemen carefully.

As he had more or less anticipated, the rebel riders had moved into a very tight formation. Their commander obviously intended to employ his entire unit as a hammer to strike a single hard blow at the Foreign Devils.

It was a simple enough tactic to counter such a move quickly and effectively, and Pieter ordered his unit to string out, leaving ample space between the individual horsemen. The experienced troops had anticipated just such a command, and they executed the move smoothly and efficiently.

The rebels, noting nothing unusual about the move, continued to advance in a unit that was bunched together. The only sign of caution that the rebels displayed was that they slowed their pace from a gallop to a walk.

Evidently the rebel leader expected the regiment to defend itself against the assault that he planned to execute at his leisure. But Pieter had other ideas. "Charge!" he shouted as he drew his saber and pointed it toward the main body of the enemy cavalry.

His bugler blew the exciting call, the most challenging maneuver that a cavalry unit could perform. In an instant, five hundred European horsemen were thundering toward the foe, all of them wielding sabers. There was no reasonable way they could miss their target, Pieter told himself, and then, suddenly, he was immersed in the heat of battle. He slashed left and right as his stallion plowed into the solidly massed ranks of Mongolian ponies. His men, too far apart to be successfully counterattacked, did the same, and the enemy brigade was thrown into chaos.

As many as four hundred rebel horsemen were unseated in the wild, grim charge, and many of that number lost their lives.

When the Foreign Devils had broken through the rear ranks of the enemy, Pieter reversed their charge, and they galloped back up the plain, again wreaking havoc on the rebel riders' formation as they wielded their sabers with deadly efficiency.

Now, Pieter decided, was the moment to attack the infantry, and he sent his unit still advancing swiftly into the massed ranks of foot soldiers. There the regiment created more havoc, and the result was mass carnage, rather than an actual battle.

The poorly trained Taiping rebel foot soldiers, most of them finding their ancient muskets useless, threw down their arms and tried in vain to get out of the path of the hard-riding horsemen.

Pieter's maneuvers had succeeded beyond his wildest hopes, and he invented new tactics to meet his improved situation, using his regiment as a pendulum that swung first to the left against the enemy cavalry, then to the right against the untrained foot soldiers. He was so busy that he had no chance to observe the approach of General Ward's infantry but the sharp crackle of rifle fire told him that the corps of Generals Tseng, Li, and Tso had joined in the battle.

As Pieter looked up, he suddenly saw General Ward himself mounted on his large stallion leading the infantry vanguard. He was leaning forward in his saddle, brandishing his bamboo cane over his head, and obviously was enjoying the experience.

He was taking a great risk, one that commanders of his rank and stature seldom assumed. But Pieter understood his reasons. The infantry maneuver he was leading was delicate, depending completely on its timing if it hoped to succeed, and the only way he could make certain that his maneuver meshed with those of the regiment of Foreign Devils was to take personal charge of the column.

Their eyes met, and they recognized each other at the same moment. Pieter grinned as he raised his saber in salute. The general's timing had been absolutely perfect, and a victory over the Taiping rebels was assured. General Ward, enjoying himself enormously, laughed aloud as he returned the salute with his own cane.

Dozens of officers and men of the Ever-Victorious Army, Chinese and foreigners alike, witnessed the exchange and had good cause to remember it. The pair were two happy warriors who had completed an exceptionally difficult exercise and were enjoying the moment of triumph. That moment seemed frozen in time.

Then tragedy struck.

A sea of retreating Taiping rebels swept across the field and, like locusts attacking ripe grain, seemed to consume everything in sight. Before Pieter Sabov quite realized what was happening, before he had an opportunity to extricate himself, he was completely surrounded by rebel soldiers, and one of them took aim from a distance of only a few feet with an old-fashioned horse pistol and put a bullet between his eyes. He died instantly, toppling from his saddle and dropping to the ground as though felled by a heavy weight.

The horrified Frederick Ward instinctively started forward, intending to help the young officer, and was himself surrounded by the panic-stricken rebels. Even the most ignorant of them could not help but recognize him as the commander in chief of the imperial forces, and in their frustration and rage a score of them attacked him simultaneously, some of them shooting their muskets, others using their clumsy, old-fashioned weapons as clubs and beating at him with the butts. He, too, was unseated, and when his body was recovered a short time later, it was found not only to be riddled with bullets but to have been stabbed innumerable times with bayonets, as well.

The imperial forces, with General Tseng assuming temporary command, occupied Ningpo and sent the survivors of the rebel garrison on a long march to Peking as prisoners of war. Most were destined to die on the road, but their captors showed them no compassion. They had killed General Ward and the army's most promising colonel.

That night General Tseng sent a victory dispatch to Prince Kung in which he informed the regent of victory and went on to give him the deplorable news of the loss of General Ward and Colonel Sabov. Then, knowing that Pieter had been close to Jade Rakehell, he stayed up until the small hours of the morning composing a letter to her. As he later confessed, it was the most difficult task he had ever performed.

IV

If Hong
Kong, with its deep-water docks, huge warehouses, and ever-increasing manufacturing plants, was the heart of Victoria Island, the Peak, the mountain that rose toward the sky on Victoria Island, was the heartbeat. The British governor-general maintained his official residence partway up the Peak, and so did virtually all of the high-ranking British colonial officials. The traders, shippers, and international bankers who were making the name of Hong Kong renowned throughout the world also lived on the Peak, where they enjoyed cooler weather in the subtropical climate and where they could relax and look out at the magnificent view of the harbor below and at Kowloon, an extension of Hong Kong, on the mainland across the bay.

The large gracious home that Jade Rakehell maintained on the Peak, complete with its informal gardens and extensive stables, fully manned by a staff of well-trained servants, was a beehive of activity. Julian Rakehell and David Boynton came and went all day, using their quarters in the mansion as their business headquarters while in Hong Kong. It was easier, David explained, to hold meetings there then to strain the facilities at the headquarters offices in downtown Hong Kong, which were too crowded to permit privacy.

Alexis and Aileen led equally busy lives. They were entertained by the wives of businessmen and colonial government officials, and they went off daily to lunches, teas, and receptions, occasionally reciprocating by asking their hostesses to join them at the house for an outdoor lunch in the garden.

Only Jade's private quarters were silent, and there was virtually no activity there. A butler appeared three times a day with meals, which he later removed with the food untouched. Serving maids entered the suite to change the bed linen and draw baths for the mistress of the house, but they rarely saw her.

Jade had withdrawn when she had received General Tseng's letter informing her of the death of Pieter Saboy, and no one, not even the members of her family, had seen her since that time.

"Leave her alone," Molinda had advised. "She must be allowed to grieve in her own way. When she's ready, she'll come back into the world again."

Jade spent most of her time sitting on a balcony, concealed by a trellis, and staring out toward the harbor. One of the maids who was interrogated at length by a deeply concerned Alexis reported that her mistress showed signs of life only when a Rakehell and Boynton ship entered or left the harbor.

Days became weeks, and finally David sent her a brief note on a tray one noon. His message was succinct: "We have news regarding Erika von Klausner that will be of interest to you."

That evening when Julian and Alexis, David and Aileen gathered in the spacious library on the ground floor for aperitifs before dinner, Jade unexpectedly appeared and stood on the threshold. She was dressed in white, the Chinese color of mourning, her Cheongsam was white, as were her silk stockings and shoes, and even her earrings and a large bracelet on one wrist were of white enameled gold.

Conversation halted abruptly when the quartet saw her.

Jade spoke with careful deliberation, apparently having rehearsed what she intended to say. "I'm sorry," she said, "if my withdrawal distressed any of you. I went off to be alone because I was not fit company, and I had to find myself and recover my equilibrium by myself."

"We understand," Alexis interrupted softly.

"Thank you, but let me finish," Jade continued. "I loved Pieter more than I knew, more than I believed possible. We shared so many dangers that we became inseparable. It was as though we had one mind, one heart, one soul. I thought my own world had come to a sudden end when I learned that he was killed in action. Now, as I regain my senses and my perspective, I know that I must live and I must exist in the present, and not in the past that I shared with him. I loved him so much that, for a time, I thought I could never love again. Then I remembered what happened to Papa. My mother, Lai-tse lu, was the great love of his life, and they had a union that was unique and extraordinary. But he was forced to continue to live after she died, and ultimately he found happiness with Elizabeth. I don't think it's possible to compare my love for Pieter with any feelings I may have toward someone else in the future." She drew a deep breath, folded her hands, and sank into a deep leather armchair.

Julian broke the ensuing silence. "Pink gin?" he asked.

She shook her head. "No, thank you. I have no need for anything that strong. I'll take a small glass of sack, if you please."

"Glad to oblige," her brother told her, and went to the bar set up on a table in the corner, where he poured her a glass of sherry.

"There's just one thing more," Jade said. "I'll be deeply obliged if you don't mention Pieter to me again. I know I have your sympathy, just as you've already shown me your patience and tolerance." She looked around the room at all of them, forced a smile, and sipped her drink.

David Boynton cleared his throat. "I suppose," he said, "you're ready to listen to the latest news on Erika von Klausner."

Jade nodded.

"She made a deal of some sort with the Taiping rebels," David explained. "Her whole fleet has been sailing into the harbor here, arriving in ones and twos, and all of them have their holds crammed with goods from rebel-held territory. Cotton and tea, silks and porcelains."

Totally absorbed, Jade raised an eyebrow. "Why in the world did she direct her fleet to come here, rather than go to Djakarta.?"

"Remember," Julian said, "the market here is far more extensive than it is in Djakarta. I would assume that she figured she would get a better price for the merchandise here."

"That's where she made her major error," David said with a dry chuckle. "As fast as she's put the various goods on the market, we've bought them up. We've used strong-arm tactics, you might say, to keep other bidders from entering the market for them, and we've bought the merchandise at rock-bottom prices."

"In other words," Julian added, "if she expected to make a killing, she's been sorely disappointed. At best, she'll break even, and I wouldn't be surprised if she takes a very considerable loss."

"Not only that," David went on, "but her whole policy must be in a state of near-collapse. The Taiping rebels are doomed. General Ward and Colonel Sabov didn't die in vain. When news of Ward's death became public, General Charles Gordon immediately offered his services to Prince Kung, and he has taken command of the Ever-Victorious Army."

Jade was surprised. "The British column that succeeded in entering Peking three years ago was led by a General Charles Gordon, an officer who was not yet thirty years old. Surely it isn't the same man?"

"Indeed it is," David told her. "In the intervening years he's stayed on here in the Orient, and he's developed a great liking and appreciation for the civilization and culture of the Middle Kingdom."

"What's more," Julian declared, "he's every bit as energetic and hard-driving as General Ward. He's given the army no chance to sit around moping, mourning the passing of Ward and of Colonel Sabov. The army is already investing Soochow, and it's certain to fall. When that happens, Nanking will be a plum ripe for plucking whenever Gordon wishes."

"I'm glad," Jade said quietly. "Pieter would have been very pleased to know that the army was that successful."

David knew better than to dwell on the subject of Pieter Sabov. "The important news about Erika von Klausner," he said, "is that she wants to see me, and I've made an appointment with her for tomorrow morning."

Jade was astonished. "You have?"

David nodded grimly. "She's coming to see me as Anna van der Luon," he said. "Surely she's aware we know the real Anna, but for some reason, that doesn't seem to faze her. Perhaps you'd like to be present."

"I wouldn't miss it for the world," Jade said, "but I've got to take certain precautions. I fully intend to make arrangements through the Oxen to have her examined for weapons before she's admitted into our presence."

"That's very wise," Alexis said. "She's a vicious, vengeful woman, and I wouldn't trust her."

"Exactly so," Jade said. "I prefer to take no risks."

"Do you actually think that she'll tolerate being searched for weapons?" David demanded.

Jade shook her head. "That won't be necessary," she said. "There will be a large crowd of people near the entrance to our offices, and she'll have to squeeze through in order to gain admission. She'll be searched without her knowledge."

The triumvirate was gathered in David Boynton's office in the Rakehell and Boynton complex near the waterfront on Victoria Island. David was seated behind his large mahogany desk, and to his left was Julian, ostensibly reclining—but actually very much on the alert—in a visitor's chair.

To his right was Jade. She was as calm as she looked, and without the knowledge of her brother or her cousin, she had an Indonesian throwing knife concealed beneath the skirt of her cheongsam. In a meeting with Erika von Klausner, she was taking no chances.

Firm believers in employing time to the best possible advantage, they each kept busy while awaiting the arrival of their unwelcome visitor. Julian went over the schedule of ships due to arrive in Hong Kong and made adjustments in their subsequent destinations. This was a process that underwent constant change and never was ended. David, who had a genius for utilizing warehouses to the greatest possible advantage, allocated space in the local buildings for newly arrived merchandise. Meanwhile, Jade scrutinized carefully a list of goods from the land held by the Taiping rebels that her cousin had bought at absurdly low prices from representatives of the woman posing as Anna van der Luon.

After a time, the principal clerk came into the room to announce that Madam van der Luon had arrived. The employee was accompanied by a pajama-clad coolie who held a broom in one hand, and he sidled up to Jade and addressed her in a low voice. "The woman carries no pistols, no knives, no weapons of any kind. Some of our most accomplished brethren put her to the test."

Jade nodded and dismissed him with a smile.

The door opened again, and Erika von Klausner swept into the office, her manner as brazenly confident as her appearance was bold. A heavy application of cosmetics coated her face, her blond hair was concealed beneath a hat with a huge cartwheel brim, and she was incongruously dressed in a gown of deep red velvet, with a very full skirt and a plunging neckline.

She looked at David, became aware of Julian's presence, and was startled to find Jade, also, sitting calmly awaiting her. All three regarded her steadily, their eyes unsmiling, their expressions revealing nothing. Her confidence began to ooze out of her. Jade's icy stare was particularly unsettling. She had become so involved in the role she was playing as Anna van der Luon that it did not occur to her until now that these Rakehells and Boyntons knew the real Anna and would see through her disguise.

"My cousins are my partners," David told her, "so I've invited them to be present for our meeting, Madam von Klausner."

Although Erika was disconcerted, she quickly recovered her poise, and her courage—that of a woman going quite mad—did not desert her. "You're mistaken regarding my name," she said evenly. "I am Anna van der Luon."

"You're wasting your time," Julian said firmly. "We happen to have been well acquainted with the real Anna van der Luon, just as we were on close terms with her uncle before her. We've gone to a great deal of trouble to learn your real identity, and you'll oblige us by not indulging in fantasies.''

"Regardless of who you are,'' David added, ''I believe you wanted to see us. Won't you sit down?'' He pointed to a chair directly opposite his desk.

Erika sank into it and smoothed her skirts and looked first at one, then at another of the trio. Only when her eyes met Jade's did she look away hastily and seem momentarily flustered. ''Your company,'' she said, ''has been buying considerable quantities of Chinese products that I've placed on the market for sale. You've paid absurdly small sums for tea, cotton, bolts of silk, and porcelain objects.''

Jade entered the conversation for the first time. ''I have a complete list of our purchases before me right now,'' she said sweetly. ''Perhaps you'd care to see them?''

"That won't be necessary,'' Erika replied, a hint of stridency in her voice. ''When I've complained to the salesmen and the auctioneers that you're paying only a fraction of what the goods are worth, they've told me, in so many words, that I can obtain no better prices anywhere, either in Hong Kong, in Singapore, or even in Djakarta, for these goods.''

David nodded equably. ''The information you've been given by the salesmen and the auctioneers is accurate,'' he told her.

Her temper flared. ''Rakehell and Boynton has threatened and otherwise intimidated other potential buyers from giving me the prices that the merchandise is worth. Thus no one wants to bid on the goods.''

"You're mistaken, Madam von Klausner,'' Julian said calmly, and smiled. ''It hasn't been necessary for us to use coercion. You forget that we're large enough and sufficiently powerful to wield considerable influence. We've just let it be known that we regard it as an unfriendly act toward our company for anyone to offer you any price whatsoever for your merchandise.''

"You're trying to ruin me!'' Erika cried.

Jade bared her teeth in a bloodless smile. ''That's one of our goals,'' she said. "The other is equally simple. We're trying to prevent the Taiping rebels from earning a profit on the goods that they've obtained by force in the areas that they occupy."

Erika knew that bluff and bluster would avail her nothing, so she abruptly changed her tactics. "Obviously there's been a terrible misunderstanding," she said, her manner suddenly humble.

Julian was unyielding, his attitude reminding Jade of their father's hard-bitten stance in business meetings. "I think not," he said. "Speaking for myself, I understand all too well from what my wife has told me in detail that you concocted a devilish plan to discredit me."

"Let me remind you, Madam von Klausner," Jade said in a surprisingly unemotional voice, "that I have an excellent memory, and I can recall all too vividly every detail of the humiliation, pain, and degradation you forced me to suffer on your usurped estate in Djakarta. Not to mention the attempt of your hired hands to murder Pieter Sabov and me in Singapore."

"I knew nothing about the attempts on your lives in Singapore until later, and that's the truth!" Erika said vehemently.

Jade's calm did not desert her. "This is a senseless conversation," she said. "You had made a standing offer for our capture, dead or alive, and it was the fact that such an offer still stood that impelled your representatives in Singapore to seek us out with such bloodthirsty vengeance."

"If you only knew the circumstances—"

"We know all we care to know, thank you very much," Jade said, cutting her off crisply. "We've learned of your attempt to inveigle my father into marrying you many years ago, and of your attempt to murder Molinda when you mistakenly thought my father was interested in her. We know you disposed of Anna van der Luon, whose place you've taken, although we're unfamiliar with the details, and we know all too well of your attempts to injure my brother and me. You made one major error. You forgot you were dealing with Rakehells. We don't frighten easily, and we're resilient."

"Furthermore," Julian added, "we deal with scum on its own level."

"In brief, Madam von Klausner," Jade said with deadly emphasis, "we determined to ruin you, to drive you out of the shipping and trading businesses, and to take from you the fortune that you unsurped."

"We've pursued that goal with single-minded determination," David said, "and we won't relax our efforts until we achieve it."

Tears appeared in Erika's downcast eyes, and she stared miserably at her hands folded in her lap. "Obviously," she said, "I've made some serious mistakes in judgment, and I regret any inconvenience that those errors may have caused you."

Jade's façade of calm was suddenly ripped away, and she rose to her feet slowly, her eyes blazing with scorn. "Inconvenience, Madam von Klausner? How dare you! I suffered more than mere inconvenience when you forced me to look like a Balinese dancing girl, and to behave with the abandon of a concubine, letting your business acquaintances make love to me and use me as they pleased. I suffered far more than inconvenience when your whips cut into my skin and left me bruised and smarting. I suffered far more than inconvenience when I was forced to abandon all hope of ever being rescued from the terrible plight I was in. Neither you nor anyone else will ever know the torments that Pieter and I were forced to endure on the uninhabited island on which we were fortunate enough to be cast up when the storm broke up our small boat. And we suffered infinitely more than inconvenience when your hired thugs pursued us through the streets and alleys of Singapore!"

Erika's mind thrashed wildly as she sought some way to justify what she had done, some way to excuse her past actions and make them seem legitimate. She could not, however, and lapsed into silence.

Julian stood, too, and pointed a finger at her. "When you were spending money on the woman who became my wife, intending to disgrace me," he said, "surely you weren't thinking in terms of any inconvenience that I might suffer. You hoped to ruin me completely for all time."

Erika's pride asserted itself, and her temper flared. "Very well," she said. "I admit the charges that both of you have made against me. Nevertheless, it should be clear that I've failed in my attempts to destroy the Rakehells and to capture your business. I really can't see why you should be so intent on trying to ruin me.''

''Forgiveness,'' Jade said harshly, ''is a Christian virtue. But I'm afraid that I'm not that good a Christian. Remember that I'm as much Chinese as I am Western, and there is a part of me that clings to the belief in the ancient gods, whom my mother and my grandfather before me worshiped. If necessary, I will endure the fires of hell for all eternity before I will forgive you or relent in my effort to destroy you. My brother and my cousin may soften if they wish, but that will in no way deter me from bending every effort toward your downfall.'' She paused and plucked her wavy-bladed *kris* from beneath her skirt.

Erika was startled by the appearance of the knife blade and rose, flinching.

Julian and David were somewhat stunned, too, both of them fearing that Jade intended to shed the blood of her tormenter right here in the Rakehell and Boynton offices.

''When I was a small child,'' she said, ''the guards on the Fat Dutchman's estate taught me to throw these knives with great accuracy. I think it would be a fitting end to your story, Madam von Klausner, if you were killed by such a knife. At the very least it would be just retribution for the Dutchman and for his poor niece, for whose death and disappearance you are undoubtedly responsible.''

Erika was terrified and began to back toward the door.

Jade took one step in her direction, and then another. ''Get out of my sight,'' she said. ''Now and for all time. My brother and my cousin seek only your financial ruin and will rejoice when they have added the shipping company, warehouses, and trading business of the Dutchman and Anna van der Luon to Rakehell and Boynton. But I will not be satisfied until I have carved out your heart and have removed it from your body.''

Erika screamed and fumbled behind her for the door latch.

"Get out of my sight," Jade said, "and never let me see you again, the next time we meet face to face, rest assured, Erika Von Klausner, that I shall kill you with no more hesitation than I would kill any other vermin!"

V

The gardens of Soochow, an ancient city in Kiangsu Province, located on the Yangtze Delta about fifty-five miles west of Shanghai, had been famous for more than three thousand years. Conscious of their renown and beauty, General Gordon issued orders accordingly before his attack on the city.

"If possible," he instructed the Ever-Victorious Army, "spare the gardens of Soochow. But do not spare the Taiping rebels. Show them no mercy. Complete victory is within our grasp if we are resolute, bold, and strong. Fight for me as you fought in the past for General Ward, and victory is assured."

The troops, astonished to discover that "Chinese" Gordon, as he was destined to become known in his long and distinguished military career, was cut from the same bolt of cloth as Frederick Ward, fought furiously and captured Soochow after a brief but decisive battle.

The remnants of the Taiping rebel military force, together with their civilian administrators and other supporters, were forced to flee to Nanking, where they would make a last stand. But the handwriting on the wall was already clear, and there was no question in the minds of any informed Chinese, as well as the ambassadors of the foreign nations in the Middle Kingdom, that the imperial forces had won the campaign, and the rebellion would be ended whenever Nanking was assaulted.

The Dowager Empress Yehonala and Prince Kung, the coregents, dined together, a frequent occurrence these days, and the good news continued to flow in to them.

As the couple dined on deep-fried dumplings made of shreaded crabmeat with fragments of kumquats and lemon rind, a delicacy served only to the very wealthy, Prince Kung smiled expansively. "The rebels," he said, "have lost their last chance to replenish their shrinking treasury."

Yehonala's eyes glowed in her masklike face. "How so?" she asked.

He explained to her the deal that General Yang had made with Anna van der Luon, the details of which he had only recently learned. "The Dutch fleet carrying the produce of the rebels sailed to Hong Kong, where an attempt was made to sell the goods in the open market. But our friends at Rakehell and Boynton not only blocked the attempt and gained possession of the tea, cotton, silks, and other merchandise, but they forced its sale at sums so low that the woman who had connived with the rebels went bankrupt. So the rebels lost the goods that they sent to Hong Kong, and they haven't received a penny in return."

Yehonala took a sip of her brown rice wine. "How lovely," she commented.

"You have yet to learn the very best part of the tale," Prince Kung told her. "In the holds of various ships, they found about two hundred and fifty casks of pure opium, which was being carried in tea chests. At the instigation of Rakehell Jade, the opium was burned in a public ceremony as a warning to all who would try to smuggle the drug in or out of the Middle Kingdom."

She studied her long, tapering fingernails, which were painted a deep green to match the emerald rings that she wore on both hands. "We have given many gifts to the Rakehells, brother and sister, and to Boynton, their cousin, in the past, just as our ancestors rewarded their father and their grandfather before them. Now we shall be obliged to make them new and significant rewards."

"I've given that problem considerable thought this very day," Kung replied. "We have presented them with valuable gems and with gifts of gold in the past. I have a somewhat better idea now, I think. All three of them hold honorary Chinese citizenship, so how would you react to the idea of giving them each one hundred acres of land from the royal preserves?"

The dowager empress looked pleased and clapped her hands together. "Perfect!" she exclaimed. "I can't think of a more fitting gift, or one that would please the recipients more."

"Good," Kung said. "That matter is settled then."

She ate the last of her dumplings, then rinsed her hands and mouth in a basin of water in which chrysanthemum petals were floating. "I wonder if a small personal gift might not be appropriate, as well," she said. "As a woman, I think I would appreciate that almost as much as I would a gift of land."

Her idea was beyond Prince Kung's comprehension, and he shrugged politely.

"Quite recently," Yehonala said, "I acquired several identical dressing gowns through a mistake in ordering that is quite irrelevant now. They are exceptionally handsome, as they are embroidered with cloth of gold, and on the back of each is emblazoned an imperial dragon in cloth-of-silver silk thread. I believe that Rakehell Jade and the wives of her brother and her cousin would be inclined to treasure such gifts."

"Then we shall send them, by all means," Prince Kung said, "and we shall include them in the same packet that contains the citations and the land deeds."

VI

The dinner party was a brilliant success. Jade, Alexis, and Aileen, identically clad in their cloth-of-gold gowns that were gifts of the Dowager Empress Yehonala, acted as joint hostesses and made certain that the guests enjoyed themselves.

The guest list was distinguished and included everyone from the governor-general of the royal Crown colony to the admiral commanding the British Far Eastern fleet, the various industrialists and shipping experts who were making Hong Kong into one of the most important commercial ports in the world, and the commander of the small United States Navy squadron stationed in the Orient.

At Jade's suggestion, enthusiastically seconded by the wives of her brother and cousin, a Western, rather than a Chinese meal was served. She based her reasoning on the fact that the guests, almost all of whom were stationed in the Orient for a number of years, were surfeited with Chinese meals and would welcome something that was reminiscent of home.

They began the meal with huge locally caught shrimp, followed by a rich and pungent gumbo, the recipe for which was one of Alexis's contributions to the meal. Then came roast beef with Yorkshire pudding prepared under Aileen's supervision, with roasted potatoes and a variety of vegetables.

Thanks to Alexis's inspiration, for dessert they served pie made with freshly picked cherries and served with large scoops of vanilla ice cream.

The wines, which included a white Burgundy, a red Bordeaux, and a dessert champagne, had all been imported from France.

Happily eating and drinking, the guests agreed that Hong Kong was no longer a frontier community but had settled down to being an adult city of international stature.

Among the innovations was one that Jade introduced: The ladies and gentlemen did not separate at the end of the meal, but all remained at the table for spirited discussion while the men drank their brandy.

One subject that intrigued everyone present was the ultimate disposition of the extensive merchant fleet that had been the property of the Fat Dutchman and, after him, of his niece! Erika von Klausner, who had been posing as Anna van der Luon, had disappeared about ten days earlier when her debts had multiplied so rapidly that they inundated her and she'd been unable to meet her obligations.

Several of her creditors, including Rakehell and Boynton, had placed liens on the ships but were unable to take possession of them pending such time as the woman was found and the courts were able to declare her legally bankrupt.

In the meantime, no one knew what had become of her. She had vanished from her hotel, leaving most of her clothing behind, and had disappeared without a trace, neither telling anyone where she had gone nor making arrangements for the various pending business matters.

Those gathered around the long table would have been shocked had they known that Erika von Klausner was listening to every word they said about her. Dressed in a black sweater and trousers and black boots, with smears of dirt on her skin to deaden her light complexion, she was crouched in the lush tropical foliage of the garden beyond the open windows of the dining room of Jade's house on the Peak. Buffeted by the severe financial losses caused by the collapse of the Taiping rebels, combined with the active opposition to her of Rakehell and Boynton, her reasoning had become even more warped.

After brooding for many days, Erika had concluded that Jade Rakehell was the cause of her miseries. So, she had told herself, if she eliminated Jade, her problems would solve themselves. Resting inside the top of her right boot was the double-edged knife—long, pointed, and supple—that would end her troubles. She would plunge the blade deep into the body of Jade Rakehell, and her torment would end. Her one regret was that she had dealt too leniently with Jade when the young woman had been in her power. Instead of simply degrading her, she should have had her put to death and been done with her. Then none of the mishaps that had befallen her would have occurred.

Erika had read about the coming dinner party in that morning's Hong Kong *Daily Telegraph*, and the rest had proved to be almost absurdly simple.

A few armed guards, members of the Society of Oxen—although Erika did not realize it—were on duty at various points along the high wall that surrounded the property. She had circumvented the guards with ease by wearing a full-skirted gown, one of the dresses she had taken with her from her hotel, over her dark attire and had walked boldly through the front gate of the property. No one had stopped her, and she had removed the dress, hiding it in the bushes, as she had moved closer and closer to the house.

Now she knew that all she needed to do was to exercise patience, and she would be richly rewarded. Strangely, it proved to be surprisingly easy for her to wait. She had only to dream about the sharp steel of her knife plunging into the flesh of Jade Rakehell, carving its way into a vital organ as she succumbed and died, and the time passed swiftly.

Ultimately, the guests rose from the dinner table, and as they trooped back to the drawing room, Erika felt a surge of elation. At last her moment of retribution was approaching!

Moving with extreme care in order to make no noise, she crept closer to the front door of the house so she could watch it as the guests departed.

At last the front door opened, the oil lamps within illuminating the front steps, and the governor-general and his lady emerged. This was in accordance with custom, as no guests could leave a social gathering until the official representative of Queen Victoria had taken his leave.

The governor-general's carriage drew to a halt at the entrance, and as he and his wife entered it, Jade Rakehell stood with her brother in the entrance, bidding them farewell.

Erika had eyes only for Jade, and the mere sight of her enemy inflamed her, took possession of her, and so enraged her that cold chills shot up and down her spine. How smug Jade looked in her dazzling cloth-of-gold gown with the cloth-of-silver dragon etched on its back. Seething with hatred, Erika watched the young woman closely, drinking in every detail of her appearance until the door closed behind her.

The mansion, like so many houses on the Peak, was constructed in such a way that a rear entrance, leading directly to the upper stories, was located higher than the front door, which stood on lower ground. So Erika edged through the foliage toward the side of the house. She had a clear picture of Jade in her mind, and that was all she needed. She climbed through the bushes and shrubs onto higher ground, and took up a position of concealment near the open terraces that led from the bedchambers. As soon as she determined which bedroom was Jade's, she would be in a position to strike.

The front door opened and closed repeatedly as other guests took their leave. But Erika paid no attention to what was happening downstairs. Instead, she concentrated her full attention on the bedchambers, and as she waited for their occupants to arrive, a fever of impatience gradually built up within her. One moment she felt cold, as though walking barefooted across an icy river in midwinter.

Then, without warning, she began to perspire heavily, soaking her black sweater. Her eyes watered as she gazed at the balconies, and in a self-rage, she wiped away the tears. Occasionally she could not resist drawing the knife from her boot and feeling the sharp edge of the blade with her thumb. Then she went all cold again as she realized that if one of the guards on the property should happen to stumble across her, she would be searched, the knife would be found, and her purpose would be given away.

Suddenly an oil lamp was lighted in the bedroom farthest from the place where Erika was concealed, and her heart hammered hard against her rib cage. Then tension became almost unbearable.

A young woman in a cloth-of-gold gown drifted onto the balcony and stood at the railing for a few moments, looking out at the view of Hong Kong and the harbor below. Her shoulders and head were hidden in shadows, but there was no mistaking the cloth-of-silver dragon that filled the back of her gown.

Erika's lips twisted in a smirking, self-satisfied grimace. At last! The moment for vengeance, for retribution, had arrived!

Climbing onto the connecting balconies, she crept from one to the next, remaining in the shadows, her eyes fixed on the silver dragon. Her breath was so short, so labored, that she was sure the Rakehell woman would hear her, and she tried in vain to breathe more quietly.

Then she reached down to draw the knife from the top of her boot for the last time, and as her fingers closed around the hilt, she felt a deep sense of gratification and of peace. For the first time since misfortune had begun to dog her existence, she was happy.

The silver dragon did not move from the rail. Its wearer was tired after discharging her duties as a hostess and was relaxing for a few brief seconds before retiring. Perhaps she was even daydreaming; whatever the cause, she did not hear her assailant approaching ever nearer.

Erika raised the dagger high in the air, then brought it down with all of her strength, striking at a spot directly to the left of the silver dragon.

As her victim screamed and sank to the floor, her blood already staining the cloth-of-gold gown, Erika saw, to her horror, that she had attacked Alexis Johnson Rakehell rather than Jade Rakehell. In her confusion, she could only look down at the woman who lay crumpled at her feet.

The sounds of shouts being exchanged, of doors opening and slamming, awakened Erika from her reverie. It was too late now to rectify her error, and she had the small consolation of knowing that at least she had evened the score with the woman she had hired to betray Julian Rakehell, but who had chosen to transfer her loyalty to him instead.

Growing panicky, Erika fled in the direction from which she had come and vanished into the tropical gardens.

At that moment the balconies filled with people. Jade, closely followed by David Boynton, peered off into the darkness below. "That was Erika von Klausner," she said softly. "I saw her and recognized her."

"So did I," David replied.

They turned and hurried to the balcony of her brother's room, where Julian and Aileen Boynton were kneeling beside Alexis.

Aileen had already taken charge, and ripping away the extensive fabric of the victim's gown, she was sponging the wound with a container of water, which was brought to the scene almost immediately by a well-trained and conscientious servant.

"She's going to be all right, Julian," Aileen said. "Fortunately, the weapon struck Alexis high in the shoulder, and although she's bleeding, it's unlikely that any real damage was done."

"Thank God for that," Julian replied hoarsely, as he cradled his wife's head in his lap.

Aileen efficiently began to tear strips to make a bandage for the victim.

Swiftly assuring herself that Alexis was in no real danger and would recover, Jade hurried into the house and ran toward the staircase, with David close beside her. "You have a *geiko*," she said. "I saw you exercising with it the other day. Fetch it for me, please." She referred to an object used in the martial arts, a stick about twenty-four inches long and about two inches in diameter at each of the ends, tapering to a width of an inch in the center, where it was grasped. It was made of mahogany, teak, or another of the hardwoods of the tropics, and was a traditional weapon that had been employed by fighting men in the Middle Kingdom for centuries.

David started to protest, thought better of it, and turning, raced off toward his own room.

"Bring me a belt or a length of rope so I can tie something around my middle, too," Jade called after him. "I don't have time to change, and with the work that I have to do, this gown is too cumbersome."

David caught up with her as she reached the front entrance, and neither was surprised to see waiting for them Lo Fang, who had been asked to take charge of the sentries this evening.

"I don't know how the woman evaded my sentries when she arrived here," Lo fang said, "but I swear to you she will not leave this property alive. She is somewhere within the walls at this very moment."

Jade nodded and buckled on David's belt, which had the effect of making her gown far less voluminous. Then she reached for the *geiko* that he held and gripped it in her hand.

Lo Fang guessed her purpose and demurred. "It is too dangerous for Missy Jade to go alone in search of her who is mad," he said. "That is why the brethren of the Oxen are here. Let them attend to this unpleasant chore for you."

Jade gently shook her head. "Surely," she said, "Lo Fang has not forgotten the rules of the Oxen that he taught me when I stood no higher than his knees. He who has a blood feud with another must avenge himself. He cannot expect his brothers in the Society of Oxen to do this work for him. The honor of his ancestors is at stake."

"That is so," Lo Fang murmured.

David Boynton was very uneasy, but he knew not only that it would be wrong of him to intervene but that such intervention would be futile.

"The woman who roams this property like a wild animal trapped in a cage," she said, "is my foe. It was she who lusted after my father many years ago and tried to murder Molinda. It was she who killed our friend, Anna van der Luon, and took her place. It was she who connived against my brother and not only hired a woman to disgrace him but, when that plan failed, has now also tried to murder that woman.

"It was she who tried in vain to capture my brother and my cousin. It was she who succeeded in enslaving me, beating me with whips, and forcing me to act the role of a concubine."

"She is armed with a sharp knife," Lo Fang protested. "You would be wise if you carried a pistol and availed yourself of the services of your good friend, the Malay *kris* that you so often have carried."

"The Oxen," Jade said, "have existed for thousands of years in the Middle Kingdom, ever since men learned the art of noting the passage of time. In all of those centuries they have served the emperors well. Throughout all of those ages, whenever an Oxen has gone out to face his personal enemy, he has been armed only with a *geiko*. I have been honored to be accepted into the Society of Oxen as a full-fledged member, without reservation. I, too, have a mortal foe. Now I go to meet my foe." She raised the *geiko* to eye level and spun it rapidly. Then the hint of a cold, merciless smile appeared in her eyes. "Concern yourself not for me, old friend," she said. "I have well and truly learned the lessons of combat that I have been taught."

"So be it," Lo Fang said.

Without further ado, Jade turned and walked off into the darkness of the garden.

"Surely you aren't going to let her face that insane woman alone," David said. "Surely your Oxen will protect her!"

Lo Fang made no move to follow Jade and folded his arms. "She knows far more than you, far more than her brother, about the martial arts. She is capable of taking care of herself, no matter what emergency may arise. Armed with a *geiko*, she is a formidable opponent. Do not worry yourself, Mr. David, and do not follow her, because you will only complicate her task. Go instead into the house and compose yourself."

David had no choice. The old man, although theoretically his inferior in class and in status, nevertheless had been his lifelong teacher, and the younger man obeyed his orders literally. Looking off into the garden, where he saw nothing and heard no sounds of life, he turned and went off to join his wife and Julian, who were tending to Alexis's needs.

Meanwhile, Jade unhesitatingly walked down a gravel path through the formal gardens until she reached a point about seventy-five yards from the house. There she halted to take stock of the situation. The blue-black sky above Hong Kong was filled with stars, as it always was, but there was no moon tonight, and as a result, it was darker than usual below.

Trying to put herself in the fleeing Erika's place, Jade decided that her one thought now would be concentrated on escape. Surely the woman knew that the entire household had been aroused by her attempted murder of Alexis and that armed sentries were searching for her. So it seemed probable that she would be lurking in the underbrush somewhere in the shadow of the wall around the property, hoping either that she could scale it or that the men at the gate would become distracted and that she could make a dash for freedom through it.

Gripping her *geiko* firmly in the center and swinging it slightly, Jade started off in the direction of the property's wall.

She thought, ruefully, that she was not dressed for an evening of action and high adventure. Her long skirt hampered her movements somewhat, and the full sleeves of her gown did not give her arms the freedom that she wished she possessed. Furthermore, the cloth-of-gold and cloth-of-silver fabric picked up and reflected whatever light was cast into the garden and made her presence rather obvious.

It was pointless, however, to indulge in wishful thinking. She had to accept the handicaps under which she labored and to make the best of the situation. If it proved necessary, she would overcome the handicaps when the time came. Such thinking gave her ideas, and she thought of a way to shorten her search for Erika von Klausner.

Moving from the relative sanctuary of a large flowering bush, she stood in the open on the gravel path about ten feet from the wall. She knew full well that, in her gown, she was now plainly visible in the event that Erika was hiding anywhere in the fairly immediate vicinity.

Seemingly careless, indifferent to her own fate, Jade approached the wall. There she halted and stood very still, straining every nerve as she listened for any sign of her enemy's approach.

Her vigil was rewarded even sooner than she had anticipated. Soon she became aware of soft, tentative footsteps approaching behind her.

She made no move, however, and in no way did she indicate that she was aware of the approach of her foe. Her back presented a tempting target, she knew, especially for someone who was armed with a dagger, but she regarded it as highly unlikely that Erika had acquired the knack of knife-throwing. That was an art that few Westerners knew, and she doubted that the woman would want to take the risk of losing her weapon.

Waiting until the last possible instant, until she judged that Erika was almost within arm's reach behind her, Jade suddenly whirled around. As she had anticipated, Erika von Klausner loomed in the darkness only a few feet from her, the gleaming knife that she held in one hand upraised, her teeth bared in a vicious snarl.

All at once Jade's *geiko* seemed to assume a life of its own, first spinning furiously, then thrusting and jabbing at the woman, and then striking like a club as it aimed itself at Erika's head and face.

Only an expert who had been drilled in the execution of the martial arts since early childhood could have performed with such brilliance and skill. Using the *geiko* first as a club, Jade wielded it with bewildering, uncanny accuracy and speed. It struck Erika repeatedly on the face and arms, chest and breasts.

But the woman, seething with hatred, was too far gone to be deterred by the *geiko*. All she knew, all she cared to know, was that she stood face to face with the person whom she held responsible for the miseries and the dismal turn of events from which she suffered. No one else was in sight, and she at last was in a position to finish off Jade Rakehell permanently.

Swearing under her breath, first in her native German and then in English, Erika lunged at her enemy with her knife.

Forced to assume the defensive, Jade barely managed to deflect the vicious blow with her *geiko* just before the knife would have entered her throat.

This near-escape sobered her and caused her to regard her opponent in a new light. She herself was tall, but Erika von Klausner was equally tall and must have weighted at least twenty pounds more than she did. Furthermore, the woman was endowed with the strength of the insane and with the reckless disregard for her own safety that only the demented could boast.

Giving ground slowly, Jade was forced again and again to use her *geiko* to deflect blows aimed at her heart, her throat, and her face. Neither then nor later did she know how she managed to escape death or serious injury. Ultimately, she realized that her training at the hands of Lo Fang and of Kai, the Rakehell family majordomo, had been more thorough than she knew. She reacted instinctively, and it was this automatic defense that saved her life.

It dawned on her, however, that in spite of her temporary success in warding off catastrophe, she remained in mortal danger every moment that the fight continued. She was seriously hampered in her ability to apply the martial arts in combat because her long full skirt prevented her from using her legs against her foe. She was confined to maneuvering her body and using her arms, and even there, the long trailing sleeves of her gown made her arm movements slower and clumsier.

Her options were so limited that she knew her only chance for survival lay in the talents she might employ in wielding her *geiko*.

Again the two-headed stick came alive in her hand. Acting with cool deliberation now, she struck the woman repeatedly on the right temple with the weapon, and then shifting her emphasis slightly, transferred her target to the left temple.

She judged her opponent wisely, and just as she had anticipated, her efforts drove Erika into a frenzy.

Trying to escape from the *geiko*, which seemed to be everywhere at once, Erika thrust and slashed repeatedly with her dangerous dagger. But thanks to the adroitness of Jade's footwork, which showed even greater agility than she herself knew, she remained unharmed.

All at once she saw an opening appear in the older woman's defenses, and she told herself: Now!

Lashing out with the *geiko* with her full strength, she brought one of its hammerlike ends down onto the bridge of Erika's nose with all the strength at her command.

A sickening cracking sound told her that she had smashed the woman's nose.

Erika moaned, then lashed out with renewed fury, striking again and again with the knife.

But Jade did not flinch or retreat. She recalled the pain and humiliation she had endured, the degradation that she had suffered, the dangers to which she and Pieter had been subjected, because of this woman. Now was the time to end the fight before she herself was injured.

Using the *geiko* in a manner that would have made her instructors proud, she struck Erika on the face and head again and again. Ultimately, she sacrificed subtlety and grace for strength, and she knew that the woman suffered from a broken jawbone and at least one smashed cheekbone.

But still Erika persisted, never slackening her pace.

In spite of the hatred she had so often felt for her tormenter, Jade was devoid of all feeling now. She felt empty inside, incapable of hatred, just as she was incapable of feeling pity.

Erika's frenzy grew as she found herself unable to reach her foe, and in her blind fury she struck out so hard that the knife slipped from her grasp.

Jade had been working toward just such an end, and caught the dagger by the handle as it fell from the woman's fingers. Now, she thought, I hold all the cards!

Grasping the *geiko* in one hand and the dagger in the other, Jade realized the moment had come to make short work of her foe and end the combat. Whirling the *geiko* rapidly as a distraction, she stepped forward and plunged the blade deep into the left side of the woman's body.

Erika von Klausner sank slowly to the ground, an expression of incredulity in her shocked eyes as her battered face fell forward and she collapsed, with the knife still protruding from her body.

Standing silently above her looking down, Jade felt neither joy nor sorrow, neither a sense of triumph nor one of vindication. She was exhausted and still felt numb after the death of Pieter. Her only sense of satisfaction was that as a member of the Oxen, she had done what it had been necessary for her to do.

Lo Fang stepped forward out of the shadows, and Jade realized he had been present throughout the fight, observing it and ready to intervene on her behalf had it proved necessary.

"Let the body of my enemy be prepared for burial," she said, and walked slowly back to the house, where, to her relief, she found that Alexis had suffered only a minor injury and was already on the road to recovery.

Erika von Klausner's body, enclosed in a simple pine coffin, was taken by ferry across the Hong Kong harbor to Kowloon, and there was carted to a pauper's burial ground. All five of the clergymen stationed in Hong Kong adamantly refused to conduct a graveside funeral service, so Erika was buried without a ceremony in unhallowed ground.

A week later, Jade, as the oriental representative of Rakehell and Boynton, appeared in court and testified, at length, under the guidance of her solicitors, in a case regarding the disposition of the property of Anna van der Luon.

After hearing testimony for several days, the court awarded the entire property of Anna van der Luon to Rakehell and Boynton, the principal creditors.

One hurdle remained to be overcome, the approval of the Dutch government. Steeling herself, Jade sailed to Djakarta, while her brother remained behind in Hong Kong with his convalescing wife. The young woman was accompanied on her journey by David and Aileen Boynton.

Jade and David met with the governor-general of the Dutch East Indies and several members of his cabinet. To their surprise and pleasure, it proved to be a simple matter to work out an arrangement that was agreeable to all. The governor-general approved of the transfer of the Fat Dutchman's entire estate to Rakehell and Boynton, provided that the shipping company they had inherited would continue to operate under Dutch law and would pay taxes to Amsterdam.

Jade and David signed papers to that effect, and the company that was responsible for the start of Rakehell and Boynton in the Far East was incorporated into the family business.

One major task remained. The property that now belonged to Rakehell and Boynton included the estate of Djakarta. So Jade went there, accompanied by the Boyntons, and was overwhelmed by bitter memories of Erika and gentler, sweeter memories of Pieter Sabov.

Summoning the concubines and eunuchs, the security guards, and the hired staff of the estate into the garden, Jade announced that it was her great pleasure to grant freedom, effective immediately, to all who were enslaved. She offered to pay for the transportation of those who wished to return to their own homes on various islands, and she promised the Malay security guards and the hired domestic help that they would have positions on the estate as long as they wanted to stay. She appointed the chief security guard as resident manager of the property.

Most of the former slaves eagerly and gratefully accepted Jade's offer, only three of the concubines and two of the eunuchs electing to go instead to the city where they intended to open a brothel.

The new owners stayed at the estate for dinner, but they departed immediately after the meal, returning to the waterfront and boarding the steamer that would return them to Hong Kong. Jade had no desire to spend any more time at the place where she was overwhelmed by her memories.

"Well," Jade said, "we've added another home to our properties in this part of the world. Papa and Elizabeth will enjoy coming to Djakarta, and so will Uncle Charles and Aunt Ruth."

"Yes," David agreed. "They all have fond memories of the Fat Dutchman and of the estate. I'm sure they'll want to come here."

"As for us," she replied with a slight smile, "we've added forty-one ships and a whole complex of warehouses to our company."

"It strikes me," David said, "that we have our work cut out for us."

The voyage to Hong Kong was uneventful, and on their arrival, Jade and David, joined by Julian, plunged into the intricate task of integrating their new acquisitions into the company. Molinda generously emerged from retirement once again to help them, and together they found that the Dutch company was in sounder condition than they had dared to hope. Not even Erika von Klausner's mismanagement had undone the many years of solid, hard work done by the Fat Dutchman and his niece, Anna van der Luon.

New shipping schedules were arranged, transfers of cargos from one warehouse to another and from one carrier to another were worked out, and the captains and crews of the Dutch fleet were placed under the jurisdiction of the Anglo-Americans. All of these activities took time to accomplish, as did the heavy correspondence with customers all over the world who were notified of Rakehell and Boynton's new acquisition.

At last the absorption was complete, and all of the newly acquired ships were scheduled to sail from Hong Kong on the same day beneath the Tree of Life banner. The best place to view the spectacle, Jade decided, was the terrace of her home on the Peak overlooking the Hong Kong harbor. She was joined there by her brother and cousin and their wives, along with Molinda, and glasses of the best available French champagne were served in honor of the occasion.

The parade of ships through the Hong Kong harbor started, and desultory conversation on the terrace stopped, with everyone present automatically rising and gazing down at the spectacle. What made the occasion memorable was the fact that so many of the ships had been built either in the Rakehell yard in New England or at the Boynton yard in London.

It seemed only right that the procession should be led by a clipper ship that had been constructed under the personal supervision of Jonathan Rakehell, who had presented it as a gift to the Fat Dutchman in response to the many kindnesses that the family had enjoyed. Her name was *Sea Cloud*, and she looked like the role assigned to her. Under full sail, she resembled a huge billowing cloud of pure white as she made her stately way majestically through the crowded waters of the harbor.

Behind her in the long line were eleven other vessels that had been built by Rakehell and Boynton, a symbol of the close ties that had existed between Jonathan Rakehell and Charles Boynton on one hand, and the Fat Dutchman and his niece on the other. It was only fitting, Jade reflected, that her company should have taken over the properties that had brought the Dutchman wealth and renown.

Above all, it was appropriate that every ship in the line should be flying the Tree of Life banner, its three branches extending from the sturdy, immovable central trunk.

Jade looked to her left and smiled at her brother. Julian stood with his arm around Alexis, now almost completely recuperated from the wound she had suffered, and he was at peace with himself and the world, proud of the past accomplishments of the family, and looking forward to even larger worlds to conquer.

Then Jade looked to her right, where David and Aileen Boynton stood arm in arm, and again she smiled. Her cousin had not only found himself but had found his perfect mate, as well. Like Julian, he was poised on the threshold of making the company bigger, more powerful, and more successful.

Conscious of the fact that she stood alone, Jade did not mind. She was strong and resilient, well able to stand on her own feet and needing no one to support and sustain her. She had learned much from Pieter Sabov, and she no longer resented his untimely death.

Realizing that she was still young, beautiful, and endowed with wisdom far beyond her years, she was content to wait, to work, and to look toward the future. Some day, perhaps, she would meet a man who, like Pieter, was worthy of her love.

Until then, like her late American and Chinese grandfathers, like her father and her late mother, she was content with her lot, happy with her existence, and secure in the knowledge that the work she accomplished was beneficial to the United States and the Middle Kingdom, the two nations whose joint product she had become.

Get the whole story of
THE RAKEHELL DYNASTY

The bold, sweeping, passionate story of a great New England shipping family caught up in the winds of change—and of the one man who would dare to sail his dream ship to the frightening, beautiful land of China. He was Jonathan Rakehell, and his destiny would change the course of history.

THE RAKEHELL DYNASTY—
THE GRAND SAGA OF THE GREAT CLIPPER SHIPS
AND OF THE MEN WHO BUILT THEM
TO CONQUER THE SEAS AND CHALLENGE THE WORLD!

Jonathan Rakehell—who staked his reputation and his place in the family on the clipper's amazing speed.

Lai-Tse Lu—the beautiful, independent daughter of a Chinese merchant. She could not know that Jonathan's proud clipper ship carried a cargo of love and pain, joy and tragedy for her.

Louise Graves—Jonathan's wife-to-be, who waits at home in New London keeping a secret of her own.

Bradford Walker—Jonathan's scheming brother-in-law who scoffs at the clipper and plots to replace Jonathan as heir to the Rakehell shipping line.

THRILLING Reading
from WARNER BOOKS

Passions For You
from WARNER BOOKS